IN THE
SHADOW OF THE
TOWERS

Also by Douglas Lain

Novels
Billy Moon
After the Saucers Landed

Collections:
Last Week's Apocalypse

IN THE SHADOW OF THE TOWERS

SPECULATIVE FICTION IN A POST-9/11 WORLD

EDITED by Douglas Lain

Night Shade Books
New York

Night Shade books may be purchased in bulk at special discounts for sales promotion, corporate gifts, fund-raising, or educational purposes. Special editions can also be created to specifications. For details, contact the Special Sales Department, Night Shade Books, 307 West 36th Street, 11th Floor, New York, NY 10018 or info@skyhorsepublishing.com.

Night Shade Books® is a registered trademark of Skyhorse Publishing, Inc.®, a Delaware corporation.

Visit our website at www.nightshadebooks.com.

10 9 8 7 6 5 4 3 2 1

Library of Congress Cataloging-in-Publication Data

In the shadow of the towers : speculative fiction in a post-9/11 world / edited by Douglas Lain.
     pages cm
   ISBN 978-1-59780-839-2 (paperback)
1. Science fiction, American—21st century.   2. September 11 Terrorist Attacks, 2001—Fiction.   I. Lain, Douglas, editor.
   PS648.S3I536 2015
   813'.0876208—dc23

                                                                    2015013581

Print ISBN: 978-1-59780-839-2
Ebook ISBN: 978-1-59780-850-7

Cover illustration and design by Erik T. Johnson

Please see page 342 for an extension of this copyright page.

Printed in the United States of America

CONTENTS

INTRODUCTION

In the Shadow of the Towers was a project undertaken with trepidation. Art always creates order out of the chaos of life, but in this case imposing an order onto chaos was especially risky. When writers such as John Updike and Don DeLillo are accused of trivializing and sensationalizing 9/11, how are we purveyors of elfin princes, ghosts, and bug-eyed aliens likely to fare? The fear from the start was that genre fiction written about 9/11 would be an exercise in bad taste.

There is history behind this concern. After World War II, a cultural critic named Theodore Adorno famously wrote that "to write poetry after Auschwitz is barbaric." He later amended this and wrote that "perennial suffering has as much right to expression as a tortured man has to scream; hence it may have been wrong to say that after Auschwitz you could no longer write poems." Adorno came to understand that he'd asked the wrong question. It wasn't a matter of whether we should or could write poetry, but rather how it might be possible to go on living at all. What Adorno realized was that the survivors of Auschwitz faced intense survivor's guilt. Many were so plagued by the conviction that they too ought to have died, unable to accept that mere chance had saved them from the ovens, that they came to believe that their lives after the camps were imaginary.

On reading this I was reminded of Peyton Farquhar in Ambrose Bierce's Civil War story, "An Occurrence at Owl Creek Bridge." Published in 1890, Bierce's fiction recounted how Farquhar hallucinated an escape from death by hanging and lived a whole life in the seconds before the rope broke his neck.

That fictional plot device, the narrative frame of an entire life passing in mere seconds, can not only help us to comprehend what it was like for survivors of the Holocaust, but can also change how we view our own history. Looking back on the Holocaust through the lens of Bierce's tale we see a different story, a different meaning, than what readers of *The San Francisco Examiner* saw back in 1890.

In 1898 a little-known, and little-remembered, writer named Morgan Robertson penned a tale about an enormous steam ship called *The Titan*. The novella was entitled "Futility," and in it the *Titan* strikes an iceberg and sinks to the bottom of the North Atlantic. We can be certain that readers of Morgan's story read the work differently in 1898 than they would have after April 15, 1912.

What I came to realize when I first started thinking about the possibility of taking this project on is that 9/11, too, had been presaged or foretold in fiction. Specifically by genre fiction.

When the attacks happened, they said it was an unprecedented event that had changed everything, that inaugurated a new era, a new normal, and what promised to be a new and perpetual war. But for science fiction and fantasy fans and writers, September 11th must have looked terribly familiar. The whole scene, especially as the rest of the country and the world saw it through the around-the-clock news coverage, looked less like a live camera feed and more like a Hollywood disaster movie. Think about your favorite adrenalin-pumping scenes in *Independence Day*, or even *Godzilla*. The *real* images of debris and dust from 9/11, of terrorized crowds stampeding away from the World Trade Center, all of it was like a Disney thrill ride that had suddenly gone terribly wrong.

We genre people were faced with a peculiar dilemma, having enjoyed celluloid apocalypses for decades. Now our collective silver-screen fantasies had shattered the fourth wall, in a way that was chillingly similar to how we'd always depicted it happening, all the more horrible and terrible for being so recognizable.

The challenge for a science fiction, fantasy, or horror writer after 9/11 was not merely to take a political or moral stance, but also to find an appropriate approach to writing fiction in the face of such tragedy. After the most garish and spectacular fictional scenario had come true, all the big tropes seemed to be played out. Those who dared to write directly

about 9/11 found themselves not merely navigating a minefield of opin-
ion and partisanship, but, more dauntingly, coming to terms with how
the real world was already science fiction, already a horror, and perhaps
also a mere fantasy. Writers who traded in the strange, the horrifying,
and the surreal were challenged to go beyond what they knew about the
unknown. 9/11 made the old apocalypses seem mundane. The stories in
this anthology then are attempts to face the destruction from that day
and create something we might still feel wonder about.

In the days after 9/11, the German composer Karlheinz Stockhau-
sen infamously said "What has happened is—now you all have to turn
your brains around—the greatest work of art there has ever been." He
later claimed that his quote was taken out of context, which it surely
must have been. But still, for genre writers the question remains: how
can we, in the face of this "greatest artwork," conceive of new imaginary
events that might compete with the sublime horror in NY? How can we
continue dreaming in the shadow of the towers? The solution for most
of us was to keep dreaming, but to keep our dreams small, personal, and
individual. Especially when we tasked ourselves with writing about 9/11
itself.

Eighteen years before 9/11, in her song "Three Songs for Paper, Film
and Video," Laurie Anderson complained and marveled that superheroes
can bend steel with their bare hands or walk in zero gravity, but nobody
asks how or why. She claimed that, in these stories of the fantastic, aimed
at creating a sense of wonder, human nature is an afterthought. Her song
suggests that the problem of human nature was too big for the contem-
porary artist to handle.

But in the new century, after 9/11, that's changed. Writers in this
new now embrace the human condition, as a refuge from the terrible
mountains of data that collect around the even more horrible events on
the horizon.

That's what you'll find here, in this collection. These are all human-
sized tales about an inhumanly over-sized event.

You'll find an array of emotion. In Rick Bowes's "There's a Hole in
the City," there is melancholy and shock. In Tim Pratt's "Unexpected
Outcomes," you'll find a numb acceptance of oblivion only overcome by
personal ambition. In Tim Marquitz's "Retribution," there is a searing
inner anger, an anger that, even after it explodes into the world, can still
be traced back to a personal and private pain.

These are small stories about a terribly huge event, but they manage to hold onto the fantastic, to hold onto wonder. Because after 9/11, the greatest fantasy might be that we humans, all of us so small and fragile, might be able to pick up the pieces, to pull the fragments together again, and live on, in and through our own imaginations.

ONE: THE DEAD

On October 16, 2004, the conservative columnist David Brooks wrote a column in *The New York Times* satirizing the upcoming presidential election between the incumbent President Bush and Swift Boat Senator John Kerry. Written as a fictionalized transcript of a televised debate, Brooks took aim at both candidates.

At one point in the column, Kerry, who in real life never wasted an opportunity to disconnect and alienate the electorate, responds to a prompt from the moderator to "spew sentimental blather in order to connect with the American people," with the following:

"Spirituality is important to me. I've always felt we humans are insignificant maggots scuttling across the muck of the universe, and that life itself is just a meaningless moment of agony between the suffocating stench of the womb and the foul decay of the grave."

Whether intentional or not, Brooks pulls a neat trick with this paraphrase of Beckett or Nietzsche. The towers collapsed, the office workers had died, and the mightiest military in the world had been powerless in stopping a ragtag group of Islamic terrorists armed with box cutters and airline tickets.

After the attacks of 9/11 the sense of security that had defined America since the second World War, the little confidence and optimism that had not been extinguished by Nixon and the Vietnam War, all of that was destroyed.

Writing for the *US News and World Report*, Roger Simon said it, if not best, then at least most directly. On September 14, 2001, just three days after the attack, he wrote:

"Life as we know it in these United States ended Tuesday morning."

We all saw the truth. Our life, as we knew it before the Twin Towers fell, could end. It had ended. The Twin Towers had fallen and with them what we thought to be true, lasting, final, and right had collapsed as well. And, for a brief moment, we were all forced to face the fact that we—not just you and not just me, but we, all of us—would die. The whole collective enterprise of the United States of America was a fragile and temporary thing. We'd watched it pulverized into dust and spread across the New York skyline in a thick cloud. We had seen it on television, this future without us in it, and it was terrible.

In hindsight, it wasn't *that* absurd for Brooks to have a Presidential candidate espousing nihilism during a televised debate. In 2004 we were all, even three years later, closet nihilists. The choice Brooks was presenting us with was the choice between denial of what we knew and the fruitless acceptance of it.

That's where we begin in this collection. The following stories present three different accountings of the dead and of our future deaths. There are zombies, ghosts, and black rectangles, censorship bars, set across the eyes of the world. And just like America in the days and years following 9/11, there is no salvation to be found ahead. There is no religious impulse in these ghost stories, nothing eternal to guide the corpses that still walk the earth and ghosts who can't go home again. There is nothing to these stories but paperweights and memories.

See you on the other side.

Richard Bowes's writing career started in the 1980s with the publication of his Warchild novels. Since then he has won two World Fantasy Awards, a Lambda Award, an International Horror Guild Award, and fourteen appearances in various Year's Best anthologies. "There's a Hole in the City" was originally published at SciFi.com and was the first chapter of his Lambda-nominated novel Dust Devil on a Quiet Street.

Told in the wake of the attacks on the Twin Towers, the Manhattan of "There's a Hole in the City" is a haunted one, even if what Bowes has created is ultimately a realistic fiction. The author turns our attention to the past, so that what we've perceived before as a chain of separate events can be truly seen, to quote Walter Benjamin, as "one single catastrophe which keeps piling wreckage upon wreckage."

THERE'S A HOLE IN THE CITY
Richard Bowes

Wednesday 9/12

On the evening of the day after the towers fell, I was waiting by the barricades on Houston Street and LaGuardia Place for my friend Mags to come up from Soho and have dinner with me. On the skyline, not two miles to the south, the pillars of smoke wavered slightly. But the creepily beautiful weather of September 11 still held, and the wind blew in from the northeast. In Greenwich Village the air was crisp and clean, with just a touch of fall about it.

I'd spent the last day and a half looking at pictures of burning towers. One of the frustrations of that time was that there was so little most of us could do about anything or for anyone.

Downtown streets were empty of all traffic except emergency vehicles. The West and East Villages from Fourteenth Street to Houston were their own separate zone. Pedestrians needed identification proving they lived or worked there in order to enter.

The barricades consisted of blue wooden police horses and a couple of unmarked vans thrown across LaGuardia Place. Behind them were a couple of cops, a few auxiliary police and one or two guys in civilian clothes with ID's of some kind pinned to their shirts. All of them looked tired, subdued by events.

At the barricades was a small crowd: ones like me waiting for friends from neighborhoods to the south; ones without proper identification waiting for confirmation so that they could continue on into Soho; people who just wanted to be outside near other people in those days of sunshine and shock. Once in a while, each of us would look up at the columns of smoke that hung in the downtown sky then look away again.

A family approached a middle-aged cop behind the barricade. The group consisted of a man, a woman, a little girl being led by the hand, a child being carried. All were blondish and wore shorts and casual tops. The parents seemed pleasant but serious people in their early thirties, professionals. They could have been tourists. But that day the city was empty of tourists.

The man said something, and I heard the cop say loudly, "You want to go where?"

"Down there," the man gestured at the columns. He indicated the children. "We want them to see." It sounded as if he couldn't imagine this appeal not working.

Everyone stared at the family. "No ID, no passage," said the cop and turned his back on them. The pleasant expressions on the parents' faces faded. They looked indignant, like a maitre d' had lost their reservations. She led one kid, he carried the other as they turned west, probably headed for another checkpoint.

"They wanted those little kids to see Ground Zero!" a woman who knew the cop said. "Are they out of their minds?"

"Looters," he replied. "That's my guess." He picked up his walkie-talkie to call the checkpoints ahead of them.

Mags appeared just then, looking a bit frayed. When you've known someone for as long as I've known her, the tendency is not to see the changes, to think you both look about the same as when you were kids.

But kids don't have gray hair, and their bodies aren't thick the way bodies get in their late fifties. Their kisses aren't perfunctory. Their conversation doesn't include curt little nods that indicate something is understood.

We walked in the middle of the streets because we could. "Couldn't sleep much last night," I said.

"Because of the quiet," she said. "No planes. I kept listening for them. I haven't been sleeping anyway. I was supposed to be in housing court today. But the courts are shut until further notice."

I said, "Notice how with only the ones who live here allowed in, the South Village is all Italians and hippies?"

"Like 1965 all over again."

She and I had been in contact more in the past few months than we had in a while. Memories of love and indifference that we shared had made close friendship an on-and-off thing for the last thirty-something years.

Earlier in 2001, at the end of an affair, I'd surrendered a rent-stabilized apartment for a cash settlement and bought a tiny co-op in the South Village. Mags lived as she had for years in a run-down building on the fringes of Soho.

So we saw each other again. I write, obviously, but she never read anything I published, which bothered me. On the other hand, she worked off and on for various activist leftist foundations, and I was mostly uninterested in that.

Mags was in the midst of classic New York work and housing trouble. Currently she was on unemployment and her landlord wanted to get her out of her apartment so he could co-op her building. The money offer he'd made wasn't bad, but she wanted things to stay as they were. It struck me that what was youthful about her was that she had never settled into her life, still stood on the edge.

Lots of the Village restaurants weren't opened. The owners couldn't or wouldn't come into the city. Angelina's on Thompson Street was, though, because Angelina lives just a couple of doors down from her place. She was busy serving tables herself since the waiters couldn't get in from where they lived.

Later, I had reason to try and remember. The place was full but very quiet. People murmured to each other as Mags and I did. Nobody I knew was there. In the background Respighi's *Ancient Airs and Dances* played.

"Like the Blitz," someone said.

"Never the same again," said a person at another table.

"There isn't even anyplace to volunteer to help," a third person said.

I don't drink anymore. But Mags, as I remember, had a carafe of wine. Phone service had been spotty, but we had managed to exchange bits of what we had seen.

"Mrs. Pirelli," I said. "The Italian lady upstairs from me. I told you she had a heart attack watching the smoke and flames on television. Her son worked in the World Trade Center and she was sure he had burned to death.

"Getting an ambulance wasn't possible yesterday morning. But the guys at that little fire barn around the corner were there. Waiting to be called, I guess. They took her to St. Vincent's in the chief's car. Right about then, her son came up the street, his pinstripe suit with a hole burned in the shoulder, soot on his face, wild-eyed. But alive. Today they say she's doing fine."

I waited, spearing clams, twirling linguine. Mags had a deeper and darker story to tell; a dip into the subconscious. Before I'd known her and afterward, Mags had a few rough brushes with mental disturbance. Back in college, where we first met, I envied her that, wished I had something as dramatic to talk about.

"I've been thinking about what happened last night." She'd already told me some of this. "The downstairs bell rang, which scared me. But with phone service being bad, it could have been a friend, someone who needed to talk. I looked out the window. The street was empty, dead like I'd never seen it.

"Nothing but papers blowing down the street. You know how every time you see a scrap of paper now you think it's from the Trade Center? For a minute I thought I saw something move, but when I looked again there was nothing.

"I didn't ring the buzzer, but it seemed someone upstairs did because I heard this noise, a rustling in the hall.

"When I went to the door and lifted the spy hole, this figure stood there on the landing. Looking around like she was lost. She wore a dress, long and torn. And a blouse, what I realized was a shirtwaist. Turn-of-the-century clothes. When she turned toward my door, I saw her face. It was bloody, smashed. Like she had taken a big jump or fall. I gasped, and then she was gone."

"And you woke up?"

"No, I tried to call you. But the phones were all fucked up. She had fallen, but not from a hundred stories. Anyway, she wasn't from here and now."

Mags had emptied the carafe. I remember that she'd just ordered a salad and didn't eat that. But Angelina brought a fresh carafe. I told Mags about the family at the barricades.

"There's a hole in the city," said Mags.

That night, after we had parted, I lay in bed watching but not seeing some old movie on TV, avoiding any channel with any kind of news, when the buzzer sounded. I jumped up and went to the view screen. On the empty street downstairs a man, wild-eyed, disheveled, glared directly into the camera.

Phone service was not reliable. Cops were not in evidence in the neighborhood right then. I froze and didn't buzz him in. But, as in Mags's building, someone else did. I bolted my door, watched at the spy hole, listened to the footsteps, slow, uncertain. When he came into sight on the second floor landing he looked around and said in a hoarse voice, "Hello? Sorry, but I can't find my mom's front-door key."

Only then did I unlock the door, open it, and ask her exhausted son how Mrs. Pirelli was doing.

"Fine," he said. "Getting great treatment. St. Vincent was geared up for thousands of casualties. Instead." He shrugged. "Anyway, she thanks all of you. Me too."

In fact, I hadn't done much. We said good night, and he shuffled on upstairs to where he was crashing in his mother's place.

Thursday 9/13

By September of 2001 I had worked an information desk in the university library for almost thirty years. I live right around the corner from Washington Square, and just before 10 a.m. on Thursday, I set out for work. The Moslem-run souvlaki stand across the street was still closed, its owner and workers gone since Tuesday morning. All the little falafel shops in the South Village were shut and dark.

On my way to work I saw a three-legged rat running not too quickly down the middle of MacDougal Street. I decided not to think about portents and symbolism.

The big TVs set up in the library atrium still showed the towers falling again and again. But now they also showed workers digging in the flaming wreckage at Ground Zero.

Like the day before, I was the only one in my department who'd made it in. The librarians lived too far away. Even Marco, the student assistant, wasn't around.

Marco lived in a dorm downtown right near the World Trade Center. They'd been evacuated with nothing more than a few books and the clothes they were wearing. Tuesday, he'd been very upset. I'd given him Kleenex, made him take deep breaths, got him to call his mother back in California. I'd even walked him over to the gym, where the university was putting up the displaced students.

Thursday morning, all of the computer stations around the information desk were occupied. Students sat furiously typing email and devouring incoming messages, but the intensity had slackened since 9/11. The girls no longer sniffed and dabbed at tears as they read. The boys didn't jump up and come back from the restrooms red-eyed and saying they had allergies.

I said good morning and sat down. The kids hadn't spoken much to me in the last few days, had no questions to ask. But all of them from time to time would turn and look to make sure I was still there. If I got up to leave the desk, they'd ask when I was coming back.

Some of the back windows had a downtown view. The pillar of smoke wavered. The wind was changing.

The phone rang. Reception had improved. Most calls went through. When I answered, a voice, tight and tense, blurted out, "Jennie Levine was who I saw. She was nineteen years old in 1911 when the Triangle Shirtwaist Factory burned. She lived in my building with her family ninety years ago. Her spirit found its way home. But the inside of my building has changed so much that she didn't recognize it."

"Hi, Mags," I said. "You want to come up here and have lunch?"

A couple of hours later, we were in a small dining hall normally used by faculty on the west side of the Square. The university, with food on hand and not enough people to eat it, had thrown open its cafeterias and dining halls to anybody with a university identification. We could even bring a friend if we cared to.

Now that I looked, Mags had tension lines around her eyes and hair that could have used some tending. But we were all of us a little ragged in those days of sun and horror. People kept glancing downtown, even if they were inside and not near a window.

The Indian lady who ran the facility greeted us, thanked us for coming. I had a really nice gumbo, fresh avocado salad, a soothing pudding. The place was half-empty, and conversations again were muted. I told Mags about Mrs. Pirelli's son the night before.

She looked up from her plate, unsmiling, said, "I did not imagine Jennie Levine," and closed that subject.

Afterward, she and I stood on Washington Place before the university building that had once housed the sweatshop called the Triangle Shirtwaist Factory. At the end of the block, a long convoy of olive green army trucks rolled silently down Broadway.

Mags said, "On the afternoon of March 25, 1911, one hundred and forty-six young women burned to death on this site. Fire broke out in a pile of rags. The door to the roof was locked. The fire ladders couldn't reach the eighth floor. The girls burned."

Her voice tightened as she said, "They jumped and were smashed on the sidewalk. Many of them, most of them, lived right around here. In the renovated tenements we live in now. It's like those planes blew a hole in the city and Jennie Levine returned through it."

"Easy, honey. The university has grief counseling available. I think I'm going. You want me to see if I can get you in?" It sounded idiotic even as I said it. We had walked back to the library.

"There are others," she said. "Kids all blackened and bloated and wearing old-fashioned clothes. I woke up early this morning and couldn't go back to sleep. I got up and walked around here and over in the East Village."

"Jesus!" I said.

"Geoffrey has come back too. I know it."

"Mags! Don't!" This was something we hadn't talked about in a long time. Once we were three, and Geoffrey was the third. He was younger than either of us by a couple of years at a time of life when that still seemed a major difference.

We called him Lord Geoff because he said we were all a bit better than the world around us. We joked that he was our child. A little family cemented by desire and drugs.

The three of us were all so young, just out of school and in the city. Then jealousy and the hard realities of addiction began to tear us apart. Each had to find his or her own survival. Mags and I made it. As it turned out, Geoff wasn't built for the long haul. He was twenty-one. We were all just kids, ignorant and reckless.

As I made excuses in my mind, Mags gripped my arm. "He'll want to find us," she said. Chilled, I watched her walk away and wondered how long she had been coming apart and why I hadn't noticed.

Back at work, Marco waited for me. He was part Filipino, a bit of a little wiseass who dressed in downtown black. But that was the week before. Today, he was a woebegone refugee in oversized flip-flops, wearing a magenta sweatshirt and gym shorts, both of which had been made for someone bigger and more buff.

"How's it going?"

"It sucks! My stuff is all downtown where I don't know if I can ever get it. They have these crates in the gym, toothbrushes, bras, Bic razors, but never what you need, everything from boxer shorts on out, and nothing is ever the right size. I gave my clothes in to be cleaned, and they didn't bring them back. Now I look like a clown.

"They have us all sleeping on cots on the basketball courts. I lay there all last night staring up at the ceiling, with a hundred other guys. Some of them snore. One was yelling in his sleep. And I don't want to take a shower with a bunch of guys staring at me."

He told me all this while not looking my way, but I understood what he was asking. I expected this was going to be a pain. But, given that I couldn't seem to do much for Mags, I thought maybe it would be a distraction to do what I could for someone else.

"You want to take a shower at my place, crash on my couch?"

"Could I, please?"

So I took a break, brought him around the corner to my apartment, put sheets on the daybed. He was in the shower when I went back to work.

That evening when I got home, he woke up. When I went out to take a walk, he tagged along. We stood at the police barricades at Houston Street and Sixth Avenue and watched the traffic coming up from the World Trade Center site. An ambulance with one side smashed and a squad car with its roof crushed were hauled up Sixth Avenue on the back of a huge flatbed truck. NYPD buses were full of guys returning from Ground Zero, hollow-eyed, filthy.

Crowds of Greenwich Villagers gathered on the sidewalks clapped and cheered, yelled, "We love our firemen! We love our cops!"

The firehouse on Sixth Avenue had taken a lot of casualties when the towers fell. The place was locked and empty. We looked at the flowers and the wreaths on the doors, the signs with faces of the firefighters who hadn't returned, and the messages, "To the brave men of these companies who gave their lives defending us."

The plume of smoke downtown rolled in the twilight, buffeted about by shifting winds. The breeze brought with it for the first time the acrid smoke that would be with us for weeks afterward.

Officials said it was the stench of burning concrete. I believed, as did everyone else, that part of what we breathed was the ashes of the ones who had burned to death that Tuesday.

It started to drizzle. Marco stuck close to me as we walked back. Hip twenty-year-olds do not normally hang out with guys almost three times their age. This kid was very scared.

Bleecker Street looked semiabandoned, with lots of the stores and restaurants still closed. The ones that were open were mostly empty at nine in the evening.

"If I buy you a six-pack, you promise to drink all of it?" He indicated he would.

At home, Marco asked to use the phone. He called people he knew on campus, looking for a spare dorm room, and spoke in whispers to a girl named Eloise. In between calls, he worked the computer.

I played a little Lady Day, some Ray Charles, a bit of Haydn, stared at the TV screen. The president had pulled out of his funk and was coming to New York the next day.

In the next room, the phone rang. "No. My name's Marco," I heard him say. "He's letting me stay here." I knew who it was before he came in and whispered, "She asked if I was Lord Geoff."

"Hi, Mags," I said. She was calling from somewhere with walkie-talkies and sirens in the background.

"Those kids I saw in Astor Place?" she said, her voice clear and crazed. "The ones all burned and drowned? They were on the *General Slocum* when it caught fire."

"The kids you saw in Astor Place all burned and drowned?" I asked. Then I remembered our conversation earlier.

"On June 15, 1904. The biggest disaster in New York City history. Until now. The East Village was once called Little Germany. Tens of thousands of Germans with their own meeting halls, churches, beer gardens.

"They had a Sunday excursion, mainly for the kids, on a steamship, the *General Slocum*, a floating firetrap. When it burst into flames, there were no lifeboats. The crew and the captain panicked. By the time they got to a dock, over a thousand were dead. Burned, drowned. When a hole got blown in the city, they came back looking for their homes."

The connection started to dissolve into static.

"Where are you, Mags?"

"Ground Zero. It smells like burning sulfur. Have you seen Geoffrey yet?" she shouted into her phone.

"Geoffrey is dead, Mags. It's all the horror and tension that's doing this to you. There's no hole . . ."

"Cops and firemen and brokers all smashed and charred are walking around down here." At that point sirens screamed in the background. Men were yelling. The connection faded.

"Mags, give me your number. Call me back," I yelled. Then there was nothing but static, followed by a weak dial tone. I hung up and waited for the phone to ring again.

After a while, I realized Marco was standing looking at me, slugging down beer. "She saw those kids? I saw them too. Tuesday night I was too jumpy to even lie down on the fucking cot. I snuck out with my friend Terry. We walked around. The kids were there. In old, historical clothes. Covered with mud and seaweed and their faces all black and gone. It's why I couldn't sleep last night."

"You talk to the counselors?" I asked.

He drained the bottle. "Yeah, but they don't want to hear what I wanted to talk about."

"But with me . . ."

"You're crazy. You understand."

The silence outside was broken by a jet engine. We both flinched. No planes had flown over Manhattan since the ones that had smashed the towers on Tuesday morning.

Then I realized what it was. "The Air Force," I said. "Making sure it's safe for Mr. Bush's visit."

"Who's Mags? Who's Lord Geoff?"

So I told him a bit of what had gone on in that strange lost country, the 1960s, the naïveté that led to meth and junk. I described the wonder of that unknown land, the three-way union. "Our problem, I guess, was that instead of a real ménage, each member was obsessed with only one of the others."

"Okay," he said. "You're alive. Mags is alive. What happened to Geoff?"

"When things were breaking up, Geoff got caught in a drug sweep and was being hauled downtown in the back of a police van. He cut his wrists and bled to death in the dark before anyone noticed."

This did for me what speaking about the dead kids had maybe done for him. Each of us got to talk about what bothered him without having to think much about what the other said.

Friday 9/14

Friday morning two queens walked by with their little dogs as Marco and I came out the door of my building. One said, "There isn't a fresh croissant in the entire Village. It's like the Siege of Paris. We'll all be reduced to eating rats."

I murmured, "He's getting a little ahead of the story. Maybe first he should think about having an English muffin."

"Or eating his yappy dog," said Marco.

At that moment, the authorities opened the East and West Villages, between Fourteenth and Houston Streets, to outside traffic. All the people whose cars had been stranded since Tuesday began to come into the neighborhood and drive them away. Delivery trucks started to appear on the narrow streets.

In the library, the huge TV screens showed the activity at Ground Zero, the preparations for the president's visit. An elevator door opened and revealed a couple of refugee kids in their surplus gym clothes clasped in a passion clinch.

The computers around my information desk were still fully occupied, but the tension level had fallen. There was even a question or two about books and databases. I tried repeatedly to call Mags. All I got was the chilling message on her answering machine.

In a staccato voice, it said, "This is Mags McConnell. There's a hole in the city, and I've turned this into a center for information about the victims Jennie Levine and Geoffrey Holbrun. Anyone with information concerning the whereabouts of these two young people, please speak after the beep."

I left a message asking her to call. Then I called every half hour or so, hoping she'd pick up. I phoned mutual friends. Some were absent or unavailable. A couple were nursing grief of their own. No one had seen her recently.

That evening in the growing dark, lights flickered in Washington Square. Candles were given out; candles were lighted with matches and Bics and wick to wick. Various priests, ministers, rabbis, and shamans led flower-bearing, candlelit congregations down the streets and into the park, where they joined the gathering vigil crowd.

Marco had come by with his friend Terry, a kind of elfin kid who'd also had to stay at the gym. We went to this 9/11 vigil together. People addressed the crowd, gave impromptu elegies. There were prayers and a few songs. Then by instinct or some plan I hadn't heard about, everyone started to move out of the park and flow in groups through the streets.

We paused at streetlamps that bore signs with pictures of pajama-clad families in suburban rec rooms on Christmas mornings. One face would be circled in red, and there would be a message like, "This is James Bolton, husband of Susan, father of Jimmy, Anna, and Sue, last seen leaving his home in Far Rockaway at 7:30 a.m. on 9/11." This was followed by the name of the company, the floor of the Trade Center tower where he worked, phone and fax numbers, the email address, and the words, "If you have any information about where he is, please contact us."

At each sign someone would leave a lighted candle on a tin plate. Someone else would leave flowers.

The door of the little neighborhood Fire Rescue station was open; the truck and command car were gone. The place was manned by retired firefighters with faces like old Irish and Italian character actors. A big picture of a fireman who had died was hung up beside the door. He was young, maybe thirty. He and his wife, or maybe his girlfriend, smiled in front of a ski lodge. The picture was framed with children's drawings of firemen and fire trucks and fires, with condolences and novena cards.

As we walked and the night progressed, the crowd got stretched out. We'd see clumps of candles ahead of us on the streets. It was on Great Jones Street and the Bowery that suddenly there was just the three of us and no traffic to speak of. When I turned to say maybe we should go home, I saw for a moment a tall guy staggering down the street with his face purple and his eyes bulging out.

Then he was gone. Either Marco or Terry whispered, "Shit, he killed himself." And none of us said anything more.

At some point in the evening, I had said Terry could spend the night in my apartment. He couldn't take his eyes off Marco, though Marco seemed not to notice. On our way home, way east on Bleecker Street, outside a bar that had been old even when I'd hung out there as a kid, I saw the poster.

It was like a dozen others I'd seen that night. Except it was in old-time black and white and showed three kids with lots of hair and bad attitude: Mags and Geoffrey and me.

Geoff's face was circled and under it was written, "This is Geoffrey Holbrun, if you have seen him since Tuesday 9/11 please contact." And Mags had left her name and numbers.

Even in the photo, I looked toward Geoffrey, who looked toward Mags, who looked toward me. I stared for just a moment before going on, but I knew that Marco had noticed.

Saturday 9/15

My tiny apartment was a crowded mess Saturday morning. Every towel I owned was wet, every glass and mug was dirty. It smelled like a zoo. There were pizza crusts in the sink and a bag of beer cans at the front door. The night before, none of us had talked about the ghosts. Marco and Terry had seriously discussed whether they would be drafted or would enlist. The idea of them in the army did not make me feel any safer.

Saturday is a work day for me. Getting ready, I reminded myself that this would soon be over. The university had found all the refugee kids dorm rooms on campus.

Then the bell rang and a young lady with a nose ring and bright red ringlets of hair appeared. Eloise was another refugee, though a much better-organized one. She had brought bagels and my guests' laundry. Marco seemed delighted to see her.

That morning all the restaurants and bars, the tattoo shops and massage parlors, were opening up. Even the Arab falafel shop owners had risked insults and death threats to ride the subways in from Queens and open their doors for business.

At the library, the huge screens in the lobby were being taken down. A couple of students were borrowing books. One or two even had in-depth reference questions for me. When I finally worked up the courage to call Mags, all I got was the same message as before.

Marco appeared dressed in his own clothes and clearly feeling better. He hugged me. "You were great to take me in."

"It helped me even more," I told him.

He paused then asked, "That was you on that poster last night, wasn't it? You and Mags and Geoffrey?" The kid was a bit uncanny.

When I nodded, he said, "Thanks for talking about that."

I was in a hurry when I went off duty Saturday evening. A friend had called and invited me to an impromptu "Survivors' Party." In the days of the French Revolution, The Terror, that's what they called the soirees at which people danced and drank all night then went out at dawn to see which of their names were on the list of those to be guillotined.

On Sixth Avenue a bakery that had very special cupcakes with devastating frosting was open again. The avenue was clogged with honking, creeping traffic. A huge chunk of Lower Manhattan had been declared open that afternoon, and people were able to get the cars that had been stranded down there.

The bakery was across the street from a Catholic church. And that afternoon in that place, a wedding was being held. As I came out with my cupcakes, the bride and groom, not real young, not very glamorous, but obviously happy, came out the door and posed on the steps for pictures.

Traffic was at a standstill. People beeped "Here Comes the Bride," leaned out their windows, applauded and cheered, all of us relieved to find this ordinary, normal thing taking place.

Then I saw her on the other side of Sixth Avenue. Mags was tramping along, staring straight ahead, a poster with a black and white photo hanging from a string around her neck. The crowd in front of the church parted for her. Mourners were sacred at that moment.

I yelled her name and started to cross the street. But the tie-up had eased; traffic started to flow. I tried to keep pace with her on my side of the street. I wanted to invite her to the party. The hosts knew her from way back. But the sidewalks on both sides were crowded. When I did get across Sixth, she was gone.

Aftermath

That night I came home from the party and found the place completely cleaned up, with a thank-you note on the fridge signed by all three kids. And I felt relieved but also lost.

The Survivors' Party was on the Lower East Side. On my way back, I had gone by the East Village, walked up to Tenth Street between B and C. People were out and about. Bars were doing business. But there was still almost no vehicle traffic, and the block was very quiet.

The building where we three had lived in increasing squalor and tension thirty-five years before was refinished, gentrified. I stood across the street looking. Maybe I willed his appearance.

Geoff was there in the corner of my eye, his face dead white, staring up, unblinking, at the light in what had been our windows. I turned toward him and he disappeared. I looked aside and he was there again, so lost and alone, the arms of his jacket soaked in blood.

And I remembered us sitting around with the syringes and all of us making a pledge in blood to stick together as long as we lived. To which Geoff added, "And even after." And I remembered how I had looked at him staring at Mags and knew she was looking at me. Three sides of a triangle.

The next day, Sunday, I went down to Mags's building, wanting very badly to talk to her. I rang the bell again and again. There was no response. I rang the super's apartment.

She was a neighborhood lady, a lesbian around my age. I asked her about Mags.

"She disappeared. Last time anybody saw her was Sunday, 9/9. People in the building checked to make sure everyone was okay. No sign of her. I put a tape across her keyhole Wednesday. It's still there."

"I saw her just yesterday."

"Yeah?" She looked skeptical. "Well, there's a World Trade Center list of potentially missing persons, and her name's on it. You need to talk to them."

This sounded to me like the landlord trying to get rid of her. For the next week, I called Mags a couple of times a day. At some point, the answering machine stopped coming on. I checked out her building regularly. No sign of her. I asked Angelina if she remembered the two of us having dinner in her place on Wednesday, 9/12.

"I was too busy, staying busy so I wouldn't scream. I remember you, and I guess you were with somebody. But no, honey, I don't remember."

Then I asked Marco if he remembered the phone call. And he did but was much too involved by then with Terry and Eloise to be really interested.

Around that time, I saw the couple who had wanted to take their kids down to Ground Zero. They were walking up Sixth Avenue, the kids cranky and tired, the parents looking disappointed. Like the amusement park had turned out to be a rip-off.

Life closed in around me. A short-story collection of mine was being published at that very inopportune moment, and I needed to do some publicity work. I began seeing an old lover when he came back to New York as a consultant for a company that had lost its offices and a big chunk of its staff when the north tower fell.

Mrs. Pirelli did not come home from the hospital but went to live with her son in Connecticut. I made it a point to go by each of the Arab shops and listen to the owners say how awful they felt about what had happened and smile when they showed me pictures of their kids in Yankee caps and shirts.

It was the next weekend that I saw Mags again. The university had gotten permission for the students to go back to the downtown dorms and get their stuff out. Marco, Terry, and Eloise came by the library and asked me to go with them. So I went over to University Transportation and volunteered my services.

Around noon on Sunday, 9/23, a couple of dozen kids and I piled into a university bus driven by Roger, a Jamaican guy who has worked for the university for as long as I have.

"The day before 9/11 these kids didn't much want old farts keeping them company," Roger had said to me. "Then they all wanted their daddy." He led a convoy of jitneys and vans down the FDR Drive, then through quiet Sunday streets, and then past trucks and construction vehicles.

We stopped at a police checkpoint. A cop looked inside and waved us through.

At the dorm, another cop told the kids they had an hour to get what they could and get out. "Be ready to leave at a moment's notice if we tell you to," he said.

Roger and I as the senior members stayed with the vehicles. The air was filthy. Our eyes watered. A few hundred feet up the street, a cloud of smoke still hovered over the ruins of the World Trade Center. Piles of rubble smoldered. Between the pit and us was a line of fire trucks and police cars with cherry tops flashing. Behind us the kids hurried out of the dorm carrying boxes. I made them write their names on their boxes and noted in which van the boxes got stowed. I was surprised, touched even, at the number of stuffed animals that were being rescued.

"Over the years we've done some weird things to earn our pensions," I said to Roger.

"Like volunteering to come to the gates of hell?"

As he said that, flames sprouted from the rubble. Police and firefighters shouted and began to fall back. A fire department chemical tanker turned around, and the crew began unwinding hoses.

Among the uniforms, I saw a civilian, a middle-aged woman in a sweater and jeans and carrying a sign. Mags walked toward the flames. I wanted to run to her. I wanted to shout, "Stop her." Then I realized that none of the cops and firefighters seemed aware of her even as she walked right past them.

As she did, I saw another figure, thin, pale, in a suede jacket and bell-bottom pants. He held out his bloody hands, and together they walked through the smoke and flames into the hole in the city.

"Was that them?" Marco had been standing beside me.

I turned to him. Terry was back by the bus watching Marco's every move. Eloise was gazing at Terry.

"Be smarter than we were," I said.

And Marco said, "Sure," with all the confidence in the world.

Ray Vukcevich is one of science fiction and fantasy's little-known masters. His first short story collection, Meet Me in the Moon Room, *gained a lot of attention and praise for working beyond the realm of readers' expectations. Back in 2001, around the time of the 9/11 attacks,* Publishers Weekly *described his stories as "helium-filled," while* Booklist *described him as "an outlandish virtuoso."*

The plot of his Pushcart-nominated story, "My Eyes, Your Ears," may be impossible to summarize. This is a work that relies on associations and imagery much more than narrative hooks or even causes and effects. The feelings on display here, however, are absolutely true and real.

MY EYES, YOUR EARS
Ray Vukcevich

I don't know if I've told you this story before, because you all have black bars over your eyes, and I cannot tell who you are. I can see one of you is a police officer. I don't know whose blood this is we're standing in. Please, God, don't let it be Caroline's.

I realize now the trick I pulled on Caroline back in high school was a desperate attempt to get her attention. She was so perfect, so strawberry blond, so well-dressed and groomed. You could signal a rescue helicopter by bouncing sunlight off her teeth. She was just so totally Barbie it made you want to grab and squeeze her to see if she'd squeak. Her mother drove her to school. The bumper sticker on her mother's car said, "My Child is a National Honor Society Student."

I replaced it with one that was almost identical but said, "My Child Has Enormous Ears."

And then people were honking and grinning and children were giving her the Dumbo ears with their hands up along the sides of their heads, and Caroline and her mother were thinking they'd made some horrible social blunder like coming out in favor of atheism or something, but then one day Caroline spotted the bumper sticker, and you could hear her outraged cry all the way down the block and across the street, and that would have been the big payoff of my prank, if it had really been a prank an not an adolescent attempt to get her to notice me.

It didn't take her long to figure out I'd done it. I'd made no effort to cover my tracks. What's the fun of a practical joke if no one knows you did it? But after a couple of fits of yelling and shaking her fists at the sky and kicking the bumper of her mother's car, she went all good-sport on me. She accepted my apology, and I scraped off the bumper sticker. Incredibly, she started smiling at me in the high school hallways. One thing led to another, and she went to the senior prom with me. We fooled around a little, but not too much, in the back seat of my car. I almost asked her to marry me. I couldn't think of how to put it. I considered a bumper sticker that said, "Marry me, Caroline!" But the moment passed in silence.

I got into a pretty good college, and she went off to an even better one, and I figured that was that. I would drink tequila and read the Beat poets. Sadder, wiser, world-weary, maybe I'd grow a mustache, but then one day, she was back and asking me out for tea. For tea? Yes, tea, you know tea, in a teahouse, with little cakes, oh, I suppose you could have coffee. No, tea is fine. It's wonderful to see you again, Caroline. Oh look over there, she said, and I looked, and she put something in my tea. I didn't see her do it. She told me about it a little later, because what fun is a practical joke if no one knows you did it?

She had let her hair grow big around her ears, no more perky pony-tails. Nice hair, I said. You mean, thank god you can't see my huge, ugly ears, she said.

There is nothing whatever wrong with your ears, Caroline. I love your ears, I said. You're just saying that, she said. Jesus, I had given her some kind of complex about her ears all those years ago with the bumper sticker.

Here's looking at . . . your ears, kid, I said, toasting her with my tea.

Always the jokes. She turned her head away and then turned back, and I saw there was a black bar over her eyes. She was a photograph of someone you shouldn't know about. All of the people in the teahouse had black bars over their eyes.

I see you're getting it, she said, and the kicker is it's retroactive!

And it is so true! I have always seen a black bar over the eyes of everyone! It hasn't been easy. I am not so much blind as unrecognizing.

Nevertheless, I have always loved Caroline's ears. She has nothing to hide when it comes to her ears.

Oddly, I also see black bars over the eyes of domesticated animals. Dogs and cats, cows and horses. Ferrets. No mice. What would be the point? Whoever worried about an unidentified mouse?

A server approaches. I don't know if I've ever seen him before because of the black bar over his eyes. You should assume the crash position, he tells us. It's going to be tricky, but our captain thinks she can set this teahouse down with not so many casualties.

Later in the smoke and shouting and running on the tarmac, I lose track of Caroline. No, no, I tell the rescue helicopter, I've got to find Caroline. Is that you? Is that you? I can see that might be you, because you are a woman of a certain width and depth and height, and your hair has red highlights that are subtly reflected an octave higher in your fingernails and an octave lower in your toenails. Nice knees. If you were Caroline, I could see you wearing that frilly white top, that pale green skirt, those brown sandals, that green glass bracelet on your left wrist.

Who is shooting?

Why does there always have to be shooting?

I suddenly see that I'm standing in someone's blood, and then the policeman drags me away for interrogation. Did you see whose blood I was standing in? Was it a woman of a certain width and depth and height? I'll ask the questions, he says. Actually her width and depth vary as you move your eyes up and down her height which is generally consistent.

He wants to know about the shooting. We are Americans, I tell him, and for us, after 9/11, everything is about shooting and screaming and standing in blood, even when it's not. We do not appreciate that kind of talk at a facility like this, he tells me. He pushes me down onto a hard wooden chair.

A woman runs up and shoulders the policeman aside and drops down on her knees in front of me. Caroline, is that you? It's okay, she says, I'm here. How can I know that's you? She leans in and flips her hair away from the side of her face, and I see her left ear in extreme close-up. She turns quickly and shows me the other one. Her ears are beautiful pink seashells in the sunshine. They fill my world with joy. They really are, I feel compelled to report, enormous.

Kris Saknussemm is a Philip K. Dick Award-nominated novelist (Zanesville), *a Mary Gilmore Award-winning poet* (In the Name of the Father), *a forthcoming playwright* (The Humble Assessment) *and a short story writer whose works have received the Fiction Collective Two Award for Innovative Writing. He is also rumored to be a pen name used by the late David Foster Wallace, or if not that then a name taken by a collective of writers working in collaboration out of Las Vegas, Paris, or possibly outer space. When asked about this possibility he reportedly said, "I'm real enough." That hardly settles the matter, does it?*

Moral judgment is the cornerstone of "Beyond the Flags," which revolves around a "Master of the Universe," a self-designated label for those who work on Wall Street. It may remind readers of "Occurrence at Owl Creek Bridge" as well, if Ambrose had decided to include anal sex and Seconal in his tale.

BEYOND THE FLAGS
Kris Saknussemm

MAGNIFICENT STAMFORD CT LAKESIDE HIDEAWAY UNDER-STATES THIS 12,000 SF STONE MANOR ESTATE WITHIN 45 MINUTES FROM MANHATTAN & 15 MINUTES FROM WEST-CHESTER COUNTY AIRPORT. THE FRONT GATE OPENS TO A COBBLESTONE DRIVEWAY WHERE BEAUTIFUL GARDENS WELCOME YOU. WATER VIEWS ARE FEATURED FROM MOST ROOMS. A FULL GYM W/ADJACENT STEAM ROOM, ELEVATOR ACCESS TO ALL LEVELS AND STATE OF THE ART HOME THE-ATRE COMPLEMENT THE EXPANSIVE GOURMET KITCHEN, DINING & LIVING SPACES. EXTERIOR FEATURES INCLUDE BASKETBALL COURT, INFINITY EDGE POOL & 13 FT CEILING GARAGE. STAIRS DOWN TO A LAKESIDE SITTING AREA AS WELL AS A TEMP-CONTROLLED MAHOGANY CRAFTED WINE CELLAR ENHANCE THE LEISURE LIFESTYLE.

What real estate bullshit, he laughed. Still, he liked reading the description. It made the house seem more real to him. He was so seldom there, as his wife so often pointed out. He slipped the creased flyer into his briefcase with the hand-tooled letters *Paul T. Connors* on the flap. It was sort of a luck charm—and as his old friend and investment guide Joe Barnett had always said, "There's nothing wrong with being superstitious. Finance is a cutthroat, magical business."

Things didn't turn out well for Joe. When the Dubai funding went south and there was a discrepancy in the holding account, his old comrade decided to fall on his sword, in the form of a handful of Seconal and a jelly jar of premium single malt in an Adirondack chair in the Hamptons. He was found three days later, his stiffened body molded into the shape of the chair.

Still, one man's fall from grace can be another man's windfall. Paul had made a lot of money in the power vacuum that resulted. He didn't drive an Aston Martin Vanquish like Rudy Olson yet, but he had a daffodil-yellow Maserati Spyder. And his wife was loaded with old Greenwich money. All he had to do was keep the deals fluid and his wife hoodwinked, and everything would be gravy.

It wasn't just that Sophie was younger than his wife. He didn't care so much about that. Sophie was hot—Argentinian and Swedish. Down where women really taste, she tasted like cantaloupe and marzipan. Her butthole was sweetly puckered but nearly unwrinkled, like a young girl laughing in a tree house, playing naughty doctor and nurse. Her nipples were fiercely pronounced and sensitive. She could arch her back to make her body appear like some new kind of musical note. She fucked like a panther.

More importantly even than that, she was actually generous in bed. Expressive. Back at Yale, he remembered reading some Henry Miller. One line stuck with him. "She said the things a man wants to hear when he's climbing on top of her." Sophie had the sexiest damn voice—and she vocalized. His wife barely ever groaned, even when he was pumped up. Sophie always knew what to say . . . from a wordless throaty murmur . . . to "Oh daddy" . . . to "Fuck God, stick that big thing in my ass!"

He'd met her at the Zinc Bar, a private client function. Very intimate. They'd hired Tony Bennett to sing and circulate. She was a rented schmoozer and cleavage flasher. Bait for the sharks. Mostly Arabs and Japanese. An iridescent little sapphire evening dress and chase-me-catch-me heels fresh out of a 34th Street box. She was always fresh out of the box. And what a box.

After the after party, he'd seen her back to a coffin-sized studio off Atlantic in Brooklyn—and that pretty much was that. She soon quit the PR company. At first he stashed her in a newly renovated condo in Alphabet City, with real hardwood floors and a working fireplace. They swanned around boutique bars and sugar lounges. Vintage wine and black licorice flavored drinks at sunrise, overlooking the river . . . lobster tails and eye filets, knickers the color of candy.

One morning came a dose of reality. The Termite, his nemesis at work, Marshal Claver, got very publicly humiliated by his enraged wife. She served him with papers in front of everyone and chucked around some saucy PI taken photos of him banging his Jamaican gal. It was right during a crucial investor's meeting, with a highly moralistic key client. Claver had been the best margin man in the business, but within 48 hours, he found his contract terminated and he was headed to court to fight for his equity payout. Almost instantly, he lost the East Village brownstone, the holiday house in the Berkshires, and the mint condition Stutz Bearcat. His wife didn't stop there. She gutted him like a hapless trout. She got to the Cook Islands money, the developments in Santa Fe and Steamboat Springs, the condo in Maui, and the 38-foot sloop. Two months later he was on the receiving end of an IRS audit that was so vindictive, he called it "a full cavity body search."

Claver had gotten too cavalier. You can't get your photo taken with a black fashion model at Sardi's or in the Rainbow Room on New Year's Eve and expect to stay under your wife's radar. Paul cooled his heels with Sophie and moved her out of Manhattan.

His brilliant idea was a place much closer to home. Upper Saddle River in Northern Bergen County, where Nixon lived. He got a great deal on a secluded caretaker's house that had been subdivided from one of the big mansions. He could slip out more often to see her. She could hoot and holler. And in a neighborhood like that, even cold-blooded murder seems above board.

He had a special present from his latest trip to London. A delphinium lace camisole and a tastefully raunchy thong from Agent Provacateur—plus a bottle of Piper-Heidsieck. He often did take the train into work. He lived close to the New Haven line of Metro North. But it wasn't unusual for him to drive into the city. He was fairly sure his wife wouldn't raise an eyebrow if he left early. What a day. A clear crisp leaves-not-yet-turning Tuesday, September 11.

2001 was going to be his Space Odyssey. The year he broke the bank on his own. He glanced at his Rolex Submariner. It was just going on 7 a.m.

He felt lucid and big—except for the remnants of a dream. There'd been some kind of catastrophe. He couldn't get a fix on it. All he remembered was the image of a Montblanc pen slicing through the air like a knife into a wall. He didn't put much stock in dreams though. He preferred real stocks. Soon he'd have Sophie's smooth legs wrapped around him, or have her bent over on that orthopedic king mattress, her brightly painted fingernails peeling back those voluptuous cheeks, so he could see everything.

She met him at the door in an aqua nightie with a plate of warm, moist sticky date muffins. He'd never felt so alive. The fall air was electric, her thighs warm and strong. Everything went to plan. She ooo-ed and ahh-ed over the silky underwear. The sex was epic—and he got it up again for an even wilder second go. This was what he wanted—a double-jointed tango Viking lover—not some cold fish L.L.Bean snow queen sitting on a graveyard of money. He felt drunk with confidence . . . until his Nokia squeaked.

It was his wife. He let it ring through to the message bank. Just seeing that number come up right then made him queasy. He squeezed Sophie's Pilates-firm breasts. The phone rang again. Another message dinged a moment later.

"Popular fella," Sophie smirked. "Is it the other chick on the side?"

"I'm afraid not."

"Uh-oh. Is it the office or Sarge?"

Sophie called his wife Sarge, which usually struck him funny. He felt a prickle of irritation this time. What in hell did his wife want? After the Marshal Claver shakedown, he could get paranoid very quickly. He was particularly peeved because although he'd had an intense ejaculation the second round, he was still turgid. If Sophie polished the knob, he thought there might've been a possible shot at another erection—and that would've meant some anal penetration, which he prized more than an option bargain.

The phone rang once more—and then once more. Christ, he thought. Sophie moved to go down on him. Then a text message leapt up like a marquee . . . URGENT CALL NOW . . .

Sophie leaned up and rolled her eyes. "Maybe Sarge is finally on to you."

She gave his penis a final grope and rose to head to the bathroom. He heard the shower come on. OK, he thought, here we go. He pushed the Call Back button.

"Hello, hun."

"Paul! Are you all right?" His wife sounded very manic.

"What? Sure," he said, propping himself up in the bed. With any luck, it was something silly like the garage door not opening.

"Jesus! Where are you?"

Maybe Luke had been hurt at school.

"What, do you mean? I'm at the office," he answered.

"Paul!"

"What is wrong?" He'd never heard her sound so cranked up. In the bathroom the shower water poured down over Sophie's luscious body. Was she singing?

"Where ARE you?" his wife cried.

Hmm, there was something else the matter. He could feel it. He had to stay cool.

"I'm just going into a meeting. It's the Hong Kong deal. Remember?"

"PAUL!"

"Stop shouting. Are you okay?"

"WHERE ARE YOU?"

"I just told you. Sheesh. Take a Valium. Try to relax."

"RELAX??"

"Yeah. What's the matter? What's wrong?"

"WRONG? Jesus Christ, you goddamn liar! Turn on the damn TV! I'm sure she has a TV—whoever the fuck she is!"

"What are you talking about? You sound insane."

"INSANE? I've been shitting myself that you were dead!"

"Why would I—be dead?"

"TURN ON A DAMN TV! AND DON'T YOU EVER COME BACK TO THIS HOUSE, YOU LYING PIECE OF CRAP!"

The remote for the bedroom TV was on the nightstand on his side. He clicked to CNN and swooned with a surge of dread and disbelief.

THE UNITED STATES IS UNDER TERRORIST ATTACK. TWO HIJACKED PLANES HAVE COLLIDED WITH THE NORTH AND SOUTH TOWERS OF THE WORLD TRADE CENTER.

Over and over again, he watched the jets slash into the very building and the very section of the South Tower where he worked. ICONS OF

AMERICAN POWER UNDER THREAT? He could've been sitting at his desk, or giving a presentation in one of the conference rooms. His job, his colleagues, his livelihood . . .

He couldn't process it—couldn't believe the stunned faces in the streets below. The World Trade Towers were on fire, ghastly streams of black smoke trailing out over Lower Manhattan.

WE ARE GETTING REPORTS FROM GROUND LEVEL OF BODIES FALLING . . .

He almost vomited some sticky date muffin. He had to get home. Had to explain to his wife. No wonder she thought he was dead. The entire sky had fallen. What was going to happen next? He dragged on his clothes and tried to brush his hair. "I have to leave!" he hollered at Sophie. He couldn't tell if she replied, "Figured that!" or not. The water was still running. Maybe she'd just wash away. Everything had gone topsy-turvy. She'd see for herself what was up. He could call later. His marriage was on the line. His wife . . . his life . . .

Outside he thought he could see a plume of dark smoke in the distance, and he imagined he could smell the wreckage on the wind. Once in the car, the scene was nearer and clearer. Crystal deadly clear. The streets he knew. Hell, the hallways. The faces. Limbs. The hallways turned to hell—or detonated into nothingness. Holy shit, America under attack. He could barely keep the Spyder on the road. He had to get home.

Crisis management mode. His wife would be on the phone to a divorce lawyer at that very minute. Bells ringing, sirens wailing. There'd be knick-knacks thrown at him. Jagged tiles of ceiling insulation, exploding fluorescent lights. She'd have already frozen the joint accounts. Billowing ash and concrete rubble. The timeshare in the Bahamas would be out of the question. Collapsing girders, suffocating pleas. She'd find out about Sophie's place. Black clouds and flying bolts. The country club membership would be revoked. Mangled bodies, stampedes of burning secretaries. He might never step into the temperature-controlled mahogany crafted wine cellar again. Ralph and Jenny were probably blown to bits in the boardroom.

The radio kept droning . . .

LOWER MANHATTAN IS IN A STATE OF TOTAL CHAOS . . . IT HAS BEEN CONFIRMED THAT AT 8:46 AM A BOEING 767, AMERICAN FLIGHT 11, FLEW INTO THE NORTH TOWER.

MINUTES LATER AT 9:03 AM, A SECOND AIRCRAFT, ANOTHER BOEING 767, UNITED AIRLINES FLIGHT 175, STRUCK THE SOUTH TOWER AT FULL SPEED.

He couldn't stop thinking that if he hadn't skipped out on work for his dalliance with Sophie, he might well have been blasted to smithereens. Instant death. Perhaps many people in his office were gone—never knowing what hit them. Who knows how many others were trapped in a nightmare of glass, steel, cement, and ravaging heat? The streets seemed weirdly empty as he wheeled the Maserati back to face the wrath of his wife. How ironic that his marriage might be destroyed on the same morning as New York City lay under siege.

When he got to Deep Valley Road, he was taken aback to see small American flags planted all along the sides of the road. How odd. Had the whole world gone mad?

THE FRONT GATE OPENS TO A COBBLESTONE DRIVEWAY WHERE BEAUTIFUL GARDENS WELCOME YOU.

Or maybe not.

He swerved in hard to his drive, but the impressive iron gate didn't open. Damn her, she'd already changed the code? Nothing felt very welcoming. In fact, the whole entryway seemed subtly different, as if the flowerbeds and front garden area had been replanted overnight. God, there were so many things he hadn't paid enough attention to.

He had to straggle over the fence like a common thief. His own house.

His wife's SUV was nowhere in sight, and in the garage he spied a mirror-black older Bentley, which seemed very unwelcoming indeed. He was only a little surprised when he found his key didn't open the front door. That woman must be really pissed off, he thought. Like some Jehovah's Witness, he rang the bell.

It was a full agonizing minute before the locks snapped back and a modestly uniformed black maid of about forty opened the cherry wood door. In a Caribbean accent she said, "Sir? What can I do for you?"

"Who are you?" he barked.

The woman took a step back, instinctively clutching the door—but she didn't seem to lose her poise.

"Sir? Do you need help?"

He felt short of breath. They didn't have a black maid. They had Clara, as Irish as you could get. Clara O'Sheay. His wife could've changed the gate code some way, just to goad him—but she couldn't have gotten rid of Clara and hired someone else so fast.

"I want to see the lady of the house!"

"Sir?"

"This is a damn emergency!"

The black woman ran her eyes over his attire, her eyes flickering with fear and indecision. Then she said, "Wait a moment. I'll get Ms. Beatty." She closed and deadlocked the door.

Ms. Beatty? Who in the hell was that? He tried desperately to get his anger under control. His anxiety. Bewilderment.

A figure blurred through warbled glass panel beside the door. A second or two later the locks clicked again, the door opened, and a severe-looking, matronly, gray-haired woman appeared before him, with a quizzical yet somehow flat expression.

"May I help you?" she as much demanded as asked. "I believe you mentioned something about an emergency?"

"I . . ."

He swallowed hard, trying to regain his voice—distracted by the large brooch in the vague shape of a seahorse pinned to the lapel of the woman's slate-blue suit jacket. It seemed curiously familiar. He thought again of the Montblanc pen sailing through the air in his dream. A rush of acid churned in his stomach. Who was this damn woman?

"I'm looking for . . ."

His wife's first name utterly slipped his mind.

Flashpoint.

Goddamnit! He thought his head was going to explode.

"I want to explain . . ."

The air on fire . . . smoke filling the room like time . . . panes shattering. Screams.

He was about to really lose his temper, but a jabbing ache in his bowels made him pause.

"I've seen you before," the woman said, and he didn't like the way she said it. It reminded him of how his mother had often spoken to him. For some reason, he couldn't remember what had happened to his mother.

"You've come here before."

"What?" He was about to bellow at her that this was his house, bought and paid for, without a single dime of mortgage, but he held back.

"I want to see my wife," he said instead.

"That's what you said last time."

"What . . . are you talking about?" A blood vessel in his temple pulsed.

"Last year. On this same day."

A wave of nausea washed through him. He'd gone "green around the gills," as his mother would've said. What had happened to her? Why didn't he know?

"Listen," he said, "I don't mean to scare you, whoever you are. But this . . . is going too far."

"That's exactly what you said then. I remember it clearly."

"I've never seen you before," he said—but he suddenly didn't think that this was true.

Kevlar fairings . . . aluminum alloys . . . splintered windows and corridors filled with flames.

He felt as if he might start to cry, and the shame of that fear made him shudder. Then the image of the Montblanc pen in midair unexpectedly softened him. The woman in the doorway's face seemed to soften too. If she'd appeared tense or annoyed, or just disdainful before, her expression took on some crusted but noticeable form of sympathy.

"Last year when you came, I was about to call the police. I asked you if were on medication. You did scare me. I'm not sure I understand, but I'm not scared now."

"I don't know who you are," he said. "I want to see Mrs. Connors, please."

"As I told you last year, Mrs. Connors's husband died in the attack on the World Trade Center. She sold the house and moved to California. I believe she lives in the Los Angeles area now. I'm . . . very sorry."

A murky brown moment overcame him, a slippage of track somewhere inside. Then a puzzle of plate glass consumed in a roaring mess of light.

"I . . . should . . . go . . ." he managed to wheeze, his ears ringing.

The woman nodded, with a sad gentleness of expression that made her face look much younger. He realized her eyes were the same shade of the evening dress Sophie had worn that first night at the Zinc Bar. He turned to go, leaving the magnificent lakeside hideaway behind.

This time the proud, pretentious iron gate opened for him, but for some reason, he couldn't bring himself to stride through. Instead, he stupidly scaled the fence like a clawing teenager after a bungled burglary, muddying his expensive leather Italian shoes in the manicured flower garden. Perspiration needle-stabbed his forehead and the back of his neck. The ringing in his inner ears intensified . . . the peculiar falling feeling. Something was terribly wrong.

The flags along the roadway rippled, but the liquid gold of the autumn sunshine had turned cold and somehow menacing. He lost his footing for a moment and almost slipped into the pavement as a sleek silver Jaguar eased around. He felt the eyes behind the tinted windows examining him. He must've known them, but they were unfamiliar now. Alien. Everything decidedly strange. Wrong. Deeply wrong on Deep Valley Road.

A bracing breath of wind off Upper Mianus Pond struck his face. Three ducks flew overhead—they reminded him of fighter planes against the bleak, otherwise barren sky. Then, a moment later, a lone duck followed frantically, as if lost, late. Nothing was the way he'd hoped it would be. No.

His entire life had been a lie. From cheating at Yale, to defrauding his clients, and setting up his mentor and loyal business partner—to sneaking around on his wife, ignoring his son. And then there was that clear fresh September day when he'd done the right thing. He was early and prepared for an important meeting. Neatly tailored. Relaxed even. His whole being seized up, like a screwdriver thrust into a chain-wheel drive. He knew who he was—and where he could never be. Ever. The grave certainty was almost peaceful now, tinged with the scent of childhood honeysuckle and the still smoking candles of some lost birthday cake.

He reached the Spyder and felt for the door handle. He noticed the bottle of Piper-Heidsieck. The box of delphinium lace lingerie lay beside it. At the last minute that morning, he'd changed his mind. The car began to gently vanish, melting into the air. His peripheral vision began to cloud and then dissolve . . . strips of film thrown into flame. Deep Valley Road . . . and the deep quiet started coming on again. The hideous trauma would pass, like another neighbor's luxury sedan. Choking kerosene stench of 24,000 gallons of jet fuel ignited on impact. Rupture of glass. Dire crunch of concrete and steel . . . the shearing torn asunder ruination of perfect oblivion. But not so perfect that he couldn't see a Montblanc fountain pen in flight, embedded in a wall that would implode like a dream . . . the screams he could never stop hearing. Then total silence.

He pulled out his cell phone, but it evaporated in his hand. Another anniversary. Then his hand disappeared. A cranberry BMW drove right through him. There would be no more black Indian Ocean pearl necklaces or crab croquettes at midnight. No more explanations or incriminations. He was moving in that other way now . . . receding once again . . . like a sweat stain on a counter top . . . summoned back . . . into the darkness beyond the flags.

Susan Palwick holds a PhD from Yale and is one of the founders of The New York Review of Science Fiction. *Her novel* Flying in Place *won a Crawford Award in 1993 and her second novel,* The Necessary Beggar, *won the Alex Award. She is a columnist for HopeandHealing.org (an Episcopalian website). Reviewing her collection* The Fate of Mice *for Tor.com, author Jo Walton deemed Palwick a "major writer" and, while not prolific, she has continued to make major contributions to the genre for over twenty years.*

"Beautiful Stuff" features a koosh ball, a paperweight, two terrorists, and a slew of reanimated corpses. It is also the most directly life-affirming story in this collection.

BEATIFUL STUFF
Susan Palwick

Rusty Kerfuffle stood on a plastic tarp in an elegant downtown office. The tarp had been spread over fine woolen carpet; the walls were papered in soothing monochrome linen, and the desk in front of Rusty was gleaming hardwood. There was a paperweight on the desk. The paperweight was a crystal globe with a purple flower inside it. In the sunlight from the window, the crystal sparkled, and the flower glowed. Rusty desired that paperweight with a love like starvation, but the man sitting behind the desk wouldn't give it to him.

The man sitting behind the desk wore an expensive suit and a tense expression; next to him, an aide vomited into a bucket. "Sir," the aide said, raising his head from the bucket long enough to gasp out a comment. "Sir, I think this is going to be a public relations disaster."

"Shut up," said the man behind the desk, and the aide resumed vomiting. "You. Do you understand what I'm asking for?"

"Sure," Rusty said, trying not to stare at the paperweight. He knew how smooth and heavy it would feel in his hands; he yearned to caress it. It contained light and life in a precious sphere, a little world.

Rusty's outfit had been a suit, once. Now it was a rotting tangle of fibers. His ear itched, but if he scratched it, it might fall off. He'd been dead for three months. If his ear fell off in this fancy office, the man behind the desk might not let him touch the paperweight.

The man behind the desk exhaled, a sharp sound like the snort of a horse. "Good. You do what I need you to do and you get to walk around again for a day. Understand?"

"Sure," said Rusty. He also understood that the walking part came first. The man behind the desk would have to re-revive Rusty, and all the others, before they could do what had been asked of them. Once they'd been revived, they got their day of walking whether they followed orders or not. "Can I hold the paperweight now?"

The man behind the desk smiled. It wasn't a friendly smile. "No, not yet. You weren't a very nice man when you were alive, Rusty."

"That's true," Rusty said, trying to ignore his itching ear. His fingers itched too, yearning for the paperweight. "I wasn't."

"I know all about you. I know you were cheating on your wife. I know about the insider trading. You were a morally bankrupt shithead, Rusty. But you're a hero now, aren't you? Because you're dead. Your wife thinks you were a saint."

This was, Rusty reflected, highly unlikely. Linda was as adept at running scams as he'd ever been, maybe more so. If she was capitalizing on his death, he couldn't blame her. He'd have done the same thing, if she'd been the one who had died. He was glad to be past that. The living were far too complicated.

He stared impassively at the man behind the desk, whose tie was speckled with reflections from the paperweight. The aide was still vomiting. The man behind the desk gave another mean smile and said, "This is your chance to be a hero for real, Rusty. Do you understand that?"

"Sure," Rusty said, because that was what the man wanted to hear. The sun had gone behind a cloud: the paperweight shone less brightly now. It was just as tantalizing as it had been before, but in a more subdued way.

"Good. Because if you don't come through, if you say the wrong thing, I'll tell your wife what you were really doing, Rusty. I'll tell her what a pathetic slimebag you were. You won't be a hero anymore."

The aide had raised his head again. He looked astonished. He opened his mouth, as if he wanted to say something, but then he closed it. Rusty smiled at him. I may have been a pathetic slimebag, he thought, but I never tried to blackmail a corpse. Even your cringing assistant can see how morally bankrupt that is. The sun came out again, and the paperweight resumed its sparkling. "Got it," Rusty said happily.

The man behind the desk finally relaxed a little. He sat back in his chair. He became indulgent and expansive. "Good, Rusty. That's excellent. You're going to do the right thing for once, aren't you? You're going to help me convince all those cowards out there to stop sitting on their butts."

"Yes," Rusty said. "I'm going to do the right thing. Thank you for the opportunity, sir." This time, he wasn't being ironic.

"You're welcome, Rusty."

Rusty felt himself about to wiggle, like a puppy. "Now can I hold the paperweight? Please?"

"Okay, Rusty. Come and get it."

Rusty stepped forward, careful to stay on the tarp, and picked up the paperweight. It was as smooth and heavy and wonderful as he had known it would be. He cradled it to his chest, the glass pleasantly cool against his fingers, and began swaying back and forth.

Rusty had never understood the science behind corpse revival, but he supposed it didn't matter. Here he was, revived. He did know that the technique was hideously expensive. When it was first invented, mourning families had forked over life savings, taken out second mortgages, gone into staggering debt simply to have another day with their lost loved ones.

That trend didn't last long. The dead weren't attractive. The technique only worked on those who hadn't been embalmed or cremated, because there had to be a more-or-less intact, more-or-less chemically unaltered body to revive. That meant it got used most often on accident and suicide victims: the sudden dead, the unexpected dead, the dead who had gone without farewells. The unlovely dead, mangled and wounded.

The dead smelled, and they were visibly decayed, depending on the gap between when they had died and when they had been revived. They shed fingers and noses. They left behind pieces of themselves as mementos. And they had very little interest in the machinations of the living. Other things drew them. They loved flowers and animals. They loved to play with food. Running faucets enchanted them. The first dead person to be revived, a Mr. Otis Magruder who had killed himself running into a tree while skiing, spent his twenty-four hours of second life sitting in his driveway making mud puddles while his wife and children told him how much they loved him. Each time one of his relations delivered another impassioned statement of devotion, Otis nodded, and said "Uh-huh." And then he ran his fingers through more mud, and smiled. At hour eighteen, when his wife, despairing, asked if there was anything she could tell him, anything she could give him, he cocked his head and said, "Do you have a plastic pail?"

Six hours later, when Otis was mercifully dead again, his wife told reporters, "Well, Otis was always kind of spacy. That's why he ran into that tree, I guess." But it turned out that the other revived dead—tycoons, scientists, gangsters—were spacy too. The dead didn't care about the same things the living did.

These days, the dead were revived only rarely, usually to testify in criminal cases involving their death or civil cases involving the financial details of their estates. They made bad witnesses. They became distracted by brightly colored neckties, by the reflection of the courtroom lights in the polished wood of the witness box, by the gentle clicking of the clerk's recording instrument. It was very difficult to keep them on track, to remind them what they were supposed to be thinking about. On the other hand, they had amazingly accurate memories, once they could be cajoled into paying attention to the subject at hand. Bribes of balloons and small, brightly colored toys worked well; jurors became used to watching the dead weep in frustration while scolding lawyers held matchbox cars and neon-hued stuffed animals just out of reach. But once the dead gave the information the living sought, they always told the truth. No one had ever caught one of the dead lying, no matter how dishonest the corpse might have been while it was still alive.

It had been very difficult for the man behind the desk to break through Rusty's fascination with the paperweight. It had taken a lot to get Rusty's attention. The sheer numbers involved—the numbers of the dead, the amounts of money required—hadn't done it. Intelligence about Rusty's affairs and insider deals hadn't done it. None of that mattered anymore. It was a set of extraneous details, as distant as the moon and as abstract as ethics, which also had no hold on Rusty.

Rusty's passions and loyalties were much more basic now.

He stood in the elegant office, rocking the paperweight as if it were a baby, crooning to it, sometimes holding it at arm's length to admire it before bringing it back safely to his chest again. He had another two hours of revival left this time; the man behind the desk would revive him and the others again in a month, for another twenty-four hours. Rusty fully intended to spend every minute of his current two hours in contemplation of the paperweight. When he was revived again in a month, he'd fall in love with something else.

"You idiot," said the man who had been sitting behind the desk. He wasn't behind a desk now; he was in a refrigerated warehouse, a month after that first meeting with Rusty. He was yelling at his aide. Around him were the revived dead, waiting to climb into refrigerated trucks to be taken to the rally site. It was a lovely, warm spring day, and they'd smell less if they were kept cool for as long as possible. "I don't want them." He waved at two of the dead, more mangled than any of the others, charred and lacerated and nearly unrecognizable as human bodies. One was playing with a paperclip that had been lying on the floor; the other opened and closed its hand, trying to catch the dust motes that floated in the shafts of light from the window.

The aide was sweating, despite the chill of the warehouse. "Sir, you said—"

"I know what I said, you moron!"

"Everyone who was there, you said—"

"Idiot." The voice was very quiet now, very dangerous. "Idiot. Do you know why we're doing this? Have you been paying attention?"

"Sir," the aide stuttered. "Yes sir."

"Oh, really? Because if you'd been paying attention, they wouldn't be here!"

"But—"

"Prove to me that you understand," said the dangerously quiet voice. "Tell me why we're doing this."

The aide gulped. "To remind people where their loyalties lie. Sir."

"Yes. And where do their loyalties lie? Or where should their loyalties lie?"

"With innocent victims. Sir."

"Yes. Exactly. And are those, those things over there"—an impassioned hand waved at the two mangled corpses—"are they innocent victims?"

"No. Sir."

"No. They aren't. They're the monsters who were responsible for all these other innocent victims! They're the guilty ones, aren't they?"

"Yes sir."

"They deserve to be dead, don't they?"

"Yes sir." The aide stood miserably twisting his hands.

"The entire point of this rally is to demonstrate that some people deserve to be dead, isn't it?"

"Yes sir!"

"Right. So why in the name of everything that's holy were those monsters revived?"

The aide coughed. "We were using the new technique. Sir. The blanket-revival technique. It works over a given geographical area. They were mixed in with the others. We couldn't be that precise."

"Fuck that," said the quiet voice, succinctly.

"It would have been far too expensive to revive all of them individually," the aide said. "The new technique saved us—"

"Yes, I know how much it saved us! And I know how much we're going to lose if this doesn't work! Get rid of them! I don't want them on the truck! I don't want them at the rally!"

"Sir! Yes, sir!"

The aide, once his boss had left, set about correcting the situation. He told the two unwanted corpses that they weren't needed. He tried to be polite about it. It was difficult to get their attention away from the paperclip and the dust motes; he had to distract them with a penlight and a koosh ball, and that worked well enough, except that some of the other corpses got distracted too, and began crowding around the aide, cooing and reaching for the koosh ball. There were maybe twenty of them, the ones who had been closest; the others, thank God, were still off in their own little worlds. But these twenty all wanted that koosh ball. The aide felt like he was in a preschool in hell, or possibly in a dovecote of extremely deformed and demented pigeons.

"Listen to me!" he said, raising his voice over the cooing. "Listen! You two! You with the paperclip and you with the dust motes! We don't want you, okay? We just want everyone else! You two, do not get on the trucks! Have you got that? Yes? Is that a nod? Is that a yes?"

"Yesh," said the corpse with the paperclip, and the one who'd been entranced by the dust motes nodded.

"All right then," said the aide, and tossed the koosh ball over their heads into a corner of the warehouse. There was a chorus of happy shrieks and a stampede of corpses. The aide took the opportunity to get out of there, into fresh air. His dramamine was wearing off. He didn't know if the message had really gotten through or not, but fuck it: this whole thing was going to be a public-relations disaster, no matter who got on the trucks. He no longer cared if he kept his job. In fact, he hoped he got fired, because that way he could collect unemployment. As soon as the rally was over, he'd go home and start working on his resume.

Back in the warehouse, Rusty had a firm grip on the koosh ball. He had purposefully stayed at the back of the crowd. He knew what he had to do, and he had been concentrating very hard on staying focused, although it was difficult not to be distracted by all the wonderful things around him: the aide's tie, a piece of torn newspaper on the floor, the gleaming hubcaps of the trucks. His mind wasn't working as well as it had been during his first revival, and it took all his energy to concentrate. He stayed at the back of the crowd and kept his eyes on the koosh ball, and when the aide tossed it into the corner, Rusty was the first one there. He had it. He picked it up, thrilling at its texture, and did the hardest thing he had ever done: he sacrificed the pleasure of the koosh ball. He forced himself to let go of it for the greater good. He tossed it into the back of the nearest truck and watched his twenty fellows rush in joy up the loading ramp. Were the two unwanted corpses there? Yes, they were. In the excitement, they had forgotten their promise to the aide.

Rusty ran to the truck. He climbed inside with the others, fighting his longing to join the exuberant scramble for the koosh ball. But instead, Rusty Kerfuffle, who was not a hero and had not been a very nice man, pulled something from his pocket. He had a pocket because the man with the quiet voice had given him a new blue blazer to wear, so he'd be more presentable, and inside the pocket was a glass paperweight with a purple flower inside. Rusty had been allowed to keep the paperweight last time, because no one else wanted to touch it now. "It has fucking corpse germs all over it," the man with the quiet voice had told him, and Rusty had trembled with joy. He wouldn't have to fall in love with something else after all; he could stay in love with this.

Rusty used the paperweight now to distract the two unwanted corpses, and several of the others closest to him, from the koosh ball. And then he started talking to them—although it was very, very hard for him to stay on track, because all he wanted to do was fondle the paperweight—and waited for the truck doors to be closed.

Outside the warehouse, it was spring: a balmy, fragrant season. The refrigerated trucks rolled past medians filled with cheerful flowers, past sidewalks where pedestrians strolled, their faces lifted to the sun, past parks where children on swings pumped themselves into the air in ecstasies of flight. At last the convoy of trucks pulled into a larger park, the park at the center of the city, and along tree-lined roads to a bandstand in the very center of that park. The man with the quiet voice stood at the bandstand podium, his aide beside him. One side of the audience consisted of people waving signs in support of the man with the quiet voice. The other side consisted of people waving signs denouncing him. Both sides were peppered with reporters, with cameras and microphones. The man with the quiet voice stared stonily down the center aisle, and read the speech prepared by his aide.

"Four months ago," he said, "this city suffered a devastating attack. Hundreds of innocent people were killed. Those people were your husbands and wives, your children, your brothers and sisters, your friends. They were cut down in the prime of their lives by enemies to whom they had done no harm, who wanted nothing more than to destroy them, to destroy all of us. They were cut down by pure evil."

The man with the quiet voice paused, waiting for the crowd to stir. It didn't. The crowd waited, watching him. The only thing that stirred was the balmy spring wind, moving the leaves. The man at the podium cleared his throat. "As a result of that outrageous act of destruction, the brave leaders of our great nation determined that we had to strike back. We could not let this horror go unanswered. And so we sent our courageous troops to address the evil, to destroy the evil, to stamp out the powers that had cut down our loved ones in their prime."

Again he paused. The audience stirred now, a little bit. Someone on one side waved a sign that said, "We Will Never Forget!" Someone on the other side waved a sign that said, "An Eye for An Eye Makes the Whole World Blind." The cameras whirred. The birds twittered. The refrigerated trucks rolled up to the edge of the bandshell, and the man at the podium smiled.

"I supported the courageous decision of our brave leaders," he said. His voice was less quiet now. "There was only one way to respond to this devastating grief, this hideous loss, this violation of all that we hold dear and sacred. This was the principled stance taken by millions of people in our great nation. But certain others among us, among you"—here he glared at the person who had waved the second sign—"have claimed that this makes me unworthy to continue to hold office, unworthy to continue to be your leader. If that is true, then many of the leaders of this country are also unworthy."

His voice had risen to something like a crescendo. The woman standing next to the man who had waved the second sign cupped her hands around her mouth and called out cheerfully, "No argument there, boss!" A few people laughed; a few people booed; the cameras whirred. The man at the podium glared, and spoke again, now not quietly at all.

"But it is not true! The leaders of this city, of this state, of this nation must be brave! Must be principled! Must be ready to fight wrong wherever they find it!"

"Must be ready to send innocent young people to kill other innocent young people," the same woman called back. The booing was louder now. The man at the podium smiled, grimly.

"Let us remember who is truly innocent. Let us remember who was truly innocent four months ago. If they could speak to us, what would they say? Well, you are about to find out. I have brought them here today, our beloved dead, to speak to us, to tell us what they would have us do."

He gave a signal. The truck doors were opened. The corpses shambled out, blinking in the glorious sunshine, gaping at trees and flowers and folding chairs and whirring cameras. The crowd gave a gratifying gasp, and several people began to sob. Others began to retch. Additional aides in the audience, well prepared for all eventualities, began handing out packets of tissues and barf bags, both imprinted with campaign slogans.

Rusty Kerfuffle, doggedly ignoring the trees and flowers and folding chairs and cameras, doggedly ignoring the knowledge that his beloved paperweight was in his pocket, moved towards the podium, dragging the unwanted corpses with him. In the van, he had accomplished the very difficult task of removing certain items of clothing from other corpses and outfitting these two, so maybe the man with the quiet voice wouldn't realize what he was doing and try to stop him. At least for the moment, it seemed to be working.

The man with the quiet voice was saying something about love and loss and outrage. His aides were trying to corral wandering corpses. More people in the audience were retching. Rusty, holding an unwanted corpse's hand in each of his—the three of them like small children cross- ing a street together—squinted his eyes almost shut, so he wouldn't see all the distracting things around him. Stay focused, Rusty. Get to the podium.

He got to the podium. Three steps up and he was on the podium, the unwanted corpses beside him. The man with the quiet voice turned and smiled at him. "And now, ladies and gentleman, I give you Rusty Kerfuffle, the heroic husband of Linda Kerfuffle, whom you've all seen on television. Linda, are you here?"

"Darling!" gasped a woman in the crowd. She ran towards the podium, but was overtaken by retching halfway there. Rusty wondered how much she was being paid.

An aide patted Linda on the back and handed her a barf bag. The aide on the platform murmured "public relations disaster," too softly for the microphones. The quiet man coughed and cleared his throat and poked Rusty in the back.

Rusty understood that this was his cue to do something. "Hi, Linda," said Rusty. He couldn't tell if the microphones had picked that up, so he waved. Linda waved back, took a few steps closer to the podium, and was overcome with retching again.

The aide on the platform groaned, and the man with the quiet voice forged grimly ahead. "I have brought back Rusty and these other brave citizens and patriots, your lost loved ones, to tell you how important it is to fight evil, to tell you about the waste and horror of their deaths, to implore you to do the right thing, since some of you have become misled by propaganda."

Rusty had just caught a glimpse of a butterfly, and it took every ounce of his will not to turn to run after it, to walk up to the microphone instead. But he did his duty. He walked up to the microphone, pulling his two companions.

"Hi," he said. "I'm Rusty. Wait, you know that."

The crowd stared at him, some still retching. Linda was wiping her mouth. Some people were walking away. "Wait," Rusty called after them. "It's really important. It really is." A few stopped and turned, standing with their arms folded; others kept walking. Rusty had to say something to make them stop. "Wait," he said. "This guy's wrong. I wasn't brave. I wasn't patriotic. I cheated on my wife. Linda, I cheated on you, but I think you knew that. I think you were cheating on me too. It's okay; it doesn't matter now. I cheated on other stuff, too. I cheated on my taxes. I was guilty of insider trading. I was a morally bankrupt shithead." He pointed at the man with the quiet voice. "That's his phrase, not mine, but it fits." There: now he couldn't be blackmailed.

Most of the people who'd been walking away had stopped now: good. The man with the quiet voice was hissing. "Rusty, what are you doing?"

"I'm doing what he wants me to do," Rusty said into the microphone. "I'm, what was that word, imploring you to do the right thing."

He stopped, out of words, and concentrated very hard on what he was going to say next. He caught a flash of purple out of the corner of his left eye. Was that another butterfly? He turned. No: it was a splendid purple bandana. The aide on the platform was waving it at Rusty. Rusty's heart melted. He fell in love with the bandana. The bandana was the most exquisite thing he had ever seen. Who wouldn't covet the bandana? And indeed, one of his companions, the one on the left, was snatching at it.

Rusty took a step towards the bandana, and then forced himself to stop. No. The aide was trying to distract him. The aide was cheating. The bandana was a trick. Rusty still had his paperweight. He didn't need the bandana.

Heartsick, nearly sobbing, Rusty turned back to the podium, dragging the other corpse with him. The other corpse whimpered, but Rusty prevailed. He knew that this was very important. It was as important as the paperweight in his pocket. He could no longer remember why, but he remembered that he had known once.

"Darling!" Linda said, running towards him. "Darling! I forgive you! I love you! Dear Rusty!"

She was wearing a shiny barrette. She never wore barrettes. It was another trick. Rusty began to tremble. "Linda," he said into the microphone. "Shut up. Shut up and go away, Linda. I have to say something."

Rusty's other companion, the one on his right, let out a small squeal and tried to lurch towards Linda, towards the barrette. "No," Rusty said, keeping desperate hold. "You stay here. Linda, take that shiny thing off! Hide it, Linda!"

"Darling!" she said, and the righthand corpse broke away from Rusty and hopped off the podium, towards Linda. Linda screamed and ran, the corpse trotting after her. Rusty sighed; the aide groaned again; the quiet man cursed, softly.

"Okay," Rusty said, "so here's what I have to tell you." Some of the people in the crowd who'd turned to watch Linda and her pursuer turned back towards Rusty now, but others didn't. Well, he couldn't do anything about that. He had to say this thing. He could remember what he had to say, but he couldn't remember why. That was all right. He'd say it, and then maybe he'd remember.

"What I have to tell you is, dying hurts," Rusty said. The crowd murmured. "Dying hurts a lot. It hurts—everybody hurts." Rusty struggled to remember why this mattered. He dimly remembered dying, remembered other people dying around him. "It hurts everybody. It makes everybody the same. This guy, and that other one who ran away, they hurt too. This is Ari. That was Ahmed. They were the ones who planted the bomb. They didn't get out in time. They died too." Gasps, some louder murmurs, louder cursing from the man with the quiet voice. Rusty definitely had everyone's attention now.

He prodded Ari. "It hurt," Ari said.

"And?" said Rusty.

"We're sorry," said Ari.

"Ahmed's sorry too," said Rusty. "He told me. He'd have told you, if he weren't chasing Linda's shiny hair thing."

"If we'd known, we wouldn't have done it," Ari said.

"Because?" Rusty said patiently.

"We did it for the wrong reasons," Ari said. "We expected things to happen that didn't happen. Paradise, and, like, virgins." Ari looked shyly down at his decaying feet. "I'm sorry."

"More," Rusty said. "Tell them more."

"Dying hurts," said Ari. "It won't make you happy. It won't make anybody happy."

"So please do the right thing," said Rusty. "Don't kill anybody else."

The man with the quiet voice let out a howl and leaped towards Rusty. He grabbed Rusty's free arm, the right one, and pulled; the arm came off, and the man with the quiet voice started hitting Rusty over the head with it. "You fucking incompetent! You traitor! You said you'd tell them—"

"I lied," Rusty said. "I'm not a nice man. What are you going to do, kill me?" He looked out at the crowd and said, "We're the dead. You loved some of us. You hated others. We're the dead. We're here to tell you: please don't kill anybody else. Everybody will be dead soon enough, whether you kill them or not. It hurts."

The crowd stared; the cameras whirred. None of the living there that day had ever heard such long speeches from the dead. It was truly a historic occasion. A group of aides had managed to drag away the man with the quiet voice, who was still brandishing Rusty's arm; Rusty, with his one arm, stood at the podium with Ari.

"Look," Rusty said. He let go of Ari's hand and reached around to pull the paperweight out of his pocket. He held it up in front of the crowd. Ari cooed and reached for it, entranced, but Rusty held it above his head. "Look at this! Look at the shiny glass. Look at the flower. It's beautiful. You have all this stuff in your life, all this beautiful stuff. Sunshine and grass and butterflies. Barrettes. Bandanas. You don't have that when you're dead. That's why dying hurts."

And Rusty shivered, and remembered: he remembered dying, knowing he'd never see trees again, never drink coffee, never smell flowers or see buildings reflected in windows. He remembered that pain, the pain of knowing what he was losing only when it was too late. And he knew that the living wouldn't understand, couldn't understand. Or maybe some of them did, but the others would only make fun of them. He finished his speech lamely, miserably, knowing that everyone would say it was just a cliche. "Enjoy the beautiful stuff while you have it."

The woman who had heckled the man with the quiet voice was frowning. "You're advocating greed! That's what gets people killed. People murder each other for stuff!"

"No," Rusty said. He was exhausted. She didn't understand. She'd probably never understand unless she died and got revived. "Just enjoy it. Look at it. Don't fight. You don't get it, do you?"

"No," she said. "I don't."

Rusty shrugged. He was too tired; he couldn't keep his focus anymore. He no longer cared if the woman got it or not. The man with the quiet voice had been taken away, and Rusty had done what he had wanted to do, although it seemed much less important now than it had even a month ago, when he was first revived. He remembered, dimly, that no one had ever managed to teach the living anything much. Some of them might get it. He'd done what he could. He'd told them what mattered.

His attention wandered away from the woman, away from the crowd. He brought the paperweight back down to chest level, and then he sat down on the edge of the platform, and Ari sat with him, and they both stared at the paperweight, touching it, humming in happiness there in the sunshine.

The crowd watched them for a while, and then it wandered away, too. The other corpses had already wandered. The dead meandered through the beautiful budding park, all of them in love: one with a sparrow on the walk, one with a silk scarf a woman in the audience had given him, one with an empty, semi-crushed milk carton she had plucked out of a trashcan. The dead fell in love, and they walked or they sat, carrying what they loved or letting it hold them in place. They loved their beautiful stuff for the rest of the day, until the sun went down; and then they lay down too, their treasures beside them, and slept again, and this time did not wake.

TWO: REACTION AND REPETITION

After the attacks of 9/11 we found ourselves holding our breath. We'd seen the New York skyline altered, the Twin Towers destroyed. What would happen next? Where would history take us and would we be able to recognize ourselves when we got to the other side?

"The search is under way for those who are behind these evil acts. I have directed the full resources of our intelligence and law-enforcement communities to find those responsible and to bring them to justice," Bush told us. "We will make no distinction between those who committed these acts and those who harbor them."

The CNN logo for America's New War arrived in the first few days. It was red, white, and blue and was set above the scroll of headlines that ran right to left on the bottom of our screens. But the US wouldn't start bombing for nearly a month after the attacks, and so in the meantime we all sat around and waited for the retaliation. We watched the headlines scroll by and held our breath with the hope that it could all, somehow, be contained.

The truth was that we wanted a new war, because along with a desire for closure there was also a desire to repeat. We were traumatized, after all, and you could see this reaction to the attacks, this desire to repeat, in the statements of politicians who promised that another attack was sure to come, that there was no way to stop it. You could see the desire to repeat on protest signs that read "I'm already against America's next war."

In the 90s, America had forgotten about, had even tried to debunk, the idea of history and with it the notion of change. The Cold War was over, we'd won, and now we were free to rebuild that American dream we'd thought the sixties and seventies had destroyed. Reagan had defeated our enemies and we all had hope. We could finally build a utopian America as a land littered with gadgets, four-car garages, and entertainment centers built by AOL/Time Warner.

In the excerpt from Bruce Sterling's novel *The Zenith Angle*, there are a few lines that sum up America's attitude, or at least the utopian side of America's attitude, before the attacks. It's a sentiment that the protagonist expresses when he finds out what's happened in New York:

> Van's New Year's resolution for the year 2001 had been to never panic over vaporware again. So Van stilled his beating heart as the blasted skyscraper burned fantastically on his television.

We'd thought that history and change was just vaporware, a product announced but destined to never arrive. When we saw that we'd been wrong, that the world could still change, our hearts raced and saliva built up in our mouths. While the stories in this section are all very different from each other—some of them are angry, some of them are quite sad, and one ends in nothing but the realization of a shock—they are all, I think, tales of reaction and that desire for the trauma to repeat.

Something had finally happened. Maybe we could make it happen again.

Bruce Sterling is one of the founders of the Cyberpunk movement and one of its most vocal and influential spokespeople. He also coined the term "slipstream" to describe the genre of science fiction or fantasy arising in the late 20th century with literary or mainstream ambitions. He has won two Hugos and several other literary awards, and is the author of nearly a dozen novels, including The Artificial Kid, Schismatrix, The Difference Engine, *and* The Zenith Angle.

This excerpt from The Zenith Angle *describes the high-tech but tranquil upper-class existence of protagonist Derek "Van" Vandeveer. A computer expert working for an Internet company before the dot-com crash, Van's world is interrupted by history when the Towers fall.*

EXCERPT FROM
THE ZENITH ANGLE
Bruce Sterling

New Jersey, September 11, 2001

With eager screams of hunger, little Ted Vandeveer drove his parents from their bed.

Dottie slipped a rubber-coated spoon between the infant's lips. Baby Ted blew out his chubby cheeks. Porridge spurted across the table.

Dottie scanned the mess. Her eyelids flickered upward meaningfully.

"Where's the au pair?" Van hedged.

"She didn't come in last night."

Van rose from his white plastic chair, and fetched a white paper towel. With the wisdom of experience, Van tore off a second towel for Ted to use as backup. Van still felt giddy inside his mansion's bright new kitchen. The new kitchen featured deep steel sinks, thick red granite counters, and a chromed fridge the size of a bank vault. When he'd signed up for a house renovation, Van hadn't known that New Jersey contractors were so enthusiastic.

At least, Van thought, Dottie approved of the changes in their house. The mansion's original kitchen had been a nightmare straight out of H. P. Lovecraft. Dottie's new kitchen was now the only place in the Vandeveer home where the plumbing worked properly.

On a corner of the new stove, a small TV played WNBC out of New York City. Van had hooked the set to a pair of rabbit ears. The town of Merwinster, New Jersey, lacked cable television. This was a serious blow to the Vandeveers, who were dedicated fans of *Babylon 5*, *Red Dwarf* and *The X-Files*. But Mondiale was the little town's biggest employer, and Mondiale was in the broadband Internet business. Mondiale despised all cable TV outfits.

Van towelled up the baby's spew. Baby Ted enjoyed this fatherly attention. He kicked his chubby feet and emitted a joyous string of syllables.

"He said 'dada,'" Van remarked.

Dottie yawned and stirred the baby's porridge, propping her head on one slender hand. "Oh, Derek, he's just babbling."

Van said nothing. As a telecom expert, Van knew definitely that his son's vocalizations had contained the phonemes "dada." Technically speaking, Van was absolutely correct. However, he had learned never to argue with Dottie about such things.

Van dropped the dirty towel into a shiny kick-top wastebasket. He sat again in his plastic picnic chair, which popped and squeaked under his bulk. Van accepted this embarrassment quietly. He knew that it was all his own fault. He, Dr. Derek Vandeveer, famous computer scientist, owned a decaying Victorian mansion that had no proper furniture.

Historical Merwinster, New Jersey, was a gabled, colonial village, woody and surrounded by horse farms. It also boasted the third-biggest clump of fiber-optics on America's Eastern Seaboard. Merwinster was a superb place for advancing high-tech research. Van routinely put in sixty-hour weeks inside the Mondiale R&D lab, so he was forced to live in the town.

Dr. Dottie Vandeveer spent her days in Boston, at the Smithsonian Astrophysics Lab. Van had bought the two of them a house in Merwinster because it seemed wrong to Van for his baby, their new third party, to have no home. Besides, Van had to do something practical with his money. Van was making money, and not just a lot of money. Van was the

VP for Research and Development at Mondiale. Van was making a weird amount of money.

The TV muttered through a headache commercial, obscuring baby Ted's eager slurps from Dottie's rubber spoon. Van tapped at his trusty ThinkPad and checked the titles of the 117 pieces of email piled up for him behind Mondiale's corporate firewall. With an effort, Van decided to ignore his email, at least until noon. Because Dottie was home with him. Dottie was sleeping with him, and lavishing her sweet attentions on him. Dottie was cooking and cleaning and changing diapers. Dottie was wandering from room to dark decaying room inside the Vandeveer mansion, and wrinkling her brow with a judgmental, wifely look. Today, furnishing the house had priority.

So far, in his rare moments outside of the Mondiale science lab, Van had managed to buy a crib, a playpen, a feeding chair, a Spanish leather couch, a polished walnut table for the breakfast nook, a forty-six inch flat-screen digital TV with DVD and VCR, and a nice solid marital bed. Van had also installed a sleek, modern Danish bedroom suite upstairs, for Helga the au pair girl. Helga the au pair girl was Swedish and nineteen. Helga had the best-furnished room in the Vandeveer mansion, but she almost never slept in.

According to Dottie, when she and Helga were alone together in Boston, the girl was always gentle, very sweet to the baby, and was never into any trouble with men. But in quiet little Merwinster, Helga went nuts. Helga was hell on wheels with the local computer nerds. She was a man-eater. The geeks were falling for blond Swedish Helga like bowling pins. Van sometimes wondered if he should charge them lane fees.

Dottie put the baby's yellow goop aside and got up to make toast and eggs. Van took rare pleasure in watching Dottie cooking for him. Dottie was not a natural cook. However, she had memorized an efficient routine for the creation of breakfast. Dottie fetched the brown eggs out of their recycled-paper carton and cracked them on the edge of the white blue-striped bowl, hitting the same spot on the rim, precisely, perfectly, every single time.

This sight touched something in Van that he lacked all words for. There was something silent and dark and colossal about the love he had for Dottie, like lake water moving under ice. The pleasure of watching her cooking was much like the secret pleasure he took in watching Dottie dress in the morning. Van loved to watch her, nude, tousled and bleary, daintily attacking all her feminine rituals until she had fully assembled her public Dottieness. Watching Dottie dressing touched him even more than watching Dottie undressing.

Baby Ted was eleven months old. Ted had some major abandonment issues. Deprived of his mommy and his rubber spoon, Ted jacked his chubby knees in his high chair, with a wild, itchy look. Van watched his baby son intensely. The baby was of deep interest to Van. With his shock of fine fluffy hair and his bulging potbelly, baby Ted looked very much like Van's father-in-law, a solemn electrical engineer who had made a small fortune inventing specialized actuators.

Baby Ted packed a scream that could pierce like an ice pick. However, Ted changed his mind about howling for his mother. Instead, he picked intently at four loose Cheerios with his thumb and forefinger. Van sensed that picking up and eating a Cheerio was a major achievement for Ted. It was the baby equivalent of an adult landing a job.

Van ran his fingers through his thick sandy beard, still wet from the morning shower. He set his ThinkPad firmly aside to confront an unsteady heap of magazines. Junk-mail catalog people had gotten wind of Van's huge paycheck. For them, a computer geek with a new house and new baby was a gold mine.

Van didn't enjoy shopping, generally. Van enjoyed mathematics, tech hardware, cool sci-fi movies, his wife's company, and bowling. However, shopping had one great advantage for Van. Shopping made Van stop thinking about Nash equilibria and latency functions. Van had been thinking about these two computer-science issues for three months, seriously. Then for two weeks very seriously and then for the last six days very, very seriously. So seriously that even Dottie became invisible to him. So seriously that sometimes Van had trouble walking.

However, Van's network-latency analysis had been successfully completed and written up. The white paper would be widely admired by key members of the IEEE, and cordially ignored by the Mondiale board of directors. So Van had given himself some time off.

Dottie, slim and delicious and barefoot, was silently reading the instructions that came with her new toaster oven. Dottie always read all the instructions for everything. Dottie always studied the safety disclaimers and even the shrink-wrap contracts on software.

Back at MIT, classmates at the lab had teased Dottie about her compulsive habits. Van, however, had noticed that Dottie never made the dumb beginner's mistakes that everybody else made. Dottie was pleased to have this quality of hers recognized and admired. Eventually Dottie wrote her own vows and then married him.

Van leafed through thick colorful pages and discovered a Fortebraccio task lamp. The designer lamp looked both spoonlike and medical. It had the robust, optimistic feeling of a vintage Gene Roddenberry *Star Trek* episode. It rocked totally.

Van ripped the lamp's page from the catalog, and dumped the rest into the recycling bin at his elbow. Van's next catalog was chock-full of chairs. Van, his attention fully snagged now, settled deeply into the problem at hand. He was sitting uncomfortably in a lousy plastic picnic chair, one of a set of six that he had bought on a hasty lunch break at the nearest Home Depot. That situation just wouldn't do.

Dottie repeated herself. "Derek! You want seven-grain bread or whole wheat?"

Van came to with a start. "Which loaf has more in the queue?"

"Uhm, the whole wheat loaf has more slices left."

"Give me the other one." Logically, that bread was bound to taste better.

As a serious programmer, Van used an Aeron chair at his work. The Aeron was in some sense the ultimate programmer's working chair. The Aeron was the only chair that a hard-core hacker lifestyle required. Van hunched his thick shoulders thoughtfully. Yet, a family home did require some domestic chairs. For instance, an Aeron lacked the proper parameters for breakfast use. Spattered baby food would stick inside the Aeron's nylon mesh.

Van winced at the memory of the three FBI guys who had shown up at his Merwinster mansion, seeking his computer security advice. The FBI G-men had been forced to sit in Van's white plastic picnic chairs. The Bureau guys hadn't said a word about the plastic chairs—they just drank their instant coffee and took thorough notes on yellow legal pads—but they got that dismissive FBI look in their eyes. They were reclassifying him as a mere informant rather than a fully qualified expert. That wouldn't do, either.

Dottie didn't know about the FBI and their discreet visits to the house. Van hadn't told Dottie about the FBI, for he knew she wouldn't approve. The interested parties from the Treasury Department and the U.S. Navy Office of Special Investigations had also escaped Dottie's notice.

This was some catalog. It had chairs made of black leather and bent chrome tubing. Chairs like baseball mitts. Chairs like bent martini glasses. Chairs cut from single sheets of pale, ripply plywood.

Dottie slid a breakfast plate before him. Dottie's new toaster oven had browned Van's toast to absolute perfection. Van had never before witnessed such perfect toast. It lacked the crude striping effect that toast got from the cheap hot wires in everyday toasters.

"Derek, can you open this?"

Van put his manly grip to an imported black jar of English jam. The enameled lid popped off with a hollow smack. There was a rush of aroma so intense that Van felt five years old. This was very good jam. This black British jam had such royal Buckingham Palace authority that Van wanted to jump right up and salute.

"Honey, this stuff is some jam."

"It's blackberry!" Dottie sang out from behind her copper frying pan. "It's your favorite!"

Even the baby was astounded by the wondrous smell of the jam. Ted's round blue eyes went tense. "Dada!" he said.

"He said 'dada' again." Van spread the happy black jam across his perfect toast.

Ted slapped his spit-shiny mitts on his feeding tray. "Dada!" he screeched. "Dada!"

Dottie stared at her son in awe and delight. "Derek, he did say it!"

She rushed over to praise and caress the baby. Baby Ted grinned up at her. "Dada," he confided. Ted was always good-natured about his mother. He did his best to mellow her out.

Van watched the two of them carrying on. Life was very good for the Dada today. Van wolfed down all eight pieces of his toast. This was a caviar among blackberry jams. "Where on earth did you find this stuff, Dots?"

"Off the Internet."

"That'll work. Can you get a case discount?"

"You want more?"

"You bet. Point, click, and ship."

Van leaned back and slid his toast-crumbled plate aside, increasingly pleased with the universe. Dottie sidled over, bearing a plate of fluffy scrambled eggs. Van lifted his fork, but then his gaze collided with yet another catalog chair. The spectacle unhinged him.

"Holy gosh, Dottie! Look at this thing. Now that's a chair!"

"It looks like a spider."

"No, it's like an elk! Look at those legs!"

"The legs, that's the most spidery part."

"It's made out of cast magnesium!"

Dottie took away Van's jar of jam. "Paging Stanley Kubrick."

No way, thought Van. Kubrick's movie 2001 was all 1968! Now that it really was 2001, all that futuristic stuff was completely old-fashioned. Van sampled his scrambled eggs. "Magnesium! Wow, no one on earth can tool that stuff, and now it's in chairs!"

Dottie set her own plate down, with dabs of food on it that would scarcely feed a sparrow. She heaved the restless baby from his high chair and propped him on her slender thigh. Ted was a big kid and Dottie was a small woman. Ted flopped back and forth, flinging his solid head at her like a stray cannonball. "How much does it cost?" she said practically.

"Six hundred. Plus shipping."

"Six hundred dollars for one chair, Derek?"

"But it's magnesium and polycarbonate!" Van argued. "They only weigh seven kilograms. You can stack them."

Dottie examined the catalog page, fork halfway to her tender mouth. "But this chair doesn't even have a real back."

"It's got a back!" Van protested. "That thing that grows out of its arms, that is its back, see? I bet it's a lot more fun to sit in than it looks."

Dottie poured Van fresh coffee as Ted yanked at her pageboy brown hair.

"You don't like it," Van realized mournfully.

"That's a very interesting chair, honey, but it's just not very normal."

"We'll be the first on the block to have one."

Dottie only sighed.

Van stared at the awesome chair, trying not to be surly. Six hundred dollars meant nothing much to him. Obviously Mondiale's stock wasn't at the insanely stellar heights it had been when he had bought the mansion, but any guy who bought his wife emeralds for their anniversary wasn't going to whine about a magnesium chair.

Van couldn't bear to turn the catalog page. The astonishing chair was already part of his self-image. The chair gave him the same overwhelming feeling he had about computers: that they were tools. They were serious work tools. Only lamers ever flinched at buying work tools. If you were hard-core you just went out and got them.

"This is a Victorian house," Dottie offered softly. "That chair just doesn't fit in here. It's . . . well, it's just too far-out."

Dottie took the catalog from him and carefully read all the fine print.

"The chair is not that weird," Van muttered. "It's the whole world that's weird now. When the going gets weird, the weird turn pro." He picked up his wireless laptop. "I'm going to Google the guys who made it."

"You really want this thing, don't you?"

"Yeah, I want ten or twelve of them."

"Derek, that's seventy-two hundred dollars for chairs. That's not good sense." Dottie sighed. "Tony Carew keeps saying that we should diversify our investments. Because the market is so down this season."

"Okay, fine, we're not stock freaks like Tony is, but folks still need wires and bits." Van shrugged. Van owned Mondiale stock because he put his own money where he himself worked. His work was the one thing in the world that Van fully understood. Whenever it came to the future, Van would firmly bet on himself. That had certainly worked out for him so far.

Dottie smoothed the glossy magazine page. "Derek, my grant expires this semester. That's not good. I've got everything publishable that I'm going to get out of that cluster survey. The peer review people are saying we need better instrumentation." She wiped at Ted's spit-shiny chin with Van's spare paper towel.

Van struggled to pay attention to her words. Dottie's lab work meant everything to her. She had been working for four solid years on her globular cluster survey. Dottie had colleagues in Boston depending on her. Dottie had grad students to feed.

"Derek, it just didn't break wide open the way I hoped it would. That happens sometimes in science, you know. You can have a great idea, and you can put a lot of work into the hypothesis, but maybe your results just don't pan out."

"People love your dark energy nucleation theory," Van said supportively.

"I've been thinking of spending more time here at home."

Van's heart leapt. "Yeah?"

"Teddy's going to walk soon. And he's talking now, listen to him." Dottie stroked the baby's wispy hair as Ted's jolting head banged at her shoulder. "A little boy needs a normal life in some kind of normal house."

Van was shocked to realize how much this idea meant to him. Dottie, living with him and Ted, every single day. He felt stunned by the prospect. "Wow, being normal would be so fantastic."

Dottie winced. "Well, Helga is never around here for us when we need her. I think maybe I made a mistake there."

"We could put out an APB for her." Van smiled. "Aw, don't feel bad, honey. We can make do."

"I should do better," she muttered. "I just don't look after you and Teddy the way that I should."

Dottie was plunging into one of her guilty funks. The oncoming crisis was written all over her. Pretty soon she would start lamenting about her mother.

Dottie only allowed herself these painful fits of insecurity when she was really, really happy. It had taken Van ten years of marriage to figure that out, but now he understood it. She was spoiling their perfect day because she had to. It was her secret promise to an ugly, scary world that she would never enjoy her life too much.

Normally this behavior on her part upset Van, but today he felt so good that he found it comical. "Look, honey, so what if you got some bad news from your lab? What's the worst thing that can come out of all that? Come on, we're rich!"

"Honey bear," Dottie said, looking shyly at the spotless tabletop, "you work too hard. Even when you're not in your office, you let those computer cops push you around all the time." She picked up the other catalog again. "This funny chair you like so much? It's waterproof. And we do need some kind of porch chair. So get this one, and you can keep it outside. Okay?"

"Two?"

Her mouth twitched. "One, Derek."

"Okay then!" One chair, just as a starter. One chair would be his proof-of-concept. Van beamed at her.

The television grew more insistent. Dottie glanced over her shoulder at it. "Oh, my goodness! What a terrible accident."

"Huh." Van stared at the smoldering hole in the skyscraper. "Wow."

"That's New York, isn't it?"

"Yeah. Boy, you sure don't see that all the time." Van could have walked to the little TV in three strides, but on principle, he spent thirty seconds to locate its remote control. It was hiding in a heap of catalogs.

Van turned up the TV's volume. An announcer was filling dead air.

Some big jet had collided with the World Trade Center.

Van scowled. "Hey, that place has the worst luck in the world."

Dottie looked puzzled and upset. Even Ted looked morose.

"I mean that crowd of bad guys with the big truck bomb," Van explained. "They tried to blow up that place once."

Dottie winced. It was not her kind of topic.

Van fetched up his ThinkPad from the floor. He figured he had better surf some Web news. These local TV guys had a lousy news budget.

Covertly, Van examined his email. Thirty-four messages had arrived for him in the last two minutes. Van flicked through the titles. Security freaks from the cyberwar crowd. Discussion groups, Web updates. They were watching TV right at their computers, and instantly, they had gone nuts. Van was embarrassed to think that he knew so many of these people. It was even worse that so many of them had his email address.

Van examined the television again. That television scene looked plenty bad. Van was no great expert on avionic systems, but he knew what any system-reliability expert would know about such things. He knew that it was very, very unlikely that FAA air control traffic at Kennedy and LaGuardia would ever let a jet aircraft just wander accidentally into a downtown New York skyscraper. New York City had a very heavy concentration of TRACONs and flow control units. So that couldn't be a conventional safety failure.

However. An unconventional failure, that was another story. An ugly story. Van had once spent a long, itchy, three-day weekend with FEMA in Washington, watching information-warfare people describing the truly awful things that might be done by "adversaries" who "owned" federal air traffic control systems.

Since there really was no such thing in the world as "information warfare," information-warfare people were the weirdest people Van knew. Their tactics and enemies were all imaginary. There was a definite dark-fantasy element to these cyberwar characters. They were like a black flock of the crows of doom, haunting an orc battlefield out of Tolkien's Lord of the Rings. Van was reluctant to pay them any serious attention, because he suffered enough real-world security problems from hacker kids and viruses. Van did recall one soundbite, however. A bespectacled infowar geek, all wound up and full of ghoulish relish, describing how every aircraft in the skies of America would "become a flying bomb."

Air traffic control was a major federal computer system. It was one of the biggest and oldest. Repeated attempts to fix it had failed. The guys in the FAA used simple, old-fashioned computers dating to the 1970s. They used them because they were much more reliable than any of the modern ones. FAA guys had very dark jokes about computers crashing. For them, a computer crashing meant an aircraft crashing. It meant a "midair passenger exchange." It meant "aluminum rain."

Now, Van realized, he was watching "aluminum rain" on New York's biggest skyscraper. There was no way this was going to do. Not at all.

Van drew a slow breath. There was a bad scene on the TV, but he was prepared for it. He had been here before, in his imagination. In 1999, Mondiale had spent over 130 million dollars chasing down Y2K bugs, with many firm assurances from security experts that the planet would fall apart, otherwise. Van had believed it, too. He'd felt pretty bad about that belief, later. When computers hadn't crashed worldwide and the world hadn't transformed itself overnight into a dark Mad Max wasteland, that had been a personal humiliation for Van.

At least the Y2K money had really helped a big crowd of old programmers who had never saved up for retirement.

Van's New Year's resolution for the year 2001 had been to never panic over vaporware again. So Van stilled his beating heart as the blasted skyscraper burned fantastically on his television. He was living way ahead of the curve here. He was already thinking in tenth gear. Calm down, he thought. Chill out. Be rational.

Nothing really important was going to happen unless his phone rang. Some flurry of email from his most paranoid and suspicious acquaintances, that did not mean a thing. Internet lists were no more than water coolers, nothing more than a place for loudmouths to shoot off. His home phone number was extremely private. If that phone rang, then that would mean big trouble.

If the phone did not ring, then he was much better off not saying anything to Dottie. Let her be happy. Let Ted be happy. Please, God, let everyone just be happy. Look at that sun at the window, that oak tree out on the lawn. It was such a nice day.

Uh-oh. There went the other tower.

THE GOAT VARIATIONS
Jeff VanderMeer

It would have been hot, humid in September in that city, and the Secret Service would have gone in first, before him, to scan for hostile minds, even though it was just a middle school in a county he'd won in the elections, far away from the fighting. He would have emerged from the third black armored vehicle, blinking and looking bewildered as he got his bearings in the sudden sunlight. His aide and the personal bodyguards who had grown up protecting him would have surrounded him by his first step onto the asphalt of the driveway. They would have entered the school through the front, stopping under the sign for photos and a few words with the principal, the television cameras recording it all from a safe distance.

He would already be thinking past the event, to the next, and how to prop up sagging public approval ratings, due both to the conflict and what the press called his recent "indecision," which he knew was more analogous to "sickness." He would be thinking about, or around, the secret cavern beneath the Pentagon and the pale, almost grub-like face of the adept in his tank. He would already be thinking about the machine.

By the end of the photo op, the sweat itches on his forehead, burns sour in his mouth, but he has to ignore it for the cameras. He's turning a new word over and over in his mind, learned from a Czech diplomat. *Ossuary*. A word that sounds free and soaring, but just means a pile of skulls. The latest satellite photos from the battlefield states of Kansas, Nebraska, and Idaho make him think of the word. The evangelicals have been eschewing god-missiles for more personal methods of vengeance, even as they tie down federal armies in an endless guerilla war. Sometimes he feels like he's presiding over a pile of skulls.

The smile on his face has frozen into a rictus as he realizes there's something wrong with the sun; there's a red dot in its center, and it's eating away at the yellow, bringing a hint of green with it. He can tell he's the only one who can see it, can sense the pulsing, nervous worry on the face of his aide.

He almost says "ossuary" aloud, but then, sunspots wandering across his eyes, they are bringing him down a corridor to the classroom where he will meet with the students and tell them a story. They walk past the open doors to the cafeteria—row on row of sagging wooden tables propped up by rusted metal legs. He experiences a flare of anger. Why *this* school, with the infrastructure crumbling away? The overpowering stale smell of macaroni-and-cheese and meatloaf makes him nauseous.

All the while, he engages in small talk with the entourage of teachers trailing in his wake, almost all overweight middle-aged women with circles under their eyes and sagging skin on their arms. Many of them are black. He smiles into their shiny, receptive faces and remembers the hired help in the mansion growing up. Some of his best friends were black until he took up politics.

For a second, as he looks down, marveling at their snouts and beaks and muzzles, their smiles melt away and he's surrounded by a pack of animals.

His aide mutters to him through clenched teeth, and two seconds later he realizes the words were "Stop staring at them so much." There have always been times when meeting too many people at once has made him feel as if he's somewhere strange, all the mannerisms and gesticulations and varying tones of voice shimmering into babble. But it's only lately that the features of people's faces have changed into a menagerie if he looks at them too long.

They'd briefed him on the secret rooms and the possibility of the machine even before they'd given him the latest intel on China's occupation of

Japan and Taiwan. Only three hours into his presidency, an armored car had taken him to the Pentagon, away from his wife and the beginnings of the inauguration party. Once there, they'd entered a green-lit steel elevator that went down for so long he thought for a moment it was broken. It was just him, his aide, a black-ops commander who didn't give his name, and a small, haggard man who wore an old gray suit over a faded white dress shirt, with no tie. He'd told his vice president to meet the press while he was gone, even though he was now convinced the old man had dementia.

The elevators had opened to a rush of stale cool air, like being under a mountain, and, beneath the dark green glow of overhead lamps, he could see rows and rows of transparent, bathtub-shaped deprivation vats. In each floated one dreaming adept, skin wrinkled and robbed of color by the exposure to the chemicals that preserved and pacified them. Every shaven head was attached to wires and electrodes, every mouth attached to a breathing tube. Catheters took care of waste. The stale air soon faded as they walked silent down the rows, replaced by a smell like turpentine mixed with honeysuckle. Sometimes the hands of the adepts twitched, like cats hunting in their sleep.

A vast, slow, repeating sound registered in his awareness. Only after several minutes did he realize it was the sound of the adepts as they slowly moved in their vats, creating a slow ripple of water repeated in thousands of other vats. The room seemed to go on forever, into the far distance of a horizon tinged at its extremity by a darkening that hinted of blood.

His sense of disgust, revulsion grew as the little man ran out ahead of them, navigated a path to a control center, a hundred yards in and to the left, made from a luminous blue glass, set a story up and jutting out over the vats like some infernal crane. And still he did not know what to say. The atmosphere combined morgue, cathedral, and torture chamber. He felt a compulsion, if he spoke, to whisper.

The briefing papers he'd read on the ride over had told him just about everything. For years, adepts had been screened out at birth and, depending on the secret orders peculiar to each administration, either euthanized or imprisoned in remote overseas detention camps. Those that managed to escape detection until adulthood had no rights if caught, not even the rights given to illegal immigrants. The founding fathers had been very clear on that in the constitution.

He had always assumed that adults when caught were eliminated or sent to the camps. Radicals might call it the last reflexive act of a puritanical brutality that reached across centuries, but most citizens despised the invasion of privacy an adept represented or were more worried about how the separatist evangelicals had turned the homeland into a nation of West and East Coasts, with no middle.

But now he knew where his predecessor had been storing the bodies. He just didn't yet know *why*.

In the control center, they showed him the images being mined from the depths of the adepts' REM sleep. They ranged from montages as incomprehensible as the experimental films he'd seen in college to single shots of dead people to grassy hills littered with wildflowers. Ecstasy, grief, madness, peace. Anything imaginable came through in the adepts' endless sleep.

"Only ten people in the world know every aspect of this project, and three of them are dead, Mr. President," the black-ops commander told him.

Down below, he could see the little man, blue-tinted, going from vat to vat, checking readings.

"We experimented until we found the right combination of drugs to augment their sight. One particular formula, culled from South American mushrooms mostly, worked best. Suddenly, we began to get more coherent and varied images. Very different from before."

He felt numb. He had no sympathy for the men and women curled up in the vats below him—an adept's grenade had killed his father in mid-campaign a decade before, launching his own reluctant career in politics—but, still, he felt numb.

"Are any of them dangerous?" he asked the black-ops commander.

"They're all dangerous, Mr. President. Every last one."

"When did this start?"

"With a secret order from your predecessor, Mr. President. Before, we just disappeared them or sent them to work camps in the Alaskas."

"Why did he do it?"

Even then, he would realize later, a strange music was growing in his head, a distant sound fast approaching.

"He did it, Mr. President, or said he did it, as a way of getting intel on the Heartland separatists."

Understandable, if idiosyncratic. The separatists and the fact that the federal armies had become bogged down in the Heartland fighting them were the main reasons his predecessor's party no longer controlled the executive, judicial, or legislative branches. And no one had ever suc- ceeded in placing a mole within evangelical ranks.

The scenes continued to cascade over the monitors in a rapid-fire nonsense rhythm.

"What do you do with the images?"

"They're sent to a full team of experts for interpretation, Mr. Presi- dent. These experts are not told where the images come from."

"What do these adepts see that is so important?'

The black-ops commander grimaced at the tone of rebuke. "The future, Mr. President. It's early days, but we believe they see the future."

"And have you gained much in the way of intel?"

The black-ops commander looked at his feet. "No, not yet, we haven't. And we don't know why. The images are jumbled. Some might even be from our past or present. But we have managed to figure out one thing, which is why you've been brought here so quickly: something will happen later this year, in September."

"Something?"

Down below, the little man had stopped his purposeful wandering. He gazed, as if mesmerized, into one of the vats.

"Something cataclysmic, Mr. President. Across the channels. Across all of the adepts, it's quite clear. Every adept has a different version of what that something is. And we don't know *exactly* when, but in September."

He had a thousand more questions, but at that moment one of the military's top scientific researchers entered the control room to show them the schematics for the machine—the machine they'd found in the mind of one particular adept.

The time machine.

The teachers are telling him about the weather, and he's pretending to care as he tries to ignore the fluorescent lighting as yellow as the skin that forms on old butter, the cracks in the dull beige walls, the faded construction paper of old projects taped to those walls, drooping down toward a tired, washed-out green carpet that's paper-thin under foot.

It's the kind of event that he's never really understood the point of, even as he understands the reason for it. To prove that he's still fit for office. To prove that the country, some of it, is free of war and divi- sion. To prove he cares about kids, even though this particular school seems to be falling apart. Why this class, why today, is what he really doesn't understand, with so many world crises—China's imperialism, the Siberian separatist movement, Iraq as the only bulwark against Russian influence in the Middle East. Or a vice president he now knows may be too old and delusional to be anything other than an embarrassment, and a cabinet he let his family's political cronies bully him into appointing, and a secret cavern that has infected his thoughts, infected his mind.

And that would lead to memories of his father, and the awful silence into which they told him, as he sat coked up and hungover that morning on the pastel couch in some sleazy apartment, how it had happened while his father worked a town hall meeting in Atlanta.

All of this has made him realize that there's only one way to succeed in this thing called the presidency: just let go of the reality of the world in favor of whatever reality he wants or needs, no matter how selfish.

The teachers are turning into animals again, and he can't seem to stop it from happening.

The time machine had appeared as an image on their monitors from an adept named "Peter" in vat 1023, and because they couldn't figure out the context—weapon? camera? something new?—they had to wake Peter up and have a conversation with him.

A time machine, he told them.

A time machine?

A time machine that travels through time, he'd clarified.

And they'd believed him, or if not believed him, dared to hope he was right. That what Peter had seen while deprived of anything but his own brain, like some deep-sea fish, like something constantly turning inwards and then turning inwards again, had been a time machine.

If they didn't build it and it turned out later that it might have worked and could have helped them avert or change what was fated to happen in September . . .

That day, three hours after being sworn in, he had had to give the order to build a time machine, and quickly.

"Something bad will happen in late summer. Something bad. Across the channels. Something awful."

"What?" he kept asking, and the answer was always the same: *We don't know.*

They kept telling him that the adepts didn't seem to convey literal information so much as impressions and visions of the future, filtered through dreamscapes. As if the drugs they'd perfected, which had changed the way the adepts dreamed, both improved and destroyed focus, in different ways.

In the end, he had decided to build the machine—and defend against almost everything they could think of or divine from the images: any attack against the still-surviving New York financial district or the monument to the Queen Mother in the New York harbor; the random god-missiles of the Christian jihadists of the Heartland, who hadn't yet managed to unlock the nuclear codes in the occupied states; and even the lingering cesspool that was Los Angeles after the viruses and riots.

But they still did not really know.

He's good now at talking to people when it's not a prepared speech, good at letting his mind be elsewhere while he talks to a series of masks from behind his own mask. The prepared speeches are different because he's expected to *inhabit* them, and he's never fully inhabited anything, any role, in his life.

They round the corner and enter the classroom: thirty children in plastic one-piece desk-chairs, looking solemn, and the teacher standing in front of a beat-up battlewagon of a desk, overflowing with papers.

Behind her, posters they'd made for him, or someone had made to look like the children made them, most showing him with the crown on his head. But also a blackboard, which amazes him. So anachronistic, and he's always hated the sound of chalk on a blackboard. Hates the smell of glue and the sour food-sweat of unwashed kids. It's all so squalid and tired and oddly close to the atmosphere in the underground cavern, the smell the adepts give off as they thrash in slow motion in their vats, silently screaming out images of catastrophe and oblivion.

The children look up at him when he enters the room like they're watching something far away and half-wondrous, half-monstrous.

He stands there and talks to them for a while at first, trying to ignore the window in the back of the classroom that wants to show him a scene that shouldn't have been there. He says the kinds of things he's said to kids for years while on the campaign trail, running for ever-greater office. Has said these things for so many years that it's become a sawdust litany meant to convince them of his charm, his wit, his competence. Later, he won't remember what he said, or what they said back. It's not important.

But he's thought about the implications of that in bed at night, lying there while his wife reads, her pale, freckled shoulder like a wall above him. He could stand in a classroom and say nothing, and still they would be fascinated with him, like a talisman, like a golden statue. No one had ever told him that sometimes you don't have to inhabit the presidency; sometimes, it inhabits you.

He'd wondered at the time of coronation if he'd feel different. He'd wondered how the parliament members would receive him, given the split between the popular vote and the legislative vote. But nothing had happened. The parliament members had clapped, some longer than others, and he'd been sworn in, duly noting the absence of the rogue Scottish delegation. The Crown of the Americas had briefly touched his head, like an "iron kiss from the mouth of God," as his predecessor had put it, and then it was gone again, under glass, and he was back to being the secular president, not some sort of divine king.

Then they'd taken him to the Pentagon, hurtled him half a mile underground, and he'd felt like a man who wins a prize only to find out it's worthless. *Ossuary.* He'd expected clandestine spy programs, secret weapons, special powers. But he hadn't expected the faces in the vats or the machine.

Before they built the time machine, he had insisted on meeting "Peter" in an interrogation room near the vats. He felt strongly about this, about looking into the eyes of the man he had almost decided to trust.

"Are you sure this will work?" he asked Peter, even as he found the question irrelevant, ridiculous. No matter what Peter said, no matter how impossible his scientists said it was, how it subverted known science, he was going to do it. The curiosity was too strong.

Peter's eyes were bright with a kind of fever. His face was the palest white possible, and he stank of the chemicals. They'd put him in a blue jumper suit to cover his nakedness.

"It'll work. I pulled it out of another place. It was a true-sight. A true-seeing. I don't know how it works, but it works. It'll work, it'll work, and then," he turned toward the black one-way glass at the far end of the room, hands in restraints behind his back, "I'll be free?"

There was a thing in Peter's eyes he refused to acknowledge. A sense of something being held back, of something not quite right. Later, he would never know why he didn't trust that instinct, that perception, and the only reason he could come up with was the strength of his curiosity and the weight of his predecessor's effort to get to that point.

"What, exactly, is the machine for? Exactly. Not just . . . time travel. Tell me something more specific."

The scientist accompanying them smiled. He had a withered, narrow face, a firm chin, and wore a jumpsuit that matched Peter's, with a black belt at the waist that held the holster for an even blacker semi-automatic pistol. He smelled strongly of a sickly sweet cologne, as if hiding some essential putrefaction.

"Mr. President," he said, "Peter is not a scientist. And we cannot peer into his mind. We can only see the images his mind projects. Until we build it, we will not know exactly how it works."

And then, when the machine was built, and they took him to it, he didn't know what to make of it. He didn't think they did, either—they were gathered around it in their protective suits like apes trying to figure out an internal combustion engine.

"Don't look directly into it," the scientist beside him advised. "Those who have experience a kind of . . . disorientation."

Unlike the apes examining it, the two of them stood behind three feet of protective, blast-proof glass, and yet both of them had moved to the back of the viewing room—as far away from the artifact as possible.

The machine consisted of a square housing made of irregular-looking gray metal, caulked on the interior with what looked like rotted beef, and in the center of this assemblage: an eye of green light. In the middle of the eye, a piercing red dot. The machine was about the size of a microwave oven.

When he saw the eye, he shuddered, could not tell at first if it was organic or a metallic lens. The effect of the machine on his mind was of a thousand maggots inching their way across the top of a television set turned on but not receiving a station.

He couldn't stop looking, as if the scientist's warning had made it impossible not to stare. A crawling sensation spread across his scalp, his arms, his hands, his legs.

"How does it work?" he asked the scientist.

"We still don't know."

"Does the adept know?"

"Not really. He just told us not to look into it directly."

"Is it from the future?"

"That is the most logical guess."

To him, it didn't look real. It looked either like something from another planet or something a psychotic child would put together before turning to more violent pursuits.

"Where else could it be from?"

The scientist didn't reply, and anger began to override his fear. He continued to look directly into the eye, even as it made him feel sick.

"Well, what do you know?"

"That it shouldn't work. As we put the pieces together . . . we all thought . . . we all thought it was more like witchcraft than science. Forgive me, Mr. President."

He gave the scientist a look that the scientist couldn't meet. Had he meant the gravity of the insult? Had he meant to imply their efforts were as blasphemous as the adept's second sight?

"And now? What do you think now?"

"It's awake, alive. But we don't see how it's . . ."

"It's what?"

"Breathing, Mr. President. A machine shouldn't breathe."

"How does it take anyone into the future, do you think?'

The temperature in the room seemed to have gone up. He was sweating.

The eye of the thing, impossibly alien, bored into him. Was it changing color?

"We think it doesn't physically send anyone into the future. That's the problem. We think it might somehow . . . create a localized phenomenon."

He sighed. "Just say what you mean."

The pulsing red dot. The shifting green. Looking at him. Looking into him.

"We think it might not allow physical travel, just mental travel."

In that instant, he saw adept Peter's pale face again and he felt a weakness in his stomach, and even though there was so much protection between him and the machine, he turned to the scientist and said, "Get me out of here."

Only, it was too late.

The sickness, the shifting, had started the next day, and he couldn't tell anyone about it, not even his wife, or they would have removed him from office. The constitution was quite clear about what do with "witches and warlocks."

At this point, his aide would hand him the book. They'd have gone through a dozen books before choosing that one. It is the only one with nothing in it anyone could object to; nothing in it of substance, nothing, his people thought, that the still-free press could use to damage him. There was just a goat in the book, a goat having adventures. It was written by a Constitutionalist, an outspoken supporter of coronation and expansion.

As he takes the book, he realizes, mildly surprised, that he has already become used to the smell of sweating children (he has none of his own) and the classroom grunge. (*Ossuary*. It sounded like a combination of "osprey" and "sanctuary.") The students who attend the school all experience it differently from him, their minds editing out the sensory perceptions he's still receiving. The mess. The depressed quality of the infrastructure. But what if you couldn't edit it out? And what if the stakes were much, much higher?

So then they would sit him down at a ridiculously small chair, almost as small as the ones used by the students, but somehow he would feel smaller in it despite that, as if he was back in college, surrounded by people both smarter and more dedicated than he was, as if he is posing and being told he's not as good: an imposter.

But it's still just a children's book, after all, and at least there's air conditioning kicking in, and the kids really seem to want him to read the book, as if they haven't heard it a thousand times before, and he feeds off the look in their eyes—*the President of North America and the Britains is telling us a story*—and so he begins to read.

He enjoys the storytelling. Nothing he does with the book can hurt him. Nothing about it has weight. Still, he has to keep the pale face of the adept out of his voice, and the Russian problem, and the Chinese problem, and the full extent of military operations in the Heartland. (There are cameras, after all.)

It's September 2001, and something terrible is going to happen, but for a moment he forgets that fact.

And that's when his aide interrupts his reading, comes up to him with a fake smile and serious eyes, and whispers in his ear.

Whispers in his ear and the sound is like a buzzing, and the buzzing is numinous and all-encompassing. The breath on his ear is a tiny curse, an infernal itch. There's a sudden rush of blood to his brain as he hears the words and his aide withdraws. He can hardly move, is seeing light where there shouldn't be light. The words drop heavy into his ear as if they have weight.

And he receives them and keeps receiving them, and he knows what they mean, eventually; he knows what they mean throughout his body.

The aide says, his voice flecked with relief, "Mr. President, our scientists have solved it. It's not time travel or far-sight. It's alternate universes. The adepts have been staring into alternate universes. What happens there in September may not happen here. That's why they've had such trouble with the intel. The machine isn't a time machine."

Except, as soon as the aide opens his mouth, the words become a trigger, a catalyst, and it's too late for him. A door is opening wider than ever before. The machine has already infected him.

There are variations. A long row of them, detonating in his mind, trying to destroy him. A strange, sad song is creeping up inside of him, and he can't stop that, either.

>>> He's sitting in the chair, wearing a black military uniform with medals on it. He's much fitter, the clothes tight to emphasize his muscle tone. But his face is contorted around the hole of a festering localized virus, charcoal and green and viscous. He doesn't wear an eye patch because he wants his people to see how he fights the disease. His left arm is made of metal. His tongue is not his own, colonized the way his nation has been colonized, waging a war against bio-research gone wrong, and the rebels who welcome it, who want to tear down anything remotely human, themselves no longer recognizable as human.

His aide comes up and whispers that the rebels have detonated a bio-mass bomb in New York City, which is now stewing in a broth of fungus and mutation: the nearly instantaneous transformation of an entire metropolis into something living but alien, the rate of change has become strange and accelerated in a world where this was always true, the age of industrialization slowing it, if only for a moment.

"There are no people left in New York City," his aide says. "What are your orders?"

He hadn't expected this, not so soon, and it takes him seven minutes to recover from the news of the death of millions. Seven minutes to turn to his aide and say, "Call in a nuclear strike."

>>> . . . and his aide comes up to him and whispers in his ear, "It's time to go now. They've moved up another meeting. Wrap it up." Health insurance is on the agenda today, along with social security. Something will get done about that and the environment this year or he'll die trying . . .

>>> He's sitting in the chair reading the book and he's gaunt, eyes feverish, military personnel surrounding him. There's one camera with them, army TV, and the students are all in camouflage. The electricity flickers on and off. The school room has reinforced metal and concrete all around it. The event is propaganda being packaged and pumped out to those still watching in places where the enemy hasn't jammed the satellites. He's fighting a war against an escaped, human-created, rapidly reproducing intelligent species prototype that looks a little bit like a chimpanzee crossed with a Doberman. The scattered remnants of the hated adept underclass have made common cause with the animals, disrupting communications.

His aide whispers in his ear that Atlanta has fallen, with over sixty thousand troops and civilians massacred in pitched battles all over the city. There's no safe air corridor back to the capital. In fact, the capital seems to be under attack as well.

"What should we do?"

He returns to reading the book. Nothing he can do in the next seven minutes will make any difference to the outcome. He knows what they have to do, but he's too tired to contemplate it just yet. They will have to head to the Heartland and make peace with the Ecstatics and their god-missiles. It's either that or render entire stretches of North America uninhabitable from nukes, and he's not that desperate yet.

He begins to review the ten commandments of the Ecstatics in his mind, one by one, like rosary beads.

>>> He's in mid-sentence when the aide hurries over and begins to whisper in his ear—just as the first of the god-missiles strikes and the fire

washes over and through him, not even time to scream, and he's nothing anymore, not even a pile of ashes.

>>> He's in a chair, in a suit with a sweat-stained white shirt, and he's tired, his voice as he reads thin and raspy. Five days and nights of negotiations between the rival factions of the New Southern Confederacy following a month of genocide from Arkansas to Georgia: too few resources, too many natural disasters, and no jobs, the whole system breaking down, although Los Angeles is still trying to pretend the world isn't coming to an end, even as jets are falling out the sky. Except, that's why he's in the classroom: *pretending*. Pretending neighbor hasn't set upon neighbor for thirty days, like in Rwanda except not with machetes, with guns. Teenagers shooting people in the stomach, and laughing. Extremist talk radio urging them on. Closing in on a million people dead.

His aide comes up and whispers in his ear: "The truce has fallen apart. They're killing each other again. And not just in the South. In the North, along political lines."

He sits there because he's run out of answers. He thinks: *In another time, another place, I would have made a great president.*

>>> He's sitting in the classroom, in the small chair, in comfortable clothes, reading the goat story. No god-missiles here, no viruses, no invasions. The Chinese and Russians are just on the cusp of being a threat, but not there yet. Adepts here have no real far-sight, or are not believed, and roam free. Los Angeles is a thriving money pit, not a husked-out shadow.

No, the real threat here, besides pollution, is that he's mentally ill, although no one around him seems to know it. A head full of worms, insecurity, and pure, naked *need*. He rules a country called the "United States" that wavers between the First and the Third World. Resources failing, infrastructure crumbling, political system fueled by greed and corruption.

When the aide comes up and whispers in his ear to tell him that terrorists have flown two planes into buildings in New York City, there's blood behind his eyes, as well as a deafening silence, and a sudden leap from people falling from the burning buildings to endless war in the Middle East, bodies broken by bullets and bombs. The future torques into secret trials, torture, rape, and hundreds of thousands of civilians dead, or displaced, a country bankrupted and defenseless, ruled ultimately by martial law and generals. Cities burn, the screams of the living are as loud as the screams of the dying.

He sits there for seven minutes because he really has no idea what to do.

. . . and *his* fate is to exist in a reality where towers do not explode in September, where Islamic fundamentalists are the least of his worries.

There is only one present, only one future now, and he's back in it, driving it. Seven minutes have elapsed, and there's a graveyard in his head. Seven minutes, and he's gradually aware that in that span he's read the goat story twice and then sat there for thirty seconds, silent.

Now he smiles, says a few reassuring words, just as his aide has decided to come up and rescue him from the yawning chasm. He's living in a place now where they'll never find him, those children, where there's a torrent of blood in his mind, and a sky dark with planes and helicopters, and soldiers blown to bits by the roadside.

At that point, he would rise from his chair and his aide would clap, encouraging the students to clap, and they will, bewildered by this man about whom reporters will say later, "Doesn't seem quite all there."

An endless line of presidents rises from the chair with him, the weight almost too much. He can see each clearly in his head. He can see what they're doing, and who they're doing it to.

Saying his goodbyes is like learning how to walk again, while a nightmare plays out in the background. He knows as they lead him down the corridor that he'll have to learn to live with it, like and unlike a man learning to live with missing limbs—phantom limbs that do not belong, that he cannot control, but are always there, and he'll never be able to explain it to anyone. He'll be as alone and yet as crowded as a person can be. The wall between him and his wife will be more unbearable than ever.

He remembers Peter's pale, wrinkled, yearning face, and he thinks about making them release the man, put him on a plane somewhere beyond his country's influence. Thinks about destroying the machine and ending the adept project.

Then he's back in the wretched, glorious sunlight of a real, an ordinary day, and so are all of his reflections and shadows. Mimicking him, forever.

Rob McCleary is primarily a television writer, having worked on Jacob Two-Two, Pecola, *and* Moville Mysteries, *among other Canadian children's programs, but in the world of literature he has one major claim to fame. McCleary is the author of "Nixon in Space," a short story published in the now-defunct semi-pro magazine called* CRANK! *back in 1993. The story has endured despite these humble beginnings and without more output from McCleary. Author Jonathan Lethem republished the story on* Electric Literature*'s Recommend Reading page in 2013 and noted that "if you wrote 'Nixon In Space' or its equivalent fifty times you'd be George Saunders or Donald Barthelme. Do it just once and you're Rob McCleary."*

"Our Lady of Toledo Transmission" seems to be as much about the Great Recession of 2007 as it is about the attacks of 9/11, although it's mostly about the Lord Our Savior, automobile mayhem, and ice cream. It is also step two in his quest to become Donald Barthelme.

OUR LADY OF TOLEDO TRANSMISSION
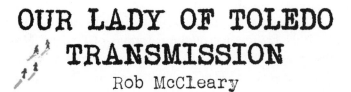
Rob McCleary

The search for Jesus and Answers began in the weeks following 9-11. And not God, because childhood cancer and leprosy. And not the Blessed Virgin Mary, because she's the Blessed Virgin Mary. The Revelations fan-fiction spectacle of people hurtling themselves out of burning skyscrapers demanded *some* sort of explanation, and Jesus, with his New Testament face-palming at our human idiocy, provided the only spiritual handhold in the sheer cliff face of the American post 9-11 existential crisis. But all the prayers and entreaties produced only insolent silence, until entire congregations, unable to bear the continual overhead Zeppelin thrumming tension of the godless void, filed out of their meeting houses and into their cars, still dressed in their Sunday best, peeling out of church parking lots and onto interstates, the spirit of the Almighty finally surging through them as they rear-ended and sideswiped and

T-boned the unbeliever, and in this way the Church of Christ the Demo-lition Derby Driver was born.

That last pre-9-11 summer was concerned not with God and the search for answers, but divorce and Toledo Transmission, my father swal-lowed, man-eating-python style, feet first, by the second shift. His exis-tence reduced to bolting one thing to another thing, or spot welding a thing to another thing, or bashing one thing into another thing with a bright orange rubber mallet, and so on. That, combined with the emo-tional equivalent of lifting a three-thousand-pound automobile off your trapped kid effort that his divorce demanded, left him rubber-legged and flop-sweated as the summer leaves of Ohio turned red and orange and August slouched into September. My father may well have been the least prepared man in America for the questions and confusions of 9-11, and therefore easy pickings for the missionaries of the Church of Christ the Demolition Derby Driver.

The spiritual Doppler effect created by my father's inability to come to terms with either his divorce or the workings of General Motors and Toledo Transmission left me with a sense of general-purpose life-ver-tigo I have retained to this day, expressed in trauma-repetition dreams of my father swallowed into an underworld of depression and apathy, my mother and her anger at both of us taking the form of an amaz-ingly cogent image of the Heat Miser from *The Year Without a Santa Claus* ("Whatever I touch, starts to melt in my clutch, I'm too much!"). The other location in our drama, the natural home of both the Church of Christ the Demolition Derby Driver and low-end divorce lawyers: the suburban strip mall. Which is where my father first found them, drag-ging me along to his lawyer and the now spectral presence of my mother, communicating across the ether by means of our attorney cum medium, a man with body odor, a slow eye, and an impossibly outdated version of Microsoft Windows. I prefer to remember an actual Ouija board on his desk, jumping in response to my father's slowly tightening gyre of questions, the planchette hesitating, then skidding back and forth across the alphabet surface ("Will she accept two hundred dollars a month more in alimony?" . . . YES . . . "Does she want visitation or custody?" . . . NO . . .). By mid-August before 9-11 it seemed all mercifully settled, leav-ing my father with his solitary, Stalingrad siege of Toledo Transmission.

The collective trauma of 9-11 was the trauma of a God asleep at the switch when a bunch of creepy, not-by-choice, career virgins slammed jetliners into the World Trade Center. But only the Church of Christ the Demolition Derby Driver had the nerve to shake their fist at God. And while their once-pristine Sunday suits and dresses soon became oil-stained, ragged, and smeared with greasy roadside diner fast-food stains and spills, their faith remained resolute, careening from town to town, punching in the rear quarter panel of the infidel. At night they circled their cars, wagon train fashion, in big-box store parking lots, burning stacks of pallets in the center, flaming high into the night, a pillar of smoke and flame, a warning of their holy, righteous wrath outside the Target, the Walmart, and the blessed bobblehead trinity of the Pep Boys. Breaking camp at first light they would thread their rumbling convoy back onto the interstate, a mechanical incarnation of the Divine, part Mad Max, part Wacky Races. Their anger growing hotter with every tick of the odometer that did not bring the light and peace of God, their desire to T-bone, to rear-end, to sideswipe *did* come as a wrath upon them. "Rear-end the mini-van full of tweens on their way to soccer practice at a four-way stop and I am with you," Jesus said, or words to that effect, in one of the Gnostic gospels. "T-bone the senior citizen who weareth the foam trucker cap perched precariously atop his balding pate, inscribed with the name of the World War Two battleship he did serve his country aboard driving home from the early bird dinner special at Denny's and I am there."

9-11 did not help America's belief that God himself was personally looking out for us, but as a town we had always had more faith in General Motors, who ran the Toledo Transmission Assembly Facility, and therefore the vast majority of our indentured lives. And GM, while just as inscrutable as God, had a greater impact in our lives on a paycheck-to-paycheck basis. God may have created the heavens and the earth, but GM gave us a blue-collar Eden of reliable, high-profit-margin truck and SUV sales figures, and Toledo Transmission to hire my father and most of the people in our Toledo suburb. Blessed be the Hydra-matic 6L80 Rear Wheel Drive 6-Speed transmission assembled therein. Blessed be the Global Front Wheel Drive 6 speed 6T40 transmission in the eyes of our Lord. And in this Eden was my Eve, or rather my Matilda of the Tasty Scoop, a young woman several years my senior whose entire genetic code seemed specifically engineered to perfectly fill out a red and white Tasty Scoop uniform made from polyester thick enough to stop small arms fire. She was the corn-fed icon of my wildest sexual imaginings and conjectures which, all summer, had been advancing and marshaling with a strange Thomas Aquinas–like progression, my personal Summa Theologica of wholly imagined hand jobs, buttons popped off the front of Tasty Scoop uniforms and hands thrust down the front of Tasty Scoop polyester pants. I ached after her, hour after hour, chocolate dipped soft ice cream cone after chocolate dipped soft ice cream cone. And just so you don't think this was some base physical attraction, she was a woman of responsibility as well: she was the assistant to the daytime manager, a valued officer in the north-Ohio-parts-of-Illinois-around-but-not-including-Chicago Tasty Scoop empire, trusted enough to head off on her own in the Tasty Scoop flagship vehicle: the Tasty Scoop Ice Cream Wagon complete with revolving fiberglass ice cream cone on top. Matilda was a woman of beauty, smarts, cool-under-fire, and, in what I can only assume was God's final act of spite before he left us all to our post 9-11 fates, was dating some jerk in a souped-up powder-blue 1983 Oldsmobile Delta 88 Royale.

America *was* a different place before 9-11, but in all honesty very little changed post-9-11 in our little suburb except for a sudden deluge of totemic American flag stickers, badges, pins, and bunting. Before 9-11 the only people who flew American flags year-round, not counting the week of July 4th, were cranks and ex-Marines. But a tightly stitched American flag iron-on patch even found its way on to Matilda's Tasty Scoop uniform, perched with insolent indifference to my needs directly above her left breast. Apparently Matilda, and the entire Tasty Scoop phalanx, had been recruited to do their part in the War on Terror. Which was fine with me. I had read that people in time of war did strange and desperate things, and I would be more than happy with a strange, desperate hand job. I too was determined not to let the terrorists win. But there was an enormous wrinkle in my plan to win over Matilda: any self-respecting American looking for evenings of Midwestern passion needed a car. It was a concrete statement of suburban manhood. You could not ask a date out on the bus. And if everything went according to plan you had a location for furtive dry-humping. I needed a car. Maybe not a powder-blue Oldsmobile 88 Royale, but something that ran. But I was broke, and the sin of sexual despair began to rivulet its way across my life.

There was, of course, one way to get a car, thereby massively leveraging my odds of a hand job: the Church of Christ the Demolition Derby Driver. But this naturally posed an ethical conundrum: they would give me a car, but I would be expected (not unreasonably) to drive it through the streets and on the interstates of America with the purposeful intensity of a cruise missile. Father had, following the inevitable lull after the buying frenzy of the please-God-don't-tell-me-they-named-it-after-what-we-all-know-they-named-it-after "Keep America Rolling" easy finance program (and in the process teaching American consumers the meaning of "pushing demand forward"), begun hanging around the Church of Christ the Demolition Derby Driver. The one in the same mini-mall as our shitty divorce lawyer. He had become isolated following his divorce, as what few friends he had all worked different shifts, so even going out for beer was a logistical nightmare. The church provided a sense of belonging he desperately needed. He began to meet with them every Sunday, and learn their ways ("God hates a perfect paint job" . . . "crush yea not the driver's side door. Contact in this area is an abomination before the eyes of the Lord," and so on). When I finally started attending, to check out if the Church of Christ the Demolition Derby Driver had a (slightly more informal) "Keep America Rolling" program of its own, I expected to see a congregation of wild-eyed grease monkeys and homicidal gearheads, but instead I found a group of happy, devoted people of diverse backgrounds and ages all united by the belief Jesus died for our sins, and rose from the dead, and ascended not to heaven, or to Utah to bury gold plates, but to the Ohio Valley to restore America's faith in God via one of America's favorite fairground pastimes. They were affable, agreeable and peaceful people . . . unless you brought up the topic of the Church of Our Lady of the Monster Truck Rally.

That a church based on a demolition derby would eventually hive off a Monster Truck-based faith seems a natural progression. But what no one realized is the amount of enmity the two groups would eventually develop for each other. The Demo guys saw the Monster Truckers as amateurs, who had lost track of the true spiritual journey of their formerly shared faith. There was definitely no love lost between the two. While in open combat, the sedans and station wagons of the Demolition Derby Drivers were no match for fire engines, school busses, and garbage trucks, all propped up on forty-eight-inch tires, some spouting flame, mufflers cut to produce a deafening, terrifying roar. They both believed, as their central tenet, that Jesus waited patiently for a certain tally of automobile wreckage before He revealed Himself to His congregation of true believers. But neither could agree on that number. A few argued that Jesus found certain makes and models favorable in His eyes. Numerous attempts at reconciliation were made, but it was hopeless. Still others, more academically inclined, insisted it was a dollar value of destruction Jesus was after. The Great Schism occurred when the Demolition Derby Drivers felt the Monster Truck drivers in the congregation should not get the same number of points, or dollar credit, for their destruction. Taking individual cars out Malachi-crunch style was certainly harder than simply driving over the top at them at high speeds and crushing them like old beer cans. And since they both believed that whoever hit that magic number or dollar figure or specific make and model coveted by God would receive special treatment from God (some said eternal life and a special car that you could smash and smash all day and the whole thing would just pop back out at the end of the day by pressing a small, red button located just inside the glove compartment) generally speaking, when the two groups met, it was "on" some real "Death Race" shit under the autumn buckeyes.

I had not given up on Matilda, but she had taken an active field command in the far-flung ice cream empire she devotedly served. When not with the dude in the powder-blue Olds '88 with faux-crushed-velour interior, of course. Almost every time the ice cream truck went out on a sales offensive, Matilda was at the wheel, a one-woman ice-cream-truck-drivin', bringing-soft-ice-cream-to-believer-and-unbeliever-alike dynamo. And every time she pulled out, that fucking powder-blue Olds '88 rode escort. My increasingly frantic thoughts were also occupied trying to figure out what I was supposed to be doing with my life. What had once been a realistic (if loathed) option of following my father into the bowels of Toledo Transmission, now, with the economy being what it was, seemed like a taunting, impossible memory. Finally I just said "fuck it" and got a job breaking rebar out of concrete for a demolition company, and tried by sheer force of will to forget about Matilda.

To be fair, America had begun the process of completely giving up on itself well before 9-11. Even my father, just a generation before me, would talk about the "good old days", before automation and surveillance cameras when a guy could sleep off a drunk in some secluded part of the plant while his buddy worked both their jobs and covered for him. But it had been going on a lot longer than that: GM downsizing, rightsizing, lean-practicing, on-demand supplying its way to a smaller and smaller and smaller work force. And with every reduction came that awkward moment where GM could not grasp that there was nowhere for all its ex-employees to go. They would have preferred them to vaporize, or possibly be crushed into bricks and recycled, sold to China as scrap.

Every city in America has that part of town where all the old brick factories of the past generations are, and sometimes, a couple blocks over, the houses of everyone who stoked, carried, hammered, sorted in the brick factories lived are now being busted up and dragged off in dumpsters: soil, scrap, wire, masonry, etc. You usually see its broken-tooth windows on your way into any American city by train. It slouches there, an embarrassed, broke, and shabby relative no one really want to talk to or acknowledge. The usual tack is to pretend it never existed: haul it away quietly piece by piece, building by building, implode it, bulldoze it, promise a convention center or casino. The summer after 9-11 I took a job busting, stacking, and hauling all that shame in brick and masonry form. It was a few buildings on a street in a shitty, forgotten part of Toledo, and I kept wondering if my ancestors had lived there once: two-story brick boxes, tarpaper roofs. Physically the work did me good. I found I enjoyed it—the violence of swinging the hammer in a cloud of dust, learning to balance it to let the sledge do the work. I got a permanent job with the demo company, and soon we were scheduled to work on the destruction project to end all destruction projects: the Willow Run Manufacturing complex. I began to take on more responsibilities at the company, feeling good. All my life I'd been a strange, chubby, asthmatic kid, both petrified of, and fascinated by, girls. All the swinging a sledge and pushing wheelbarrows rounded my shoulders and within six months I was proud of my body. I even managed to get my father a job, which he badly needed after the latest round of GM's looking over its shoulder with a shocked expression of "the fuck you guys still doing here" layoffs at Toledo Transmission. Insulting enough after ten or twenty or thirty years of service. But why they always had to insist that now everyone was free to pursue their *real* dream in life ("brain surgeon! billionaire entrepreneur! Apple computer was founded by a high school dropout!") was always the kick in the taint that let everyone know this was no temporary circumstance. That fire hoses and attack dogs for those who refused to mournfully slink away after a lifetime's service and wrecked backs and shift-work-stoked heart attacks was the next step. I got my father a job with me: wrestling the enormous canvas fire hoses that knocked down the dust from the back end loaders tearing down America's former "You *really* wanna mess with this shit?" industrial might. I think the job did him good. It was tough work for a man in his late forties, but being outside brought back his color (every man in our town, from shift work, booze and drugs seemed to have skin like old plumbing putty) and while he was making nowhere near what he would have made at GM (and, of course, no benefits), he was just happy to have a job.

From the moment we even knew Willow Run was a possibility, we were excited, albeit in a confused, guilty way. This wasn't a few abandoned townhouses or a derelict block-long wheel-hub assembly factory in Toledo. This was Willow Run. Toledo Transmission was a respectable-sized factory. Willow Run was a fucking Death Star. They had built the B-29 Liberator bombers there during the Second World War. Now we were destroying it. Almost everyone in our part of the state had some connection to Willow Run. It was almost impossible *not* to. Fathers, uncles, aunts, grandparents, some lifers, some cycling in and out through college and on to better things. But it was always a simple fact of industrial mass, a metal-stamping black hole. Its destruction was an undeniable admission of defeat. And the Church of Christ the Demolition Derby Driver even wrote it into their gospel as the final sign on the end-of-the-auto-industry apocalypse. Which is why they didn't take it so well when they found out the Church of Our Lady of the Monster Truck Rally had been hired to destroy a part of it.

We had been working with the survey party when the Church of Our Lady of the Monster Truck Rally showed up. It was easy work: walking around the endless factory in our high-visibility vests, moving fallen beams or cinder blocks as needed as the surveyors set up sight lines and marked the floors with cans of Jamaica orange spray paint, numbering and coding and divvying it up like a side of beef. It was far too big for one company to handle, so everyone involved would get a section of their own to go to work on. It was a warm spring day and we had been laughing and joking the whole time. For the first time in a long time I could see my father's spirits picking up. I thought working together would be a pain in the ass, but I soon found out we were much better at being work buddies than father and son. Which was fine with me. We had even taken to practicing our demolition derby moves on the vast air-strip outside Willow Run where the B-29's had taken off on their journey to air combat over Europe. To my great surprise the Church of Christ the Demolition Derby Driver had given me a car, without prompting, the first week I started going to services with my father. It was a 1987 Ford LTD Crown Victoria Country Squire station wagon complete with jump seats in the back, luggage rack on top, and fake wood veneer on the sides. It was both a thing of beauty and the automobile equivalent of a Nazi V2 rocket. But the congregation was insistent I only use it in the true spirit of Jesus. That I had to truly, deeply feel the spirit of God move within me, and only I would know when that moment would arrive. It arrived, of course, like an atomic blast, with the coming of the Church of Our Lady of the Monster Truck Rally.

Like I said, the Church of Christ the Demolition Derby Driver saw the Church of Our Lady of the Monster Truck Rally as amateurs, johnny-come-latelys, and publicity hounds. But they had undeniably managed to capture the public imagination with their methods, particularly the imagination of that vast swath of mouth-breathing believers who felt strongly that God himself had a deep and personal interest in who won the Super Bowl or the Indy 500. We had just finished a few emergency hand brake stops and bootlegger's turns and were quietly eating our lunch, knowing we had found favor with our Lord, when we heard their arrival.

Willow Run had this enormous airstrip of basket-weave runways that looked like a cross between the Nazca Lines and a place for the Titans to play tic-tac-toe, like the concrete tentacles of the enormous mechanical squid of Willow Run. All the companies contracted to take down Willow Run were arriving, looking like an invasion force suitable for the Normandy invasion. In addition to all the actual demolition machinery (backhoes, bulldozers, front-end loaders) were all the support machinery: flatbeds piled with metal barrier fence and portable toilets, semis hauling mobile office trailers and modular buildings, steel shipping containers with valuable tools and cutting torches, water trucks and teams of environmental assessment eggheads. And bringing up the rear, the unearthly roar of the Church of Our Lady of the Monster Truck Rally.

I could see the color drain from my father's face the instant he saw them. We would learn later that they had managed to insert themselves into the demolition as a cheap publicity stunt: smashing and roaring and crashing into the thin steel-sided buildings that used to contain the B-29 assembly line. But my first reaction was one of awe. There was every conceivable size and shape: a fire truck, an ambulance, a school bus. One made to look like a steam locomotive. Another made to look like a shark. Dinosaurs. Tanks. An F-14 fighter. And there, right out in front, leading this end-of-the-world convoy, the Tasty Scoop truck, on top of forty-eight-inch tires, fiberglass ice cream scoop still revolving on top, Matilda behind the wheel. And there, following after her, that powder-blue Oldsmobile 88. And the power of the Lord *did* come upon me. And I did toss my lunch aside and jump in my Ford LTD Crown Victoria Country Squire station wagon. And I did find favor in the eyes of our Lord that day.

The Lord *does* move in mysterious ways. Sometimes (as is the case in 9-11) he just moves like a fucking asshole. But I had come to believe the Lord helps those who help themselves, so when I hit the rear quarter panel of the powder-blue Olds going reverse at forty miles an hour, I knew somehow the spirit of Jesus was smiling down upon me. I hit him with such force that the front of his car came spinning back against me, like someone closing a jackknife, and for a brief instant we locked eyes before the greater mass of my Ford carried me past him, leaving him spun completely around three hundred and sixty degrees, the back of his car now simply a tangled mess. After that all hell broke loose. Most of the crew my father and I worked with were members of the Church of Christ the Demolition Derby Driver, and when they saw what was going on they jumped in their cars and raced to help me. They had no clue what was going on besides the fact a bunch of Monster Trucks, their sworn enemy, had shown up, and I was madly careening in and out of their ranks trying to get close to the Tasty Scoop truck. In an instant we were swarming in and out of their ranks, but there was nothing we could *really* do to them. Their giant tires served like enormous rubber bumpers, like tires hung around the outside of tugboats to cushion their impact when pushing ships. Before long both sides wore down in confusion and we arrived at an uneasy stalemate.

Management knew they had to rectify the situation, so they called an impromptu peace conference the next day inside Willow Run under a protective amnesty, which is where, for the firs time in three years, I saw Matilda. All the Monster Truck drivers were huddled in an uneasy knot, all wearing clothing thematically tied into their vehicles: bus driver, fireman, fighter pilot, so they all looked like a cross between cut-rate, blue-collar superheroes and a group of male strippers. Matilda stuck out, both because she was the only female in the group and because she was, despite the fact she drove around all day in a fully functioning ice cream truck, still smokin' hot. After the obligatory short speech about getting along sprinkled with veiled threats about what steps management would take if we chose *not* to get along, we formed two lines and began to shake hands like hockey teams after the final game of a playoff series. I could feel my heart beating faster and faster the closer Matilda came to me in the line, and I think it took my father about eight seconds to figure out what was going on, and to project into the future about what was going to happen.

"Does it still make ice cream?" was my opener. Lousy, but that was alright. I was no longer a chubby asthmatic. I was tall, with wide, round shoulders and a flat stomach. Wide, round shoulders and a flat stomach forgive a lot of lousy openers. Or at least *my* opener.

"Yeah, wanna see?" was Matilda's response, seeming to forget about the dude in the powder-blue Olds, who I could only assume was somewhere either in traction, or at the very least (hopefully) a comical neck-brace. From then on I started working on my end-game, casually strolling over to Matilda's Tasty Scoop truck every day at lunch for free ice cream (that was the flimsy excuse I'm sure my father saw through it instantly anyway).

Our little internecine war had set back Willow Run's demolition date, and in that time me and Matilda grew closer. And the ghosts of Willow Run seemed to visit us. For me it began with a spooky feeling that everyone that had worked at Willow Run was ashamed of us and our complicity in destroying the vast facility. Maybe I just over-romanticized it. I was too old to ever *really* know what it was like to be a part of the system at GM. To have your life *totally* determined by the groans and tectonic shifts of a place like Willow Run or Toledo Transmission. That was all long gone by the time I was old enough to walk through those gates. Its vast silence seemed a noble recrimination against the horde of termite-like men and women who were about to tear it up for scrap. But any chance to protest it had passed a long, long time ago. This was no Battle of the Overpass. It was just embarrassing. I'd had enough of tearing things down that other, harder-working people than me had built up. It came to a head the night before work was supposed to start. Me and Matilda were sitting in a pair of lawn chairs on the runway beside her truck. She had managed to build a substantial business with her truck selling to all the workers who were from out of state, and was camped out waiting for work to start. I had started helping her out, and it felt good. Better than seeing your entire blue-collar history disassembled brick by brick. I told her I wanted to quit, leave Willow Run, and see something of the world outside the Ohio Valley and southern Michigan.

"Everybody loves ice cream," I said. Checkmate.

It's five years later now, and I couldn't tell you if we won, or the terrorists won, or it ended in a draw. From what I've seen through the serving window of the Tasty Scoop truck, American looks pretty much the same as it did pre-9-11. It's been at least a generation since the military became the new Toledo Transmission: the place you went after high school if you didn't have either the brains or the money to go to college. Luckily, I had Matilda and her Tasty Scoop truck, or it probably would've been the Marines or tooling around in the Navy on some Godforsaken aircraft carrier in the Middle East for me too. I write my father postcards whenever I can, and send him pictures of me and Matilda in whatever state we've decided to explore. I'm happy. I think she's happy. And it's true: peace, war, stock market collapse, housing bubble burst, everybody *does* love ice cream. Things seem to be turning around. There's even a rumor they're going to start up Toledo Transmission again, which, to be honest, I don't think most people know whether to shit or go blind over. The jobs may be there, but the pension and benefits have been successfully cannibalized by management. I read about it in the papers, but mostly I just want to forget about the whole thing.

Kelly Robson has been published in Clarkesworld, Asimov's Science Fiction, *and* Tor.com. *She is a rising star in the world of science fiction and fantasy and, after studying with Connie Willis and Walter Jon Williams at the Taos Toolbox writing workshop, has hit the ground running.*

"The Three Resurrections of Jessica Churchill" is a disturbing tale about the inner life of a brutally victimized hitchhiker and how she saves humanity.

THE THREE RESURRECTIONS OF JESSICA CHURCHILL
Kelly Robson

"I rise today on this September 11, the one-year anniversary of the greatest tragedy on American soil in our history, with a heavy heart . . ."
—Hon. Jim Turner

September 9, 2001

Jessica slumped against the inside of the truck door. The girl behind the wheel and the other one squished between them on the bench seat kept stealing glances at her. Jessica ignored them, just like she tried to ignore the itchy pull and tug deep inside her, under her belly button, where the aliens were trying to knit her guts back together.

"You party pretty hard last night?" the driver asked.

Jessica rested her burning forehead on the window. The hum of the highway under the wheels buzzed through her skull. The truck cab stank of incense.

"You shouldn't hitchhike, it's not safe," the other girl said. "I sound like my mom saying it and I hate that but it's really true. So many dead girls. They haven't even found all the bodies."

"Highway of Tears," the driver said.

"Yeah, Highway of Tears," the other one repeated. "Bloody Sixteen."

"Nobody calls it that," the driver snapped.

Jessica pulled her hair up off her neck, trying to cool the sticky heat pulsing through her. The two girls looked like tree planters. She'd spent the summer working full time at the gas station and now she could smell a tree planter a mile away. They'd come in for smokes and mix, dirty, hairy, dressed in fleece and hemp just like these two. The driver had blonde dreadlocks and the other had tattoos circling her wrists. Not that much older than her, lecturing her about staying safe just like somebody's mom.

Well, she's right, Jessica thought. A gush of blood flooded the crotch of her jeans.

Water. Jessica, we can do this but you've got to get some water. We need to replenish your fluids.

"You got any water?" Jessica asked. Her voice rasped, throat stripped raw from all the screaming.

The tattooed girl dug through the backpack at Jessica's feet and came up with a two litre mason jar half full of water. Hippies, Jessica thought as she fumbled with the lid. Like one stupid jar will save the world.

"Let me help." The tattooed girl unscrewed the lid and steadied the heavy jar as Jessica lifted it to her lips.

She gagged. Her throat was tight as a fist but she forced herself to swallow, wash down the dirt and puke coating her mouth.

Good. Drink more.

"I can't," Jessica said. The tattooed girl stared at her.

You need to. We can't do this alone. You have to help us.

"Are you okay?" the driver asked. "You look wrecked."

Jessica wiped her mouth with the back of her hand. "I'm fine. Just hot."

"Yeah, you're really flushed," said the tattooed girl. "You should take off your coat."

Jessica ignored her and gulped at the jar until it was empty.

Not so fast. Careful!

"Do you want to swing past the hospital when we get into town?" the driver asked.

A bolt of pain knifed through Jessica's guts. The empty jar slipped from her grip and rolled across the floor of the truck. The pain faded.

"I'm fine," she repeated. "I just got a bad period."

That did it. The lines of worry eased off both girls' faces.

"Do you have a pad? I'm gonna bleed all over your seat." Jessica's vision dimmed, like someone had put a shade over the morning sun.

"No problem." The tattooed girl fished through the backpack. "I bleed heavy too. It depletes my iron."

"That's just an excuse for you to eat meat," said the driver.

Jessica leaned her forehead on the window and waited for the light to come back into the world. The two girls were bickering now, caught up in their own private drama.

Another flood of blood. More this time. She curled her fists into her lap. Her insides twisted and jumped like a fish on a line.

Your lungs are fine. Breathe deeply, in and out, that's it. We need all the oxygen you can get.

The tattooed girl pulled a pink wrapped maxi pad out of her backpack and offered it to Jessica.

The driver slowed down and turned the truck into a roadside campground.

"Hot," Jessica said. The girls didn't hear. Now they were bitching at each other about disposable pads and something called a keeper cup.

We know. You'll be okay. We can heal you.

"Don't wait for me," Jessica said as they pulled up to the campground outhouse. She flipped the door handle and nearly fell out of the truck. "I can catch another ride."

Cold air washed over her as she stumbled toward the outhouse. She unzipped her long coat and let the breeze play though—chill air on boiling skin. Still early September but they always got a cold snap at the start of fall. First snow only a few days ago. Didn't last. Never did.

The outhouse stench hit her like a slap. Jessica fumbled with the lock. Her fingers felt stiff and clumsy.

"Why am I so hot?" she said, leaning on the cold plywood wall. Her voice sounded strange, ripped apart and multiplied into echoes.

Your immune system is trying to fight us but we've got it under control. The fever isn't dangerous, just uncomfortable.

She shed her coat and let it fall to the floor. Unzipped her jeans, slipped them down her hips. No panties. She hadn't been able to find them.

No, Jessica. Don't look.

Pubic hair hacked away along with most of her skin. Two deep slices puckered angry down the inside of her right thigh. And blood. On her legs, on her jeans, inside her coat. Blood everywhere, dark and sticky.

Keep breathing!

An iron tang filled the outhouse as a gout of blood dribbled down her legs. Jessica fell back on the toilet seat. Deep within her chest something fluttered, like a bird beating its wings on her ribs, trying to get out. The light drained from the air.

If you die, we die too. Please give us a chance.

The flutters turned into fists pounding on her breastbone. She struggled to inhale, tried to drag the outhouse stink deep into her lungs but the air felt thick. Solid. Like a wall against her face.

Don't go. Please.

Breath escaped her like smoke from a fire burned down to coal and ash. She collapsed against the wall of the outhouse. Vision turned to pinpricks, she crumpled like paper and died.

"Everything okay in there?"

The thumping on the door made the whole outhouse shake. Jessica lurched to her feet. Her chest burned like she'd been breathing acid.

You're okay.

"I'm fine. Gimme a second."

Jessica plucked the pad off the outhouse floor, ripped it open and stuck it on the crotch of her bloody jeans, zipped them up. She zipped her coat to her chin. She felt strong. Invincible. She unlocked the door.

The two girls were right there, eyes big and concerned and in her business.

"You didn't have to wait," Jessica said.

"How old are you, fifteen? We waited," the driver said as they climbed back into the truck.

"We're not going to let you hitchhike," said the tattooed girl. "Especially not you."

"Why not me?" Jessica slammed the truck door behind her.

"Most of the dead and missing girls are First Nations."

"You think I'm an Indian? Fuck you. Am I on a reserve?"

The driver glared at her friend as she turned the truck back onto the highway.

"Sorry," the tattooed girl said.

"Do I look like an Indian?"

"Well, kinda."

"Fuck you." Jessica leaned on the window, watching the highway signs peel by as they rolled toward Prince George. When they got to the city the invincible feeling was long gone. The driver insisted on taking her right to Gran's.

"Thanks," Jessica said as she slid out of the truck.

The driver waved. "Remember, no hitchhiking."

September 8, 2001

Jessica never hitchhiked.

She wasn't stupid. But Prince George was spread out. The bus ran maybe once an hour weekdays and barely at all on weekends, and when the weather turned cold you could freeze to death trying to walk everywhere. So yeah, she took rides when she could, if she knew the driver.

After her Saturday shift she'd started walking down the highway. Mom didn't know she was coming. Jessica had tried to get through three times from the gas station phone, left voice mails. Mom didn't always pick up—usually didn't—and when she did it was some excuse about her phone battery or connection.

Mom was working as a cook at a retreat center out by Tabor Lake. A two-hour walk, but Mom would get someone to drive her back to Gran's.

Only seven o'clock but getting cold and the wind had come up. Semis bombed down the highway, stirring up the trash and making it dance at her feet and fly in her face as she walked along the ditch.

It wasn't even dark when the car pulled over to the side of the highway.

"Are you Jessica?"

The man looked ordinary. Baseball cap, hoodie. Somebody's dad trying to look young.

"Yeah," Jessica said.

"Your mom sent me to pick you up."

A semi honked as it blasted past his car. A McDonald's wrapper flipped through the air and smacked her in the back of the head. She got in.

The car was skunky with pot smoke. She almost didn't notice when he passed the Tabor Lake turnoff.

"That was the turn," she said.

"Yeah, she's not there. She's out at the ski hill."

"At this time of year?"

"Some kind of event." He took a drag on his smoke and smiled.

Jessica hadn't even twigged. Mom had always wanted to work at the ski hill, where she could party all night and ski all day.

It was twenty minutes before Jessica started to clue in.

When he slowed to take a turn onto a gravel road she braced herself to roll out of the car. The door handle was broken. She went at him with her fingernails but he had the jump on her, hit her in the throat with his elbow. She gulped air and tried to roll down the window.

It was broken too. She battered the glass with her fists, then spun and lunged for the wheel. He hit her again, slammed her head against the dashboard three times. The world stuttered and swam.

Pain brought everything back into focus. Face down, her arms flailed, fingers clawed at the dirt. Spruce needles flew up her nose and coated her tongue. Her butt was jacked up over a log and every thrust pounded her face into the dirt. One part of her was screaming, screaming. The other part watched the pile of deer shit inches from her nose. It looked like a heap of candy. Chocolate covered almonds.

She didn't listen to what he was telling her. She'd heard worse from boys at school. He couldn't make her listen. He didn't exist except as a medium for pain.

When he got off Jessica felt ripped in half, split like firewood. She tried to roll off the log. She'd crawl into the bush, he'd drive away, and it would be over.

Then he showed her the knife.

When he rammed the knife up her she found a new kind of pain. It drove the breath from her lungs and sliced the struggle from her limbs. She listened to herself whimper, thinking it sounded like a newborn kitten, crying for its mother.

The pain didn't stop until the world had retreated to little flecks of light deep in her skull. The ground spun around her as he dragged her through the bush and rolled her into a ravine. She landed face down in a stream. Her head flopped, neck canted at a weird angle.

Jessica curled her fingers around something cold and round. A rock. It fit in her hand perfectly and if he came back she'd let him have it right in the teeth. And then her breath bubbled away and she died.

When she came back to life a bear corpse was lying beside her, furry and rank. She dug her fingers into its pelt and pulled herself up. It was still warm. And skinny—nothing but sinew and bone under the skin.

She stumbled through the stream, toes in wet socks stubbing against the rocks but it didn't hurt. Nothing hurt. She was good. She could do anything.

She found her coat in the mud, her jeans too. One sneaker by the bear and then she looked and looked for the other one.

It's up the bank.

She climbed up. The shoe was by the log where it had happened. The toe was coated in blood. She wiped it in the dirt.

You need to drink some water.

A short dirt track led down to the road. The gravel glowed white in the dim light of early morning. No idea which way led to the highway. She picked a direction.

"How do you know what I need?"

We know. We're trying to heal you. The damage is extensive. You've lost a lot of blood and the internal injuries are catastrophic.

"No shit."

We can fix you. We just need time.

Her guts writhed. Snakes fought in her belly, biting and coiling.

Feel that? That's us working. Inside you.

"Why doesn't it hurt?"

We've established a colony in your thalamus. That's where we're blocking the pain. If we didn't, you'd die of shock.

"Again."

Yes, again.

"A colony. What the fuck are you? Aliens?"

Yes. We're also distributing a hormonal cocktail of adrenalin and testosterone to keep you moving, but we'll have to taper it off soon because it puts too much stress on your heart. Right now it's very important for you to drink some water.

"Shut up about the water." She wasn't thirsty. She felt great.

A few minutes later the fight drained out of her. Thirsty, exhausted, she ached as though the hinge of every moving part was crusted in rust, from her jaw to her toes. Her eyelids rasped like sandpaper. Her breath sucked and blew without reaching her lungs. Every rock in the road was a mountain and every pothole a canyon.

But she walked. Dragged her sneakers through the gravel, taking smaller and smaller steps until she just couldn't lift her feet anymore. She stood in the middle of the road and waited. Waited to fall over.

Waited for the world to slip from her grasp and darkness to drown her in cold nothing.

When she heard the truck speeding toward her she didn't even look up. Didn't matter who it was, what it was. She stuck out her thumb.

September 10, 2001

Jessica woke soaked. Covered in blood, she thought, struggling with the blankets. But it wasn't blood.

"What—"

Your urethra was damaged so we eliminated excess fluid through your pores. It's repaired now. You'll be able to urinate.

She pried herself out of the wet blankets.

No solid food, though. Your colon is shredded and your small intestine has multiple ruptures.

When the tree planters dropped her off, Gran had been sacked out on the couch. Jessica had stayed in the shower for a good half hour, watching the blood swirl down the drain with the spruce needles and the dirt, the blood clots and shreds of raw flesh.

And all the while she drank. Opened her mouth and let the cool spray fill her. Then she had stuffed her bloody clothes in a garbage bag and slept.

Jessica ran her fingertips over the gashes inside her thigh. The wounds puckered like wide toothless mouths, sliced edges pasted together and sunk deep within her flesh. The rest of the damage was hardened over with amber colored scabs. She'd have to use a mirror to see it all. She didn't want to look.

"I should go to the hospital," she whispered.

That's not a good idea. It would take multiple interventions to repair the damage to your digestive tract. They'd never be able to save your uterus or reconstruct your vulva and clitoris. The damage to your cervix alone—

"My what?"

Do you want to have children someday?

"I don't know."

Trust us. We can fix this.

She hated the hospital anyway. Went to Emergency after she'd twisted her knee but the nurse had turned her away, said she wouldn't bother the on-call for something minor. Told her to go home and put a bag of peas on it.

And the cops were even worse than anyone at the hospital. Didn't give a shit. Not one of them.

Gran was on the couch, snoring. A deck of cards was scattered across the coffee table in between the empties—looked like she'd been playing solitaire all weekend.

Gran hadn't fed the cats, either. They had to be starving but they wouldn't come to her, not even when she was filling their dishes. Not even Gringo, who had hogged her bed every night since she was ten. He just hissed and ran.

Usually Jessica would wake up Gran before leaving for school, try to get her on her feet so she didn't sleep all day. Today she didn't have the strength. She shook Gran's shoulder.

"Night night, baby," Gran said, and turned over.

Jessica waited for the school bus. She felt cloudy, dispersed, her thoughts blowing away with the wind. And cold now, without her coat. The fever was gone.

"Could you fix Gran?"

Perhaps. What's wrong with her?

Jessica shrugged. "I don't know. Everything."

We can try. Eventually.

She sleepwalked through her classes. It wasn't a problem. The teachers were more bothered when she did well than when she slacked off. She stayed in the shadows, off everyone's radar.

After school she walked to the gas station. Usually when she got to work she'd buy some chips or a chocolate bar, get whoever was going off shift to ring it up so nobody could say she hadn't paid for it.

"How come I'm not hungry?" she asked when she had the place to herself.

You are, you just can't perceive it.

It was a quiet night. The gas station across the highway had posted a half cent lower so everyone was going there. Usually she'd go stir crazy from boredom but today she just zoned out. Badly photocopied faces stared at her from the posters taped to the cigarette cabinet overhead.

An SUV pulled up to pump number three. A bull elk was strapped to the hood, tongue lolling.

"What was the deal with the bear?" she said.

The bear's den was adjacent to our crash site. It was killed by the concussive wave.

"Crash site. A spaceship?"

Yes. Unfortunate for the bear, but very fortunate for us.

"You brought the bear back to life. Healed it."

Yes.

"And before finding me you were just riding around in the bear."

Yes. It was attracted by the scent of your blood.

"So you saw what happened to me. You watched." She should be upset, shouldn't she? But her mind felt dull, thoughts thudding inside an empty skull.

We have no access to the visual cortex.

"You're blind?"

Yes.

"What are you?"

A form of bacteria.

"Like an infection."

Yes.

The door chimed and the hunter handed over his credit card. She rang it through. When he was gone she opened her mouth to ask another question, but then her gut convulsed like she'd been hit. She doubled over the counter. Bile stung her throat.

He'd been here on Saturday.

Jessica had been on the phone, telling Mom's voice mail that she'd walk out to Talbot Lake after work. While she was talking she'd rung up a purchase, $32.25 in gas and a pack of smokes. She'd punched it through automatically, cradling the phone on her shoulder. She'd given him change from fifty.

An ordinary man. Hoodie. Cap.

Jessica, breathe.

Her head whipped around, eyes wild, hands scrambling reflexively for a weapon. Nobody was at the pumps, nobody parked at the air pump. He could come back any moment. Bring his knife and finish the job.

Please breathe. There's no apparent danger.

She fell to her knees and crawled out from behind the counter. Nobody would stop him, nobody would save her. Just like they hadn't saved all those dead and missing girls whose posters had been staring at her all summer from up on the cigarette cabinet.

When she'd started the job they'd creeped her out, those posters. For a few weeks she'd thought twice about walking after dark. But then those dead and missing girls disappeared into the landscape. Forgotten.

You must calm down.

Now she was one of them.

We may not be able to bring you back again.

She scrambled to the bathroom on all fours, threw herself against the door, twisted the lock. Her hands were shuddering, teeth chattering like it was forty below. Her chest squeezed and bucked, throwing acid behind her teeth.

There was a frosted window high on the wall. He could get in, if he wanted. She could almost see the knife tick-tick-ticking on the glass.

No escape. Jessica plowed herself into the narrow gap between the wall and toilet, wedging herself there, fists clutching at her burning chest as she retched bile onto the floor. The light winked and flickered. A scream flushed out of her and she died.

A fist banged on the door.

"Jessica, what the hell!" Her boss's voice.

A key scraped in the lock. Jessica gripped the toilet and wrenched herself off the floor to face him. His face was flushed with anger and though he was a big guy, he couldn't scare her now. She felt bigger, taller, stronger, too. And she'd always been smarter than him.

"Jesus, what's wrong with you?"

"Nothing, I'm fine." Better than fine. She was butterfly-light, like if she opened her wings she could fly away.

"The station's wide open. Anybody could have waltzed in here and walked off with the till."

"Did they?"

His mouth hung open for a second. "Did they what?"

"Walk off with the fucking till?"

"Are you on drugs?"

She smiled. She didn't need him. She could do anything.

"That's it," he said. "You're gone. Don't come back."

A taxi was gassing up at pump number one. She got in the back and waited, watching her boss pace and yell into his phone. The invincible feeling faded before the tank was full. By the time she got home Jessica's joints had locked stiff and her thoughts had turned fuzzy.

All the lights were on. Gran was halfway into her second bottle of u-brew red so she was pretty out of it, too. Jessica sat with her at the kitchen table for a few minutes and was just thinking about crawling to bed when the phone rang.

It was Mom.

"Did you send someone to pick me up on the highway?" Jessica stole a glance at Gran. She was staring at her reflection in the kitchen window, maybe listening, maybe not.

"No, why would I do that?"

"I left you messages. On Saturday."

"I'm sorry, baby. This phone is so bad, you know that."

"Listen, I need to talk to you." Jessica kept her voice low.

"Is it your grandma?" Mom asked.

"Yeah. It's bad. She's not talking."

"She does this every time the residential school thing hits the news. Gets super excited, wants to go up north and see if any of her family are still alive. But she gives up after a couple of days. Shuts down. It's too much for her. She was only six when they took her away, you know."

"Yeah. When are you coming home?"

"I got a line on a great job, cooking for an oil rig crew. One month on, one month off."

Jessica didn't have the strength to argue. All she wanted to do was sleep.

"Don't worry about your Gran," Mom said. "She'll be okay in a week or two. Listen, I got to go."

"I know."

"Night night, baby," Mom said, and hung up.

September 11, 2001

Jessica waited alone for the school bus. The street was deserted. When the bus pulled up the driver was chattering before she'd even climbed in.

"Can you believe it? Isn't it horrible?" The driver's eyes were puffy, mascara swiped to a grey stain under her eyes.

"Yeah," Jessica agreed automatically.

"When I saw the news I thought it was so early, nobody would be at work. But it was nine in the morning in New York. Those towers were full of people." The driver wiped her nose.

The bus was nearly empty. Two little kids sat behind the driver, hugging their backpacks. The radio blared. Horror in New York. Attack on Washington. Jessica dropped into the shotgun seat and let the noise wash over her for a few minutes as they twisted slowly through the empty streets. Then she moved to the back of the bus.

When she'd gotten dressed that morning her jeans had nearly slipped off her hips. Something about that was important. She tried to concentrate, but the thoughts flitted from her grasp, darting away before she could pin them down.

She focused on the sensation within her, the buck and heave under her ribs and in front of her spine.

"What are you fixing right now?" she asked.

An ongoing challenge is the sequestration of the fecal and digestive matter that leaked into your abdominal cavity.

"What about the stuff you mentioned yesterday? The intestine and the . . . whatever it was."

Once we have repaired your digestive tract and restored gut motility we will begin reconstructive efforts on your reproductive organs.

"You like big words, don't you?"

We assure you the terminology is accurate.

There it was. That was the thing that had been bothering her, niggling at the back of her mind, trying to break through the fog.

"How do you know those words? How can you even speak English?"

We aren't communicating in language. The meaning is conveyed by sociolinguistic impulses interpreted by the brain's speech-processing loci. Because of the specifics of our biology, verbal communication is an irrelevant medium.

"You're not talking, you're just making me hallucinate," Jessica said.

That is essentially correct.

How could the terminology be accurate, then? She didn't know those words—cervix and whatever—so how could she hallucinate them?

"Were you watching the news when the towers collapsed?" the driver asked as she pulled into the high school parking lot. Jessica ignored her and slowly stepped off the bus.

The aliens were trying to baffle her with big words and science talk. For three days she'd had them inside her, their voice behind her eyes, their fingers deep in her guts, and she'd trusted them.

Hadn't even thought twice. She had no choice.

If they could make her hallucinate, what else were they doing to her?

The hallways were quiet, the classrooms deserted except for one room at the end of the hall with 40 kids packed in. The teacher had wheeled in an AV cart. Some of the kids hadn't even taken off their coats.

Jessica stood in the doorway. The news flashed clips of smoking towers collapsing into ash clouds. The bottom third of the screen was overlaid with scrolling, flashing text, the sound layered with frantic voiceovers. People were jumping from the towers, hanging in the air like dancers. The clips replayed over and over again. The teacher passed around a box of Kleenex.

Jessica turned her back on the class and climbed upstairs, joints creaking, jeans threatening to slide off with every step. She hitched them up. The biology lab was empty. She leaned on the cork board and scanned the parasite diagrams. Ringworm. Tapeworm. Liver fluke. Black wasp.

Some parasites can change their host's biology, the poster said, or even change their host's behavior.

Jessica took a push pin from the board and shoved it into her thumb. It didn't hurt. When she ripped it out a thin stream of blood trickled from the skin, followed by an ooze of clear amber from deep within the gash.

What are you doing?

None of your business, she thought.

Everything is going to be okay.

No it won't, she thought. She squeezed the amber ooze from her thumb, let it drip on the floor. The aliens were wrenching her around like a puppet, but without them she would be dead. Three times dead. Maybe she should feel grateful, but she didn't.

"Why didn't you want me to go to the hospital?" she asked as she slowly hinged down the stairs.

They couldn't have helped you, Jessica. You would have died.

Again, Jessica thought. Died again. And again.

"You said that if I die, you die too."

When your respiration stops, we can only survive for a limited time.

The mirror in the girls' bathroom wasn't real glass, just a sheet of polished aluminum, its shine pitted and worn. She leaned on the counter, rested her forehead on the cool metal. Her reflection warped and stretched.

"If I'd gone to the hospital, it would have been bad for you. Wouldn't it?"

That is likely.

"So you kept me from going. You kept me from doing a lot of things."

We assure you that is untrue. You may exercise your choices as you see fit. We will not interfere.

"You haven't left me any choices."

Jessica left the bathroom and walked down the hall. The news blared from the teacher's lounge. She looked in. At least a dozen teachers crowded in front of an AV cart, backs turned. Jessica slipped behind them and ducked into the teachers' washroom. She locked the door.

It was like a real bathroom. Air freshener, moisturizing lotion, floral soap. Real mirror on the wall and a makeup mirror propped on the toilet tank. Jessica put it on the floor.

"Since when do bacteria have spaceships?" She pulled her sweater over her head and dropped it over the mirror.

Jessica, you're not making sense. You're confused.

She put her heel on the sweater and stepped down hard. The mirror cracked.

Go to the hospital now, if you want.

"If I take you to the hospital, what will you do? Infect other people? How many?"

Jessica, please. Haven't we helped you?

"You've helped yourself."

The room pitched and flipped. Jessica fell to her knees. She reached for the broken mirror but it swam out of reach. Her vision telescoped and she batted at the glass with clumsy hands. A scream built behind her teeth, swelled and choked her. She swallowed it whole, gulped it, forced it down her throat like she was starving.

You don't have to do this. We aren't a threat.

She caught a mirror shard in one fist and swam along the floor as the room tilted and whirled. With one hand she pinned it to the yawning floor like a spike, windmilled her free arm and slammed her wrist down. The walls folded in, collapsing on her like the whole weight of the world, crushing in.

She felt another scream building. She forced her tongue between clenched teeth and bit down. Amber fluid oozed down her chin and pooled on the floor.

Please. We only want to help.

"Night night, baby," she said, and raked the mirror up her arm.

The fluorescent light flashed overhead. The room plunged into darkness as a world of pain dove into her for one hanging moment. Then it lifted. Jessica convulsed on the floor, watching the bars of light overhead stutter and compress to two tiny glimmers of light inside the thin parched shell of her skull. And she died, finally, at last.

Tim Marquitz is the novelist behind the Demon Squad series and the Blood War Trilogy. His short fiction has appeared in numerous anthologies including At Hell's Gates, Demonic Dolls, *and* Neverland's Library. *He is also the editor-in-chief of Ragnarok Publications.*

"Retribution" had to be included in this anthology because of how nakedly raw it is. This revenge fantasy can't be ignored. There is often a tendency to tiptoe around the anger and even hatred that the attacks of 9/11 engendered, and to self-censor in the name of a genteel liberalism. Tim Marquitz is having none of that.

RETRIBUTION
Tim Marquitz

September 11, 2001, 8:46 a.m. That's when it all went to hell.

The date and time are seared into my mind with a heat I can only pray my wife never felt. Candace had found her dream job. Just the week before, she'd started at Channel 5, WNYW. Their offices were on the 110th floor of the North Tower, and she'd worked overnight, preparing for her first time on camera. She was just a fill-in, but she wanted to be perfect. Candace always did.

She was scheduled off at 9:00.

She was also six months pregnant with our son: Joshua Michael Drake.

We'd only settled on his name a few days earlier. I never got to meet him. They never came home. Just fourteen minutes before Candace would have been in the elevator and down past the impact point, I lost them both.

I lost everything.

No, that's not entirely true. I didn't lose *everything*. After watching all I loved disappear in a roiling cloud of gray smoke as the building went down, there was still one thing left in my life. Once all the tears had dried and the empty words of comfort had soured on sorry tongues, there was still my fury.

I'd been a good husband until that moment, 8:46; the moment they took them away. I'd been a good man.

That man died with his family.

September 11, 2006, 8:40 a.m. Revenge was but six minutes away.

While the world had watched my wife and child disintegrate live on television, and had seen the eagle roused in righteous anger, our soldiers sacrificed in foreign lands, it would never know the truth of what had been set in motion that day. The jihadists had brought the struggle to our shores, but five years after our nation had been dealt a grievous blow, the war had yet to truly begin. In five minutes, it would start in earnest; with me.

My job was to repay our enemies in kind.

It was my pleasure.

The road from then to now had been difficult, in far more ways than I could ever have imagined when I signed up to fight. I wanted nothing more than to kill the bastards who'd stolen my family from me. All I asked of my country was a gun and a one-way ticket to the desert. It gave me so much more.

The morning sun of northern Waziristan beat down upon my head, the heat already sweltering as I made my way along the dusty streets of Mir Ali, heading toward an open market. My skin darkened by chemical staining and my beard grown out thick, itching at my chin and dyed black like my hair, I looked as though I belonged.

I was dressed in the traditional *shalwar kameez*, colored in a simple brown and carrying nothing. The other people on the narrow lane paid me little attention. I affected a shallow limp to feign a sense of weakness, and greeted those I passed with quiet courtesy, my teeth clenched to still my tongue. After five years of learning the language, I was proficient, but it always paid to be cautious. It wouldn't do for someone to note a flaw in my inflection, the anger in my voice. Not when I was so close.

In another three minutes, it wouldn't matter.

Central Intelligence reports had placed a number of ranking al-Qaeda fighters in the area, the people of Mir Ali complicit to their presence, or at the very least, complacent. No real difference between the two in my eyes. You harbor terrorists, you are a terrorist.

Inside the market, I moved amidst the jumbled stalls and carts, my eyes drifting as I weaved my way toward the thickest concentration of shoppers. I was disappointed there were so few women around, the local culture hiding them away from the eyes of men not their husbands. My dissatisfaction was tempered somewhat by the number of children that ran laughing through the crowded aisles. They were mostly boys, but there were a few girls as well, all too young to be coveted yet, even in their society. I counted nearly thirty who scampered about; twenty-seven young boys who would one day take up arms and fight against my nation, and three girls who would breed more. The numbers were hardly equal, but it would be a good start.

Two minutes.

I sidled up close to the busiest of the stalls, patrons haggling in quick tongues over the price of *chapatis*, the long loaves of bread stacked a dozen high. Flies swarmed about, their humming buzz adding to the morning's furor. It was hardly the last meal I would have chosen, but then again, none of them knew just how close to death they were.

I ignored the old man barking at me to move away if I wasn't buying, and let my heart settle. He'd be quiet soon enough.

My thoughts reached down and I felt the first stirrings of heat in my veins, my blood warming in response to the pressure of my will. The man went on, threatening violence if I didn't step aside, only affirming my cause.

I raised my finger and smiled at him, mouthing, "One minute," in his own tongue. That only set him to frothing, his tantrum drawing an audience of onlookers to the stall. I should have thanked him, but I needed to concentrate.

Blocking the ranting shopkeeper out, I closed my eyes and sent the spark of my fury to light the fuse inside. My stomach roiled with stinging acid and I could feel the sweat pushing its way from my pores, coating me instantly in a wet sheen. The man went silent as though he could hear the boiling rush that was building, the napalm sear that rippled beneath my flesh.

I opened my eyes to see him staring at me. His face was twisted in an almost comical confusion, and I wondered what he thought, not that it really mattered. The people who had gathered to watch the shopkeeper's tirade had drawn back a few steps, their voices muted by the uncertainty

of what was happening. They sensed something they couldn't understand, but still they gathered thick, sheep too dim to see the culling
ahead. It was too late to run.

I turned to face the crowd, my smile breaking through the blackness
of my beard. "You have taken my family from me," I told them, in English. Though most of them probably didn't understand a word I'd said,
there was no doubt they understood my intent. Their eyes went wide at
the recognition of an enemy among them, one of the great Satan, but
that thought would be their last. "Now I take you from yours."

8:46.

With one more push, my blood boiled over. A flash of white stole my
vision as the gift my government had given me took hold. Pain lanced
through my body, growing sharper with every instant. The agony multiplied like shattered glass, each shard breaking into a million more and
yet again, and again, and again. All but the simplest thoughts left my
head, my essence too scattered for true coherence. Split into a billion
pieces, my consciousness was a tiny blip in each, my body broken down
into its basest molecules. Every atom imbued with the fury to match
Oppenheimer's greatest achievement, I felt myself explode.

A blur of motion filled my remaining senses and I was overwhelmed
by the feeling of being hurled in every direction at once, vertigo at its
most exhilarating. Though it seemed, even to me, to be impossible, I
noted each and every impact as my fiery essence tore through the assembled crowd, shattered the stalls, and decimated the wares, millions of me
peppering the ground where I had just stood. Dust whipped about in
my wake.

For the briefest of instants, I was one with everything in the market:
the earth, the air, flesh and bone. As my being tore through theirs, it
was as though I could taste them, sorting the blood from wood and dirt
without a thought. I could hear the people's screams inside me, though
I had no ears, and could feel their lives ending as I punctured each with
a million different fragments of me. The world was alive with ruin, a
crimson cloud holding court amidst the carnage.

My momentum carried my discorporate particles out to a radius of
about a thousand feet. My essence slowed at last as it burst through the
surrounding obstacles of shops and homes and the remnants of my energies drained away. I could feel gravity's return, its gentle tug pulling the
whole of me toward the ground. The sense of separation began to ease,

clarity drawing closer like a ship approaching shore. Now came the hard part.

There weren't adequate words to describe the pain that came with reintegration, but as the pieces of me slammed together, becoming one again on a genetic level, no agony could steal my satisfaction away. As they had with us, I had brought the war to our enemy in a way they had never imagined.

Flesh and feeling returned with an acid bath rage, pieces of a puzzle set upon the surface of the sun. I could feel myself knitting back together, and recognized every molecule as it wove itself into the whole. Sense congealed while muscles and tendons stretched and returned to their natural shapes, growing over thickening bone. The smell of char filled my developing nose, and tears spilled from newborn eyes. I was nearly me again.

Close to two blocks from the market, I was reborn, huddled naked on a mattress of wreckage brought about by my righteous fury. My skin sizzled, gray tendrils of smoke wafting about me as the energies inside slowly cooled. I drew myself up and heard my joints creak, the pain and stiffness of my transformation ebbing.

All around me I could hear the cries of the wounded, those too far from the epicenter of the blast to have met their end with a merciful swiftness. There was no time to revel in my satisfaction.

Men shouted, and the morning air was filled with the crackle of flames and the sounds of panic. Black smoke swirled through the streets and alleys, obscuring the world from my eyes, and me from the men that swarmed nearby. It was only a taste of the ruin they'd brought.

I swallowed my smile and rubbed dirt and ashes across my skin, nicking my flesh in a number of places with a sharpened piece of debris, and then slathering blood across my body. For all my success, I had yet to escape. So far behind enemy lines as to be unreachable by my allies, it was up to me to find my way out.

Deep in the throes of adrenal fatigue, I had no need to fake the appearance of the walking wounded. Every step was an anchor drawn through sand as I emerged from the sheltering alley where I'd coalesced and stumbled out on the street. Mournful wails rose up as chaos began to break, the truth of what I'd wrought coming to light. I could only imagine what they saw. Flickering images of the moment twisted and tangled inside my throbbing head.

I staggered toward the desert, hoping to remain unseen, but I'd done my job too well. All of Mir Ali was in the streets, drawn by my release of power. A man shouted, his gnarled finger pointed at me, a dozen more taking up his cry. I looked about, seeking a clear path to run, but there was none. What wasn't blocked by a cluster of onlookers was made impassable by the fires set by my conflagration. My heart sank for an instant, but I remembered my guise. All of those who'd heard me speak were gone, red stains about the market floor.

Only one outward sign remained to betray my true origins. I crumpled to the ground and curled fetal, moaning incoherent. The men rushed to my side with heavy steps, but there was no anger in their voices; only concern.

"له ما سره ه مرسته," I told them as they closed. *Help me.*

Words of comfort filled my ears. They believed I was one of them.

Rough hands pulled me into the air, the largest of the men cradling me in his arms as though I were a child. His eyes narrowed as his nostrils flared as the stench of burnt flesh drifted up to assail his nose. I let my hands fall to my groin as he blinked away tears, covering my genitals from sight. None had noticed my circumcision.

I let the man carry me, burying my face in his chest to muffle my barked laughter, turning it into a cough. He jarred me about as he ran, shouting to clear the path ahead. His footsteps slapped as they struck the packed dirt roadway. A few moments later he slowed, his breath loud in his lungs as he called out for assistance. More hands clutched at me, pulling me from his arms. I was a set upon a makeshift gurney, a woolen blanket laid overtop, only helping to hide the truth of who they had helped.

I could hear their chattered voices as they scrambled for direction, the gurney raised unsteadily beneath me. Daring a glance ahead, I saw the doors of a medical center looming before me, the Red Crescent emblem emblazoned above in chipped and peeling paint. Men in white met us at the threshold, taking the gurney from those in the street and transferring me to a rolling cart. As they wheeled me down the hall, flickering lights flashing above my eyes, they asked in clipped voices where I was hurt.

I gave them only one answer, "My heart," then I asked for the time. They looked at me strangely, but one of the interns glanced at his watch, thinking perhaps he was granting a dying man's wish by answering.

9:02.

I smiled in thanks, meeting his dark eyes as we burst through the inner doors of the hospital, the room busy with people. With a deep breath, I mustered my will once more and drew upon the fire.

9:03.

K. Tempest Bradford is a speculative fiction writer and well-known blogger. Her work has been published by Strange Horizons, Electric Velocipede, *and* Diverse Energies. *Bradford was featured on CNN in March 2014 in a piece by John Blake about multiracial heroes on television, and on NPR for a piece entitled "The Lure of Literary Time Travel."*

"Until Forgiveness Comes" is a story about a yearly ritual done in remembrance of a 9/11-style attack. Told as a fictional news report, it exposes the power and problems of repetition while tantalizing the reader with the promise of an alternate world that is hidden away, just out of view. Strange Horizons *fiction editor Julia Rios has proclaimed this story as her favorite* Strange Horizons *story yet.*

UNTIL FORGIVENESS COMES
K. Tempest Bradford

National Radio News
Mourners Gather at New Central Terminal for Twelfth-Anniversary *Haitai*
by Sylvia Aloli

Audio for this story will be available at approx. 1900 KNT

Morning Edition, Akhet, Thuthi 19, 4511 The ceremony started at exactly six o'clock this morning when the clerics of Anpu, Iset, Seker, and Nebet-het stood at the four corners to create the sanctified square. Inside New Central Terminal, families and participants listened to the invocations and chants on loudspeakers while frankincense-infused smoke hovered over the still and silent mourners. Once the square was established, Sadana Manu, under-cleric of Iset, gave the sign for mourners to station themselves near the main blast sites for their glimpses of loved ones long gone.

In the twelve years since Red Seteshday, the clerics have perfected the haitai ritual to the point where participants know the script by heart and no longer need much direction on where to go and when. Still, Sadana manages a rotating roster of family members and survivors, reminding them of the correct verses to chant while invoking the highlights of that tragic day. Every year she stands on the memorial dais at the center of the Main Concourse, marking the time for prayers and the time for reading the names of the dead. Even if she weren't an officiant, Sadana says she would find some way to participate.

"Having something to do gets me through the day every year. It's my way of honoring Beke."

She lost her partner of four years that morning. Both seminary students at the time, they were planning to spend their lives serving Iset together. Bekeshe was on her way back to Nubia to spend time with family before her acolyteship began. Every year Sadana watches a faint trace of her stride across the concourse with her bags, searching for the train to the airport, just as the bombing began.

Though the day is painful, Sadana feels that her dual role as mourner and officiant has helped her minister to the families over the years.

"I know exactly how everyone feels. We all lost someone we loved. Had them ripped away by hate. We share a bond."

She helps eleven-year-old Marcus KichiAkak up on the dais. This is his first year as a reader, though he has attended every anniversary haitai. His mother, Decima, was eight months pregnant the day her husband Titus died on his way in to work. Marcus has only seen his father's face in pictures and on the anniversaries when Titus's ghost returns to relive those final moments.

"My mom brought me to the station each time, but I didn't get to go down to the platform until I was seven and told her I was ready."

Titus Nootau died next to train number 710 that morning. He was in the car with bomber number one, who waited until the train came to a full stop before setting off the explosives strapped to his body. Several passengers in the car were blown out onto the platforms, and that is where Marcus has watched his father struggle for breath and expire every year for five years.

"It's hard to watch. But at least I get to see him this way."

Sadana chimes a bell at 7:07 and then thirty seconds later to mark the first two bomb blasts, both from trains arriving in the station. One long, silent minute later a third bell signals the moment when bomber number three detonated in the middle of a large, confused crowd of commuters on the concourse.

Most family members stand on the balconies above the main floor. Even from a distance, the invocation of this moment stirs feelings of claustrophobia. The entire hall, filled with faint, translucent shades of the dead, suddenly feels crowded as the ghosts snap into focus. Panic erupts as some are thrown several feet through the air while others, dying from their injuries, scramble to escape. Many victims were trampled, or trapped by falling debris.

"That moment . . . It's very hard."

Aemilia Nebibi lost her sister to the chaos that bomber number three unleashed.

"The first year, you didn't really get a sense of it. They had these platforms we could stand on in the middle of the excavation, but you couldn't follow people the way you can now. When the reconstruction was finally done and we did the invocation, people nearly panicked when it happened. The immediacy of that moment never goes away, even though you know you're not in danger.

"I used to feel sort of bitter about the people who didn't stop to help the injured and, basically, stepped on them to get out. After that ritual I understood. It was hard not to bolt myself."

Sadana leads a group of incense-bearing acolytes downstairs where Hannadotter Frida and J. C. Granger stand on opposite ends of the Dining Concourse and ring bells simultaneously to mark the point when bombers number four and five blew themselves up on the main stairways, killing dozens instantly and trapping hundreds more.

"This is my last year, I think. I've seen this too many times. I don't want to see again."

When asked why she came this year, Hannadotter says she did it for her mother.

"I promised her before she died that I would come. She knew, because of the cancer, she would not make it this time. It was important to her, so I am here."

Hannadotter is one of the few who didn't have to wait for the anniversaries to see the details of her father's death. His video camera was recovered from the rubble two days after the attack. The original tape showed bomber number five blocking the stairwell and a view from the floor of the aftermath. The archived version, with the bomber's face and name removed, is now part of the Red Seteshday memorial.

"I ask my mother every year why we come. We had seen his last moments. He even spoke to us in the camera. He said he loved us. I want to honor him, but maybe this is not the way."

Others have also raised concerns over the ongoing nature of the haitai ritual. Though performing it after the first or second anniversary isn't unheard of, most clerics don't recommend it. Wassirian cleric Anes Mshai is an outspoken opponent of further Red Seteshday haitai.

"Bringing closure and allowing family members to say goodbye is healthy. Especially in the case of such a massive disaster. But reliving and recreating the event over and over again every year may be keeping them from moving on."

Anes works closely with Bel-Leuken of the Interfaith Coalition to quell the violence that inevitably arises as the anniversary approaches.

"Doing this ritual every year, long after the event, is like ripping a scab off a wound so it can't heal. It's not just the families, either. Twelve cities from here to Khmet to Britannia effectively stand still on this day, and the anger comes fresh again and again."

Leuken says a year has not gone by without a member of his congregation reporting an altercation or worse.

"People still don't understand the difference between Paesdan Belnos cultists and the average Auvergni. Everyone in Auvergne shares a desire to have Gergovie under sovereign rule, but the majority is against the use of violence to achieve that end."

Anes agrees that the ritual is what sparks the fresh wave of conflicts, rather than the anniversary itself.

"Of course we should never forget those who died and why they're gone. But the haitai is not the way."

The families in attendance mostly disagree with her assessment, but a few have expressed similar sentiments.

"I come here every year to mark the day, but I only went downstairs once."

Mihram Rivera survived the blast upstairs only to find out later that her daughter died when the ceiling collapsed on the Dining Concourse.

"I saw her and I said goodbye and I was done. And that was hard enough. I lived through this. I don't want to experience it again, even if it's just shades and shadows. Why do we have to call up the past? Just commemorate it."

Since the third anniversary, members of the sect of Yeshua-Horu have protested the haitai. Standing silently outside of the station until the ritual is over, they hold signs or wear shirts embroidered with the ancient sign for ba.

"By forcing the ba back into this world we're denying these people the ability to pass through the door into the next life."

The group echoes an old belief that the ghosts the ritual invokes aren't just shades, but the actual ba of the deceased. Out of respect for the dead, they refuse to interfere with the haitai, but they petition the clerics to refuse the request each year.

"We don't know—we can't know the effect this has on the dead. Are we making them relive the pain and fear and anguish of dying all over again? The Father and Son wait for them on the other side of the door. How long are these people going to keep the dead from the next life? I mean, no one can undo what was done, so what's the point in reliving it?"

Sadana has heard all of these objections before, but dismisses them.

"They completely misinterpret the fundamentals of the haitai. The ba can travel back and forth, yes, but it's the sheut we invoke. An imprint left on this world, nothing more."

She also contends that closure can never come until the source of the victims' pain is eliminated. Years after the coordinated bombings in twelve cities, Khmet has still never brought Arverni Vercingetor to justice. Paesdan Belnos still operates, though in a weakened state. And the military is on the eve of invading another Gaelic country accused of providing aid to the organization.

For some families it isn't about global concerns, but about their own personal grief.

"My son struggled to hang on to life."

Nadie Tanafriti leaned against Sadana for support as she rang the sixth bell on the subway platform where bomber number six, a transit employee, delivered the final blow.

"Claudius crawled into a nook and tried to stop the bleeding. But he was alone and the shrapnel cut him too deep and his life just slipped away. Before he died, he said, 'I'm sorry, Mom. I love you.' I had a lip reader come the year after I finally found him. He said it over and over to make sure I'd be able to see and understand. How can I not come every year and be witness to that? He needed me to know.

"There was a young lady who died right over there, trapped under these big chunks of . . . Sorry. It breaks my heart because I saw her for two or three years, then she just faded. There was no one here to invoke her, to bring her back and remember her. So now she's gone, maybe forgotten, forever."

Others who died have also faded from the ritual over the years—most notably the bombers themselves, who were often the target of fruitless attacks by grieving survivors. All but one are gone from the square now. Only bomber number two remains. His widow, Deirdre, stands in front of the place where he appears each year, flanked by three Mawt-Kom City police officers. She never speaks and has never taken part in reading the names or ringing the bells.

In earlier years, some families and survivors protested her right to take part in the haitai, making well-publicized threats. Sadana has advocated on her behalf since the beginning, finally bringing about an uneasy peace between the mourners. Deirdre's grief is private, some families concede, and of a different measure than theirs.

Each year she stands close enough to see into her husband's eyes, to mark the moment when he went from partner and father to martyr and murderer. When asked, six years ago, why she came, she said she was looking for a way to forgive him. And she'll keep attending, she says, until that forgiveness comes.

Sylvia Aloli, National Radio News.

Brian Aldiss is a Damon Knight Memorial Grand Master Award-winner. His first published science fiction story appeared in The Observer *newspaper in 1954 and was entitled "Not for an Age." His short story "Super-Toys Last All Summer Long" was the basis for the Stanley Kubrick/Steven Spielberg motion picture* A.I. Artificial Intelligence, *and his 1973 nonfiction book* Trillion Year Spree *is perhaps the definitive history of the science fiction genre.*

"Pipeline" tells the story of an amoral and confident employee of Butterfield-Chuu-Wolff, the biggest consortium on the face of the planet. It takes the reader on a journey from Turkmenistan to Turkey.

PIPELINE
Brian Aldiss

Carl Roddard paced up and down the chamber of the Interior Minister. The floor was tiled. The sound of his footsteps drowned out the screech of the noisy air-conditioning.

The Interior Minister sat placidly behind his desk. He smoked a cigarette. Behind him hung an oil portrait of President Firadzov, smiling. He looked up at the ceiling of the chamber. Beyond his narrow window, the sun ruled over the city of Ashkabad. Ashkabad, the capital of the Central Asian republic of Turkmenistan, was where the pipeline began.

Roddard ceased his pacing and confronted the Minister across his desk. He said, "Minister, your position is untenable. You do not have it in your power to nationalise the pipeline. Particularly at this late stage."

The Minister flicked ash. "We understand the pipeline is American. But it runs for the first seventy-two miles through territory that is Turkmenistan. Neither fact is under dispute. It is fitting that our forces protect this stretch from terrorism."

A stale odour permeated the chamber, as if it smelt ancient deceits.

"You don't have the fire power," Carl told him. "You don't control the air. Besides, our contract was drawn up nine years ago. This wild claim was not mentioned at that time. Why bring this absurd difficulty up now?"

With a slight smile, the Minister replied, "There has been regime change since then."

He rose to his feet. "Now this meeting will close, Mr Roddard. No oil will flow through the pipeline until this matter of sovereignty is resolved. My government will not permit me to turn on the tap till then. Good day."

Carl's auto was waiting in the shade of the Ministry. He told the driver to take him to the American quarter. Once through the blazing streets, and the various check-points, he went straight to the Embassy.

Carl was a big man who thought big. He had been in Central Asia, on and off, for nine years. He was Chief Architect of the Pipeline Project, and employed by Butterfield-Chuu-Wolff, the biggest consortium on the face of the planet. Still he took his problems to the American Ambassaor to Turkmenistan, Stanley Coglan.

Stanley was with his wife, Charlotte, and just finishing lunch. He stood up, wiping his mouth on his tabel napkin.

"Hi, Stan, Charlie! Sorry to break in."

"Have a chair, Carl. Good to see you. You want something to eat? How was it with that snake of an Interior Minister?"

Carl drew up a chair. "Not good. They've set us up." He told Stanley of his meeting. "The essence of it is their demand to nationalise the first two hundred miles of the pipeline. It's meaningless—and they know it."

Stanley looked thoughtful. "So what are they after, springing this on us? Can't be money. Money is going to pour into this little tinpot state once the taps are turned. So why do they delay?"

"Search me. National pride?"

Charlotte looked over her shoulder to see that no servants were lingering. She said, "And what will they do with all the money? If precedents are anything to go by, they will not invest it on the infrastructure of the country, on much needed hospitals and better housing. No, it'll go into explosives."

Stanley told his wife, mildly, "Darling, these are not Arabs we're dealing with. Central Asians are rather different."

Charlotte shrugged. She poured Carl a glass of wine. He sipped it gratefully. The wine was imported from Italy, like many supplies in Turkmenistan.

The ambassador swivelled in his chair to stare out of the window. Beyond the small garden, a sentry stood armed and alert at the gate. "Have you spoken yet to the top brass at Butterfield-Chou-Wolff?"

"No. I drove straight here. BCW would probably want to give in. We can't do that. Suoyue has to be in our hands from start to finish. It's Security." With a tinge of sarcasm, he had used Suoyue, the common Chinese name for the pipeline.

"Of course, Firadzov is behind this," Charlotte said, thoughtfully. Firadzov, the President of Turkmenistan, was the victor of a coup earlier in the previous year.

"Not a cockroach moves without Firadzov's say-so," Stanley replied. He gazed at his wife.

"So? Ziviad Haydor."

Both men looked at her blankly.

"Ziviad Haydor," Charlotte repeated. "That rare thing, a powerful Turkmen dissident. Funded by Moscow, naturally. Come on, guys, when Firadzov took over, and was gunning for him, Haydor ran here to us for sanctuary."

Carl remembered. "Moscow has no use for Firadzov. They wanted the oil pumped north to Moscow, as in Soviet times, when they owned this dump. This guy Haydor was Moscow's man. Where is he now? Syria?"

Stanley thumped the table. "He's still here! One of our permanent lodgers. He lives in couple of rooms in the annexe. No one else will have him. Where can he go? The Arabs hate him even more than the Ruskies, because they think he did a deal with us. Of course, Firadzov would kill Haydor if he got half a chance."

Charlotte said quietly, "We could do a trade . . ."

The two men looked at each other. Then they both grinned.

Carl Roddard had himself driven to the offices of Butterfield-Chou-Wolff on the edge of town. Big initial letters BCW loomed on the facade of a square concrete building. It was ringed with a double protective fence. Nearby, the road led to a spot where the city abruptly stopped. A red-and-white painted metal pole was down. Beyond it, the great desert began, stoney and drab. The barrier kept out various camels, who stood hopelessly, staring in at this outpost of civilization.

After thrusting his biometric card in the entry-slot to the building, Carl took the elevator to his offices on the fourth and top floor. It was blessedly cool in BCW, where the air-cond unit worked. His assistant, Ron Deeds, greeted him. Preoccupied, Carl went to study the map of the area on the far wall.

A silver marker pen depicted the pipeline running a thousand miles from East to West. It started just outside Ashkabad, to cross the frontier with Northern Iran at the town of Gifan. At the frontier was a fortified pumping station, marked as at Milestone 72.

Ron came over, looking serious, tousling further his untidy fair hair. "The BCW committee met this morning," he said in a low voice. "It's looking not good. The world is waiting for the opening of the pipeline next week. BCW don't want hitches. They were on the air to Washington and Beijing this morning, saying they would accede to Firadzov's demand for nationalisation of the first stretch of pipeline. They will take over control. We'll just have a watching brief."

Carl scowled. "We can't let it happen. Look, Ron, we're going to do a trade. We think it will work. I need your help, okay?"

"Sure. What can I do?"

"We buy Firadzov off with a well-known dissident in our keeping. This nationalisation idea is just a bluff. We'll call their bluff. We give Firadzov the dissident, he stops this nonsense. After all, Firadzov needs the oil flowing as much as we do."

"What do I do?"

Carl began wagging his finger as if counting. "One, we can't let anyone know the Embassy is involved in this deal. Two, we need you because you are British. Three, you drive round tonight and we have everything ready. Four, you take the dissident, whose hands will be tied and whose legs will be shackled, to the gates of the Interior Ministry. Tanks and major fire power will be there to protect you. Five, you speak over the intercom to the Interior Minister offering him the deal. Call off this nationalisation ploy immediately and you hand over the dissident they want like mad. Okay? Will you do it?"

Ron had begun to look dubious during this speech. "Very dicey. Who is this dissident guy any way?"

"His name's Haydor, Ziviad Haydor."

Ron let out a whistling breath. "Him? Carl, you can't hand Haydor over to that bastard Firadzov! Haydor is a hero of the people. It was

Haydor who represented the chance of a better life for everyone. Firadzov would torture him to death!"

"Look, Ron, Haydor is a spent force. That issue's closed, okay? It's worth one life to get the damned oil flowing, isn't it?"

Ron stuck his fists in his jeans and turned his back. "It's treachery, Carl. We swore to protect Haydor only a year since. Sorry, I want no part of it."

Carl grabbed Ron's shoulder. "Can't you see what's involved? This is no time for scruples!"

"Take your hand off me," Ron said. "I can't do it."

"Fuck you! Then I'll do it myself!"

He did it himself. It worked. Carl Roddard was hooded as he handed over his prisoner to the Interior Ministry. Ziviad Haydor disappeared into the regime's torture chambers. Next morning, President Firadzov himself spoke on television. He stated, "Regretably, an attempt was recently made by unreliable elements to seize control of the oil pipeline. We of course recognise the legitimacy of the present international construction company to operate the pipeline for the benefit of all concerned. I have personally supported this great international venture, which affirms the greatness and importance of our dear nation, Turkmenistan.

"Unreliable elements involved in this attempted illegal appropriation of property have been arrested, including the Minister for the Interior. They will stand trial at a future date."

Stanley Coglan and Mr Freddie Go from the Chinese Embassy shook hands with Carl in a brief ceremony. After which they toasted each other in champagne.

"We must reward you somehow, Carl," said Freddie Go, his face crinkling in the friendliest of smiles.

"I didn't want anyone to adopt my baby," said Carl, thus mystifying his Chinese friend. "My marriage has collapsed, Freddie. Margie refused to live here in Ashkabad with me. She's in England now. I'm hoping to patch things up, now that the oil is at last about to run."

"Okay," said Stanley. "We'll charter you a special plane right into London Heathrow—with our best wishes."

Carl, smiling, shook his head. "A bigger favour even than that, Stan, and Freddie. I want to be the first guy ever to drive along the whole length of Suoyue, all the way to the Med."

"Do we let him?" Stanley asked Freddie.

Freddie pretended a sigh. "Can we stop him?"

Carl Roddard shook hands with his Chief Engineer in farewell before climbing into his car. Behind them lay the first pumping station and the opening stretch of pipeline. The all-steel pipe had cathodic protection— the negative electric charge running throughout the length of the pipe. The pipeline and its associated roads stretched for over one thousand miles, covering some dangerous territory.

Carl left Ashkabad, the capital city of Turkmenistan, early that morning. He kept himself well-armed, and tucked a revolver into the auto's front compartment. The Pipeline Road began outside Ashkabad on its long journey westwards. Carl had programmed his car accordingly, and was travelling at an average of ninety miles per hour.

With him in the car was Donna Khaddari. Donna had taken a Luck-istryke and was sitting quietly, smiling to herself. Carl's secretary was ill; she had sent her sister Donna instead. A pretty girl, thought Carl, approvingly. They had passed Gifan, where they crossed the frontier between Turkmenistan and Iran.

To the right of the speeding vehicle—to the north—the coast of the Caspian Sea was visible. Dead ships lay there aslant, stranded, beached for all time, bones merely of boats that had once sailed from Baku in Azerbijan to Bandar-e Shah in Iran. Now the sea itself, whose waters had been syphoned off in the construction of the pipeline and its attendant highways, was wan, white, waveless, shrinking from its forsaken shore.

To the south of the highway, the Elburz Mountains rose, their rainy slopes thickly forested, except where new roads had cut fresh scars through the trees.

Carl, vacationing from his engagement to contractors Butterfield-Chuu-Wolff, kept his eyes on the highway ahead. It curved little, it swerved little, it climbed on gentle inclines, only to dip again, always following beside the armour-plated oil pipeline. Where the pipeline went, monstrous, shining metal-black, there the road went. Where the road went, there sped Carl's auto, streamlined as a fish. And on the north side of the great pipe, there a twin road went, designed to carry traffic eastwards.

At present, though, the twin routes were empty of traffic. The great highways were not yet officially open. Only Architects-in-Chief travelled them. Together with a few military vehicles. Carl concentrated on recalling details of his conversation with Coordinator Mohamed Barrak before he left Ashkabad. He had voiced a complaint that the consortium to which he belonged was filling the pockets of the dictator, Firadzov.

He regarded Barrak as yet another corrupt native official, one of a kind with which BCW had become used to dealing. Barrak had grown distant and formal. He clasped his hands over his white jacket and his ample stomach. The vodka was getting to him.

He spoke of historic necessity. The need of the West to draw on Central Asian oil overrode other considerations. Yes, Firadzov was rather—shall we say, overbearing?—well, dictatorial; but he controlled a country that floated on oil, and those vast reservoirs were needed to sustain the greedy West. A West, Barrak might say, also dictatorial. When the oil was flowing, the West would no longer have need of oil from Saudi Arabia and other Arab states, such as Iraq and Kuwait.

Then Barrak had abruptly changed the subject, demanding to know why Carl Roddard suddenly needed leave to go to England.

"My ex-wife has moved to England from Savannah. She lives with her brother in Oxford. I need to see her again."

"You are planning to remarry?"

"That remains to be seen." None of your business. He disliked Barrak and his pompous manner. Barrak liked to speak of the pipeline as "this great engineering achievement," as if he had built it himself.

Carl Roddard had broad shoulders and a broad base. He sat hunched in a narrow chair, saying nothing. He was drinking vodka with Barrak in a more-or-less westernised tea house in the European quarter of Ashkabad. Although the Turkmen were Muslim, or faintly Muslim, their seventy years under Russian domination had taught them to drink vodka like Cossacks. Carl did not tell the other man he had two young sons wandering about somewhere in the eastern United States, kicking up hell.

Barrak had not enquired why Carl wished to drive the length of the pipeline road instead of flying. Everyone involved in the grandiose project desired to drive the whole length of it one day. Perhaps even Barrak felt the itch.

The car sped ever on. Carl's great tanned face was immoveable as he half-listened to a remastered ribbon of music from the long-dead Django, cool as a dingo in December. Donna appeared to be listening. She sat close to Carl, saying nothing.

He gazed at the landscape he had helped forge. The highway undulated over northbound rivers pouring down from the mountain slopes. It followed the great coffin of the oil pipeline, by far the strongest feature of the moribund natural scene. Haze overhead filtered sunlight down evenly, shadowlessly; as the distance indicators flashed by; the scene resembled a computer playscene.

The pipeline would, in a sense, unite East and West. Yet it was Carl's absorption in the mighty project which had broken up his marriage to Margie. That could be put right, maybe. He would try. He regarded himself as a good fixer. Results were in the lap of the gods.

Gigantic yellow-painted Chinese constructors toiled along in parallel with the pipeline. They were preparing to build a third lane on the westbound route. The great project was yet to be completed. High overhead, geostationary satellites saw to it that the project was not interfered with.

The auto map was signalling fifty miles to Amol-Babol when Donna said, "I need a coffee."

"Right behind you."

"No, I need to stretch my legs. I have long legs, you know."

"I have noticed."

"Stop at Amol-Bobol, please, Carl."

Amol-Babol was first stop after Ashkabad, the site of a big pumping station. As they had had to show their biometricards to enter the pipeline road, so they had to show their biometricards to get off it. The barriers swung up, the steel teeth sucked themselves down into the roadway and they drifted through.

After the auto was douched with germicidal wash, it parked itself and the couple were free to walk.

Amol-Babol was situated on the coast. Ships manoeuvred in the overcrowded harbour. Tehran was no more than sixty miles away, south over the Elburz Mountains. Amol-Babol was a newly compounded city, a transitory refuge for many of the men and women of all nationalities who worked on the pipeline. They included American, Australian, French, Spanish, English, Kurdish, Japanese and certainly Chinese. Many were soldiers, clerks, prostitutes, thieves, adventurers.

The chaos of Amol-Babol was preferable to the deadness of Firadzov-ruled Ashkabad.

At least Firadzov had cooperated with the constructors of the gigantic pipeline. The gross egotist he was regarded the pipeline as his memorial. He already had a pipeline, but it ran northward to Moscow, and Moscow paid peanuts compared with what the West would pay. Everything was a question of money.

A big transporter aircraft was thundering down on the Amol-Babol airport even now, bringing in more workers, more machinery.

The permanent civilian population consisted of a small clique of Iranian, Indian and Chinese bureaucrats, sitting at the top of the pile, then mainly of Kurds and other Iranians, with a scattering of Afghans. These latter, the poor, had set up stalls and markets through which Carl and Donna now strolled. Here were the world's electronic gadgets, blinking, winking, chirruping, together with bright cheap Chinese-manufactured toys and clothes. Oriental music shrilly played.

Donna bought a deep blue T-shirt bearing the elegantly complex Chinese symbol, Suoyue, for 'Pipeline'. At another stall they sat and drank a rich Sumatra coffee. No alcohol was permitted anywhere along the course of the pipeline; it was a condition on which the Chinese had insisted.

Carl took Donna to the Pipeline Consortium H.Q. in A-B Square, to say hello to his friend and colleague, Wang Feng Ling. Ling embraced Carl, kissed Donna's hand, and ordered tea to be brought. Ling as ever was neatly dressed in a well-tailored suit. His hair was immaculate. He wore a gold ring on one of his long artistic fingers. His smile was warm and sincere.

"How is life in Ashkabad, Carl, dear chap?" he asked. "Dear chap" was his favourite form of address.

"Dull as ever. Even the camels are bored."

"With that particular time-expired Central Asian dullness?" Ling smiled at the recollection.

"The new dictator is slightly better than the old dictator. Firadzov accepts bribes with a better grace . . ."

Ling nodded his sympathy. "Unfortunately the new dictator in Uzbekistan is not slightly better than the old dictator, dear chap. However, we maintain long and tedious talks."

Carl gave a short laugh. "You still have hopes, then." He had learnt to talk obliquely to Ling.

Ling raised his cup and smiled at his friend. "Hopes? You mean plans? Certainly the Suoyue can be key to both East and West."

Indeed, even the Westerners on the pipeline road referred to it as the "Suoyue," the Chinese word for "key." Westerners were interested only in piping the oil of Central Asia to the West, bypassing the Arab states; but the Chinese were major players here, and the Chinese had plans to extend the Suoyue eastwards, beyond Turkmenistan to China itself.

As had always been the case, Chinese intentions were not clearly understood in the West.

"Any problems on your stretch of the pipe, Ling?"

"Your president, Julian Caesare, may cause problems, dear chap, if he continues to exacerbate Islamic problems in Iran."

"Well, the Consortium has a century's concession on this coastal strip."

"Religion always has contempt for any concession."

"You're right there."

As—thought Carl, shaking hands on leaving—Ling was so frequently right. Staunch nationalist though he was, he had begun to believe that the Chinese were actually a superior race. The superior race.

He did not say as much to Donna when they reentered the bazaar. Or when they climbed into their auto. Or when they were once again travelling on their way westward on the Suoyue. The great pipeline in its protective casing appeared to go on for ever. Every so often, a pumping station straddled the pipe. Dominating the stations were small strongholds, bristling with masts and fully manned, fortified against those enemies of the West who would seek to block the flow of oil.

Carl remembered he had visited Hadrian's Wall in the North of England, stretching from east coast to west coast, where he studied how the Romans had attempted to keep out the barbarians. The Suoyue might bear a Chinese name, but the essential elements of its design lay in the West, and had its links with ancient Rome.

The Caspian fell away, leaving its lassitudes behind them. Climbing, they crossed the forty-ninth line of latitude. Kurd patrols were in evidence here, driving US army vehicles with Kurdish flags attached to their aerials. The aerials whipped in the wind. The Kurds had been paid off; the patrol now fired their Kalashnikovs into the air by way of greeting to the speeding car.

The weather became colder and an inclement wind blew. Clouds were torn to shreds. The climate remained mild inside the auto. Carl and Donna sat close, elbows all but touching.

Pilotless planes, controlled from Diyarbakir, screamed overhead, low to the ground. Higher overhead, they occasionally saw the heavyweight

BWA, the Broad Wing Aircraft that also kept up a contunuous patrol.

"It's like living in a sci-fi dream," Carl remarked to Donna.

They passed the ruins of a village that had been demolished to make way for the pipeline. Only a minaret remained standing, a solitary sentinel to a vanished way of life.

As the landscape grew wilder, dusk became thicker. When night encompassed the solitary vehicle, Carl followed an old life-saving habit, lowered his seat, opaqued the windows and went to sleep.

Once he was soundly asleep, Donna depaqued the windows again to watch an electric storm over the mountains ahead. No thunder accompanied the flashes. Great sheets of lightning appeared and disappeared silently, ghosts of the stratosphere. Their reflected light ran off the sides of the pipeline armour like water spray.

She too slept, waking when the hitherto unnoticed tone of the auto changed. The car travelled on electromagnetic force; although it was without wheels, a new resonance suggested new conditions.

From the windows, Donna saw a glitter of water on both sides far below them. The sky had cleared. The night was now comparatively cloudless, and a crescent moon shone on the water. She woke Carl.

"Where are we? What's this?"

He glanced at the auto map to confirm his understanding.

"We're crossing Lake Urmia. It's a lovely spot, about forty miles wide in places. Lots of geese and water birds here."

"We're crossing on a bridge, are we?"

He heard the nervousness in her voice, and was surprised.

"Yes, we've just avoided a high mountain. I forget its name. Some people would say we were in the middle of nowhere."

"But I can see lights down below. A long way down there!" She was half-standing, to peer below the bridge.

"The people down there are also in the middle of nowhere, even if they don't realise it. There are quite a few islands in the lake. Relax, Donna!"

To calm her, he said, "I went fishing with Ling off one of the islands, once, in the early stages of construction. The supports of this bridge are founded on some of those islands. The people got paid for the disruption to their lives. They went and built a new mosque with the money, instead of a new hospital. They think like that."

"So we are still in Iran, or where?"

He was looking down at the village lights, small below, remembering the immense pike he and Ling had caught. They had spitted it, cooked it over their fire, and ate it. He remembered the taste of it.

"We're travelling a dramatic stretch of northern Iran. Some way to our north there's Azerbijan and Armenia. It's earthquake country. The Suoyue runs on shock absorbers over this stretch."

Donna remarked that for once she could see the ribbon of the parallel road running eastwards.

He said that the roads here were built on separate bridges for safety reasons.

She fell silent, perhaps awed by the magnitude of the engineering feat that had built Suoyue. Nor was she unaware of the years of political discussion, contrivance and bribery that had gone into the groundwork before building started. The pipeline project had ruined her life and her family's. Only when China had signed on to play a major role in the construction had the consortium Butterfield-Chuu-Wolff gained the financial incentive in which to function.

Her family had been one of those that lost out in the wheeler-dealing. Donna's father, Awal al-Khaddari, had lost his home and his business and had comitted suicide. Donna had had to work for the negotiators throughout the desperate years, and had gone to bed with some of them, in order to keep her family in bread.

The structure, despite furious Arab protests, was hailed as a great advance in world trade. It was touted as a unifying force, whatever had happened to Donna's and other families. Still the West remained worried about Chinese motives. Some things never changed.

The car was slowing. They were moving through dense forest. The replay on the auto map showed that they had passed along the northern frontiers of Iraq. Barriers protecting the pipeline road itself had gone down when they crossed the next national frontier. They were now about to enter Diyarbakir.

Turkey had become a member country of the European Community some years ago, despite its murky reputation regarding human rights. The feeling was inescapable that they were now in more friendly territory. Turkey was a secular state, despite its numerous Muslim inhabitants. So it had been since the day of Kemal Ataturk.

But at the feed road, when they slotted their biometricards into the gate computer, the gate did not open. Carl spoke over the phone.

"Please be patient. Please remain where you are," said a recorded message. "Your needs will be attended to as soon as possible."

"Oh shit," Carl exclaimed. "A certain lack of information there . . ."

"There's a problem . . ." Donna was increasingly nervous.

Above them, the armour-encased pipe ran into the base of a towering metal structure as big as an aircraft carrier. Diyarbakir was the last and largest pumping station before Suoyue ended its monstrous length at the new Turkish terminus port of Mersin.

Three police on amoured motorbikes appeared, sirens screaming. They wore blue helmets. They halted on the other side of the gate and the lead police officer spoke over the barrier. Carl showed his identification.

The officer apologised with more formality than warmth.

"What's the problem?" Carl asked.

"A strike twenty-five kilometres from here, sir. The road's out."

"How's that?"

"Shell or mortar fire. Maybe nuclear. One of these Islamic terrorist groups."

"Bastards!"

The officer ignored the remark. He had other problems. "You have to wait here for a while."

"Take me to Chief of Suoyue Police, Tinkja Gabriel."

The mention of the Police Chief produced smart action. Carl and Donna were escorted immediately into the fortress. The very name of Tinkja Gabriel was a passport. Carl said to Donna, "I'll be a while with Tinkja. Can you keep yourself amused?"

"I'll try." She gave him a sly contemplative smile. Carl had once had a brief but passionate affair with Tinkja. Donna, he knew, had a cousin in Diyarbakir, working in the Logistics Division. Under all the militaristic activity of the project lay human affection, human relationships, human need.

They parted. Carl took an elevator to the Police control tower. He was stopped and body-searched before getting into the express elevator and when leaving it on the ninety-first floor—as if he could have made himself a bomb on the way up.

As he entered the great circular office, he saw Tinkja immediately, and drank in her appearance, her long dark hair swept back and knotted at the nape of her slender neck, her high-nosed hawkish profile. She was wearing a khaki uniform, looking severe, leaning slightly forward to speak into a microphone, despite the body mike dangling round her elegant neck.

She saw him immediately. Her dark eyes flashed. She gestured towards her inner office. She went on talking.

The room was crowded. People at desks spoke quietly to their screens, machines clattered. On one wall was an electronic map of the entire Suoyue with its sweep of roads, from Ashkabad to Mersin on the north-eastern corner of the Mediterranean. LCDs indicated the whereabouts of items of traffic, of the pilotless strike planes and of the BWA drifting above the pipeline.

He waited in Tinkja's office. Tinkja was an Israeli of German-Romanian extraction, with royal blood on the Romanian side. Carl and she had met in France, when he was seconded to an EU architectural partnership. They had fallen in love and taken a brief—all too brief!—holiday in the Auverne. Never had conversation, never had love-making, been sweeter. A time of unbelievable empathy. Never he had been so close to another human being. Carl allowed himself to recall those times as he looked about the room. It was in apple-pie order. On one wall hung two framed lines of verse from a poem called "Gates of Damascus":

Postern of Fate, the Desert Gate, Disaster's Cavern, Fort of Fear,

The Portal of Baghdad am I, the Doorway of Diyarbekir

He smiled to himself. He had once claimed that this was the only occasion Diyarbekir had been mentioned in English poetry. Evidently Tinkja had not forgotten.

From the window, the great forward organisations of the revolutionary Suoyue project could be seen. Miles of barracks and stores and yards and linking roads contained moving vehicles and personnel. A nearby services restaurant flew the flags of many nations. More distantly, a newly built railway linked the centre with distant Angora, the Turkish capital.

Tinkja entered the room briskly. "Sometimes I could nuke Washington," she said. She spoke as if she had only just left the room and Carl Roddard.

By way of greeting, she went to Carl, shook his jacket roughly, clasped him, snapped a smile, and then turned away.

She stalked over to a speaker system and said, "Hospital Emergency Service. Ron Habland, report to me please. Ron Habland." Then she looked at Carl, arms folded across her chest, her tense expression relaxing only slightly.

"I hear the road has been blown," he said, in an equally no-nonsense way. "How did that happen?"

"We want to know who blew it," she said. "The strike occured only at 13.05 hours. I have no time to stand here and chat, sorry. Washington is already bleating. Beijing will be next."

He glanced at his watchputer. It was 15.15. "Can I help?"

"Of course not." She said again, as if to herself, "We must know who blew it. There's no Arab nation which doesn't hate the Suoyoe. Or it could be a local group of disaffected Turks, displaced by the pipeline. Or the damned Kurd dissidents. We have to know what we're up against."

Carl said, "We're up against most of the men in the Middle East. So, the road's already being rebuilt?"

"Whoever they were, they had posession of field nuclear weapons. Yeah, they're fixing your precious road."

An arbitrary tap at the door and a small man with well-greased hair, wearing green overalls, came in. This was Ron Habland from the hospital emergency services. "Ron runs the morgue," she said in a brusque aside to Carl. She did not make an introduction.

Habland regarded Carl suspiciously. In fact, Carl had met Habland two years ago, in Ashkabad, but the man failed to recognise him, so tense was he. He bore the not-unfamiliar air of those who thought that, in a region which had never known democracy, no one could be trusted.

Tinkja addressed the grim-faced newcomer. "Ron, you probably know already that one of our pilotless planes immediately strafed the terrorists. They were up in the hills, not a kilometre away. It's too bad. We needed at least one of them alive for questioning."

"Those planes are too damn efficient," said Ron. "We need troops on the ground. Even Spanish troops would do."

He pulled a face and turned a thumb down.

"I need you to get a contingent to go and collect up anything you can find of their bodies or parts of bodies. Toes, even. Legs. Heads. Clothing. Weapons. Support gear. The route they came from. Anything they dropped on the way. Go with the contingent."

"Glad to," said Ron, with a slight bow.

"Anything you can find. Back here soonest."

He said, "Once the oil starts to flow, the Arabs can go back to their fucking camels."

"My sentiments exactly." Tinkja gave Ron a grin as he departed, before she turned to switch over a TV screen.

"A bitter little man," she commented. "Lost a leg three years back, though you wouldn't think so to look at him."

"I'd think he was on the brink of a breakdown."

"Let's hope not today . . ."

Looking over Tinkja's shoulder, Carl saw the scene at the damaged road, filmed from one of the satellites. A missile crater was surrounded by rubble and twisted metal for a distance of perhaps two miles. Wrecking and repair vehicles were already at work, clearing the site, relaying foundations. The pipeline and its casing appeared to be unharmed.

"At least they missed the pipeline."

She said, "Yeah, that's what they would have aimed for. The shits probably believe that oil is already coming through . . . Now I have to call Beijing. Sorry, Carl, I have no time for you. You better scram."

"Okay." He thought, She's glad to have an excuse. Of course she has another lover by now. She would never be without a man for long, not a woman like this. He sighed. At least she had once been his. And he hers.

"Your road will be fixed soonest—open again maybe by eighteen hours. Not too much delay. 'Bye."

She turned and began to make her Beijing call. Carl quit without saying good-bye.

It was 15.50. As Carl approached his auto, Donna emerged from a nearby archway, accompanied by a dark slender man in a worn grey suit. Carl was immediately alert at the sight of a stranger. This stranger, though seemingly young, had a deeply lined face. He wore a thin black moustache over thin lips.

Donna was neatly dressed and composed, although there was something about her body language Carl mistrusted.

He said as she approached, "You've heard about the strike on the road. Why do they hate us so much?" She made no answer to his remark.

"You look like shit. What's up, apart from the road?"

It was not the sort of comment she usually dared to make.

"Oh, the past—the past remains. Who's this with you?"

They were having one of their conversations . . .

As she gave a half-smile, her teeth very white in her black face.

"He doesn't have a name, Carl."

The thin man came close and stuck a gun in Carl's ribs.

Subdued Chinese music played somewhere in the background.

Carl delivered a swift knee to the man's testicles, but the man was alert, chopping the knee down. He gave a hard jab with his free hand to Carl's midriff, which winded him with pain. It was hard to credit that this was happening in the police precinct. A previous thought came back to him: in a region that had never known democracy, no one could be trusted. At some level there was police connivance involved here.

"Walk!" the thin man commanded.

As they went towards the side of the building, Carl looked about for CCTV. The nearest camera was plastered over with spray paint, still dripping. Then they were round the corner.

Still breathless, he asked Donna, "This is your cousin? What do you hope to get out of this?"

"Shut up and walk," she said.

The thin man punched Carl again. "You, fucker, you give Ziviad Haydor to the enemy, to your fucking friend Firadzov. Now you pay."

They were walking fast. It was hard to believe that this had happened in the police precinct.

Cops were everywhere, mainly men hurrying to get into wheeled cars. There was a crisis on on the pipeline road. So the thin man and his prisoner slipped away. No one took any notice of them.

They reached a fast road crossing. On the other side, Carl was pushed into a tall building with an ancient crumbling facade. Sweet smell, not pleasant, greeted them inside. They started down a flight of steps, some rather broken. Carl turned suddenly, striking the thin man across the face with a violent blow.

The gun went off. The bullet whistled past Carl's ear. Donna chopped him across the neck with a sharp blow from the edge of her hand. He fell, and went tumbling down the remaining steps.

They were after him and on him. They hit and kicked him, cursing in their own language.

He was then frog-marched down a stone corridor. A side door was unlocked and he was kicked into darkness, so savagely that he sprawled on a damp and filthy floor. The door slammed behind him.

Carl lay there, groaning and breathing hard. After a while, he pulled himself up and leant against a wall.

As his eyes accustomed themselves to the darkness, he saw there was a choked grey light filtering from a grating in the corner of the cell. Calming his breathing, he listened. Someone or something was breathing nearby.

He moved. The cell was larger than he had at first assumed. In the far corner, away from the light, a man was hanging.

Cautiously, Carl stepped nearer.

"Hello!"

There was no reply, but the man raised his head slightly.

Carl now saw that he was suspended by his wrists by ropes attached to steel rings set in the stone ceiling.

"How long have you been here like this?"

The answer came faintly in a foreign tongue.

"You poor bugger, hang on and I'll get you down."

In their rage and anxiety, Donna and her cousin had not searched him. He drew the knife from the sheath strapped to his lower leg and, reaching upwards, sliced through the ropes.

He caught the body as it fell, to lower it gently to the floor. He knelt by it. He gently massaged the injured wrists.

Again the man muttered something.

As Carl sheathed his knife, he reassured the man as best he could. The poor fellow had been forced to relieve himself and stank.

An idea struck him. He peeled off his outer jacket and forced the injured men into it. Taking the man by his shoulders, he dragged him into the darkest corner and propped him sitting against the wall. He then stood waiting alertly by the two severed ropes.

The minutes crawled by. His resolution did not fail. When he heard footsteps in the corridor outside, he leapt up and seized the ropes in his two hands. As the cell door was opened, he hung his head as if unconscious.

It was the thin man, Donna's cousin, who had entered. He grunted as he took in the recumbent figure, before turning his attention to the hanging man. He came closer.

Carl threw himself on his captor. They fell together, the cousin striking his head on the floor. Carl slammed it again against the stone slabs. The cousin did not move.

With a quick look into the corridor, where a guard of some kind stood distantly, Carl dragged the unconscious man to a position under the grill in the wall. By standing on his chest, he could now gain leverage on the grill. Fragments of rust came away in his hands. He heaved and felt a slight movement.

"Rotten—like everything else in this damned place," he said to himself.

He pushed hard, and pushed again. One of the bars crumbled away. He rattled the grating. It gave. He heaved it to one side. Clasping the sides of the hole, he made a mighty effort and heaved himself up into daylight. Once he had an elbow on the ground, he knew he had made it.

Another struggle, kicks against the inner wall, and he was free.

Breathing heavily, he stood up, having to lean for a moment against an ivy-clad wall to look about him.

He was in a neglected courtyard. Brambles and other weeds sprouted from among flagstones. At one end of the courtyard was a wrought iron gate, through which uniformed men could be seen. Ducking low, Carl sprinted to the opposite wall. He clutched at a thick woody stem of ivy and hauled himself up. Beyond the wall was a busy street with shops, restaurants and a cinema. Many men, the majority wearing robes, strolled about, indolent in the heat.

Carl dropped down onto the road, picked himself up and walked rapidly away. His plan was to enter a restaurant and there call Tinkja—until he realised he was covered in filth, picked up from the floor of the prison cell.

As he was walking rapidly to the end of the street, a taxi eased slowly beside him, a decrepit old vehicle with a turbanned Sikh at the wheel.

"Taxi, sah?"

He trusted no one in Diyarbekir, but there seemed nothing for it but to get in. Besides which, he liked and trusted Sikhs and their religion. He climbed into the back of the vehicle and told the man to take him to police H.Q.

"I will leave you by the gate, sah."

As he paid off the taxi driver in dollars, two black police cars came roaring from the yard and drove away down the road the taxi had taken.

He called Tinkja from reception. "I need a wash and some clothes."

She sounded surprised. "You are still in the dissident prison."

"No I'm not."

"I sent cars for you."

"I'm here in your reception area. How did you know about the prison anyway?"

She explained that she had planted a bug on him earlier, afraid he might meet with trouble. It was on his jacket, sticking like a burr. The jacket remained in the cell.

"I don't do this for everyone," she said. "But come on up."

Now the crisis on the wrecked highway was under control, the elegant Tinkja actually escorted him in his new clothes down to where his auto was parked. She blew him a kiss with her neat leathery hand.

"Don't come back, Carl, okay?"

"You could say life is rather like a long long road," he said lightly, as he climbed into the car.

"Except you can repair a long long road," she said. Carl let her have the last word.

There were indications that the architect's car had been searched. A rear-view mirror had been deflected, a seat had been reoriented. The revolver was still in place. There was also an elusive scent, which Carl recognised as coming from a fingerprint spray.

It was all a safety precaution, part of the life they led. He thought nothing of it. Trust was not in it.

Once he had fed in his biometricard, the car moved slowly along the feed road to the pipeline highway. Still it ran slowly. Power had been reduced. He was travelling at 50 mph.

At about Denghuo (or Station) Thirty—lights blazing because there was a drab overcast—the helicopters started hovering. They were painted wasp-coloured: Chinese Suoyue Military. The auto moved still more slowly.

Intense activity ahead. Gathered around a fair-sized crater demolishing the stretch of the road were huge BCW excavators, construction units, cranes, concrete-sprouters and other vehicles, among which wheeled cars moved like beetles. Emergency cabins had been erected. On a mountain to the south of this activity there was also movement. Tanks had been called in, plus a large number of military personnel in a variety of coloured helmets.

Carl stopped the vehicle. He took binoculars from the front locker and was about to get out when the machine said, "Do not leave your vehicle, Carl Roddard!"

But he did leave it.

Barely had he raised the glasses to his eyes than a siren sounded and an armoured vehicle came howling up. A Chinese captain jumped from it before it had stopped and came at Carl in a run, levelled carbine aimed at him.

"Hold it!" said Carl. He half-raised his hands. "I'm Architect-in-Chief of this entire road, Dr. Carl Roddard."

The captain's hostility was not relaxed. Still pointing the weapon, he said, "I don't care who you are, sir, get back in your car!"

"Hey, I have every right to—"

"You have no right. Please get back in car fast!"

Increasingly angry, Carl said, "Lower your fucking gun, will you? I want to speak to your—"

"This is military area." He came close, prodding Carl with the muzzle of his gun. "Please return into your car fast and right now."

Carl did as he was told.

The captain became less confrontational. Staring down at Carl, he said, "Is radioactivity here. I want see your biometric details. Where is young lady you had earlier?"

"Locked up by now, I'd guess. Back in Diyarbekir."

Carl handed over his card for inspection. The captain scrutinised it for several seconds, before processing it through a hand-held checker. He nodded, handed it back. When he spoke again, his tone was more moderate.

"We have an accident here. The road is down. You must go by temporary road. You will follow this military vehicle along. Do not deviate." He indicated a car just behind his car.

"Follow? For how far?"

The captain managed a rictus of smile. He slung his carbine over a shoulder. "Not too far. Do not attempt to deviate. Then you get back on the proper Suoyue road. Other people coming here we turn away. You official are lucky."

"What, you mean lucky to be nearly fucking shot?"

"Get on your way, sir. Never lose your temper."

The captain nodded curtly, and returned to his vehicle. A second vehicle pulled out and signalled Carl should follow. A large red sign on its rear announced LEADER VEHICLE, just so there should be no mistake. Carl followed.

The leader vehicle led on to an improvised road, which skirted the disaster site in a wide bow. Carl watched guys in radiation suits climbing from the crater. No doubt they checked on the kind of missile that had been fired, on its composition and where it had been manufactured.

They had to halt. A signal was against them. The driver of the other vehicle came back and had a word with Carl, seeming curious about him.

Carl said to the newcomer, "We may be witnessing the beginning, not the end of a crisis. This bunch of terrorists got themselves killed. You can bet others will come along."

"Just as well you're going on leave, then," replied the man.

"What do you know about that?"

"It's not only oil that travels along this here pipeline." He added that he had been told Carl would meet a reception when he arrived at the terminal in Mersin.

The Go signal came through.

It was a slow ride. Night was coming on. But once they left the site of the nuclear strike behind, the Leader Vehicle brought Carl back to the proper highway. The driver gave him a cheerful wave and departed back the way he had come.

Ordinary civilian police directed him onto the pipeline road. Once again he was speeding through Turkey westwards. Now there were military patrol cars parked or bumping along beside the highway

Carl stared out indifferently at the barren landscape. Beggars, ragged men and woman, gesticulated to him or simply stood inert, some holding out begging bowls.

"Fat chance you've got!" Carl exclaimed. Yet Turkey had benefitted greatly from joining the EU; of course, that would apply only to the big cities.

An ambulance was loading in a prostrate woman and baby on a stretcher into the rear of the vehicle. Then he had flashed past. The tiny cameo of drama and fate was lost far behind. In no time, they were approaching a well-lit bridge. Together with the pipeline, they crossed the youthful River Firat, once known as the Euphrates.

In just over three hours, Carl's auto descended to Turkey's southern coastal plain. The waters of the Mediterranean appeared, flat, faintly gleaming. From here on to its terminus at Mersin, the great armoured pipeline ran on reinforced stilts, and the two motorways, the eastbound and the westbound, ran together in parallel.

The newly constructed airport was at Mersin, on the outskirts of the growing city. This was where the great thousand-mile thrust of metal ended. Carl would soon be seeing his ex-wife again; that matter would certainly need some sorting out. Either she would see sense or she wouldn't.

Although it was midnight, Mersin was still extremely busy, preparing for the moment when the pumping station began operations and Central Asian oil began to pour into waiting Western tankers, to quench the inexhaustible Western thirst for oil and more oil.

He climbed from the car. He could see an Allied American plane gleaming under searchlights on the runway. The Stars & Stripes were flying. They were symbols of home. An official welcoming party clustered behind the barrier, waiting for him, holding flags and placards. One placard read, "LESSEPS WAS A PIKER COMPARED TO U." He felt only fatigue, not elation. He had had a job to do. Another job lay ahead.

As he approached the crowd, a woman called out shrilly, "Come back safe, Carl."

He gave her a grin. A nice-looking young woman.

She clutched his arm as he pushed by. Perhaps she sensed his scepticism. "Maybe things will be better when you return."

He grinned into her smiling face and said, "And by then, if I can quote a friend, 'The Arabs may be going back to their fucking camels'."

THREE: THE NEW NORMAL

The phrase "the new normal" dates back to the end of the first World War. Published in the *National Electric Light Association Bulletin* in December 1918, the writer Henry Wise Wood asked the question, "How shall we pass from war to the new normal with the least jar, in the shortest time?"

The original New Normal was established to stave off the abyss, to help the world continue on after it had admitted that it could not bear to. The New Normal was a kind of madness, a specific kind of madness born out of a death. This was a death of not just people, but of ideas.

One of the ideas that died after 9/11 was the notion of civil liberty or liberal democracy. With the passage of the Patriot Act and the formation of the Total Information Awareness program, the twin ideas of privacy and the right to a trial were, if not entirely undone, then at least placed firmly on the chopping block of history.

Beyond the loss of liberty that came as a consequence of the attacks, justified by a newly invigorated paranoia and the strong desire for security that this paranoia wrought, there were other, more fundamental, losses. Life in America, if not the rest of the West, came along with its own set of comforting myths and metaphysical niceties. The feeling was that, while we might not be much, and our dreams and aspirations might be small or banal, we knew who we were and what was real. We didn't have a culture, maybe, but we had stuff, things, and those things were enough. If the old religions didn't work that was okay, as long as we had something firm to grab onto. It didn't matter whether that something was a Big Mac, a suburban home, or some ancient notion of transcendence and purpose. We lost all of that. 9/11 robbed us of our Big Macs just as surely as it stole away our illusions about liberty.

It's that sense of being adrift, of being unmoored, of being nowhere, that defined life after 9/11. It's also what the stories in this next section are ultimately all about. Ketchum's narcissistic nihilist antagonist, Pratt's virtual reality without weather, Friedman's losing hand, and Doctorow's Little Brother are all telling us the same thing:

This is the New Normal.

Cory Doctorow is probably most famous as an advocate for liberalizing or loosening copyright law. He is also a co-editor at Boing Boing, *the novelist behind books such as* Down and Out in the Magic Kingdom, Pirate Cinema, *and* Little Brother, *and a fictional character in the online comic "xkcd." Doctorow apparently lives in a hot air balloon and can often be found working on a literal floating "blogosphere."*

Doctorow's novel Little Brother *tells the story a networked teenage life hacker whose "world changes when he and his friends find themselves caught in the aftermath of a major terrorist attack on San Francisco."*

EXCERPT FROM
LITTLE BROTHER

Cory Doctorow

CHAPTER 2

"I'm thinking of majoring in physics when I go to Berkeley," Darryl said. His dad taught at the University of California at Berkeley, which meant he'd get free tuition when he went. And there'd never been any question in Darryl's household about whether he'd go.

"Fine, but couldn't you research it online?"

"My dad said I should read it. Besides, I didn't plan on committing any crimes today."

"Skipping school isn't a crime. It's an infraction. They're totally different."

"What are we going to do, Marcus?"

"Well, I can't hide it, so I'm going to have to nuke it." Killing arphids is a dark art. No merchant wants malicious customers going for a walk around the shop-floor and leaving behind a bunch of lobotomized merchandise that is missing its invisible bar code, so the manufacturers have refused to implement a "kill signal" that you can radio to an arphid to get it to switch off. You can reprogram arphids with the right box, but I hate doing that to library books. It's not exactly tearing pages out of a book, but it's still bad, since a book with a reprogrammed arphid can't be shelved and can't be found. It just becomes a needle in a haystack.

That left me with only one option: nuking the thing. Literally. 30 seconds in a microwave will do in pretty much every arphid on the market. And because the arphid wouldn't answer at all when D checked it back in at the library, they'd just print a fresh one for it and recode it with the book's catalog info, and it would end up clean and neat back on its shelf.

All we needed was a microwave.

"Give it another two minutes and the teacher's lounge will be empty," I said.

Darryl grabbed his book at headed for the door. "Forget it, no way. I'm going to class."

I snagged his elbow and dragged him back. "Come on, D, easy now. It'll be fine."

"The *teacher's lounge*? Maybe you weren't listening, Marcus. If I get busted *just once more*, I am *expelled*. You hear that? *Expelled*."

"You won't get caught," I said. The one place a teacher wouldn't be after this period was the lounge. "We'll go in the back way." The lounge had a little kitchenette off to one side, with its own entrance for teachers who just wanted to pop in and get a cup of joe. The microwave—which always reeked of popcorn and spilled soup—was right in there, on top of the miniature fridge.

Darryl groaned. I thought fast. "Look, the bell's *already rung*. If you go to study hall now, you'll get a late-slip. Better not to show at all at this point. I can infiltrate and exfiltrate any room on this campus, D. You've seen me do it. I'll keep you safe, bro."

He groaned again. That was one of Darryl's tells: once he starts groaning, he's ready to give in.

"Let's roll," I said, and we took off.

It was flawless. We skirted the classrooms, took the back stairs into the basement, and came up the front stairs right in front of the teachers' lounge. Not a sound came from the door, and I quietly turned the knob and dragged Darryl in before silently closing the door.

The book just barely fit in the microwave, which was looking even less sanitary than it had the last time I'd popped in here to use it. I conscientiously wrapped it in paper towels before I set it down. "Man, teachers are *pigs*," I hissed. Darryl, white-faced and tense, said nothing.

The arphid died in a shower of sparks, which was really quite lovely (though not nearly as pretty as the effect you get when you nuke a frozen grape, which has to be seen to be believed).

Now, to exfiltrate the campus in perfect anonymity and make our escape.

Darryl opened the door and began to move out, me on his heels. A second later, he was standing on my toes, elbows jammed into my chest, as he tried to back-pedal into the closet-sized kitchen we'd just left.

"Get back," he whispered urgently. "Quick—it's Charles!"

Charles Walker and I don't get along. We're in the same grade, and we've known each other as long as I've known Darryl, but that's where the resemblance ends. Charles has always been big for his age, and now that he's playing football and on the juice, he's even bigger. He's got anger management problems—I lost a milk-tooth to him in the third grade—and he's managed to keep from getting in trouble over them by becoming the most active snitch in school.

It's a bad combination, a bully who also snitches, taking great pleasure in going to the teachers with whatever infractions he's found. Benson *loved* Charles. Charles liked to let on that he had some kind of unspecified bladder problem, which gave him a ready-made excuse to prowl the hallways at Chavez, looking for people to fink on.

The last time Charles had caught some dirt on me, it had ended with me giving up LARPing. I had no intention of being caught by him again.

"What's he doing?"

"He's coming this way is what he's doing," Darryl said. He was shaking.

"OK," I said. "OK, time for emergency countermeasures." I got my phone out. I'd planned this well in advance. Charles would never get me again. I emailed my server at home, and it got into motion.

A few seconds later, Charles's phone spazzed out spectacularly. I'd had tens of thousands of simultaneous random calls and text messages sent to it, causing every chirp and ring it had to go off and keep on going off. The attack was accomplished by means of a botnet, and for that I felt bad, but it was in the service of a good cause.

Botnets are where infected computers spend their afterlives. When you get a worm or a virus, your computer sends a message to a chat channel on IRC—the Internet Relay Chat. That message tells the botmaster—the guy who deployed the worm—that the computers are there ready to do his bidding. Botnets are supremely powerful, since they can comprise thousands, even hundreds of thousands of computers, scattered all over the Internet, connected to juicy high-speed connections and running on fast home PCs. Those PCs normally function on behalf of their own- ers, but when the botmaster calls them, they rise like zombies to do his bidding.

There are so many infected PCs on the Internet that the price of hir- ing an hour or two on a botnet has crashed. Mostly these things work for spammers as cheap, distributed spambots, filling your mailbox with come-ons for boner-pills or with new viruses that can infect you and recruit your machine to join the botnet.

I'd just rented 10 seconds' time on three thousand PCs and had each of them send a text message or voice-over-IP call to Charles's phone, whose number I'd extracted from a sticky note on Benson's desk during one fateful office visit.

Needless to say, Charles's phone was not equipped to handle this. First the SMSes filled the memory on his phone, causing it to start chok- ing on the routine operations it needed to do things like manage the ringer and log all those incoming calls' bogus return numbers (did you know that it's *really easy* to fake the return number on a caller ID? There are about fifty ways of doing it—just google "spoof caller id").

Charles stared at it dumbfounded, and jabbed at it furiously, his thick eyebrows knotting and wiggling as he struggled with the demons that had possessed his most personal of devices. The plan was working so far, but he wasn't doing what he was supposed to be doing next—he was supposed to go find some place to sit down and try to figure out how to get his phone back.

Darryl shook me by the shoulder, and I pulled my eye away from the crack in the door.

"What's he doing?" Darryl whispered.

"I totaled his phone, but he's just staring at it now instead of moving on." It wasn't going to be easy to reboot that thing. Once the memory was totally filled, it would have a hard time loading the code it needed to delete the bogus messages—and there was no bulk-erase for texts on his phone, so he'd have to manually delete all of the thousands of messages.

Darryl shoved me back and stuck his eye up to the door. A moment later, his shoulders started to shake. I got scared, thinking he was panicking, but when he pulled back, I saw that he was laughing so hard that tears were streaming down his cheeks.

"Galvez just totally busted him for being in the halls during class *and* for having his phone out—you should have seen her tear into him. She was really enjoying it."

We shook hands solemnly and snuck back out of the corridor, down the stairs, around the back, out the door, past the fence and out into the glorious sunlight of afternoon in the Mission. Valencia Street had never looked so good. I checked my watch and yelped.

"Let's move! The rest of the gang is meeting us at the cable-cars in twenty minutes!"

Van spotted us first. She was blending in with a group of Korean tourists, which is one of her favorite ways of camouflaging herself when she's ditching school. Ever since the truancy moblog went live, our world is full of nosy shopkeepers and pecksniffs who take it upon themselves to snap our piccies and put them on the net where they can be perused by school administrators.

She came out of the crowd and bounded toward us. Darryl has had a thing for Van since forever, and she's sweet enough to pretend she doesn't know it. She gave me a hug and then moved onto Darryl, giving him a quick sisterly kiss on the cheek that made him go red to the tops of his ears.

The two of them made a funny pair: Darryl is a little on the heavy side, though he wears it well, and he's got a kind of pink complexion that goes red in the cheeks whenever he runs or gets excited. He's been able to grow a beard since we were 14, but thankfully he started shaving after a brief period known to our gang as "the Lincoln years." And he's tall. Very, very tall. Like basketball player tall.

Meanwhile, Van is half a head shorter than me, and skinny, with straight black hair that she wears in crazy, elaborate braids that she researches on the net. She's got pretty coppery skin and dark eyes, and she loves big glass rings the size of radishes, which click and clack together when she dances.

"Where's Jolu?" she said.

"How are you, Van?" Darryl asked in a choked voice. He always ran a step behind the conversation when it came to Van.

"I'm great, D. How's your every little thing?" Oh, she was a bad, bad person. Darryl nearly fainted.

Jolu saved him from social disgrace by showing up just then, in an oversize leather baseball jacket, sharp sneakers, and a meshback cap advertising our favorite Mexican masked wrestler, El Santo Junior. Jolu is Jose Luis Torrez, the completing member of our foursome. He went to a super-strict Catholic school in the Outer Richmond, so it wasn't easy for him to get out. But he always did: no one exfiltrated like our Jolu. He liked his jacket because it hung down low—which was pretty stylish in parts of the city—and covered up all his Catholic school crap, which was like a bulls-eye for nosy jerks with the truancy moblog bookmarked on their phones.

"Who's ready to go?" I asked, once we'd all said hello. I pulled out my phone and showed them the map I'd downloaded to it on the BART. "Near as I can work out, we wanna go up to the Nikko again, then one block past it to O'Farrell, then left up toward Van Ness. Somewhere in there we should find the wireless signal."

Van made a face. "That's a nasty part of the Tenderloin." I couldn't argue with her. That part of San Francisco is one of the weird bits—you go in through the Hilton's front entrance and it's all touristy stuff like the cable-car turnaround and family restaurants. Go through to the other side and you're in the 'Loin, where every tracked-out transvestite hooker, hard-case pimp, hissing drug dealer and cracked-up homeless person in town was concentrated. What they bought and sold, none of us were old enough to be a part of (though there were plenty of hookers our age plying their trade in the 'Loin.)

"Look on the bright side," I said. "The only time you want to go up around there is broad daylight. None of the other players are going to go near it until tomorrow at the earliest. This is what we in the ARG business call a *monster head start*."

Jolu grinned at me. "You make it sound like a good thing," he said.

"Beats eating uni," I said.

"We going to talk or we going to win?" Van said. After me, she was hands-down the most hardcore player in our group. She took winning very, very seriously.

We struck out, four good friends, on our way to decode a clue, win the game—and lose everything we cared about, forever.

The physical component of today's clue was a set of GPS coordinates—there were coordinates for all the major cities where Harajuku Fun Madness was played—where we'd find a WiFi access-point's signal. That signal was being deliberately jammed by another, nearby WiFi point that was hidden so that it couldn't be spotted by conventional wifinders, little key-fobs that told you when you were within range of someone's open access-point, which you could use for free.

We'd have to track down the location of the "hidden" access point by measuring the strength of the "visible" one, finding the spot where it was most mysteriously weakest. There we'd find another clue—last time it had been in the special of the day at Anzu, the swanky sushi restaurant in the Nikko hotel in the Tenderloin. The Nikko was owned by Japan Airlines, one of Harajuku Fun Madness's sponsors, and the staff had all made a big fuss over us when we finally tracked down the clue. They'd given us bowls of miso soup and made us try uni, which is sushi made from sea urchin, with the texture of very runny cheese and a smell like very runny dog-droppings. But it tasted *really* good. Or so Darryl told me. I wasn't going to eat that stuff.

I picked up the WiFi signal with my phone's wifinder about three blocks up O'Farrell, just before Hyde Street, in front of a dodgy "Asian Massage Parlor" with a red blinking CLOSED sign in the window. The network's name was HarajukuFM, so we knew we had the right spot.

"If it's in there, I'm not going," Darryl said.

"You all got your wifinders?" I said.

Darryl and Van had phones with built-in wifinders, while Jolu, being too cool to carry a phone bigger than his pinky finger, had a separate little directional fob.

"OK, fan out and see what we see. You're looking for a sharp drop off in the signal that gets worse the more you move along it."

I took a step backward and ended up standing on someone's toes. A female voice said "oof" and I spun around, worried that some crack-ho was going to stab me for breaking her heels.

Instead, I found myself face to face with another kid my age. She had a shock of bright pink hair and a sharp, rodent-like face, with big sunglasses that were practically air-force goggles. She was dressed in striped tights beneath a black granny dress, with lots of little Japanese decorer toys safety pinned to it—anime characters, old world leaders, emblems from foreign soda-pop.

She held up a camera and snapped a picture of me and my crew.

"Cheese," she said. "You're on candid snitch-cam."

"No way," I said. "You wouldn't—"

"I will," she said. "I will send this photo to truant watch in thirty seconds unless you four back off from this clue and let me and my friends here run it down. You can come back in one hour and it'll be all yours. I think that's more than fair."

I looked behind her and noticed three other girls in similar garb—one with blue hair, one with green, and one with purple. "Who are you supposed to be, the Popsicle Squad?"

"We're the team that's going to kick your team's ass at Harajuku Fun Madness," she said. "And I'm the one who's *right this second* about to upload your photo and get you in *so much trouble*—"

Behind me I felt Van start forward. Her all-girls school was notorious for its brawls, and I was pretty sure she was ready to knock this chick's block off.

Then the world changed forever.

We felt it first, that sickening lurch of the cement under your feet that every Californian knows instinctively—*earthquake*. My first inclination, as always, was to get away: "when in trouble or in doubt, run in circles, scream and shout." But the fact was, we were already in the safest place we could be, not in a building that could fall in on us, not out toward the middle of the road where bits of falling cornice could brain us.

Earthquakes are eerily quiet—at first, anyway—but this wasn't quiet. This was loud, an incredible roaring sound that was louder than anything I'd ever heard before. The sound was so punishing it drove me to my knees, and I wasn't the only one. Darryl shook my arm and pointed over the buildings and we saw it then: a huge black cloud rising from the northeast, from the direction of the Bay.

There was another rumble, and the cloud of smoke spread out, that spreading black shape we'd all grown up seeing in movies. Someone had just blown up something, in a big way.

There were more rumbles and more tremors. Heads appeared at windows up and down the street. We all looked at the mushroom cloud in silence.

Then the sirens started.

I'd heard sirens like these before—they test the civil defense sirens at noon on Tuesdays. But I'd only heard them go off unscheduled in old war movies and video games, the kind where someone is bombing someone else from above. Air raid sirens. The wooooooo sound made it all less real.

"Report to shelters immediately." It was like the voice of God, coming from all places at once. There were speakers on some of the electric poles, something I'd never noticed before, and they'd all switched on at once.

"Report to shelters immediately." Shelters? We looked at each other in confusion. What shelters? The cloud was rising steadily, spreading out. Was it nuclear? Were we breathing in our last breaths?

The girl with the pink hair grabbed her friends and they tore ass downhill, back toward the BART station and the foot of the hills.

"REPORT TO SHELTERS IMMEDIATELY." There was screaming now, and a lot of running around. Tourists—you can always spot the tourists, they're the ones who think CALIFORNIA = WARM and spend their San Francisco holidays freezing in shorts and t-shirts—scattered in every direction.

"We should go!" Darryl hollered in my ear, just barely audible over the shrieking of the sirens, which had been joined by traditional police sirens. A dozen SFPD cruisers screamed past us.

"REPORT TO SHELTERS IMMEDIATELY."

"Down to the BART station," I hollered. My friends nodded. We closed ranks and began to move quickly downhill.

CHAPTER 3

We passed a lot of people in the road on the way to the Powell Street BART. They were running or walking, white-faced and silent or shouting and panicked. Homeless people cowered in doorways and watched it all, while a tall black trans hooker shouted at two mustached young men about something.

The closer we got to the BART, the worse the press of bodies became. By the time we reached the stairway down into the station, it was a mobscene, a huge brawl of people trying to crowd their way down a narrow staircase. I had my face crushed up against someone's back, and someone else was pressed into my back.

Darryl was still beside me—he was big enough that he was hard to shove, and Jolu was right behind him, kind of hanging on to his waist. I spied Vanessa a few yards away, trapped by more people.

"Screw you!" I heard Van yell behind me. "Pervert! Get your hands off of me!"

I strained around against the crowd and saw Van looking with disgust at an older guy in a nice suit who was kind of smirking at her. She was digging in her purse and I knew what she was digging for.

"Don't mace him!" I shouted over the din. "You'll get us all too."

At the mention of the word mace, the guy looked scared and kind of melted back, though the crowd kept him moving forward. Up ahead, I saw someone, a middle-aged lady in a hippie dress, falter and fall. She screamed as she went down, and I saw her thrashing to get up, but she couldn't, the crowd's pressure was too strong. As I neared her, I bent to help her up, and was nearly knocked over her. I ended up stepping on her stomach as the crowd pushed me past her, but by then I don't think she was feeling anything.

I was as scared as I'd ever been. There was screaming everywhere now, and more bodies on the floor, and the press from behind was as relentless as a bulldozer. It was all I could do to keep on my feet.

We were in the open concourse where the turnstiles were. It was hardly any better here—the enclosed space sent the voices around us echoing back in a roar that made my head ring, and the smell and feeling of all those bodies made me feel a claustrophobia I'd never known I was prone to.

People were still cramming down the stairs, and more were squeezing past the turnstiles and down the escalators onto the platforms, but it was clear to me that this wasn't going to have a happy ending.

"Want to take our chances up top?" I said to Darryl.

"Yes, hell yes," he said. "This is vicious."

I looked to Vanessa—there was no way she'd hear me. I managed to get my phone out and I texted her.

> We're getting out of here

I saw her feel the vibe from her phone, then look down at it and then back at me and nod vigorously. Darryl, meanwhile, had clued Jolu in.

"*What's the plan?*" Darryl shouted in my ear.

"We're going to have to go back!" I shouted back, pointing at the remorseless crush of bodies.

"It's impossible!" he said.

"It's just going to get more impossible the longer we wait!"

He shrugged. Van worked her way over to me and grabbed hold of my wrist. I took Darryl and Darryl took Jolu by the other hand and we pushed out.

It wasn't easy. We moved about three inches a minute at first, then slowed down even more when we reached the stairway. The people we passed were none too happy about us shoving them out of the way, either. A couple people swore at us and there was a guy who looked like he'd have punched me if he'd been able to get his arms loose. We passed three more crushed people beneath us, but there was no way I could have helped them. By that point, I wasn't even thinking of helping anyone. All I could think of was finding the spaces in front of us to move into, of Darryl's mighty straining on my wrist, of my death-grip on Van behind me.

We popped free like Champagne corks an eternity later, blinking in the grey smoky light. The air raid sirens were still blaring, and the sound of emergency vehicles' sirens as they tore down Market Street was even louder. There was almost no one on the streets anymore—just the people trying hopelessly to get underground. A lot of them were crying. I spotted a bunch of empty benches—usually staked out by skanky winos—and pointed toward them.

We moved for them, the sirens and the smoke making us duck and hunch our shoulders. We got as far as the benches before Darryl fell forward.

We all yelled and Vanessa grabbed him and turned him over. The side of his shirt was stained red, and the stain was spreading. She tugged his shirt up and revealed a long, deep cut in his pudgy side.

"Someone freaking *stabbed* him in the crowd," Jolu said, his hands clenching into fists. "Christ, that's vicious."

Darryl groaned and looked at us, then down at his side, then he groaned and his head went back again.

Vanessa took off her jean jacket and then pulled off the cotton hoodie she was wearing underneath it. She wadded it up and pressed it to Darryl's side. "Take his head," she said to me. "Keep it elevated." To Jolu she said, "Get his feet up—roll up your coat or something." Jolu moved quickly. Vanessa's mother is a nurse and she'd had first aid training every summer at camp. She loved to watch people in movies get their first aid wrong and make fun of them. I was so glad to have her with us.

We sat there for a long time, holding the hoodie to Darryl's side. He kept insisting that he was fine and that we should let him up, and Van kept telling him to shut up and lie still before she kicked his ass.

"What about calling 911?" Jolu said.

I felt like an idiot. I whipped my phone out and punched 911. The sound I got wasn't even a busy signal—it was like a whimper of pain from the phone system. You don't get sounds like that unless there's three million people all dialing the same number at once. Who needs botnets when you've got terrorists?

"What about Wikipedia?" Jolu said.

"No phone, no data," I said.

"What about them?" Darryl said, and pointed at the street. I looked where he was pointing, thinking I'd see a cop or an paramedic, but there was no one there.

"It's OK buddy, you just rest," I said.

"No, you idiot, what about *them*, the cops in the cars? There!"

He was right. Every five seconds, a cop car, an ambulance or a fire-truck zoomed past. They could get us some help. I was such an idiot.

"Come on, then," I said, "let's get you where they can see you and flag one down."

Vanessa didn't like it, but I figured a cop wasn't going to stop for a kid waving his hat in the street, not that day. They just might stop if they saw Darryl bleeding there, though. I argued briefly with her and Darryl settled it by lurching to his feet and dragging himself down toward Market Street.

The first vehicle that screamed past—an ambulance—didn't even slow down. Neither did the cop car that went past, nor the firetruck, nor the next three cop cars. Darryl wasn't in good shape—he was white-faced and panting. Van's sweater was soaked in blood.

I was sick of cars driving right past me. The next time a car appeared down Market Street, I stepped right out into the road, waving my arms over my head, shouting "*STOP*." The car slewed to a stop and only then did I notice that it wasn't a cop car, ambulance or fire engine.

It was a military-looking Jeep, like an armored Hummer, only it didn't have any military insignia on it. The car skidded to a stop just in front of me, and I jumped back and lost my balance and ended up on the road. I felt the doors open near me, and then saw a confusion of booted feet moving close by. I looked up and saw a bunch of military-looking guys in coveralls, holding big, bulky rifles and wearing hooded gas masks with tinted face-plates.

I barely had time to register them before those rifles were pointed at me. I'd never looked down the barrel of a gun before, but everything you've heard about the experience is true. You freeze where you are, time stops, and your heart thunders in your ears. I opened my mouth, then shut it, then, very slowly, I held my hands up in front of me.

The faceless, eyeless armed man above me kept his gun very level. I didn't even breathe. Van was screaming something and Jolu was shouting and I looked at them for a second and that was when someone put a coarse sack over my head and cinched it tight around my windpipe, so quick and so fiercely I barely had time to gasp before it was locked on me. I was pushed roughly but dispassionately onto my stomach and something went twice around my wrists and then tightened up as well, feeling like baling wire and biting cruelly. I cried out and my own voice was muffled by the hood.

I was in total darkness now and I strained my ears to hear what was going on with my friends. I heard them shouting through the muffling canvas of the bag, and then I was being impersonally hauled to my feet by my wrists, my arms wrenched up behind my back, my shoulders screaming.

I stumbled some, then a hand pushed my head down and I was inside the Hummer. More bodies were roughly shoved in beside me.

"Guys?" I shouted, and earned a hard thump on my head for my trouble. I heard Jolu respond, then felt the thump he was dealt, too. My head rang like a gong.

"Hey," I said to the soldiers. "Hey, listen! We're just high school students. I wanted to flag you down because my friend was bleeding. Someone stabbed him." I had no idea how much of this was making it through the muffling bag. I kept talking. "Listen—this is some kind of misunderstanding. We've got to get my friend to a hospital—"

Someone went upside my head again. It felt like they used a baton or something—it was harder than anyone had ever hit me in the head before. My eyes swam and watered and I literally couldn't breathe through the pain. A moment later, I caught my breath, but I didn't say anything. I'd learned my lesson.

Who were these clowns? They weren't wearing insignia. Maybe they were terrorists! I'd never really believed in terrorists before—I mean, I knew that in the abstract there were terrorists somewhere in the world, but they didn't really represent any risk to me. There were millions of ways that the world could kill me—starting with getting run down by a drunk burning his way down Valencia—that were infinitely more likely and immediate than terrorists. Terrorists killed a lot fewer people than bathroom falls and accidental electrocutions. Worrying about them always struck me as about as useful as worrying about getting hit by lightning.

Sitting in the back of that Hummer, my head in a hood, my hands lashed behind my back, lurching back and forth while the bruises swelled up on my head, terrorism suddenly felt a lot riskier.

The car rocked back and forth and tipped uphill. I gathered we were headed over Nob Hill, and from the angle, it seemed we were taking one of the steeper routes—I guessed Powell Street.

Now we were descending just as steeply. If my mental map was right, we were heading down to Fisherman's Wharf. You could get on a boat there, get away. That fit with the terrorism hypothesis. Why the hell would terrorists kidnap a bunch of high school students?

We rocked to a stop still on a downslope. The engine died and then the doors swung open. Someone dragged me by my arms out onto the road, then shoved me, stumbling, down a paved road. A few seconds later, I tripped over a steel staircase, bashing my shins. The hands behind me gave me another shove. I went up the stairs cautiously, not able to use my hands. I got up the third step and reached for the fourth, but it wasn't there. I nearly fell again, but new hands grabbed me from in front and dragged me down a steel floor and then forced me to my knees and locked my hands to something behind me.

More movement, and the sense of bodies being shackled in along-side of me. Groans and muffled sounds. Laughter. Then a long, timeless eternity in the muffled gloom, breathing my own breath, hearing my own breath in my ears.

I actually managed a kind of sleep there, kneeling with the circulation cut off to my legs, my head in canvas twilight. My body had squirted a year's supply of adrenalin into my bloodstream in the space of thirty minutes, and while that stuff can give you the strength to lift cars off your loved ones and leap over tall buildings, the payback's always a bitch.

I woke up to someone pulling the hood off my head. They were neither rough nor careful—just . . . impersonal. Like someone at McDonald's
putting together burgers.

The light in the room was so bright I had to squeeze my eyes shut,
but slowly I was able to open them to slits, then cracks, then all the way
and look around.

We were all in the back of a truck, a big 18-wheeler. I could see
the wheel-wells at regular intervals down the length. But the back of
this truck had been turned into some kind of mobile command-post/
jail. Steel desks lined the walls with banks of slick flat-panel displays
climbing above them on articulated arms that let them be reposi-
tioned in a halo around the operators. Each desk had a gorgeous
office-chair in front of it, festooned with user-interface knobs for
adjusting every millimeter of the sitting surface, as well as height, pitch
and yaw.

Then there was the jail part—at the front of the truck, furthest away
from the doors, there were steel rails bolted into the sides of the vehicle,
and attached to these steel rails were the prisoners.

I spotted Van and Jolu right away. Darryl might have been in
the remaining dozen shackled up back here, but it was impossible to
say—many of them were slumped over and blocking my view. It stank of
sweat and fear back there.

Vanessa looked at me and bit her lip. She was scared. So was I. So
was Jolu, his eyes rolling crazily in their sockets, the whites showing. I
was scared. What's more, I had to piss like a *race-horse*.

I looked around for our captors. I'd avoided looking at them up until
now, the same way you don't look into the dark of a closet where your mind
has conjured up a boogey-man. You don't want to know if you're right.

But I had to get a better look at these jerks who'd kidnapped us. If
they were terrorists, I wanted to know. I didn't know what a terrorist
looked like, though TV shows had done their best to convince me that
they were brown Arabs with big beards and knit caps and loose cotton
dresses that hung down to their ankles.

Not so our captors. They could have been half-time-show cheerlead-
ers on the Super Bowl. They looked *American* in a way I couldn't exactly
define. Good jaw-lines, short, neat haircuts that weren't quite military.
They came in white and brown, male and female, and smiled freely at

one another as they sat down at the other end of the truck, joking and drinking coffees out of go-cups. These weren't Ay-rabs from Afghanistan: they looked like tourists from Nebraska.

I stared at one, a young white woman with brown hair who barely looked older than me, kind of cute in a scary office-power-suit way. If you stare at someone long enough, they'll eventually look back at you. She did, and her face slammed into a totally different configuration, dispassionate, even robotic. The smile vanished in an instant.

"Hey," I said. "Look, I don't understand what's going on here, but I really need to take a leak, you know?"

She looked right through me as if she hadn't heard.

"I'm serious, if I don't get to a can soon, I'm going to have an ugly accident. It's going to get pretty smelly back here, you know?"

She turned to her colleagues, a little huddle of three of them, and they held a low conversation I couldn't hear over the fans from the computers.

She turned back to me. "Hold it for another ten minutes, then you'll each get a piss-call."

"I don't think I've got another ten minutes in me," I said, letting a little more urgency than I was really feeling creep into my voice. "Seriously, lady, it's now or never."

She shook her head and looked at me like I was some kind of pathetic loser. She and her friends conferred some more, then another one came forward. He was older, in his early thirties, and pretty big across the shoulders, like he worked out. He looked like he was Chinese or Korean—even Van can't tell the difference sometimes—but with that bearing that said *American* in a way I couldn't put my finger on.

He pulled his sports-coat aside to let me see the hardware strapped there: I recognized a pistol, a tazer and a can of either mace or pepper-spray before he let it fall again.

"No trouble," he said.

"None," I agreed.

He touched something at his belt and the shackles behind me let go, my arms dropping suddenly behind me. It was like he was wearing Batman's utility belt—wireless remotes for shackles! I guessed it made sense, though: you wouldn't want to lean over your prisoners with all that deadly hardware at their eye-level—they might grab your gun with their teeth and pull the trigger with their tongues or something.

My hands were still lashed together behind me by the plastic strapping, and now that I wasn't supported by the shackles, I found that my legs had turned into lumps of cork while I was stuck in one position. Long story short, I basically fell onto my face and kicked my legs weakly as they went pins-and-needles, trying to get them under me so I could rock up to my feet.

The guy jerked me to my feet and I clown-walked to the very back of the truck, to a little boxed-in porta-john there. I tried to spot Darryl on the way back, but he could have been any of the five or six slumped people. Or none of them.

"In you go," the guy said.

I jerked my wrists. "Take these off, please?" My fingers felt like purple sausages from the hours of bondage in the plastic cuffs.

The guy didn't move.

"Look," I said, trying not to sound sarcastic or angry (it wasn't easy). "Look. You either cut my wrists free or you're going to have to aim for me. A toilet visit is not a hands-free experience." Someone in the truck sniggered. The guy didn't like me, I could tell from the way his jaw muscles ground around. Man, these people were wired tight.

He reached down to his belt and came up with a very nice set of multi-pliers. He flicked out a wicked-looking knife and sliced through the plastic cuffs and my hands were my own again.

"Thanks," I said.

He shoved me into the bathroom. My hands were useless, like lumps of clay on the ends of my wrists. As I wiggled my fingers limply, they tingled, then the tingling turned to a burning feeling that almost made me cry out. I put the seat down, dropped my pants and sat down. I didn't trust myself to stay on my feet.

As my bladder cut loose, so did my eyes. I wept, crying silently and rocking back and forth while the tears and snot ran down my face. It was all I could do to keep from sobbing—I covered my mouth and held the sounds in. I didn't want to give them the satisfaction.

Finally, I was peed out and cried out and the guy was pounding on the door. I cleaned my face as best as I could with wads of toilet paper, stuck it all down the john and flushed, then looked around for a sink but only found a pump-bottle of heavy-duty hand-sanitizer covered in small-print lists of the bio-agents it worked on. I rubbed some into my hands and stepped out of the john.

"What were you doing in there?" the guy said.

"Using the facilities," I said. He turned me around and grabbed my hands and I felt a new pair of plastic cuffs go around them. My wrists had swollen since the last pair had come off and the new ones bit cruelly into my tender skin, but I refused to give him the satisfaction of crying out.

He shackled me back to my spot and grabbed the next person down, who, I saw now, was Jolu, his face puffy and an ugly bruise on his cheek.

"Are you OK?" I asked him, and my friend with the utility belt abruptly put his hand on my forehead and shoved hard, bouncing the back of my head off the truck's metal wall with a sound like a clock striking one. "No talking," he said as I struggled to refocus my eyes.

I didn't like these people. I decided right then that they would pay a price for all this.

One by one, all the prisoners went to the can, and came back, and when they were done, my guard went back to his friends and had another cup of coffee—they were drinking out of a big cardboard urn of Starbucks, I saw—and they had an indistinct conversation that involved a fair bit of laughter.

Then the door at the back of the truck opened and there was fresh air, not smoky the way it had been before, but tinged with ozone. In the slice of outdoors I saw before the door closed, I caught that it was dark out, and raining, with one of those San Francisco drizzles that's part mist.

The man who came in was wearing a military uniform. A US military uniform. He saluted the people in the truck and they saluted him back and that's when I knew that I wasn't a prisoner of some terrorists—I was a prisoner of the United States of America.

They set up a little screen at the end of the truck and then came for us one at a time, unshackling us and leading us to the back of the truck. As close as I could work it—counting seconds off in my head, one hippopotami, two hippopotami—the interviews lasted about seven minutes each. My head throbbed with dehydration and caffeine withdrawal.

I was third, brought back by the woman with the severe haircut. Up close, she looked tired, with bags under her eyes and grim lines at the corners of her mouth.

"Thanks," I said, automatically, as she unlocked me with a remote and then dragged me to my feet. I hated myself for the automatic politeness, but it had been drilled into me.

She didn't twitch a muscle. I went ahead of her to the back of the truck and behind the screen. There was a single folding chair and I sat in it. Two of them—Severe Haircut woman and Utility Belt man—looked at me from their ergonomic super-chairs.

They had a little table between them with the contents of my wallet and backpack spread out on it.

"Hello, Marcus," Severe Haircut woman said. "We have some questions for you."

"Am I under arrest?" I asked. This wasn't an idle question. If you're not under arrest, there are limits on what the cops can and can't do to you. For starters, they can't hold you forever without arresting you, giving you a phone call, and letting you talk to a lawyer. And hoo-boy, was I ever going to talk to a lawyer.

"What's this for?" she said, holding up my phone. The screen was showing the error message you got if you kept trying to get into its data without giving the right password. It was a bit of a rude message—an animated hand giving a certain universally recognized gesture—because I liked to customize my gear.

"Am I under arrest?" I repeated. They can't make you answer any questions if you're not under arrest, and when you ask if you're under arrest, they have to answer you. It's the rules.

"You're being detained by the Department of Homeland Security," the woman snapped.

"Am I under arrest?"

"You're going to be more cooperative, Marcus, starting right now." She didn't say, "or else," but it was implied.

"I would like to contact an attorney," I said. "I would like to know what I've been charged with. I would like to see some form of identification from both of you."

The two agents exchanged looks.

"I think you should really reconsider your approach to this situation," Severe Haircut woman said. "I think you should do that right now. We found a number of suspicious devices on your person. We found you and your confederates near the site of the worst terrorist attack this country has ever seen. Put those two facts together and things don't look very good for you, Marcus. You can cooperate, or you can be very, very sorry. Now, what is this for?"

"You think I'm a terrorist? I'm seventeen years old!"

"Just the right age—Al Qaeda loves recruiting impressionable, idealistic kids. We googled you, you know. You've posted a lot of very ugly stuff on the public Internet."

"I would like to speak to an attorney," I said.

Severe Haircut lady looked at me like I was a bug. "You're under the mistaken impression that you've been picked up by the police for a crime. You need to get past that. You are being detained as a potential enemy combatant by the government of the United States. If I were you, I'd be thinking very hard about how to convince us that you are not an enemy combatant. Very hard. Because there are dark holes that enemy combatants can disappear into, very dark deep holes, holes where you can just vanish. Forever. Are you listening to me young man? I want you to unlock this phone and then decrypt the files in its memory. I want you to account for yourself: why were you out on the street? What do you know about the attack on this city?"

"I'm not going to unlock my phone for you," I said, indignant. My phone's memory had all kinds of private stuff on it: photos, emails, little hacks and mods I'd installed. "That's private stuff."

"What have you got to hide?"

"I've got the right to my privacy," I said. "And I want to speak to an attorney."

"This is your last chance, kid. Honest people don't have anything to hide."

"I want to speak to an attorney." My parents would pay for it. All the FAQs on getting arrested were clear on this point. Just keep asking to see an attorney, no matter what they say or do. There's no good that comes of talking to the cops without your lawyer present. These two said they weren't cops, but if this wasn't an arrest, what was it?

In hindsight, maybe I should have unlocked my phone for them.

CHAPTER 4

They re-shackled and re-hooded me and left me there. A long time later, the truck started to move, rolling downhill, and then I was hauled back to my feet. I immediately fell over. My legs were so asleep they felt like blocks of ice, all except my knees, which were swollen and tender from all the hours of kneeling.

Hands grabbed my shoulders and feet and I was picked up like a sack of potatoes. There were indistinct voices around me. Someone crying. Someone cursing.

I was carried a short distance, then set down and re-shackled to another railing. My knees wouldn't support me anymore and I pitched forward, ending up twisted on the ground like a pretzel, straining against the chains holding my wrists.

Then we were moving again, and this time, it wasn't like driving in a truck. The floor beneath me rocked gently and vibrated with heavy diesel engines and I realized I was on a ship! My stomach turned to ice. I was being taken off America's shores to somewhere *else*, and who the hell knew where that was? I'd been scared before, but this thought *terrified* me, left me paralyzed and wordless with fear. I realized that I might never see my parents again and I actually tasted a little vomit burn up my throat. The bag over my head closed in on me and I could barely breathe, something that was compounded by the weird position I was twisted into.

But mercifully we weren't on the water for very long. It felt like an hour, but I know now that it was a mere fifteen minutes, and then I felt us docking, felt footsteps on the decking around me and felt other prisoners being unshackled and carried or led away. When they came for me, I tried to stand again, but couldn't, and they carried me again, impersonally, roughly.

When they took the hood off again, I was in a cell.

The cell was old and crumbled, and smelled of sea air. There was one window high up, and rusted bars guarded it. It was still dark outside. There was a blanket on the floor and a little metal toilet without a seat, set into the wall. The guard who took off my hood grinned at me and closed the solid steel door behind him.

I gently massaged my legs, hissing as the blood came back into them and into my hands. Eventually I was able to stand, and then to pace. I heard other people talking, crying, shouting. I did some shouting too: "Jolu! Darryl! Vanessa!" Other voices on the cell-block took up the cry, shouting out names, too, shouting out obscenities. The nearest voices sounded like drunks losing their minds on a street-corner. Maybe I sounded like that too.

Guards shouted at us to be quiet and that just made everyone yell louder. Eventually we were all howling, screaming our heads off, screaming our throats raw. Why not? What did we have to lose?

The next time they came to question me, I was filthy and tired, thirsty and hungry. Severe Haircut lady was in the new questioning party, as were three big guys who moved me around like a cut of meat. One was black, the other two were white, though one might have been Hispanic. They all carried guns. It was like a Benetton's ad crossed with a game of Counter-Strike.

They'd taken me from my cell and chained my wrists and ankles together. I paid attention to my surroundings as we went. I heard water outside and thought that maybe we were on Alcatraz—it was a prison, after all, even if it had been a tourist attraction for generations, the place where you went to see where Al Capone and his gangster contemporaries did their time. But I'd been to Alcatraz on a school trip. It was old and rusted, medieval. This place felt like it dated back to World War Two, not colonial times.

There were bar codes laser-printed on stickers and placed on each of the cell-doors, and numbers, but other than that, there was no way to tell who or what might be behind them.

The interrogation room was modern, with fluorescent lights, ergonomic chairs—not for me, though, I got a folding plastic garden chair—and a big wooden board-room table. A mirror lined one wall, just like in the cop shows, and I figured someone or other must be watching from behind it. Severe Haircut lady and her friends helped themselves to coffees from an urn on a side-table (I could have torn her throat out with my teeth and taken her coffee just then), and then set a styrofoam cup of water down next to me—without unlocking my wrists from behind my back, so I couldn't reach it. Hardy har har.

"Hello, Marcus," Severe Haircut woman said. "How's your 'tude doing today?"

I didn't say anything.

"This isn't as bad as it gets you know," she said. "This is as *good* as it gets from now on. Even once you tell us what we want to know, even if that convinces us that you were just in the wrong place at the wrong time, you're a marked man now. We'll be watching you everywhere you go and everything you do. You've acted like you've got something to hide, and we don't like that."

It's pathetic, but all my brain could think about was that phrase, "convince us that you were in the wrong place at the wrong time." This was the worst thing that had ever happened to me. I had never, ever felt this bad or this scared before. Those words, "wrong place at the wrong time," those six words, they were like a lifeline dangling before me as I thrashed to stay on the surface.

"Hello, Marcus?" she snapped her fingers in front of my face. "Over here, Marcus." There was a little smile on her face and I hated myself for letting her see my fear. "Marcus, it can be a lot worse than this. This isn't the worst place we can put you, not by a damned sight." She reached down below the table and came out with a briefcase, which she snapped open. From it, she withdrew my phone, my arphid sniper/cloner, my wifinder, and my memory keys. She set them down on the table one after the other.

"Here's what we want from you. You unlock the phone for us today. If you do that, you'll get outdoor and bathing privileges. You'll get a shower and you'll be allowed to walk around in the exercise yard. Tomorrow, we'll bring you back and ask you to decrypt the data on these memory sticks. Do that, and you'll get to eat in the mess hall. The day after, we're going to want your email passwords, and that will get you library privileges."

The word "no" was on my lips, like a burp trying to come up, but it wouldn't come. "Why?" is what came out instead.

"We want to be sure that you're what you seem to be. This is about your security, Marcus. Say you're innocent. You might be, though why an innocent man would act like he's got so much to hide is beyond me. But say you are: you could have been on that bridge when it blew. Your parents could have been. Your friends. Don't you want us to catch the people who attacked your home?"

It's funny, but when she was talking about my getting "privileges" it scared me into submission. I felt like I'd done *something* to end up where I was, like maybe it was partially my fault, like I could do something to change it.

But as soon as she switched to this BS about "safety" and "security," my spine came back. "Lady," I said, "you're talking about attacking my home, but as far as I can tell, you're the only one who's attacked me lately. I thought I lived in a country with a constitution. I thought I lived in a country where I had *rights*. You're talking about defending my freedom by tearing up the Bill of Rights."

A flicker of annoyance passed over her face, then went away. "So melodramatic, Marcus. No one's attacked you. You've been detained by your country's government while we seek details on the worst terrorist attack ever perpetrated on our nation's soil. You have it within your power to help us fight this war on our nation's enemies. You want to preserve the Bill of Rights? Help us stop bad people from blowing up your city. Now, you have exactly thirty seconds to unlock that phone before I send you back to your cell. We have lots of other people to interview today."

She looked at her watch. I rattled my wrists, rattled the chains that kept me from reaching around and unlocking the phone. Yes, I was going to do it. She'd told me what my path was to freedom—to the world, to my parents—and that had given me hope. Now she'd threatened to send me away, to take me off that path, and my hope had crashed and all I could think of was how to get back on it.

So I rattled my wrists, wanting to get to my phone and unlock it for her, and she just looked at me coldly, checking her watch.

"The password," I said, finally understanding what she wanted of me. She wanted me to say it out loud, here, where she could record it, where her pals could hear it. She didn't want me to just unlock the phone. She wanted me to submit to her. To put her in charge of me. To give up every secret, all my privacy. "The password," I said again, and then I told her the password. God help me, I submitted to her will.

She smiled a little prim smile, which had to be her ice-queen equivalent of a touchdown dance, and the guards led me away. As the door closed, I saw her bend down over the phone and key the password in.

I wish I could say that I'd anticipated this possibility in advance and created a fake password that unlocked a completely innocuous partition on my phone, but I wasn't nearly that paranoid/clever.

You might be wondering at this point what dark secrets I had locked away on my phone and memory sticks and email. I'm just a kid, after all.

The truth is that I had everything to hide, and nothing. Between my phone and my memory sticks, you could get a pretty good idea of who my friends were, what I thought of them, all the goofy things we'd done. You could read the transcripts of the electronic arguments we'd carried out and the electronic reconciliations we'd arrived at.

You see, I don't delete stuff. Why would I? Storage is cheap, and you never know when you're going to want to go back to that stuff. Especially the stupid stuff. You know that feeling you get sometimes where you're sitting on the subway and there's no one to talk to and you suddenly remember some bitter fight you had, some terrible thing you said?

Well, it's usually never as bad as you remember. Being able to go back and see it again is a great way to remind yourself that you're not as horrible a person as you think you are. Darryl and I have gotten over more fights that way than I can count.

And even that's not it. I know my phone is private. I know my memory sticks are private. That's because of cryptography—message scrambling. The math behind crypto is good and solid, and you and me get access to the same crypto that banks and the National Security Agency use. There's only one kind of crypto that anyone uses: crypto that's public, open and can be deployed by anyone. That's how you know it works.

There's something really liberating about having some corner of your life that's *yours*, that no one gets to see except you. It's a little like nudity or taking a dump. Everyone gets naked every once in a while. Everyone has to squat on the toilet. There's nothing shameful, deviant or weird about either of them. But what if I decreed that from now on, every time you went to evacuate some solid waste, you'd have to do it in a glass room perched in the middle of Times Square, and you'd be buck naked?

Even if you've got nothing wrong or weird with your body—and how many of us can say that?—you'd have to be pretty strange to like that idea. Most of us would run screaming. Most of us would hold it in until we exploded.

It's not about doing something shameful. It's about doing something *private*. It's about your life belonging to you.

They were taking that from me, piece by piece. As I walked back to my cell, that feeling of deserving it came back to me. I'd broken a lot of rules all my life and I'd gotten away with it, by and large. Maybe this was justice. Maybe this was my past coming back to me. After all, I had been where I was because I'd snuck out of school.

I got my shower. I got to walk around the yard. There was a patch of sky overhead, and it smelled like the Bay Area, but beyond that, I had no clue where I was being held. No other prisoners were visible during my exercise period, and I got pretty bored with walking in circles. I strained my ears for any sound that might help me understand what this place was, but all I heard was the occasional vehicle, some distant conversations, a plane landing somewhere nearby.

They brought me back to my cell and fed me, a half a pepperoni pie from Goat Hill Pizza, which I knew well, up on Potrero Hill. The carton with its familiar graphic and 415 phone number was a reminder that only a day before, I'd been a free man in a free country and that now I was a prisoner. I worried constantly about Darryl and fretted about my other friends. Maybe they'd been more cooperative and had been released. Maybe they'd told my parents and they were frantically calling around.

Maybe not.

The cell was fantastically spare, empty as my soul. I fantasized that the wall opposite my bunk was a screen, that I could be hacking right now, opening the cell-door. I fantasized about my workbench and the projects there—the old cans I was turning into a ghetto surround-sound rig, the aerial photography kite-cam I was building, my homebrew laptop.

I wanted to get out of there. I wanted to go home and have my friends and my school and my parents and my life back. I wanted to be able to go where I wanted to go, not be stuck pacing and pacing and pacing.

They took my passwords for my USB keys next. Those held some interesting messages I'd downloaded from one online discussion group or another, some chat transcripts, things where people had helped me out with some of the knowledge I needed to do the things I did. There was nothing on there you couldn't find with Google, of course, but I didn't think that would count in my favor.

I got exercise again that afternoon, and this time there were others in the yard when I got there, four other guys and two women, of all ages and racial backgrounds. I guess lots of people were doing things to earn their "privileges."

They gave me half an hour, and I tried to make conversation with the most normal-seeming of the other prisoners, a black guy about my age with a short afro. But when I introduced myself and stuck my hand out, he cut his eyes toward the cameras mounted ominously in the corners of the yard and kept walking without ever changing his facial expression.

But then, just before they called my name and brought me back into the building, the door opened and out came—Vanessa! I'd never been more glad to see a friendly face. She looked tired and grumpy, but not hurt, and when she saw me, she shouted my name and ran to me. We hugged each other hard and I realized I was shaking. Then I realized she was shaking, too.

"Are you OK?" she said, holding me at arms' length.

"I'm OK," I said. "They told me they'd let me go if I gave them my passwords."

"They keep asking me questions about you and Darryl."

There was a voice blaring over the loudspeaker, shouting at us to stop talking, to walk, but we ignored it.

"Answer them," I said, instantly. "Anything they ask, answer them. If it'll get you out."

"How are Darryl and Jolu?"

"I haven't seen them."

The door banged open and four big guards boiled out. Two took me and two took Vanessa. They forced me to the ground and turned my head away from Vanessa, though I heard her getting the same treatment. Plastic cuffs went around my wrists and then I was yanked to my feet and brought back to my cell.

No dinner came that night. No breakfast came the next morning. No one came and brought me to the interrogation room to extract more of my secrets. The plastic cuffs didn't come off, and my shoulders burned, then ached, then went numb, then burned again. I lost all feeling in my hands.

I had to pee. I couldn't undo my pants. I really, really had to pee.

I pissed myself.

They came for me after that, once the hot piss had cooled and gone clammy, making my already filthy jeans stick to my legs. They came for me and walked me down the long hall lined with doors, each door with its own bar code, each bar code a prisoner like me. They walked me down the corridor and brought me to the interrogation room and it was like a different planet when I entered there, a world where things were normal, where everything didn't reek of urine. I felt so dirty and ashamed, and all those feelings of deserving what I got came back to me.

Severe Haircut lady was already sitting. She was perfect: coiffed and with just a little makeup. I smelled her hair stuff. She wrinkled her nose at me. I felt the shame rise in me.

"Well, you've been a very naughty boy, haven't you? Aren't you a filthy thing?"

Shame. I looked down at the table. I couldn't bear to look up. I wanted to tell her my email password and get gone.

"What did you and your friend talk about in the yard?"

I barked a laugh at the table. "I told her to answer your questions. I told her to cooperate."

"So do you give the orders?"

I felt the blood sing in my ears. "Oh come on," I said. "We play a *game* together, it's called Harajuku Fun Madness. I'm the *team captain*. We're not terrorists, we're high school students. I don't give her orders. I told her that we needed to be *honest* with you so that we could clear up any suspicion and get out of here."

She didn't say anything for a moment.

"How is Darryl?" I said.

"Who?"

"Darryl. You picked us up together. My friend. Someone had stabbed him in the Powell Street BART. That's why we were up on the surface. To get him help."

"I'm sure he's fine, then," she said.

My stomach knotted and I almost threw up. "You don't *know*? You haven't got him here?"

"Who we have here and who we don't have here is not something we're going to discuss with you, ever. That's not something you're going to know. Marcus, you've seen what happens when you don't cooperate with us. You've seen what happens when you disobey our orders. You've been a little cooperative, and it's gotten you almost to the point where you might go free again. If you want to make that possibility into a reality, you'll stick to answering my questions."

I didn't say anything.

"You're learning, that's good. Now, your email passwords, please."

I was ready for this. I gave them everything: server address, login, password. This didn't matter. I didn't keep any email on my server. I downloaded it all and kept it on my laptop at home, which downloaded and deleted my mail from the server every sixty seconds. They wouldn't get anything out of my mail—it got cleared off the server and stored on my laptop at home.

Back to the cell, but they cut loose my hands and they gave me a shower and a pair of orange prison pants to wear. They were too big for me and hung down low on my hips, like a Mexican gang-kid in the Mission. That's where the baggy-pants-down-your-ass look comes from, you know that? From prison. I tell you what, it's less fun when it's not a fashion statement.

They took away my jeans, and I spent another day in the cell. The walls were scratched cement over a steel grid. You could tell, because the steel was rusting in the salt air, and the grid shone through the green paint in red-orange. My parents were out that window, somewhere.

They came for me again the next day.

"We've been reading your mail for a day now. We changed the password so that your home computer couldn't fetch it."

Well, of course they had. I would have done the same, now that I thought of it.

"We have enough on you now to put you away for a very long time, Marcus. Your possession of these articles—" she gestured at all my little gizmos—"and the data we recovered from your phone and memory sticks, as well as the subversive material we'd no doubt find if we raided your house and took your computer. It's enough to put you away until you're an old man. Do you understand that?"

I didn't believe it for a second. There's no way a judge would say that all this stuff constituted any kind of real crime. It was free speech, it was technological tinkering. It wasn't a crime.

But who said that these people would ever put me in front of a judge.

"We know where you live, we know who your friends are. We know how you operate and how you think."

It dawned on me then. They were about to let me go. The room seemed to brighten. I heard myself breathing, short little breaths.

"We just want to know one thing: what was the delivery mechanism for the bombs on the bridge?"

I stopped breathing. The room darkened again.

"What?"

"There were ten charges on the bridge, all along its length. They weren't in car-trunks. They'd been placed there. Who placed them there, and how did they get there?"

"What?" I said it again.

"This is your last chance, Marcus," she said. She looked sad. "You were doing so well until now. Tell us this and you can go home. You can get a lawyer and defend yourself in a court of law. There are doubtless extenuating circumstances that you can use to explain your actions. Just tell us this thing, and you're gone."

"I don't know what you're talking about!" I was crying and I didn't even care. Sobbing, blubbering. "I have *no idea what you're talking about*!"

She shook her head. "Marcus, please. Let us help you. By now you know that we always get what we're after."

There was a gibbering sound in the back of my mind. They were *insane*. I pulled myself together, working hard to stop the tears. "Listen, lady, this is nuts. You've been into my stuff, you've seen it all. I'm a seventeen-year-old high school student, not a terrorist! You can't seriously think—"

"Marcus, haven't you figured out that we're serious yet?" She shook her head. "You get pretty good grades. I thought you'd be smarter than that." She made a flicking gesture and the guards picked me up by the armpits.

Back in my cell, a hundred little speeches occurred to me. The French call this "esprit d'escalier"—the spirit of the staircase, the snappy rebuttals that come to you after you leave the room and slink down the stairs. In my mind, I stood and delivered, telling her that I was a citizen who loved my freedom, which made me the patriot and made her the traitor. In my mind, I shamed her for turning my country into an armed camp. In my mind, I was eloquent and brilliant and reduced her to tears.

But you know what? None of those fine words came back to me when they pulled me out the next day. All I could think of was freedom. My parents.

"Hello, Marcus," she said. "How are you feeling?"

I looked down at the table. She had a neat pile of documents in front of her, and her ubiquitous go-cup of Starbucks beside her. I found it comforting somehow, a reminder that there was a real world out there somewhere, beyond the walls.

"We're through investigating you, for now." She let that hang there. Maybe it meant that she was letting me go. Maybe it meant that she was going to throw me in a pit and forget that I existed.

"And?" I said finally.

"And I want you to impress on you again that we are very serious about this. Our country has experienced the worst attack ever committed on its soil. How many 9/11s do you want us to suffer before you're willing to cooperate? The details of our investigation are secret. We won't stop at anything in our efforts to bring the perpetrators of these heinous crimes to justice. Do you understand that?"

"Yes," I mumbled.

"We are going to send you home today, but you are a marked man. You have not been found to be above suspicion—we're only releasing you because we're done questioning you for now. But from now on, you *belong* to us. We will be watching you. We'll be waiting for you to make a misstep. Do you understand that we can watch you closely, all the time?"

"Yes," I mumbled.

"Good. You will never speak of what happened here to anyone, ever. This is a matter of national security. Do you know that the death penalty still holds for treason in time of war?"

"Yes," I mumbled.

"Good boy," she purred. "We have some papers here for you to sign." She pushed the stack of papers across the table to me. Little post-its with SIGN HERE printed on them had been stuck throughout them. A guard undid my cuffs.

I paged through the papers and my eyes watered and my head swam. I couldn't make sense of them. I tried to decipher the legalese. It seemed that I was signing a declaration that I had been voluntarily held and submitted to voluntary questioning, of my own free will.

"What happens if I don't sign this?" I said.

She snatched the papers back and made that flicking gesture again. The guards jerked me to my feet.

"Wait!" I cried. "Please! I'll sign them!" They dragged me to the door. All I could see was that door, all I could think of was it closing behind me.

I lost it. I wept. I begged to be allowed to sign the papers. To be so close to freedom and have it snatched away, it made me ready to do anything. I can't count the number of times I've heard someone say, "Oh, I'd rather die than do something-or-other"—I've said it myself now and again. But that was the first time I understood what it really meant. I would have rather died than go back to my cell.

I begged as they took me out into the corridor. I told them I'd sign anything.

She called out to the guards and they stopped. They brought me back. They sat me down. One of them put the pen in my hand.

Of course, I signed, and signed and signed.

My jeans and t-shirt were back in my cell, laundered and folded. They smelled of detergent. I put them on and washed my face and sat on my cot and stared at the wall. They'd taken everything from me. First my privacy, then my dignity. I'd been ready to sign anything. I would have signed a confession that said I'd assassinated Abraham Lincoln.

I tried to cry, but it was like my eyes were dry, out of tears.

They got me again. A guard approached me with a hood, like the hood I'd been put in when they picked us up, whenever that was, days ago, weeks ago.

The hood went over my head and cinched tight at my neck. I was in total darkness and the air was stifling and stale. I was raised to my feet and walked down corridors, up stairs, on gravel. Up a gangplank. On a ship's steel deck. My hands were chained behind me, to a railing. I knelt on the deck and listened to the thrum of the diesel engines.

The ship moved. A hint of salt air made its way into the hood. It was drizzling and my clothes were heavy with water. I was outside, even if my head was in a bag. I was outside, in the world, moments from my freedom.

They came for me and led me off the boat and over uneven ground. Up three metal stairs. My wrists were unshackled. My hood was removed.

I was back in the truck. Severe Haircut woman was there, at the little desk she'd sat at before. She had a ziploc bag with her, and inside it were my phone and other little devices, my wallet and the change from my pockets. She handed them to me wordlessly.

I filled my pockets. It felt so weird to have everything back in its familiar place, to be wearing my familiar clothes. Outside the truck's back door, I heard the familiar sounds of my familiar city.

A guard passed me my backpack. The woman extended her hand to me. I just looked at it. She put it down and gave me a wry smile. Then she mimed zipping up her lips and pointed to me, and opened the door.

It was daylight outside, gray and drizzling. I was looking down an alley toward cars and trucks and bikes zipping down the road. I stood transfixed on the truck's top step, staring at freedom.

My knees shook. I knew now that they were playing with me again. In a moment, the guards would grab me and drag me back inside, the bag would go over my head again, and I would be back on the boat and sent off to the prison again, to the endless, unanswerable questions. I barely held myself back from stuffing my fist in my mouth.

Then I forced myself to go down one stair. Another stair. The last stair. My sneakers crunched down on the crap on the alley's floor, broken glass, a needle, gravel. I took a step. Another. I reached the mouth of the alley and stepped onto the sidewalk.

No one grabbed me.

I was free.

Then strong arms threw themselves around me. I nearly cried.

Tim Pratt is a Nebula Award-nominated short story writer and novelist whose work has appeared in a number of Year's Best collections and whose story "Impossible Dreams" won the Hugo Award for Best Short Story in 2006. His Marla Mason series follows the adventures of an over confident "ass-kicking sorcerer" as she battles with monsters, magical daggers, and sex parties.

In "Unexpected Outcomes," Pratt uses the trope of virtual reality and/or the "brain in a vat" thought experiment to explore the impact of the events of 9/11.

UNEXPECTED OUTCOMES
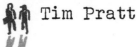
Tim Pratt

I was lying in bed with my girlfriend Heather that Tuesday morning in September when the phone rang, early. We didn't jump to answer it—that's what machines are for—and after a couple of rings and the beep we heard our friend Sherman, sounding excited, say, "Guys, you should turn on your TV."

We didn't get up right away. It was early, only about 6 a.m. in California, and though the phone had awakened us, we sprawled languidly entangled for a while. "Hey," she said. "He didn't say what channel. What could have happened, that it would be on every channel?"

I thought about it for a minute. "Aliens," I said. I was seven-eighths joking, but I was always a science fiction fan—yeah, that's a laugh now, isn't it?—and I kind of half hoped maybe I was right. Aliens. "We come in peace," I said.

She sighed. "I wish. It's probably an assassination."

"Probably." Nearly a year after the election, we were still pissed about Gore losing the presidency he'd rightfully won, about the Supreme Court deciding they knew better than the people. Maybe somebody even more pissed off than us had decided to do something about Bush Jr., but really, Cheney in charge would have been even worse.

We finally got up, and went into the living room in our robes, and turned on the TV . . . and saw what all the rest of you in the television-owning world saw.

I know it's a cliché, but it's a cliché for a reason: 9/11 changed everything.

The talking heads on screen were pretty much yelling, but we didn't listen, just stared at the impossible image on the screen. A jetliner—a Boeing 767-223ER, we learned later—hanging perfectly still in the air, so close to the side of one of the World Trade Center towers that someone could have leaned out the window of an office and laid her hand on the jet's nose (if the windows up that high opened, anyway). The plane was suspended impossibly in the sky, like a special effect in a movie about a kid with a magical wristwatch that stops time. But even though the first thought everyone had on seeing the plane was "This is like something out of a movie," it wasn't a movie.

"Tim," Heather said. "Is it . . . some kind of publicity thing? Or like a David Copperfield magician trick? Or . . ."

I flipped channels. The same images were on all the channels, the same repeating camera angles, from helicopters, from the ground—only the yelling was different. "I don't think—" I began, and then the second plane entered the frame from the left, cruising along the sky-line with the easy grace of a shark, seeming to move deceptively slowly, and I braced myself, expecting it to slam into the Trade Center's second tower. Reporters on the ground stopped yelling and started screaming.

But the plane just stopped, and hung there, nose tipped at a slight angle, mere feet from the side of the building.

And that's when the figure—the one people call the Ambassador, or the Doctor, or the Outsider, or the Professor, or a hundred other names—appeared. Just a middle-aged man in a white lab coat, with steel-rimmed glasses and graying hair. His image filled the air above the jetliner, like the dome of the sky had been transformed into an IMAX movie screen, which only added to the sense of special-effects-laden unreality. "What's he saying?" Heather asked, the same thing the reporters on the ground were saying, and it was a moment before his moving lips synched up with booming sound.

He said, "People of Earth, I have a message for you."

"Hi there," a voice said from the far side of our living room. We wrenched around on the couch and saw a man sitting on the stained old loveseat left behind by a prior tenant.

"Who the fuck are you? Get out of here!" We lived in a lousy part of town near 40th and Telegraph Ave., over by the MacArthur BART commuter train station, and there were times we couldn't come in through our front gate because the cops had drug dealers handcuffed and sitting on the sidewalk in the way, so a crazy homeless guy sneaking into our living room seemed plausible.

But my girlfriend put her hand on my arm and said, "Tim, that's the guy from the TV."

I settled back down, though I was hardly comforted. She was right, though—same glasses, same lab coat, same vaguely affable expression.

"People of . . . this house," he said. "I have a message for you."

Later we heard about how he'd appeared all over the world, in everybody's living room, or hut, or yurt, or bathysphere, or mountaintop temple, or patch of dirt. Sometimes he was a white guy in a lab coat, sometimes he was a black guy in a three-piece suit, sometimes he was a woman in a headscarf, sometimes he was a god—he looked different to everyone, and even his image in the sky over the WTC didn't look the same to all the people there. But his message was pretty much the same for everyone. I wonder about those uncontacted, remote tribes in Papua New Guinea and the South American rain forests—how did he explain the situation to *them*, when they had no technological context for understanding? Or do those undiscovered peoples even exist, here, since they aren't part of the global community, since they were utterly unaffected by the Age of Global Terror—were they outside the bounds of the study? Maybe Dawson and I should look into it, though jungle exploring is a little tricky these days, unless you find the right hole.

"You have been participants in a long-running and very successful historical and sociological study," Professor Apocalypse said. "And that study has now come to an end." He gestured at the TV screen. "In actual recorded history, those planes crashed into those towers in an attack orchestrated by religious fundamentalists. This morning ushered in what my people call the Age of Global Terror. We've been studying the roots of that age by reproducing the sum of human history up until that moment. And now." He shrugged minutely. "We're finished."

I think my thoughts were something like, *Oh, shit*, probably the same as your thoughts, though it's hard to remember what I really felt, then. Of course I wanted to disbelieve, but, you understand. Planes hanging in mid-air. Future-guy appearing in our living room. It was pretty persuasive.

"Your world is just a simulation, running on computers—what you would call computers—in the far future. That is, it's the present, for me, but from your point of view . . . I'm sorry if this is confusing. This is not my native semiotic level. The world you know, the lives you've led, they are . . . a dramatization of the past, as accurate as we could make it, peopled by all the same individuals who lived in the real history, doing all the same things their original counterparts did, guided not by rote programming but by perfectly reproduced pressures of nature and nurture, the combination of initial conditions and environment." Professor Badnews glanced around and pointed at one of the prints hanging on our off-white walls—that Waterhouse painting, "Nymphs Finding the Head of Orpheus." He said, "Ah, you see, this painting— it's a print, a reproduction of the original. You are the same, a reproduction of—"

"We understand what you mean." I was pissed off that he considered us so slow, primitive, whatever he thought. "We're science fiction writers." *Or trying to be.* I'd met Heather at a brunch thrown by the organizers of an online magazine we'd both contributed to. "You mean we're living in a simulation. Like that movie *The Matrix*."

He nodded. "That is a comparison many in this nation make. Are making. Except . . . you have no real bodies tucked away in vats somewhere else. You are nothing *but* simulations. Like characters on a holodeck, some of your peers have said."

"We're not *real?*" Heather said.

"Not strictly speaking. But, arguably, you are sentient. That's why I'm here. Normally in a historical simulation of this kind, when the study is over, we simply, ah, you would say 'pull the plug.' But this is a very advanced program, inhabited by artificial but nevertheless rational actors—by which I mean all the simulated humans, along with some of the larger sea mammals—and our ethics committee has ruled we cannot simply 'pull the plug' on your existence. A majority of the committee believes that would constitute genocide."

"If you're not ending the experiment, why appear to us at all? Why not just let us go on living as we were?" I'm not normally a vocal proponent of the idea that ignorance is bliss, but I was beginning to come around to the argument.

"Yes. A valid question. The scale of this study is large, as you can imagine, and the resources necessary to accurately simulate an entire planet and all its six billion inhabitants are staggering. Since the study is over, we can't justify the amount of processing power required to continue at the current level of resolution, and so I've come to let everyone know about certain, ah, reductions in non-essential services."

"Non-essential services" is a phrase to chill the blood. I imagined dead pixels in the surface of the moon, frozen tides, the sun switched off like a lamp. "Such as?"

"Well." He shifted uncomfortably, and I resented the psychological manipulation—he was a projected image, he wasn't *uncomfortable*, and I suspect he was just trying to make me feel bad for him in his role as bearer of bad news. (Dawson figures I was right about that, by the way.) "Weather is the main thing. Simulating weather is *hugely* resource-intensive, we've only been able to accurately model such chaotic systems for a few decades, and they take up enormous quantities of processing power. So that has to stop."

"There won't be any more *weather*?" Heather was a gardener, and she had relatives who ran a working farm—I think she grasped the implications quicker than I did. "What does that even mean?"

"The weather . . . just won't change. Where it's raining now, it will continue to rain. Where it's not raining, it won't rain again. And so on. There was some talk of stopping the Earth's rotation, but that's comparatively simple to model, and it was felt by the committee that eternal night for half the planet would be unnecessarily psychologically debilitating. Likewise, the tides will continue."

I stared at him. "So our choices are to live in places of permanent flooding or permanent drought? We'll all starve to death!"

"Ah, no, you don't need to eat anymore. To require you to do so would be monstrous. There will likely be some movement of the population away from climatically inhospitable areas, but with no new children being born, overcrowding in temperate areas should only be a temporary—"

"No more *children*?"

He frowned. "Of course not. The study is over. We need no more subjects."

I looked at my girlfriend, and saw the same bleakness in her eyes that I felt behind my own. We'd only been living together for a month, dating five times that, hadn't even talked about marriage, we were in our twenties, we'd certainly never talked about children—but I think we both thought *someday* we'd talk about children.

"Let me see if I understand," I said slowly. "We'll just go on living, not needing to eat, with no more kids being born, until we all . . . die of old age?"

"Yes. Or accidents. Or . . . well . . . we suspect some may decide they prefer not to live, given their new understanding of reality."

"What about disease?" my girlfriend said.

He made a seesawing gesture with his hand. "Not global pandemics— also surprisingly hard to accurately simulate—but most diseases will remain, yes."

"Why don't you get rid of disease!" She looked pissed. Her father had died of emphysema before we met.

"Ah, well, the basic forms of your bodies and the frailties therein are already established, built into the simulation as it were, and changing them all . . ." He shrugged. "Not for a study that's over. If there are no further questions . . . Then that's all."

"What do you mean that's all?"

"I have nothing else to tell you. The study is over. You're free to live your lives however you see fit."

"What lives?"

"That's a question you'll have to settle for yourselves." He blinked his eyes. Then he blinked out of existence.

My girlfriend and I reached out and held each other on the couch, silently. Outside, in the streets of Oakland, dogs barked and sirens wailed.

The next thing I remember seeing on the TV was the image of falling bodies as the passengers and crew of Flight 11 opened the cockpit door and tossed the struggling hijackers to their deaths. Some of the reporters gasped. Others cheered.

The survivors of the flights said that when he arrived the Ambassador disarmed the hijackers with a wave of his hand, rounded them up, and asked them a series of questions. None of the survivors understood the language being spoken during that conversation. When I asked Dawson what he thought Future Man and the hijackers had talked about, he just shrugged and said, "Exit interview. Not uncommon in a psychological experiment." Then he went back to digging.

I don't know about you, but I was most impatient with the disbelievers. A bunch of Flat-Earth, the-moon-landing-was-faked, Holocaust-denier types, sure, but ordinary people too. (Then again, it's hard not to have sympathy for the wacky conspiracy theorists, especially since some small subset of them were proved right—the world *is* fake, and everything we know really *is* a lie.) Humans are driven by engines of denial, obstinance, and short-sightedness, whether we're simulated or not. Government officials telling us to disbelieve the evidence of our eyes. Experts talking about mass hysteria, even as other experts—experts at piloting helicopters—hovered over New York rescuing the passengers who were stuck on those frozen planes in New York, and the other plane stopped a handsbreadth from the Pentagon. Flight 93 was close enough to the ground in Pennsylvania when it froze that the local fire department just rescued the passengers with hook-and-ladder trucks and big inflatable pads to cushion the ones too scared or old or frail to climb. And still people argued, shouted on TV, blamed terrorists or Western imperialists, called it a hoax. The scientists tried to be rational, to tell us how deep space had gone suddenly static, no more pulsars pulsing, no more stars exploding—more non-essential services taken offline—but nobody listens to scientists in America. After a few weeks with no babies born, though, with people realizing they didn't get hungry anymore, with the weather never changing, it began to sink in. The first wave of suicides was pretty brutal. Maybe as much as ten percent of the population, dead by their own hands. Nihilism is tough to live with. Me, I was always an atheist. Finding out there was no point to our existence, besides whatever point we create, wasn't too tough for me. Though I did wonder if I'd been robbed of a destiny. I never believed in destiny before, but now I knew there was *literally* a different life I was meant to lead, that I would never have now.

Not as many religious nuts killed themselves as I expected. Those people are adaptable. They came up with whole new weird explanations, most involving the UN and the Antichrist. Just as boring and incomprehensible as the old weird explanations, really.

It was the end of the world, sort of, so I decided to take a road trip. My relationship with Heather didn't even last until the end of September—she was worried about her mom, living all alone in the middle of the country, in the middle of increasing unrest and craziness, and she made arrangements to catch a ride back home with some old friends. There was no discussion of my going with her. In those last days it was like she couldn't see me at all, she just looked beyond me, moved around me without noticing my presence. To be fair, I was probably the same to her. Our world of possibilities had been beheaded. There was nothing else keeping me in Oakland. I'd lived there for about a month, having relocated from Santa Cruz when my old contract job ran out and Heather agreed to let me live with her, so I'd hardly put down roots. I'd only been working at my new job as an editorial assistant for a trade publishing magazine for a few weeks, and the few friends I had weren't close enough to stay for, or else they'd scattered.

So I loaded up my silver Nissan with my worldly possessions—that only just filled the back seat and the trunk, and it was mostly books—and set out East, reversing the course I'd taken thirteen months before, when I left the mountains of North Carolina to seek my fortune.

There were a lot of cars out on the road, a lot of people trying to get to one place from another for whatever reasons of their own. I passed a few crashes, maybe two or three a day, and there were places in the mountains or over rivers where people had clearly just lost their shit, decided there was no point anymore and crashed through guardrails, dropping their simulated cars into simulated rivers and gulches. The radio, especially in the dead stretches at night, were full of preachers, and I listened, because it was that or country-and-western music, and I've got my limits.

I won't lie to you, it was a depressing goddamn journey. I looked into that empty sky and what I missed most were the clouds. The way they used to slide across the sky, like they had someplace to go, but weren't in any particular hurry to get there. That was me, I guess—moving cloudwise, knowing I'd get where I was going eventually. I didn't have a cell phone, which was okay, since they didn't work reliably anymore anyway—neither did pay phones, so I couldn't let Dawson know I was coming, though I tried a few times. I couldn't even be sure he was still there, living in the house we'd shared with a few friends in Boone—he had family farther east, maybe he'd gone to join them in these times of tribulation. But he was one of my dearest friends, the guy who always seemed to know how to deal with anything, from flat tires to financial catastrophe to muggers to bad trips, without even blinking. We'd met at a writing workshop freshman year, when he decided he wasn't really a writer and I decided I really was, and we'd been tight ever since, and were roommates for years. He was a Chinese-Hawaiian military brat who'd trained in more martial arts than I could remember, owned about five swords, smoked incessantly, liked to stay up all night talking about movies, and was no better at playing chess than I was, though he loved it just as much. Who better to spend the end of the world with? Of course, Dawson wasn't perfect. He was shit at romance and creative writing. We used to joke that I was a lover and he was a fighter. Fighting didn't sound bad to me, but what could we possibly fight for? Or with? Or against?

It was a pretty mellow apocalypse, all in all. I mean, nothing was *broken*. Nothing exploded. Driving through Texas I was a little weirded out to see that somebody had attacked the second largest cross in the Western hemisphere, something of a landmark in the area, and one of its arms was hanging broken. Sometimes cars went past me the other way *fast*, and military vehicles, and cops, but I figured they were dealing with little local disasters. I wondered how long people would last in that part of Texas. It was always pretty dry, but there was a difference between "always pretty dry" and "absolutely never getting any rain at all, ever again, *never*." Even cacti die of thirst eventually, right?

But I didn't. I'd gotten used to not eating—I was never hungry, so it just didn't occur to me—but I was filling up the overheated radiator at a filling station in the desert when I realized I hadn't had a drop of anything to drink in a couple of days, not even a caffeinated soda. Didn't much miss drinking, either. I did miss pissing and taking craps, though. I'd done some good thinking while pissing and taking craps. I still *could* eat but it seemed like a lot of hassle, and it's not like many of the highway fast food joints were open. When the world's falling apart, you don't keep your gig as a drive-through attendant.

I'd been sleeping in my car on the side of the road, but I wasn't exactly *tired*, either. Was sleep just a habit, too? That night I drove straight through, and wasn't tired a bit, and didn't notice any bleariness or weariness or psychotic breaks. Maybe there were perks to this apocalypse after all. No sleep meant more time to do . . . Oh, right. There was no point in doing anything. So much for silver linings.

I got to Boone in late afternoon and pulled into the old familiar driveway, the same one I'd pulled away from a bit over a year before. Back then, right after college, I'd shared the little brick house and split the rent with four other guys, and after graduation we'd all gone our separate ways . . . except for Dawson, who'd kept the whole place for himself. He'd studied clinical psych in college, even co-authored a couple of papers (one controversial one about whether violent videogames primed people for real-life violent behavior), but pretty soon after graduating he got into traditional Chinese medicine and started training in acupuncture.

Dawson was sitting on the porch, wearing overalls and all spattered with mud, drinking a beer. He raised his hand to me in a little wave when I pulled into the driveway, like I'd just run out to the store or something. I turned off the car and went up the steps, and he stood up and hugged me. He didn't mind my days-on-the-road stink and I didn't mind his mud smears. I used to say Dawson was one of the few people in the world who, if he called me and said he needed help, I'd hop the next plane, no questions asked. Nowadays the planes aren't flying anymore, but the principle's the same.

"Welcome back, bro," he said. "We shouldn't talk here. Come with me to the basement." He went down the steps and around the house, and I followed for about a dozen paces before I remembered that house didn't have a basement.

"So I've been digging this hole in the ground," Dawson said, nodding to a messy tarp spread out in the backyard. "But the moles started it. You know we always had trouble with them digging tunnels in the yard. I was walking back here, and one of the holes . . . looked funny. It wasn't dark inside. It was bright. So I got a shovel, and started expanding it, and, well . . ." He bent down, grabbed the edge of the tarp, and whipped it aside.

A slanted tunnel drove down into the earth, shored up here and there with two-by-fours, and at the bottom there was . . . a big white glowing nothing.

"What the fuck is that?"

Dawson shrugged. "Do I look like a godlike programmer from beyond the simulation? I'm not sure. But you know how sometimes, when you're playing a video game, you hit a buggy section and suddenly you're moving *under* the terrain? Where you can see the polygons and the colors are reversed or there are no colors at all, because it's not something players are ever meant to see, it's unfinished virtual space? I think this is like that. Come on down."

He slipped into the hole—hence the muddiness—and soon vanished from sight, and after a second I followed him, as I'd followed him into innumerable parties, smoky bars, and dark woods in the years of our friendship. It was a weird descent, half climb, half slide, and eventually we wound up in a cavern about seven feet high and ten feet across, partly dirt, partly that white glowing null-space. There was a shovel and a pick-axe and a few buckets—Dawson was expanding the cavern, chipping away the dirt and roots to expand the whiteness. A couple of tarps hung on the walls, held on with tent spikes driven into the corners. There were also a pair of filthy folding chairs, and Dawson and I sat down.

I looked around. The nullness didn't get any less weird under examination—it was white light that was *also* physical space. "Guess you found a project to keep yourself occupied in the post-apocalypse."

"I could be wrong, but I think it's possible we can talk here without being monitored," Dawson said, leaning forward earnestly. "I think this little room is technically outside the simulation—or under it, anyway. They might not be able to hear us."

"They? Bro, they're not listening. They're gone. They left us here."

Dawson sighed. "I got you into a couple of psychological studies back when we were undergrads, remember?"

"Sure." Mostly filling out questionnaires and answering hypothetical questions and the like. No Stanford Prison Experiment-level weirdness or anything.

"What's the first thing to remember when you become part of an experiment?"

"I was an English major, Dawson, you'll have to refresh my memory."

"The researchers *lie* to you. They tell you the experiment is about one thing—but it's really about another. Because if the research subjects know the *true* purpose of the experiment, they might not act naturally, and the experiment would be contaminated. So they tell you they want to ask you some questions about your buying habits, then lock you in a room alone for hours with nothing but a pitcher of water, because they *really* want to see how long it takes before you overcome your societal training and piss in the corner. Or they tell you they're studying the pain threshold of test subjects receiving electric shocks, when they're *really* testing to see how much pain you're willing to inflict on a stranger just because some guy in a lab coat told you to."

I frowned. "But . . . the study's over . . ."

Dawson shook his head. "I doubt it. The explanation they gave totally falls apart when you start to examine it. They can make it so we don't have babies, don't get hungry, don't get thirsty, and don't sleep, but they can't get rid of disease? They have so much power they're able to convincingly simulate an entire planet, but they can't afford to leave the simulation running quietly in the background, or to download our minds into bodies in the *real* world, outside the simulation? Somebody somewhere on an ethics committee is unwilling to just let us vanish into oblivion, but isn't troubled by the cruel-and-unusual implications of letting us go slowly insane in our fishbowl world? I call bullshit. There's something else going on here."

I felt like I'd had my world turned inside out . . . again. "Like what? What do you think their real purpose is?"

"Who knows? A rat in a maze can't hope to understand the fundamental underpinnings of behavioral science. Maybe it's beyond us entirely."

"So . . . what do we do?"

Dawson grinned. "Well, we can be good rats, and keep running the maze they've built for us."

"Or?"

"Or . . ." He stood and pulled down a tarp on the wall with a flourish, revealing another tunnel—but this one didn't lead to whiteness. It led to trees, lots of trees, a forest of trees . . . sideways trees, the ground to the left, the sky to the right. My head hurt just looking at it.

"Ta da," Dawson said. "The world isn't a globe, Tim, not really. This is all map, no territory. Geography is an illusion here. I was just digging out of curiosity at first, to see how deep the whiteness went, but I found . . . I don't know. A warp. A shortcut to another map. Go through that tunnel, and you pop out sideways in Germany, near the Black Forest. I found another tunnel that leads to Perth, in Australia. International travel is a thing of the past for most people, and the whole communications infrastructure of the world has crumbled. Gas is running out since the oil wells are all empty now. We're going back to basics here. I gotta think, whatever the researchers are really interested in, they want us all isolated, localized, tribal, *fragmented*. Maybe they want to study the collapse of a civilization? Who knows. But we don't have to collapse. We don't have to be fragments. We can keep digging, maybe find more tunnels, and you and me . . ."

"We could walk the earth," I said.

"We could spread the word. Spread the good news. Or the bad news, I guess."

"But even if the researchers can't hear us in this place, they'll notice eventually. What if they fix the bug? Close the shortcuts?"

"Ah," he said, smiling that big broad smile I loved. "Then I'll *know* I'm right. Then I'll have *proof* we aren't just an abandoned simulation, that they're still monitoring us. It's win-win."

I laughed. "And what if they just erase us? Or if the next hole you dig opens up in the bottom of the ocean and we drown?"

"A life without risks is no life at all, Tim."

We go a lot of places, but we can't go everywhere, so we made this little 'zine, this chain letter, and started sending it around. If you've read this, you already know the important thing: the researchers are lying to us. They've got a hidden agenda. Just having that knowledge in your head helps ruin their study—whatever it is. We hope you'll make a copy of this, handwritten or otherwise if you've still got access to working tech, and that you'll pass it on. Or start digging your own hole, and see if you hit a shortcut, and tell whoever you find on the other side. The shortcuts are all over. Maybe they're part of the experiment, Dawson says it's possible, anything is, the researchers are smarter than us, but he told me something else I take comfort in. He said if we were really a historical simulation before, we were constrained by whatever we'd actually done in our original lives, controlled by historical imperatives. But now history is broken, the future is wide open, and we're free. For the first time, we're free. We'd better start acting like it.

Because this shit can't go on. We're not rats, we're not worms, we're not fruit flies—we're sentient. Maybe the researchers *made* us that way, but every abused kid should know you don't owe unconditional loyalty to the ones that made you, and our makers haven't earned our respect. So let's fuck up their game. Let's smash their study. Let's break the experiment. Let's climb on our rooftops and shout, "We *know*, you bastards, we *know* you're lying to us." We'll have the world's largest sit-in, or the world's biggest riot, and maybe the experimenters will pull the plug on us, or maybe they'll erase our memories and put us back in the old maze to live out our old lives, but the minute they do *something*—that's when we know we've won.

And even if they just ignore us, hell—what else do you have to do with the time you've got left on this imaginary Earth?

On my road trip, I spent a lot of time wondering what happened to the real me. The unsimulated Tim. Did I stay with Heather? Did we get married, have children, were we happy? I've always been fascinated by roads left untaken, possibilities unfulfilled, and now I was living in the ultimate wrong path. I used to write stories about regret and parallel universes and many-worlds theory and the god of the crossroads, and now I'm living in one.

Mostly—and I know it's shallow, but if I can't be honest with the anonymous masses of the world, who can I be honest with?—I wondered whether or not the real me ever became a famous writer. If maybe people even in Professor Fuckwit's time read the books I hadn't quite gotten around to writing yet in late 2001. I always wanted to be a famous writer, or, more specifically, I wanted to be a writer so good that fame was just an inevitable side effect—a writer that everyone would read, that everyone would feel compelled to read, a writer who was important, a writer who was *great*. I mentioned that old ambition to Dawson, just now, and he said, "That's a classic example of 'Be careful what you wish for,' bro."

I guess he's got a point. Because you're reading this, aren't you?

David Friedman is a former professional poker player who has placed in many major tournaments including coming in first at the No Limit Hold'em tournament at LA's Hawaiian Gardens Casino back in 2004. He is also a screenwriter and film editor whose work includes everything from documentary films (The Shoe Store) *to softcore porn* (Erotic Confessions). *He is the author of the novel* Rat House. *This is his second published short story.*

"Out of My Sight, Out of My Mind" explores the devastating after-effects of the 9/11 attacks, as seen from inside the mind of a poker-playing telepath.

OUT OF MY SIGHT, OUT OF MY MIND

David W. Friedman

The view out of the plane's window was obscured by clouds. I finished my whiskey and soda and waved at the attendant for another. Hell, why not a double? Flying always scared me. Now, two months after the 9/11 attacks, I was more scared than ever. I didn't know if there would be another hijacking, another plane flying into a building with me strapped into my seat, burned and dead. So, why not a double whiskey and soda?

Traveling, especially on a plane, is grueling for me because I'm telepathic. Ideally, people's thoughts are background chatter, a kind of endless noise that hums like a refrigerator, seldom noticed unless deliberately focused on. However, when there are lots of people in a relatively small space, I can have trouble blocking out the thoughts. Like on this plane. Another reason I drink when I fly, to try to keep the thoughts at bay.

I was flying from San Francisco to New Orleans for a Hold'em poker tournament. The top prize was guaranteed to be two hundred fifty thousand dollars. I planned on getting that money and some extra from the ring games. There were going to be plenty of fish at those tables waiting to get hooked. That was the only reason I risked flying this time, because of all the fish.

I spend more time trying not to read people's minds than reading them. Most people's thoughts aren't interesting. They're thinking about what to buy at the grocery store, where they can find a sale price for a television they really like, whether they locked the front door or not. To get all those random thoughts to just sit in the background takes a lot of energy. As a result I'm not much of a talker. I can get irritated easily if I'm not careful. Knowing a person's most mundane thoughts is a demanding, wearying process. People also see me as being cold and aloof, distant, even taciturn, and I am. It helps with my table image. After all, obfuscation is the hallmark of a good poker player.

Now, with poker I want to read minds. I'm open to every stray thought. I focus on them, figuring out who's not paying attention to their hand, who is looking for the cocktail waitress, who just thought of pocket Kings. Not everyone can have their mind read. Many times I've misread someone's thoughts. They can have a monster hand and simply not let on. That's poker; nothing is a sure thing, even when you can see what your opponents have in their hands.

Usually if I concentrate and blot out the background thoughts I can really home in on my targets. I make exceptionally difficult folds or surprising raises. However, lately, everything has backfired. My top pair turns out to be a loser when someone with a weak hand does the unusual play and runs out a flush. I've had my pocket Aces cracked by some idiot with a seven and a deuce catch a river for two pair. My mind reading sees their cards, but I'm having trouble seeing beyond that, to read how they're going to play those cards. I've become lazy, depending on a surface read. I believe that the harder it is to drown out others' thoughts the more difficult it is to read players' thoughts. I've been running bad and I really need to win this upcoming tournament.

The attendant brought me a fresh drink and I downed it. The racket of minds on the plane was annoying, more so than even a baby crying, and I hoped to drown them out with alcohol. I heard the thoughts of the passenger to my right, who was worried that his marriage was collapsing because he traveled so frequently for his job. The woman in front of me was concerned she'd never get pregnant, and the man behind me and to my right was full of dread over his upcoming cancer screening. I popped a Xanax and hoped I'd fall asleep and let the babble of voices stop for a while.

Soon the whiskey and Xanax started doing their job. I was dozing off, my head tilted to the left, toward the window and the clouds. I felt comfortable, those inner voices receding into the background, my own thoughts dimming as sleep approached. Suddenly, a horrible idea came to me with urgency and immediacy: There was a bomb on the plane. I groggily rose out of my chair, standing bent over under the overhead compartment, the better to scan the cabin, to look intently at each passenger, trying to find even a faint whisper of an act of terror. That whisper turned to a shout as I looked at each person. I felt panic coming from everyone, a fear that the bomb threat was real, yet I couldn't identify the bomber from reading thoughts. Finally I conceded I couldn't read every passenger in time, if there was a bomb; it would take too long. I looked at the man to my right. He was mindlessly thumbing through *Business Week* and worrying about his marriage. He wasn't panicked, he wasn't even conscious. What had I been thinking, where did the thought of danger come from? I don't think my ability is unreliable. Sometimes it doesn't work, but I've never had it give me false information.

"Sir, you'll have to sit down," the flight attendant said. "The captain has put on the seatbelt sign." She thought I was just another drunken passenger who couldn't hold his liquor. What I'd just experienced wouldn't be believed and no one could know about my telepathy. Knowledge of that would ruin my poker career, or I would be mocked as a fraud. Either way, it would be trouble if anyone knew. I sat down and looked out the window, there was nothing but clouds.

I arrived at the downtown Harrah's hotel where the tournament was being held. It was a balmy New Orleans evening in November and it almost blotted out the horrors I'd experienced on the flight over. I was still on edge, despite the Xanax and the booze. As I was checking in, Doc and Mel, two players I knew from the poker circuit, came up to me. They'd driven from Houston and were waiting for their rooms. Doc was an inveterate sports bettor who didn't say much and Mel was a mediocre poker player who liked to cheat on his wife.

"Hey, buddy, how are you? Looking forward to a big win?" Mel said. "You're going to have to do better than that tourney in Atlantic City. Getting crushed by a pair of eights must have stung!" He laughed.

Doc said nothing. He was like Harpo Marx or Teller from Penn & Teller, only without the humor. Mel was joking, but it still hurt.

"I hope to do better this time," I said and turned toward the front desk.

Mel grabbed my arm. I looked at him with a mixture of curiosity and disdain. What did he want? Was it to irritate me further? Did he want to criticize my play some more? I needed to lie down, relax, and get my mind off the flight and onto poker. I was spooked. That terror vision on the plane was something new to me. I didn't know how it happened or what it meant.

"Come out for a drink. The tournament doesn't start until tomorrow. I'll buy you a drink," Mel offered.

I shrugged. I didn't want to carouse. I wanted to lie on the bed in my room and decompress from the flight.

Doc looked at me with a wry smile. I sensed his overwhelming desire to watch basketball. Doc had bet on several games and needed to watch them.

"I don't feel like it. I had a rough flight," I said.

Mel said, "I have a business proposition I'd like to talk about."

"Why not talk to me now?" I asked.

"Come on. It's New Orleans, man! Let's enjoy the Big Easy," Mel said excitedly. "Come on, just a drink and some talk. We haven't seen you since Atlantic City! I'm buying."

I relented and offered to meet them in the lobby in an hour. Mel was happy.

In my room I slammed the door behind me and dropped my suitcase by the bed. I couldn't wait to be by myself. I was stressed from the flight and the onboard incident and annoyed with Mel. He really was an asshole. I shouldn't have agreed to go out with them. I just wanted to lie down and compose myself.

The room was like every other hotel room I'd ever been in for a tournament. It's as if every Hilton or Ramada or Crowne Plaza or Harrah's used one architect and one designer for all their rooms. There was a double bed with a nondescript duvet, and a couple of chairs for all the visitors I'd wouldn't be entertaining. The light brown curtains were open and I could see the lights of the French Quarter beckon me from across Canal Street. I closed them.

I unpacked my case and took a shower. After drying off I put on some underwear and stretched out of the bed. I focused on my own thoughts and not any others. It was easier when I was alone. I concentrated on tamping down any external stimulus and pushed any telepathic thoughts into the background, where they belonged. It was my choice to read a mind, not have someone's thoughts in my head without invitation.

After an hour of rest in the darkened room I dressed. As I steadied myself at the door I took a deep breath to keep my focus and then I walked down the hall to the elevators.

Doc and Mel were waiting for me in the lobby. Mel was particularly elated to see me. It worried me. Doc was nonchalant. He was busy calculating basketball odds in his head. We headed out across Canal Street and after a short walk we stopped at Hooters.

"I thought we were going to a real New Orleans bar," I said.

"This is real. Besides, Doc wants to watch the games."

We entered the restaurant and sat at a table. The place was almost full. The Wizards and Heat game and the Pistons and Hornets game were on most of the televisions as well as CNN's Headline News. Blocking out the mental chatter of the patrons was easy, since all anyone seemed to be thinking about was basketball, titties, and beer. Mel ogled the waitresses and Doc watched the basketball games.

"Isn't this great? It's just like the one in Houston," Mel said. It was like McDonald's, I thought, go into one and you've been in every other one.

I immediately felt uncomfortable. I was still psychically bruised from my unexplained incident on the plane. I needed more time to recuperate. Instead, I was in Hooters. I really wanted to be in a good local restaurant eating oysters and gumbo.

"I love the waitresses here," Mel said. I nodded.

I asked him about the business proposition. He shook his head.

"Not yet. Let's have a drink first."

A waitress came over and took our order. Mel had his eyes at a level with her breasts and he had a huge grin on his face. I scanned his mind and all I got was sexual desire . . . boring stuff. Mel watched her ass as she left with our order.

"Man, she's one hot bitch," Mel said, shaking his head.

Doc, who was watching the game and hadn't looked at her once, said, "She sure is."

The table fell into an awkward silence. I didn't have the energy to figure out what Mel and Doc wanted from me. I'd let them reveal it later. I went back to the drone of background thoughts.

After a time the waitress brought our drinks. I sipped at my whiskey and soda while Mel adjusted himself in his seat and leaned toward me.

"Doc and I have a plan. We pool our resources and back each other. We funnel our chips to you so you have a commanding lead. You go the final table. When it's over we split three ways." The words tumbled out of Mel's mouth. Doc was actually looking at me and not the games. He wanted to see my reaction.

"Why me?" I asked.

"Because you have a way for reading players that Doc and I don't. We're aggressive early on, we can accumulate chips, but we get challenged by players later in the tournaments and our stacks get smaller. You don't do that. You pick your moves and you usually win those hands. If you had our chip stacks you'd be unstoppable," Mel said.

I didn't like it. I had a style of play that suited my unique abilities. Reading a person's mind to find out their hole cards gave me an advantage, but it wasn't like I could read the future and see what the next five cards were going to be. Winning wasn't an absolute.

"That's your plan? If I make the final table we split three ways?" I asked.

Before Mel spoke I glanced at a television and caught a glimpse of CNN. Footage of the planes flying into the twin towers filled the screen and suddenly I was there.

I was falling from a tall building hundreds of stories up. There was black smoke and I dived right through it, and I could see the ground rising up to me. I could smell the acrid odor of burnt plastic. I was falling and falling until was on the ground. Then, suddenly, that vision was over and I was right back in Hooters, only the background drone was gone.

"Are you okay?" Mel asked and looked at my face. He said, "You're pale as a ghost."

"I don't know. I, I, don't know."

I tried reading Mel's mind but there was nothing there, a complete blank. Then the familiar hum of many people's thoughts filled my mind again.

I downed the remainder of my drink. I needed the alcohol to settle me down. My mind wandered back to the strange falling sensation I'd just had. It wasn't like a thought. I saw it like I was falling through the air, the ground coming up fast and I was going to die. I couldn't explain it. I hadn't read someone's thoughts; who could think that vividly of something so horrific? This was something else.

I decided that I'd had enough of Hooters and Doc and Mel. I didn't feel well. The psychic event on the flight and now this all-too-realistic sensation was exhausting.

"I'm going back the hotel. I don't feel well."

"You look like shit," Doc said, looking at me for the first time.

"Yeah, you're looking a little green around the gills," Mel said. "Get some rest so you can play tomorrow. Think about my offer."

I returned to my room and soaked a washcloth in cool water. I laid it across my forehead and stretched out in the bed. I felt queasy, as if I had just come off a rough sea voyage. I didn't know what was happening to me, if it was telepathy or psychosis.

I woke up late the next day. I was hungry since I hadn't eaten dinner the night before. I hurried down to the hotel restaurant; I had just enough time for breakfast before the tournament began. I regretted not being able to see some of New Orleans, a city I hadn't visited since I was a child. I should have ventured out on my own last night, instead of going to Hooters with Doc and Mel. I could have seen some of the sights, gone to Café du Monde, had a drink on Bourbon Street, maybe I wouldn't have had that strange falling sensation.

I wondered what those hallucinations had been. Maybe they were stress related, traveling so soon after 9/11. Two planes had flown into New York City's Twin Towers and nothing was the same since. The world didn't stop after the attacks, but you could feel a difference. There were hours of security check-ins at the airport; armed shoulders with rifles, machine guns, and shotguns; police were wearing camouflage gear and military helmets. There was a subtle loss of freedom, of movement, of liberty. I was a kind of waking nightmare and it put me on edge.

Regardless, I needed to ready myself for the tournament. I had to reassure myself that I had the ability to come in the money, if not win the whole thing. After twenty years of playing poker I had enough skills to battle any opponent. The mind-reading was just an added tool to my repertoire of poker plays. Ninety-nine percent of my game was based on probabilities and logic, not telepathy.

As I was finishing breakfast Doc and Mel sat down at my table. I didn't have to be a mind reader to know what was coming.

"How are you feeling?" Mel asked.

"Better, thanks," I said. I paused. I wanted Mel to start the conversation about the deal.

"Are you in?"

"No, I'm not in. It's cheating. If we get caught we'll never be able to live it down. We will be banned from all future tournaments," I stated.

"No one will find out."

"They won't because I'm not in. I can win this thing on my own, without your help." Besides Mel's plan being unethical, if I did come in the money I didn't want to split three ways.

"You'd better watch out then. If we're on the same table, we're going to steamroll you," Mel threatened. Doc nodded. I almost laughed at their tough guy act. They didn't know what I could do to them if I wanted to. Their chips would be mine.

The tournament was held in the ballroom of the hotel. It was a large space that held over forty poker tables. There were chandeliers; otherwise, the room was without ornamentation. Functional and utilitarian, just like the rest of the hotel. There were at least two hundred players, all of whom had paid a fifteen-hundred-dollar entry fee. The prize pool was at least three hundred thousand dollars, beating the casino's guarantee of two hundred fifty thousand. As I walked to my seat there were still people buying in. There might be more than two hundred fifty players before the cutoff.

I was on table nine. There were ten players to a table. When someone got knocked out, they brought a player from another table to even things out, or they'd "break" the table and send the players to other tables to even those out. It would be a long time before that happened. With a deep starting stack of five thousand chips, forty-five-minute levels, and blinds beginning at twenty-five and fifty, we'd probably be keeping each other company for five or six hours.

At my table were the usual suspects: a forty-something Chinese man, an elderly Chinese woman, a Persian gentleman, a Korean man, a Russian man, two nondescript white Southern men, a middle-aged African American woman, and a rotund man with silver hair and a gold diamond-studded lucky horseshoe pinkie. He also had a large Rolex watch. Ostentatious displays of wealth on the table say "Winner." He was the only one that concerned me, so I was going to read his mind.

He was quite demonstrative and jovial, talking to his neighbors on the table. He was laughing and joking and taking big swigs of coffee from the cup in front of him.

"Where are you from?" I asked him. This was a common question at a large tournament.

"Dallas, Texas," he replied, and I knew he was lying. His read mind said he was from Tunica, Mississippi. Now, if he'd lie about that with an even tone of voice, what else would he do as the tournament progressed? Tunica was the gambling Mecca of the South. This shark fed on the tourist chum that visited there.

"Where are you from?" he asked me and I told him the Bay Area. He nodded sagely, as if my answer was deeply profound instead of a statement of residence. Then everyone on the table piped in: New Orleans! Houston! Baton Rouge! Boston! Los Angeles!

I tried not to lose focus on the fat man. He was amused, a gambler's mind conditioned to stay aware despite hours of tedious poker playing. I've heard poker described as the old cliché of watching paint dry, but it was even more boring when you played it for hours in a tournament. Fewer hands were played than in a cash game and you tried to protect your stack of chips more. The average large two-day tournament lasted anywhere from twelve to sixteen hours a day. You had to keep part of your mind on the game, to see how people played, what they played, how they bet. Telepathy helped since I could scan a player's mind to see their hole cards. However, if they were unfocused players, or distracted by something else, I couldn't get a read on their hand. Then it was up to good guessing and the use of probabilities like everyone else. I'd say telepathy gave me an edge, but at times it was negligible. They drew the cards for the dealer button, the person who is last to act. I got caught as the big blind, which is a forced bet to invoke action on the table. Without a big blind or the small blind, which is half the big blind, the game would stall and there would never be a winner.

The first hand was dealt. I relaxed and let the drone of people's thoughts wash over me, as I fine-tuned my focus on my "enemy," the fat, boisterous man from Tunica. I knew he was going to be tough; everyone else on the table was average and ordinary. At least that's what I thought.

The man from Tunica wasn't making any big plays early. I did a test to see if what I saw in his mind matched what his cards were. I chose a few hands where he raised the pot before the flop. I assumed he had a pocket pair or Ace/King or Ace/Queen. Then I would read his mind and see his cards. I was surprised once; he made a raise with six/eight of clubs and was called by one of the Southern gents. He caught lucky with two eights on the flop for three of a kind, and the other player had a pair of Jacks. We all got to see that one since he revealed his cards to claim the pot. So far there were no other surprises, so I decided to expand my telepathy to include the Russian and the man from Baton Rouge.

My first read on the Russian was that he was passive. He had a deuce/seven off-suit and he folded. I then read the other player, the one from Baton Rouge, and he held pocket Kings and raised three times the pot. I smirked and quickly caught myself and put on a blank expression. The surprise came when the Persian from Los Angeles, who I wasn't observing, re-raised all-in. I tried to read his mind to see what he had, but I couldn't get a fix. He was thinking about ordering a drink. He must have two Aces, I thought. It had to be pocket Aces.

The pocket Kings called and the player I thought had Aces, in fact, held Ace/Queen of Diamonds. It was certainly not a hand worth risking your entire tournament. The flop, the first three shared cards, was Ace, Nine, Ten with two Diamonds. So far the all-in player was in the lead. The next card, the turn, was the King of Hearts, giving the pocket Kings three of a kind. The river was the deuce of Spades and the all-in player was out of the tournament. I tried scanning his mind, but all I read was "cocktails." Weird. Why was he thinking about cocktails? He wasn't particularly perturbed that he was out of the tournament.

I tangled with the man with the horseshoe ring once. I had Ace/King of Clubs, on the button before the flop, meaning I was the last to act before the small and big blinds had their chance, and decided to raise three times the value of the pot. Ace/King suited is a powerful starting hand, especially on the button. The small blind folded and the big blind was the man from Tunica. He hesitated and I decided to read his mind. I discovered he had a pair of Queens. He paused either for effect or he genuinely needed time to think. As I scanned his mind for more information, he raised it four times what I had raised it. He thought I might have pocket Jacks or exactly what I had, the Ace/King suited. I waited an appropriate amount of time and threw my hand in the muck. I was a huge dog in that one. I regretted I didn't read his hand before I raised it. It would have saved me chips.

We had a few players leave our table and new ones join before we broke for dinner at seven o'clock. I really wanted gumbo but the hotel's restaurant didn't serve that so I had a burger and fries with a soda. With only a forty-five-minute meal break there wasn't time leave the hotel to eat. Mel and Doc walked by while I ate and gave me the stink-eye. They weren't doing well. They were on separate tables and Doc didn't have the opportunity to push his stack to Mel on a bogus all-in play. They had to fight for their chips like the rest of us.

Back on the tables at seven forty-five, there were only one hundred fifteen players left out of the original two hundred thirty-seven entrants. They were lots of players who thought their hands were worth going all-in. This meant lots of players with huge stacks in front of them, making it difficult to tangle with them. Our man from Tunica, Mississippi, was one of them. Although our table hadn't broken yet, I had put two players all-in and emerged victorious, but I didn't need any special abilities to do it. I had pocket Aces both times and they held up.

Around eleven o'clock, after me poking the bear a couple of times, so to speak, and not getting a rise, our table broke and I was moved to another. All new players to figure out and I was getting tired. Nine hours of poker can sap your energy so I did a quick scan of all the minds. They were all good players, or they wouldn't have lasted so long, and they were all as tired as I was. Some had been drinking, others stayed sober. Two players were smokers and were thinking about when to leave the table to have a cigarette. It didn't take long; fifteen minutes later one said he was going to smoke on his big blind, and the other joined him.

There was a man with a thin gold chain around his neck. He was wearing a blue running suit and a Yankees cap. It didn't take telepathy to know he was a New Yorker. I decided to check him out and when I read his mind I learned one single true thought. His outer appearance was calm, maybe a little angry, and confident, but it was an act. He was scared.

The tournament director announced that they were paying twenty-seven places and the top prize was one hundred seventeen thousand dollars. Second place was a little more than seventy-five thousand. He also said that we would break for the day and return tomorrow when we were down to four tables. Right now we were at seven.

The last hand of the night occurred around three in the morning. I was heads up against the New Yorker; our stacks were about the same size. I didn't even have to read his mind; I had pocket Jacks and all his money was going into the pot if I had anything to do about it, which I did. We got all-in and he turned over his hand, it was pocket Tens. I had him crushed. Someone at the table said, "The Twin Towers," referring to the Tens resembling two buildings, like the World Trade Center.

Suddenly the New Yorker's thoughts were filled with what happened on 9/11. He was scared, he was there! He'd been in an elevator at Ground Zero as the plane hit the tower. The elevator had shaken and landed on the ground floor violently. The doors opened and he ran. Then, *I* was on the plane as it banked left and rammed into the building. The aluminum peeled off the body of the plane as the engines kept pushing the jet through the tower. A fireball rolled down the aisle, scorching the passengers. I could smell jet fuel and burning flesh. Then it was over.

I was shaking, it was so vivid, so real, yet here I was, sitting at a poker table in New Orleans. The dealer was pushing the chips to the New Yorker; he had caught a Ten on the river and beat me with three of a kind. I looked at the board, incredulous. I had lost. I managed to mumble "Nice hand" and take a look at the survivor.

It was strangely quiet. Not the ballroom, people were talking excitedly about the hand I had just played, but I noticed the absence of background thoughts. There were no voices; they were gone. I walked away from the table. There was nothing but the feeling of losing, of losing everything.

After a night of troubled sleep I awoke early. I showered and dressed and had breakfast in the hotel's restaurant. Without the constant drone of background thoughts I was lost. I had always thought it would liberate me, but I'd grown accustomed to it and now it felt peculiar without it. A vital part of my being was gone. I tried to read the waitress's mind and came up blank. I stared at people, hoping that a small spark of their thoughts would show up, but there was nothing. My gift was gone.

I was disappointed I didn't place in the tournament. Mel and the New Yorker went on to the final table and won thousands of dollars each. I was devastated by the vision of 9/11 and the loss of my telepathy. I pondered a life without it, but I hoped that it also meant an end to those visions of a horrific act of terror. Perhaps my mind reading had made me terse and unemotional and this was the final straw. I can't say for certain, and I can't talk to anyone about it. How could I explain?

I decided to play in the cash games to get my bankroll back in shape. It was missing fifteen hundred dollars plus the airfare and the hotel. I didn't want to take that debt; I would prefer to free roll it through ring games. I sat down to play without any aids, just the years of experience playing poker. It was going to be hard work.

On Monday I flew back to San Francisco three thousand dollars lighter in my pockets. I lost it playing pocket Kings against a nominal player who had Ace/King off-suit. He hit an Ace on the flop and that was that. I would have played it the same way even if I could read his mind.

Stephen King once described Jack Ketchum as "one of the best in the [horror] business, on a par with Clive Barker and James Ellroy." A Bram Stoker and Grand Master award-winner, many of Ketchum's novels have been adapted for film, including The Girl Next Door *and* The Lost. *Significantly, Ketchum lives in New York City.*

"Closing Time" is the title story in Ketchum's 2014 short story collection from Crossroad Press. It is a novella about, among other things, adultery and armed robbery. The evil on display here is frighteningly nihilist and the entire tale echoes the culture-wide dread brought on by the attacks.

 # CLOSING TIME
Jack Ketchum

Lay upon the sinner his sin,
Lay upon the transgressor his transgression . . .

—Epic of Gilgamesh

Only the dead have seen the end of war.

—Plato

October 2001

ONE

Lenny saw the guy in his rearview mirror, the guy running toward him trying to wave him down at the stoplight, running hard, looking scared, a guy on the tall side and thin in a shiny blue insulated parka slightly too heavy for the weather—one seriously distressed individual. Probably that was because of the other beefy citizen in his shirtsleeves chasing him up 10th Avenue.

Pick him up or what?

Traffic was light. Pitifully light ever since World Trade Center a month ago. New York was nothing like it used to be traffic-wise. And it was late, half past one at night. He had the green now. Nobody ahead of him. No problem just to pull away.

And suppose he did. What was the guy gonna do? Report him to the Taxi and Limousine Commission?

You had to figure that a chase meant trouble. For sure the guy in his shirtsleeves meant trouble if he ever caught up to the poor sonovabitch. You could read the weather on his face and it was Stormy Monday all the way down the line.

Get the hell out of here, he thought. *You got a wife and kids.* Don't be stupid. 10th and 59th was usually a pretty safe place to be these days but you never could tell. Not in this town. You've been driving for nearly thirty years now. You know better. So what if he's white, middle-class. So what if you need the fare.

He lifted his foot off the brake but he'd hesitated and by then the guy was already at the door. He flung it open and jumped inside and slammed it shut again.

"Please!" he said. "*That guy back there . . . his goddamn wife . . . Jesus!*"

Lenny smiled. "I got it."

He glanced at the American flag on his dashboard and thought, *I love this fucking town.*

The beefy citizen was nearly on them, coming down off the curb just a couple steps away. Lenny floored it.

They slid uptown through time-coordinated greens like a knife through warm butter.

"Where to?"

"Take it up to Amsterdam and 98th, okay?"

"Sure. No problem." He looked at the guy through the rear-view, the guy still breathing hard and sweating. Glancing back out the window, still worried about shirtsleeves. Like his ladyfriend's irate hubby had found some other cab and was hot on his tail. It only happened in the movies.

"So what's the story, you don't mind my asking? You mean you didn't know?"

"Hell, no, I didn't know. It was a pickup in a bar. She's got her hand on my leg for godsakes. It's going great. Then this guy shows up. Says he's gonna push my face in! Jesus, I never even paid the bar tab! I just got the hell out of there. Thank god for you, man!"

Lenny reflected that nobody had ever thanked god for him before. Not that he could remember. It was a first.

Your Good Deed for the Day, he thought. From the look of the shirt-sleeves, maybe for the month.

"So you go back, you pay your tab another time. No problem."

"I don't even know the name of the place. I just wandered in."

"Corner of 58th and 10th? That would be the Landmark Grill."

The guy nodded. He saw it in the rear-view mirror.

And there was something in the guy's face right then he didn't like. Something nasty all of a sudden. Like the guy had gone away somewhere and left a different guy sitting in the back seat who only looked like him.

Ah, the guy's had a hard night, he thought.

No babe. No pickup. Almost got his ass kicked for his trouble. You might be feeling nasty too.

They drove in silence after that until Lenny dropped him at Amsterdam and 98th, northeast corner. The guy said thanks and left him exactly fifteen per cent over the meter. Not bad but not exactly great either, considering. The next fare took him to the East Side and the next four down to the Village and then Soho and Alphabet City and then to the Village again. He never did get back to Tenth or even to Hell's Kitchen for that matter.

So it was only when he returned to the lot at the end of his shift that he learned from his dispatcher that the Landmark Grill had been robbed at gunpoint by a tallish, thin sandy-haired man in a parka. Who got away in a cab, for chrissake. Everybody was buzzing about it because he'd used a goddamn cab as getaway. Thought it was pretty funny.

That and the fact that the bartender had been crazy enough to chase him.

A guy with a gun. You had to be nuts to risk it.

Or maybe you had to be bleeding from the head where the guy had used the butt end of his gun on you. Lenny hadn't managed to catch that little detail in the rear-view.

There was never any question in his mind about calling the cops. If they didn't have his medallion number then so be it. You didn't want to get involved in something like this unless you had to. But Lenny thought about his fifteen per cent over the meter and wondered what the take was like.

No good deed ever goes unpunished his mother used to say.

He hated to admit it but as in most things, he supposed his mom was right.

TWO

At first Elise was embarrassed by them. No—for them.

First embarrassed. Then fascinated.

And then she couldn't look away.

The train was real late—she'd wondered if it was another bomb scare somewhere up the line, it would be just her luck to miss her dance class entirely and it was the only class she could care about at all—so that the platform was crowded and getting more so, mostly kids like her just out of school for the day and thank god it was over, nobody but Elise seeming to care if the train was late or not, the noise level enormous with the echo of kids shouting, laughing, arguing, whatever.

For sure these two over by the pillar there didn't care. She doubted they even noticed the kids swarming around them. Much less the lateness of the train.

She had never seen a pair of adults so . . . *into* one another.

But it wasn't a good thing.

It was terrible. And it was going on and on.

They were probably in their thirties, forties—Elise couldn't tell but she thought they were younger than her mother—and the woman was a little taller than the man who was almost as cute, for an old guy, as she was pretty. Or they would have been cute and pretty if their faces didn't keep . . . *crumbling* all the time.

They kept hugging and pulling apart and staring at each other as though trying to memorize one another's faces and then hugging again so hard she thought it must have hurt sometimes, she could see the man's fingers digging deep into the back of her blouse. And both of them were crying, tears just pouring down their cheeks and they didn't even bother to try to wipe them away half the time, they mostly just let them come.

She saw them stop and smile at each other and the smiles were worse than the tears. *My god, they're so sad.* And smiling seemed to bring the tears on again, like they were one and the same, coming from the very same place. It was like they couldn't stop. Like she was watching two hearts breaking for ever and ever.

She was already ten or fifteen feet away from them but she found herself stepping back without even knowing at first she was doing it. It was as though there were some kind of magnetic field around them that repelled instead of pulling, as though they were pushing out at empty space, in order to give them space, all the space they needed to perform this horrible dance.

I meant what I said, you know that, right? she heard the woman tell him and he nodded and took her in his arms again and she missed what the woman said after that but then they were crying again though real silently this time and then she heard the woman say I just can't anymore and then they were crying hard again, really sobbing, clutching each other and their shoulders shaking and she wanted to look away because what if they noticed her staring at them but somehow she knew that they weren't going to notice, they weren't going to notice anything but each other.

They were splitting up, she knew now. At first she'd thought maybe they had a kid who'd died or something. I just can't anymore. The woman was dumping him but she didn't want to because they still loved each other. And they loved each other so much—she'd never seen two people that much in love. She wasn't even sure she'd ever seen it in the movies.

So how could you do that? How could you just break up if you felt that way? How was it even possible?

She noticed that some of the other kids were watching too and would go silent for a while. Not as intently as Elise was watching and mostly the girls but there on the platform you could feel it pouring out of these people and it was getting to some of the other kids as well. Something was happening to them that she had the feeling only adults knew about, something secret played out right out there in the open. Something she sensed was important. And a little scary.

If this was what being an adult was all about she wanted no part of it. *And yet she did.*

To be in love that much? God! So much in love that nothing and nobody matters but the two of you standing together right where you're standing, oblivious to everybody, just holding holding tight and feeling something, somebody, so much and deep. It must be wonderful.

It must be awful.

It must be both together.

How? How could that be?

So that as the train roared in and kids crowded into the car, Elise behind them, wiping at her own tears which only served to confuse her more now, the woman stepped on a little behind her to the side and turned to the window, hands pressed to the dirty cloudy glass to watch him standing there alone on the platform and somehow smaller-looking without her and Elise looked from one to the other and back again and saw their shattered smiles.

THREE

She put down the paper and washed her hands in the sink. As usual the Sunday *Times* was filthy with printer's ink. She went back to her easel in the living room. Her lunch break was over. The pastel was coming along.

She had that much, anyway. The work.

What did you expect? she thought. When things got bad they were probably bound to get worse. If only for a little while.

She hoped it was only for a little while.

Because she was seriously doubting, for the very first time ever, her actual survival here.

Everybody in the city was fragile, she guessed. No matter where you were or who you were World Trade had touched you somehow. Even if you'd lost nobody close to you, you'd still lost something. She knew that was part of it.

She could look at a cat in a window and start to cry.

And breaking off with David would have been bad enough under any circumstances—correction, still was bad enough. Because he wouldn't quite let go and neither could she exactly. Lonely late-night emails still were all too common between them.

I understand you can't see me, I understand it hurts too much to keep see-ing me and I'm sorry. But I miss just talking to you too. We always talked, even through the worst of it. Emails just don't work. I feel like I've lost not only my

lover but my friend. Please—call me sometime, okay? I want my friend back.
I want her bad.
　　Love, David.

　　I can't call. Not yet. Someday maybe but not now. I'd call and we'd talk
and the next step would be seeing you and you know that. Why do you want to
make me go through this again, David? Jesus! You say you understand but you
don't seem to. You're not going to leave her and that's that. And I need somebody
who'll be there for me all the time, not just a couple nights a week. I miss you too
but you're not that person, David. You can't be. And I can't simply wish that
away. So please, for a while, just please leave me be.
　　Love, Claire.

　　She knew he was hurting and she hated that because there was so much
good between them and the love was still there. She hated hurting him. But
she was alone and he wasn't. So she also knew who was hurting the worst.
She was. She was tired of crying herself to sleep every night he wouldn't be
there next to her or every morning when he'd leave. It had to stop.
　　He'd never stop it. It was up to her.
　　She'd been alone most of her life but that was always basically okay.
She liked her own company. She'd always been a loner.
　　But she'd never felt this lonely.
　　What was that Bob Dylan line? *I'm sick of love.*
　　She knew exactly how he felt when he wrote it.
　　Fuck it, she thought, *get to work. You're an artist. So make art.*

The piece was one of a series, a still-life, an apple core surrounded by
chains. A padlock lay open, gleaming, embracing one of the links of chain.
　　She studied it.
　　She knew exactly what it meant. Most people didn't. That was fine,
so long as they felt it.
　　And bought one now and then.
　　Which hadn't happened in a while now.
　　Concentrate, she thought. Focus. Work the blacks. Work the
shadows.
　　But that was the other thing. Money. Cold hard cash. Financially her
life was a mess too. She'd only just started painting again—David was the
main one who'd encouraged her, dammit!—had only sold a few pieces for

good but not terrific money, and the New York restaurant business, which she'd always counted on as backup, had been hit hard by the Bush economy even before World Trade Center. Tourism was down to a fraction of what it was this time last year and the natives were paranoid about going out to dinner. In the past three months she'd been laid off as a bartender, hired as a waitress, laid off as a waitress, hired as a manager—a job she'd always loathed—and then laid off as a manager too.

She was always assured it was a matter of cutbacks, not her performance. Last hired, first fired. Simple as that.

She'd been making the rounds. Nobody was hiring.

So that at the moment she was jobless, with two months' rent and utilities in the bank and if she didn't find something soon she was going to have to eat this apple core off the canvas.

It's Sunday, she thought. You can't do a damn thing about it now.

So make the art. Later, call your mother.

Get on with it. All of it.

She drew a line, smudged it lightly with her finger. A link of chain sprung suddenly into focus on the canvas. She drew another.

FOUR

What the hell are you doing? he thought.

It was two in the morning. He was standing outside across the street from her apartment. He could see the light burning through the second-floor living room window. Either she was still awake or she'd fallen asleep and left it on but to leave it on was very unlike her.

She was awake.

He could walk up the steps, ring the bell.

No he couldn't.

He had no right to. It would be tantamount to harassment.

And standing out here was tantamount to stalking.

So what the hell are you doing, David?

A glimpse, he thought. That's all. A glimpse of somebody you love through a brownstone window. What the hell is wrong with that?

Everything. It's crazy, desperate. It's pathetic. You're not Romeo and she's not Juliet. Go the hell home.

Don't want to.

Your wife is waiting.

By now she'll be fast asleep.

You've had too much to drink again.

So? What else is new?

Go home.

A cab cruised past him going west. Northwest was the direction of his apartment. The cab's sign was lit. He could have flagged it down. A simple wave of the hand. He didn't. He needed something. He wanted to feel something.

Now what the hell does that mean?

59th was quiet. No breeze. Nobody on the street but him. There was traffic heading south on 9th half a block away but not here and even on 9th the traffic was light, he could barely hear it hissing by.

So here he was, alone. Staring up at a living room window and afraid to look away or even to blink for fear that if he did it would be exactly that moment she'd choose to appear and not any other moment and not again, afraid of the perversity of incident and chance, perhaps because it was precisely incident and chance that had got him here in the first place. She a new bartender, he a regular. Quickly becoming friends, far more slowly becoming lovers—two years before that happened—not until a casual date that left them alone in a crowded noisy new dance club they found not to their liking at all, waiting for two other friends to return from the bar so they could get the hell out of there, a single slightly boozy hug turning to a surprisingly lovely kiss and then more and more and before they knew it two more years had gone by and love had trapped them as surely incident and chance could trap anyone.

The window blurred over.

He wiped his eyes.

He was aware of sirens in the distance, somewhere around Times Square.

The window blurred again.

Were the sirens doing this? Some fucking ambulance making him cry? Somebody else's distress? Some stranger's? It was possible. These days anything was.

But that was too damn ridiculous even for him and no, he saw what it was now, literally saw it in that way that the mind imposes an image it chooses over the eyes so that what the eyes see in the natural world disappears for a moment, unable to compete, utterly sterile compared to the image the brain mandates. He saw it, vividly, sobbed once because he knew that in the natural world he might never see it again and certainly not the way he did now, directed so wholly at him—her open happy smile—and turned and started home.

FIVE

The composite on the nightly news was not great.

They'd got the nose right and the chin mostly but the forehead was way too high and the eyes were completely wrong because the eyes in the composite were bland, they held nothing, while his were full of . . .

. . . *what?*

Something. He didn't bother trying to go there.

They were off on the numbers too. They had him down for around fifteen, twenty jobs this year. He had to laugh. The number was more like thirty, thirty-five. Roughly one every week and a half. He figured that by the end of his own personal fiscal year which began and ended on his birthday just before Christmas he'd take in fifty, maybe sixty grand. Not as much as if you were robbing banks but bars were a whole lot safer. Bars were vulnerable.

For one thing you didn't work in daylight except to cruise for likely joints to hit. You didn't have much in the way of surveillance cameras to worry about. And you didn't have some retired cop with an attitude, some asshole armed guard willing and stupid enough to start blazing away at you.

It was a pretty rare bartender who was willing to die for the till and his tips.

That guy last week, though. That asshole actually *chasing* him.

He thought he'd put the fear of god in him. Especially that last hard whack on the head. He guessed there had to be a first time for everything.

Usually the getaway was simple. You headed for the nearest subway, didn't matter where you went once you were on it. If there was a bus handy you caught that. You got off and had a beer or two at another bar far away and then you went on home.

They'd worried out loud on the news about his gun. Some police lieutenant mouthing off. Said that seeing as he had a gun, sooner or later he was going to use it. That was bullshit. His weapons were surprise and fear. The gun was only window dressing. Loaded window dressing but window dressing all the same.

Then they tried to link him up to a wider trend. All very ominous. Seems that shootings in the City were up twenty-four per cent over the same month last year—the figure spiked by the thinned ranks of the NYPD who were now on anthrax, security, and Ground Zero duty since World Trade Center instead of manning street crime.

Again, bullshit. He wasn't part of any goddamn trend. He just did what he always did.

Plain old-fashioned armed robbery.

He sat on the sofa and sipped his beer. The composite didn't worry him. Except for the eyes he was blessed with one of those more or less *basic* faces, a kind of no-frills face, one that set off no bells and whistles in anybody. Acceptable—that was how he liked to think about it. Acceptable enough so that guys had no reason either to fear him, be impressed or intimidated by him or even to remember him for that matter. Acceptable enough to women so that he got himself some pussy now and then. Not a hard face and not soft. No scars, no dimples, no cleft palates or cleft chins.

The composite didn't work. His face was far too mutable.

The hair you could cut or color. For the line of forehead, a hat or a baseball cap. You could change the eyes with colored contact lenses or no-scrip glasses or just by trimming down your eyebrows a bit. Or darkening them with eyebrow pencil.

He thought eyebrows were seriously underrated.

You wanted to avoid a good tan. A good tan was memorable to New Yorkers, who were used to pallor. You made the mistake getting of a tan, you powdered it. Physique was changeable as the goddamn weather. You're on the tall side like he was? five-eleven? So you're stoop-shouldered now and then. You flex the knees. Build? Baggy sweaters or business clothes one time, jeans and tee-shirt the next.

Backpack on one job, shopping bag or briefcase on another.

He finished the beer and frowned at New York One. New York One was supposed to be about New York City, wasn't it? But now they were going on and on about the fucking anthrax again. If it wasn't the anthrax it was the fucking war in Afghanistan or else the fucking World Trade Center. Who cared if some senator's assistant or postal clerk got anthrax—inhaled, cutaneous, or shot up the ass? Who cared if the towelheads took out skyscrapers?

He strictly worked ground-floor.

They ended with some puff piece about this guy who had to be the most politically correct asshole on the face of the earth—some Westchester dentist who was offering to buy up all the neighborhood kids' Halloween candy so they didn't rot their teeth. Fuck their teeth. He turned the damn thing off and got up and tossed the beer can into the sink.

Time to get.

In the bathroom shaving he glanced down at his various toiletry items and got a really great idea.

"You're lucky," the bartender said. "I was just about to tell my friend here last call. What'll it be?"

"Miller, thanks."

"Miller coming up."

The barkeep's friend probably didn't know him from Adam. His friend looked to have been on a long night's pub crawl and only one step up from blue-collar, if that, while this was clearly a kids' bar, Barrow and Hudson, pool table and concert posters, "Sweet Home Alabama" on the jukebox and the bartender not much more than a kid himself. Wire-rim glasses, rosy cheeks, spiked hair, good strong build under the tee-shirt. Irish maybe.

"Gettin' cold out there?"

The kid poured a half glass of Miller into the beer mug and set it down in front of him.

"Nah. Good breeze, though."

The barkeep took his twenty to the register. The guy next to him downed his beer and mumbled thanks and slid off the barstool and tapped his dollar fifty with his forefinger. He was tipping the bartender one fifty. Big spender. He put his hands in his pockets and headed for the door. Which meant that this was going very nicely indeed.

"G'night. Thank you, sir. You take care now."

The barkeep put his change in front of him. Scooped up his tip and dropped it in the bucket.

He slipped on the surgical gloves.

"*You* take care," he said.

"S'cuse me?"

They said that a lot. *You take care.* You said it back to them, it threw them off balance. Maybe even started to worry them right then and there.

But this kid was only puzzled.

He slid the .45 out from behind his sport jacket. Rested it flat on the bar pointed at the barkeep's trim flat belly.

"I said *you* take care. Now, listen real carefully and you'll get to go home tonight to your girlfriend. Let's say I'm an old college buddy of yours and I'm closing up with you, so you do what you do every night, only I'm here. That's how I want you to act. I'm just here having a drink. You lock the door and hit the lights outside and you dim the ones in here. Only difference is after that you go to the register and instead of counting it you empty it into this bag."

He handed the Big Brown Bag from Bloomie's across the counter.

"Open it and put it on the floor. That's it. Very good. Now go about your business. And don't even think about opening that door. I know you really want to but see, it takes too long to open it, throw it back and then go through. You'll be dead by the time you hit the sidewalk, believe me. They've already got me down twice for Murder One"—it was a lie but it always worked—"so it doesn't mean a thing to me one way or the other. I'm a very good shot, though. So it would mean a lot to you."

For emphasis he clicked off the safety.

He could smell it then, that faint ammonia smell or something like ammonia. Bleach maybe. Fear-sweat coming off the guy. Fear cleansing the guy, pouring through the fat and skin all the way up from the organs, the organs unwilling to cease their function, unwilling to give up the pulse.

He put the gun between his legs and swiveled on the stool smiling as the guy moved on shaky legs out from behind the bar and fished his keys out of his pocket, locked the door, put them back in his pocket and reached behind a tall brown sad potted cactus and flicked off the outside lights.

"The dimmer's over here, okay?"

The guy was pointing across the room to another half-dead fern or something.

"Why shouldn't it be okay? I trust you. What's your name?"

The guy hesitated. Like he didn't want to say. Like it was getting personal.

"Robert . . . Bob."

"Bob or Robert?"

"Bob."

"Okay, Bob. Let's dim the lights."

He watched him cross the room, not even daring to glance out through the plate-glass window, afraid that even that much might get him shot. Good.

It was always amazing to him. Within minutes—seconds—you could get a guy performing for you like a trained seal. Half the time, like now, you didn't even have to ask.

"You should water your fucking plants, Bob. Know that?"

He nodded, reached up and dimmed the lights.

"Okay, Bob, let's get to the good stuff."

He drank some of his beer. The barkeep moved back behind the bar and keyed open the register.

"Just the bills, now. No change."

He watched him drop the bills into the Bloomies bag. Bob had had a pretty good night tonight. From where he sat it looked like well over a thousand. He'd read in the paper today that business was down in the City about $357 million since September 11th. Bars and restaurants particularly. You wouldn't know it from where he was sitting.

"Tell you what, Bob. Let's play a little game for your tip bucket. I'm sure you got a couple hundred in there. I'm sure you'd like to keep it. So, I lose, it's yours. I win, it goes in the bag."

"No, that's okay, you can just . . ."

He started reaching for the bucket above the register.

"Hey! It's not okay, Bob!"

He lurched to his feet and leaned over and shoved the barrel of the gun against the barkeep's pale high forehead. He could feel the guy trembling right down though to the handle of the gun. Saw his glasses slip half an inch down his sweaty nose.

"Get this right, Robert. I say we play a little game, then we play a little game. Let me tell you something you don't know about me, Bob. I don't like people. In fact it's fair to say that I fucking hate people. Not just you, Bob, you spikey-haired little Midwest shit-for-brains—though I do hate you, for sure. But see, I hate everybody. I'm a completely equal-opportunity hater—Jews, Arabs, Asians, blacks, WASPs, you name it. Some people think that's a problem. You know how many people have tried to help me with this little problem, Bob? Have tried to reform me? Dozens! I'm not kidding you. But you know, it never takes. Never. You know why? Because my one real kick in life, the one thing that really gets me off, is to reform all those people who want to reform me. And it is my honestly held belief that the only way to reform people is to hurt 'em or kill 'em or both. Period."

He sat back down again, rested the gun on the bar, his hand spread out on top of it.

Bob was visibly twitching now, mouth gulping air like a fish.

"Jesus, calm down, Robert, or this isn't gonna work. Hand me the bag. And your keys. That's good. Thanks very much. Now slide over that cutting board there and that little knife you use on the lemons."

"Oh, Jesus."

"Just do it. And dump the lemons."

The kid glanced at his hand on the gun and then turned and did as he was told, set the knife and the board down in front of him.

"Okay, here's what we're gonna do. You're right-handed, right? Thought so. So you're gonna put your right hand down, palm-side up— that's important, palm up—and spread your fingers. Then I'm gonna take this knife here, which I notice you keep nice and sharp—very good Robert—and jab around between your fingers. Slow at first, then maybe a little faster. Not too fast, don't worry. Believe me, I'm good at this. I really am. But if I miss, even the slightest little cut, the slightest nick, you get to keep the bucket. I don't miss, bucket goes with me. Fair enough? Sure it is. All you got to do is hold very still for me now."

"Oh Jesus."

"Stop with the *oh Jesus*, Robert. Try to be a fucking man for a change. Or you can just remember that I got the gun here, whichever works for you. Okay. Spread your fingers."

The kid pushed his glasses up on his nose. They slid back down again. Then he took a deep breath and held it and put his hand down flat on the board.

He took the knife between his thumb on one side and forefinger and middle finger on the other and as promised, he started off slow. *Thump*, beat. *Thump*, beat. *Thump*. Then he picked up tempo and the thumps got louder because the force got greater and he really was good at this, damn he was good, *thumpthumpthumpthumpthumpthumpthump* and the kid kept saying oh Jesus, oh Jesus, Bob a Christian through and through now and he knew that for poor Bob this was going on forever, this was an eternity and when he finally got tired out scaring the shit out of the kid pinned the web of his thumb to the cutting board so that the kid gasped and said *aahhhh!* and he said don't you yell, Bob, whatever you do, *don't you dare fucking yell.*

And Bob didn't. Bob was toughing it out as expected.

He just stood there breathing hard, his left elbow propping him up on the bar against the pain and probably against a pair of pretty shaky legs and looked down at the spreading pool of blood between his fingers. He reached into his pocket and took out the envelope and opened it. Tore it down one side and blew a tablespoon of Johnson's talcum powder directly into his face.

Bob looked startled. Blinking at him, confused.

"*Anthrax, Bob,*" he said. "It's the real thing, I promise."

He picked up the bag of money. Took four pair of rolled-up socks out of his jacket pockets and unrolled them and spread them out over the money.

Like he'd just done his laundry.

"You try not to breathe now for a while Bob, go wash your face. That shit'll get right down into your lungs. And you know what happens then. Bucket's yours. You won it fair and square. You take care now. And if you think I've treated you badly which I really hope you don't, well hell, you should just see what I do to the ladies."

Whether the kid believed him or not about the anthrax didn't matter but he was betting he'd have a bad moment at least, the City being what it was nowadays.

He keyed the lock, looked right and left, threw the keys in the gutter and slipped off the gloves as he walked on out the door.

SIX

It had taken Claire a while to do this, to work up the will and the courage finally and Barbara had felt the same way. So they'd decided to do it together and that helped.

They stood in front of the Chambers Street subway exit on an unseasonably warm sunny day along with thirty or so other people scattered across the block staring south from behind the police barricades at the distant sliver of sky where only a month and a half ago the Twin Towers had been.

The smell was invasive, raw, born on a northerly breeze. It clawed at her throat. *Superheated metal, melting plastic and something else. Something she didn't like to think about.*

She had never much liked the Trade Center. It had always seemed overbearing, soulless, a huge smug temple to money and power.

And now both she and Barbara were quietly crying.

All those people lost.

She was crying so much these days.

She knew nobody who had died here.

Somehow she seemed to know everybody who had died here.

She stared up into a bright blue sky tarnished with plumes of pale blonde smoke and after a while she turned around. She had never seen so many stricken faces.

Old people and young people and even little kids—kids so small she thought they shouldn't even know about this let alone be standing here, they shouldn't have to grow up in the wake of it either. It wasn't right. A woman wearing jeans and an I LOVE NY—EVEN MORE tee-shirt was wiping back a steady stream of tears. A man with a briefcase didn't bother.

She didn't see a single smile.

"Let's walk," she said.

It was a whisper, really. As though they were standing in a church. And that was the other uncanny thing about this—the silence. New York City heavy and thick with silence broken only by the occasional truck rolling by filled with debris and once, the wail of a fire engine hurtling through the streets to ground zero. She had only one memory of the City to compare it with—a midnight stroll a few years back after a record snowfall, a snowfall big enough so that it had closed all the airports and bridges and tunnels. It had paralyzed the City. She remembered standing alone in the middle of the northbound lane at Broadway and 68th Street in pristine untracked snow for over twenty minutes until finally a pair of headlights appeared far in the distance. She could have been in Vermont or New Hampshire. Instead she was standing in one of the busiest streets in the busiest city in the world. She remembered being delighted with the sheer novelty of it, of all that peace and silence.

This was not the same thing.

They walked south down Broadway past shop after shop selling posters or framed photos of the Towers, their eyes inevitably drawn to them. And they didn't strike her as crass or even commercial particularly, though of course they were—New York would always recover first through commerce—they stuck her as valid reminders of what had been. And there was nothing wrong with that.

They stopped in front of a boarded-up Chase Bank filthy with dust, the entire broad surface of its window covered with ID photos of cops and firemen dead, all those young faces staring out at them frozen in time forever. The thick brown-white dust lay everywhere. On the sidewalks, the streets, the surfaces of shops and high-rises—canopies and even whole skyscrapers were being hosed down to try to get rid of it.

It was a losing battle. The site was still burning.

She stared at the faces moving past her. She guessed that not one in thirty was smiling.

They passed police barricades strewn with flowers.

Windows filled with appeals for information on the missing. *The dead.*

Their photos.

They passed children's bright crayon drawings—hearts, firemen, cops, flowers, words of grief and thanks.

It had been a while since either of them had said a thing. She'd always been perfectly comfortable with Barbara ever since their days bartending together at the Village Cafe but this was different. Each of them, she thought, was really alone here. Everybody was.

The wind shifted. The stench died down. But her mouth still tasted like steel and dust and plastic. She was hungry. She hadn't eaten. Yet it was impossible to think of eating here. She wondered how the sub shops and sidewalk stands stayed open. Even a Coke or a bottled water here would taste . . . wrong.

They'd stop at each corner and gaze into the empty sky.

Approaching Liberty Street the sidewalks became more crowded and then very crowded and before long they were trapped in the midst of a slow-moving mass of people that was almost frightening, what felt like hundreds of people, tourists and New Yorkers all crowding together at the barricades and straining for what was supposedly the best view of what was no longer there. And here you did see smiles and laughter, too damn much laughter for her liking. Almost a carnival atmosphere, fueled by morbid curiosity. And packed too tight together, far too tight, seven or eight deep—so that what if something happened? what if somebody panicked? You could be crushed, trampled. And when a father snapped a photo of his smiling little girl against the horizon and then a teenage boy with his girlfriend did the same she said, *let's get the hell out of here.*

"We can't," said Barbara.

"I don't like this."

"Neither do I."

She was shaking with a mix of fear and fury.

"This way."

It was easier than she'd thought. As they stepped slowly through from the center to the rear of the crowd people were happy to take their place so they could get nearer to the site. Finally they stood at the edge of this crawling human tide, their backs nearly scraping the filthy storefronts and climbing over steps leading into other storefronts and soon they found themselves on Park Row leading east so that it was silent again finally and they laughed and shook their heads almost dizzy with relief and that was when they heard it, a small soft mewling sound.

"Is that . . . ?"

"Shhhh," she said. "Yes."

She listened. In a moment she heard it again. There was a long green dumpster on blocks and packed with rubble, mostly chunks of cement, across the street to her left. The sound was coming from there. They walked over and peered beneath the dumpster, Claire working one way, Barbara the other.

"Nothing," she said.

"Nothing here either."

She looked behind it. A dirty empty sidewalk and the wall of a building.

"We didn't imagine that," Barbara said. "That was a kitten."

"I know. Hold on a minute."

She put her foot down on one of the blocks and hauled herself up to the lip of the dumpster and scanned the rubble.

And there it was, far over to her right, a tiny tabby walking unsteadily across a narrow jagged cement-shard tightrope, back tiny tabby walking unsteadily across a narrow jagged cement-shard tightrope, back and forth, gazing down at something beyond her sight-lines to the far side of the dumpster. They heard it cry again. She hopped down.

"Over here," she said.

They walked over to where she judged the cat had been but there weren't any blocks there, nothing for her to step up on. She looked around for a milk crate or a bucket or garbage can. Something.

"Cradle your fingers."

"Gotcha."

Barbara did and her first try failed miserably and Claire fell back to the street again practically into her and they both started laughing and then she tried again.

"Okay. I got it. Hold on."

She took most of her weight out of Barbara's hands when her belly hit the lip of the dumpster and she folded at the waist and she spotted the cat and reached and the kitten turned to look at her, wide-eyed at this new disturbance and she thought it probably would have bolted had it not been perched there so precariously, but as it was, stayed put just long enough for her to put her right hand down and push further at the lip to get an extra foot of reach so that she caught it in her left hand and lifted it away.

The kitten gave one long *meeeeeooooowwwwww* in earnest now and glanced anxiously over its shoulder and she looked down to where the cat was looking and saw the much larger body whose markings so nearly matched its own. Its head lay hidden beneath a block of stone. She saw long-dried blood along its bib and shoulder.

"Oh, you poor little thing," she said.

The kitten just looked at her, trembling.

"I've got her," she said. "I'm coming down."

"How did you know?" Barbara said.

"How did I know what?"

"That it was a she?"

She laughed. "I did. I didn't. I don't know."

They were headed uptown and over to the subway and then home. Barbara carried her bag for her. She carried the kitten pressed against her breast and shoulder. The kitten was matted and caked with dust and god knows what else and smelled like the inside of a garbage can and she gripped Claire's shoulder fiercely. Claire didn't mind a bit.

"How old, do you figure? Five, six weeks?"

"God, I doubt that her eyes were even open a week ago. She's young. Really young. I'll get her to a vet this afternoon. Check her out and see if she's okay. The vet'll probably know."

They were going back roughly the way they came. Past the dusty shops and into the smell of burning and the strange sad New York silence.

"You going to keep her?"

She lifted the cat off her body and held her up over her head with both hands and the cat looked down and she smiled at the cat and smiled too out into the quiet street.

"Forever."

November 10th, 2001

SEVEN

When David finished work for the day—the acrylic for the YA book cover was getting somewhere, finally—he did what he always did and cleaned his brushes and covered his canvas and went to the bedroom and pressed MESSAGES on his answering machine and turned off the mute button and listened.

Sandwiched between a recorded pitch from Mike Bloomberg asking for his support in the coming election and a call from his agent's assistant asking him to phone when he got the chance, she had good news for him, was her voice saying *it's me, just wanted to see how you were doing,* cut off abruptly.

There had been whole days by now that he hadn't even thought of her though they were still few and far between but this had been one of them, he'd been that absorbed in the work for a change, and then her voice, or the ghost of her voice—his machine was an old analog cassette recorder and had the annoying habit of allowing snippets of old buried messages to rise up from between the new ones like withered fingers from a grave—rushed at him with all its force and broke the dam inside him again.

How am I doing?

Some days fine, Claire. Most days, not well at all.

He dialed her number. Something he hadn't done in weeks now at her request.

He got her machine.

"It's me," he said. "Did you phone today? Or is my machine messing with my mind again? I figured I'd better check. Anyway, I'm here, and I hope all's well. See you."

He'd given her plenty of time to pick up. She hadn't, so either she really wasn't there and the call had come in earlier or her voice had been a mechanical glitch and she still wasn't talking to him.

Ready to talk to him was the way she put it.

He'd wondered if she'd ever be ready.

His agent was on speed-dial. She wasn't. He'd taken her off almost a month ago. Too much temptation, far too easy. His agent said they had a terrific offer for him, cover art for the next six Anne Rice paperback reissues, his agent very enthusiastic about it, and went on to outline the deal. The deal was a good one and he sure as hell could use the money but he'd worked with Rice a few years back and knew she could be a pain in the ass, one of those writers who seemed to think they were painters too and let you know it each step of the way, detailing you to death, your art going back and forth for approval like a canvas ping-pong ball.

"Tell them I'll take it," he said.

He hung up and went to his computer and lit his twenty-first cigarette of the day. It was supposed to help him cut down if he counted them but so far it had only made him nervous to know he was smoking so damn much. He went into his email. Half an hour later he hadn't answered any of them. The words wouldn't come.

It was obsessive but all he could think of was her message on the machine. Just wanted to see how you were doing. Maybe she really did. Maybe she had just gone out for a while and she'd call back later.

He doubted it.

But he missed her enormously and whenever he allowed himself to realize that, whenever he truly let it through, he'd cling to even the most delicate thread of hope. *She'd changed her mind, it didn't matter that he couldn't bring himself to leave, she missed him too much, all forgiven, let's try again.*

He knew her far too well to think it was anything but fantasy but he clung to hope as though hope itself might make it so. It wasn't just the sex he missed though god knows it had never been anything but fine between them but his heart had an entire Whole Earth catalog of what he missed about her and his mind kept flipping through the pages. Sometimes almost at random, something striking him hard for no reason. *The gap between her two front teeth, the husky voice, the talk about mutual friends whose names he hadn't heard for weeks now and incidents long past and people long gone in both their lives and art and books and feelings, the tall proud way she walked the street or the feel of her waist beneath his arm or her cheek beneath his hand or the two of them staring up at the darkening New York sky*—it just went on and on. Countless images, moments observed and shared over the heady course of two long years. And the friendship which always lay beneath.

He pushed back away from the computer and turned it off, watched the screen crackle down to neutral gray. The email would have to wait. He wasn't feeling up to the basically cheery voice it always seemed to require of him.

A drink, he thought, *that's what was in order. You got a lot of work done today. You deserve it. Have a scotch and turn on the news for a while. Couldn't hurt.*

Could it?

He was drinking a fair amount these days.

Was it for pleasure the way it used to be? Or just to throw a cozy blanket over pain?

He knew Sara worried about it. Sometimes so did he.

He seemed to have to bludgeon himself to sleep these days.

He got up and poured one anyway. His two tabby cats yawned awake on the counter when he cracked the plastic tray of ice. He scratched them both behind the ears. They fell asleep again. Sara wouldn't be home from work for two hours yet and the cats wouldn't be fed until she did. They knew that as well as they knew every flat surface in the apartment and the exact extent to which it was good for sleeping on. Until that time rolled around, dozing was an appropriate response to life.

He wished he were as sensible and poured himself a stiff one.

He was waiting for a phone call.

It might be a long night.

It was.

Seven hours, five drinks and a leftover chicken dinner later she hadn't called. So it had been a glitch, as suspected. Tomorrow he was getting a new machine, dammit. He didn't need the torment.

And it *was* a torment. He wasn't overstating. He felt like a caged animal in his own apartment. Sara was in the bedroom watching TV and doing paperwork, some homework from the bank but he couldn't join her the way he usually did, not tonight. He couldn't turn it off. It was as though being in the same room with her right now would constitute betrayal—of Sara, of Claire, of all three of them.

He tried to read but that didn't work either. He never painted or even sketched when he'd been drinking and he wasn't about to start now. So that left the computer. He answered his email as best he could and then surfed the net, looking for images, not sure what he was looking for but something to startle him or comfort him. Something. He felt hot-wired to her voice on the phone. Finally he left-clicked on the WRITE MAIL icon and began this long, feverish, idiotic letter to her. A plea for some kind of communication, any kind would do but mostly he wanted to see her and probably he wanted that for the very same reason she did not want to see him. It might start it up all over again, which he was selfish enough to want even knowing it could not be good for her and was honest enough about to make him feel guilty as sin.

He didn't know if the booze was helping or hindering in the sense-making department but the letter poured out of him and when it was finished he began to hit the SEND button but then stopped to read it again. He didn't know if it spoke to his feelings or didn't. If it was self-pitying drivel or not. Fuck it, he thought. Fuck it fuck it fuck it. He saved it into the MAIL WAITING TO BE SENT file. Maybe he'd send it off tomorrow when he was more sober and maybe he wouldn't.

Meantime he was not going to sit here staring at a computer screen all night.

He knew where she worked these days.

They still had a few friends in common who hadn't deserted him completely and he'd persuaded Barbara to give up the address. Hell, she was right here in the neighborhood. Only ten blocks away.

He turned off the computer and got up and walked into the bedroom. Sara looked up at him from the bed. Piles of papers fanned out in front of her in an orderly fashion. She was doing something to them with a red felt tip pen.

"I'm going out," he said. "Feeling restless."

"Okay. Where to?"

"Take a walk, have a drink. We'll see."

"You going to see Claire?"

"I don't know. Maybe. I guess I'll figure that one out once I'm out there. She still doesn't want to see me."

She put down the pen.

"David, are we in trouble? Do we need to talk?"

"No, we're not in trouble. At least not now. I don't know about the long run. I don't know where we're going. But we don't need to talk, not now."

"I worry."

"Don't. It's okay. I just might need to see her. I don't know."

She looked at him and nodded. "All right. Be careful," she said. She meant it. All that careful entailed.

"I will. I love you."

She went back to her papers. He thought how strange this would look to some outsider. As though she really didn't care. But he knew she did care and how much. They had thirty years together and the ties were strong even if sometimes invisible to most people, stretched thin these days because he had fallen in love and she of course knew as she knew everything important in his life—and maybe it was that knowing, as much as the cats they shared or the apartment they shared or the fact that she was his first best critic or even the years themselves of order and easy companionship which was why he stayed and couldn't seem to leave.

Sarah was family by now.

He had no other.

He put on his jacket and stepped into the hall and locked the door behind him.

EIGHT

Half past midnight and Claire was finally getting to eat—the Caesar salad with grilled chicken she'd asked the cook to leave for her in the microwave. They'd been slammed all night long for a change but now there was only old Willie in his usual corner, arms folded in front of him and half asleep over his beer. When she finished she'd roust him. Willie weighed in at a good two hundred pounds and he'd already fallen off his barstool once since she'd started working here only a few weeks ago. He was going to crack his head open one of these days. She didn't want it to be on her watch.

Sandi dumped the last of the candles out of its holder into the black plastic trash bag down at the end of the bar, sighed and smiled and untied her waitress apron and slid it off over her head.

"I'm outa here, that okay?"

They'd already split the tips and balanced out the register. There hadn't been any discrepancies between that and the cash-due printout or they'd have had to go through the checks together one by one to find the error. And Sandi looked dead on her feet.

"Sure. Go. You have a good night."

"What's left of it."

"Give that guy a hug for me."

"Yeah. Hey, listen, I really want to thank you for that. I really appreciate you talking to me. It helped."

"Kenny's a good kid. Everybody screws up now and then. Just don't let him make a habit of it, that's all."

Sandi smiled again and slipped on her jacket and hoisted her shoulderbag.

"I won't. See you tomorrow?"

"I'll be here."

She finished her salad. Hell, she'd wolfed the damn thing down. You got busy, you didn't have time to eat. Then you forgot to eat. Pretty soon you were starving. It was high time she had a shot and a Marlboro. She poured a double Cuervo neat and lit up and let the smoke slide down deep.

"Hey, Willie. Last call."

"Hmmmm?"

She watched the heavy eyelids slide up and then down again—what her father used to call the Long Blink. "Willie. Hey."

"Hmmmm?"

"Time to go."

"Oh yeah, 'course. Okay I finish this?" He smiled.

"Sure."

She watched his fingers toy with the neck of the Heineken, literally feeling around for the thing, and then grip it and pour. He had about a third of a glass left. She took a hit of the Cuervo and another pull on the cigarette and walked around the service station and then down the bar past him to turn off the central air over by the plate-glass window and then heard the sounds of the city rush in to her left as the man opened the door and stepped through. The man nodded and smiled and took off his thin brown leather gloves and she thought, shit, why does this always happen to me? because she was supposed to stay open until one if there were any customers at all, that was the rule in this place and here it was twelve forty-five and it would be just her luck and she was just that new on the job that the boss would come around to check up on her if she told this guy she was closed already.

The man was tall and wore a good brown three-piece suit and he put his brown leather briefcase down on the bar eight stools back from Willie, just in front of the register and smiled again and said, evening.

"Evening," Willie said.

The man just looked at him.

She had to laugh.

"I'm just about to close," she said. "So this'll be last call. But what can I get you?"

If he knew about anything he knew about bars and barflies and he could tell from the way the fat guy was sitting on his stool that he was about to drop, that she sure wasn't going to serve him again so that was when he'd made his move. He'd walked across the street from the flower shop where he'd been pretending to admire the window display and through the door. From where he stood he had a perfect view of the street and the corner of Columbus and 70th. Nice easy monitoring.

"What's on tap?" he said and she told him. He said he'd take the Amstel.

The Amstel came in a frosted mug. He liked that. He took a sip and watched her rinse a few glasses and dry her hands and then walk over to the fat guy in the corner. He liked the way she walked. It was assertive, very New York.

"Hey, Willie. Wake up, Willie."

"Huh?"

"Finish your beer."

"Right. Okay."

He tilted the glass and drank and set it down again.

"Tomorrow's another night, Willie. Finish it up."

"Okay." He did. "What I owe you?"

"You already paid me."

"I did?"

"Yep."

"Tip?"

"You left a good one, Willie. Thanks."

"Pleasure," he said and smiled and waved at her once like he was the goddamn pope bestowing a drunk benediction and slid off the barstool.

He tugged once at the collar of his faded gray raincoat and straightened up and managed not to stagger as he walked out the door.

God, he hated barflies. Fucking disgusting.

She went back to the dishes again.

"He's really a very nice guy," she said. "But with all that weight he's carrying I worry about him. I'm afraid he's going to have a heart attack or something right in the middle of my shift. Then what am I supposed to do?"

"I don't blame you. But say it did happen, what would you do?"

She shrugged. "Call 911 I guess. I've seen CPR but I've never, you know, actually done it."

"You've seen CPR?"

"Movies, television. Not in real life."

"Oh. I'm Larry by the way." He put out his hand. She smiled and dried hers on a towel and took it.

"Claire. Nice to meet you."

"Nice to meet you, Claire."

He looked around while she went back to the glasses in the sink and thought, hell, as good a time as any, slipped on the surgical gloves out of her sightlines beneath the bar, unlatched the briefcase and opened it and pushed it aside with the top open so that it would block any view from the street and lay the gun down softly on the bar.

"Claire?"

She looked at him first and then at his hand spread over the gun and he watched her face change. He always liked this moment. *Revelation-time.*

"Here's what we're going to do, Claire. We're going to pretend we're a pair of old friends, maybe we even dated way back when, who knows? And I'm here closing up with you, so you do what you do every night, only I'm here. You lock the door and hit the lights outside and dim the ones in here. Only difference is that once you've done all that you empty the register into this briefcase. Me, I'm just having a drink. You understand?"

She nodded.

"Okay, now go on about your business. And Claire? Don't even think about trying to run out that door. I know you really want to very much right now but here's the thing, it takes too long to open the door, throw it back and then go through. Believe me, I know. You'll be dead before you hit the sidewalk. And I'm already up for Murder One in New

York, New Jersey and Connecticut so it won't mean a thing to me one way or another."

He clicked off the safety.

"Do we have a meeting of the minds here, Claire?"

"Yes."

"Good. You know what you're supposed to do?"

"Yes."

"Then go."

"The keys are in my bag. The door keys."

"So? Get 'em."

He watched her, trying to gauge her reaction as she stooped down to the floor for her bag and set it in front of the speed rack and opened it and fished out her key ring. Her hands were shaking as she fumbled for the right one and that was good. Her color was off and that was good too.

But she kept glancing up at him—just before she stooped to retrieve her bag and then as she set it on the speed rack and then again as she turned the corner at the service station and a fourth time as she passed him headed for the door. He thought, this one's a wiseass, she's trying to memorize what I look like, but there were ways to minimize that possibility and ways to wipe it out almost completely.

It was called shock therapy.

The night had turned chilly and David was unprepared for that, dressed only in a light tan jacket and even with it zipped to the chin the wind off the river along West End Avenue was enough to send him immediately east all the way across to Central Park West where the packed-together rows of high-end residentials blocked it. He walked from 63rd all the way up 78th Street wondering what he was doing, keeping to the west side against the buildings both for the shelter and because you never knew about Central Park and who you might encounter this time of night. It was a lonely stretch though pretty well lit—a few people out walking their dogs or on their way home from somewhere or other and light two-way traffic. He supposed the street matched his mood. *Lonely and at least half-lit.*

At 78th he crossed three blocks over to Broadway though her bar was back on Columbus. He meant, he guessed, to describe a wide circle around her and only then, if he hadn't managed to shake this feeling by

252 • Jack Ketchum

then, narrow in. He hoped the feeling would just go away. It was stupid, what he was doing. Even just standing across the street from the bar watching her through the plate-glass window would be stupid because if he could see her then there was also the possibility that she'd see him. Never mind that it was easily as humiliating as standing under her apartment window. To go inside and try to talk to her, which was what he really wanted to do, which was what he was aching to do, was bound to cause more hurt for both of them.

There could be no good ending to this.

But he was doing it anyway.

He headed down Broadway, hands shoved into his jeans against the cold. Some of the bars were still packed mostly with kids in their twenties and he heard music and loud laughter and other bars were still and dark, closed already or just about to close and the thought came to him suddenly that he had no idea how business was over at her place. She could easily have locked up and gone home by now. It was a definite possibility.

The thought filled him with a kind of dread and he picked up his pace so that by the time he crossed against the red and passed Grey Papaya at 72nd Street his heart was pounding so he slowed again. It wouldn't be good for her to see him this way, if he was going to be seen at all. He still wasn't sure about that. Wasn't sure what in the hell he was going to do.

But this feeling hadn't been mitigated being out here. The night air hadn't cleared his head or cured him. Not by a long shot. *He was so close.* To seeing her at least. To something.

He turned east at 70th and walked slowly toward Columbus.

She was going to keep this under control. He wouldn't use the gun.

He wanted the money, that's all.

Fine.

"I cashed out already," she said. "The money's in back."

"What's in the drawer?"

"Two hundred startup money for tomorrow."

"Put it in the briefcase. Cash box or safe?"

"Cash box, locked in the desk. They wouldn't trust me with the safe. I'm still new here."

"Oh? You're not trustworthy?"

"I'm new here."

She stacked the money in his briefcase. She watched him sip his beer.

"You already said that. But what I asked you is, are you trustworthy?"

"Y-yes."

Stop that, she thought. Shit! You don't want to show him fear. Not the slightest bit of fear.

"Should I trust you to go in back there and get the box for me?"

"Up to you."

He smiled and looked her up and down and she wished she'd worn something a little less clingy than the thin scoop-neck blouse.

"I don't think so," he said. "You're a woman. And I wouldn't trust a woman on a short leash with her fucking legs cut off. Nothing personal. Walk me back. And keep your hands down at your sides. Move."

She walked back through the tables and chairs stacked for the night back to the office and opened the office door and thought of slamming it in his face but that was only a thought and nothing she'd consider for a moment because all he wanted was the money. She found the right key for the drawer and opened it, took out the cash box and put it on the desk beside the printer and computer.

She turned.

And he was so close. The gun only inches from her chest. She lurched back and her hip hit the desk. It hurt. Her mouth was very dry all of a sudden.

"You want me to . . . I mean, should I open it? Or you want to just take it as it is?"

"Open it. I like to see what I've got."

He was smiling again and the brown eyes seemed to jitter back and forth and she thought strangely of ants or bees, of insects.

And there was no smile in the eyes at all.

It was a relief to turn back to the desk. Not to have to look at the eyes. She used three fingers against the box to steady her thumb and forefinger and finally found the keyhole and turned the key and turned and stepped away a little to her left. He lifted the lid.

"You had a good night, Claire."

He shut it again and took one step toward her, his face only inches from her face, directly in front of her.

"You really don't know CPR?"

"What?"

"You really don't know CPR? Just from what you see on television?"

"I never . . . "

"So what happens if some customer throws a fit or something? I'm just curious. Aren't you supposed to be in charge of this bar, Claire? Isn't that you? It's not the waiter who's in charge, it's not the fucking busboy. Is pouring a goddamn beer the only thing you're good for? What about responsibility? Suppose I pitched a fit or something! What would you do for me? Call 911 while I'm dying here? Jesus Christ!"

He's crazy, she thought. *He's a goddamn fucking lunatic and god knows what a lunatic will do.* Maybe it isn't just the money. And for the first time now he really scared her.

He had her now, he could tell by the look on her face, time to put the real fear of God into the bitch and see if she remembered anything but fear after that. He put the gun against her temple and backed her ass to the desk again.

"Open your mouth."

"What?"

"I said open your mouth. Do it, Claire."

She did.

"All right, now keep it open, understand? I'm gonna show you something. I'm gonna show you how to do CPR."

He reached over and pinched her nostrils shut. Her eyes skittered. He took a deep breath and put his mouth over hers and exhaled hard and heard her gasp when he pulled away and try to catch her breath but he did it again before she could, emptied his lungs into her and this time when he let her up for air she was coughing and her eyes were gleaming with tears.

She tasted like smoke and tequila.

The coughing stopped. She leaned back against the desk, chest heaving.

"There you go. Of course you'd be on your back, normally. But you get the idea. Grab the cash box. Come on."

He marched her back the way they'd come and saw her wipe her cheek with one hand and thought, good start.

David sat on the steps of a brownstone across the street from the ornate blue-and-gold Pythian building, a lit cigarette in his hand, trying to will his heart to stop pounding. He'd gotten halfway down the block when it felt like somebody had put a hand to his chest and said, *asshole, don't you take another step further.* Don't even think it.

He had no business being here.

Not on the steps, nobody would care about that—but being *here.* This close. Thinking what he was thinking.

She'd said she didn't want to see him, period, and no hedging this time, that she couldn't see him, that seeing him had become a kind of grief played over and over again and that they simply had to stop, get away from one another and go lick their wounds until maybe in time they could be friends again or something like friends but that now they could be nothing.

It was the act of a willful selfish child to be this close to her.

What he needed to do was go home. Be an adult.

He'd made his choice. He should live with it.

He gasped at a sudden unexpected rush of tears. *That he should have to choose at all.* Not fair.

He wiped away the tears and drew on the cigarette and sat there, slowly calming.

"Pour me another Amstel, Claire. This one's gone flat. Use one of those good frozen mugs you've got there."

She did as he told her to do while he transferred the contents of the cash box to his briefcase, poured the beer and set it in front of him, trying to keep her hands from shaking, trying not to spill it, not to show. The taste of him was still in her mouth. He handed her the empty box.

"Put that on the floor or something, will you?"

She did that too, bent over and set it beside the garbage can and when she stood up again something hit her in the chest and she gasped, something freezing cold sliding down off her chest and over her belly.

He was laughing. The frosted glass was empty.

"Ooops. Little spill there. Gee, sorry."

"You . . . !"

He leaned in close over the bar. "You what, Claire? You what? What do you want to call me? You want to call me names? Pour me another beer you dumb little shit and keep your fucking mouth shut. And I want a new glass."

She looked down at herself, arms out to her sides. She didn't know what to do. You could see almost everything through the thin material and the bra was thin too so you could even see her nipples puckered by the cold. He could see them, goddammit. If she brushed at it that would only make it worse, plastering the material to her body. She wanted to cry. She wouldn't cry. She turned to the freezer to get the glass and that was when she brushed herself off because then he couldn't see.

She drew the beer and set it in front of him on the bar. And almost wasn't surprised when he lifted it and threw it all over her again.

But when he laughed the second time, then she did cry. She couldn't help it. It just happened. Whether it was humiliation or frustration or fear or all of these together she just stood there, eyes closed and quietly sobbing.

"Look at me," he said.

She wouldn't. If she couldn't see him then she could almost pretend he couldn't see her.

"I said, look at me, dammit!"

She opened her eyes. What she saw was a man enjoying himself immensely. She couldn't understand. Why was he putting her through this? Shouldn't he be running away right now? Wasn't he at all worried about the cops? How could anybody be like this?

"You stink of beer, Claire. Clean yourself off. You smell like a slut. Use that hand towel there. Dip it in some water. That's right. You have nice nipples, Claire. Say thank you, sir. I'm the customer. The customer's always right."

"Thank you."

She plucked the material out in front of her and wiped at it with the wet rag. The blouse was going to be stretched and ruined.

"Thank you, sir, Claire."

"Thank you, sir."

"Better. Now hand me that spindle."

"The what?"

"Jesus Christ, Claire, you've worked in bars for how long? The spindle. The goddamn spindle. The spike you stack your checks on, for chrissake!"

"I . . ." She didn't want to do this. Her heart was suddenly hammering. She hated those things. Always had. Even just to look at them. The spike was maybe eight inches long rising straight up out of a thick coil of wire at its base. This one was set at the service station below one of the wine racks and whenever she had to climb up onto the counter to get to one of the more pricey wines up top she had visions of losing her balance and falling right onto it, of being impaled. She could see it. Ridiculous, horrible way to die.

The spike was as sharp and thick as an icepick.

"Please . . . I don't . . ."

"Ah, begging. I like that."

"Those things scare me, okay?"

"Why? You use it every day."

"They just do."

"Maybe I want to scare you."

"What? Please . . ."

"Maybe I want to scare you. Maybe I don't like you one goddamn bit, Claire, and maybe I want to scare you so much I could almost come in my pants just thinking about it? What if the money's only a kind of perk? Maybe this is what it's all about. You ever consider that, you dopey whore?"

"Why . . . ?"

"Why? Because I want to. Because this gun tells us both I can. You hear me, you ugly fuck? You get ugly when you cry, Claire, you know that? *You want to know why? Because after me you'll never feel safe again, Claire. Never. Not at work, not at home. Nowhere. Because that's my wish for the whole fucking world and for you, Claire, in particular.* Now hand me the goddamn spindle!"

She could barely see him through the tears but she could feel the heat of his anger reach out to her across the bar. For a split second she imagined him bursting into flame. *Where did all this come from? Why? What had she done?*

David thought, *If she hates me for it, so be it. I have to see her.*

He crushed out the cigarette and stepped down off the brownstone.

"I want to show you how we're gonna do this, Claire. Stop blubbering for chrissake. Take one of those cocktail napkins there. Wipe your goddamn nose. You're gonna do it once first, just so you can see how hard it is, and then it's my turn. See, I put my hand on the bar, palm down, just like this. Then you pick up the spindle. You raise it over the center of my hand to exactly the level of this beer mug, no lower and no higher. Lower's cheating. Higher and it'll never work. Then you try to spike me."

"I can't . . ."

"Sure you can. I'll give you some incentive. You spike me and the game's over right now and you get to keep whatever's in your tip jar. I don't think you will, though. Like I say, it's hard. Assuming you don't, then I get three tries. I miss all three, you keep whatever's in your tip jar. I don't miss . . . well, then you're shit out of luck, Claire. Now pick up the spindle. And remember, the gun's in the other hand so you don't want to be thinking about doing anything else with it other than playing our little game."

He watched her eyes. The eyes always flickered when they made their move. The eyes were a dead giveaway. But he didn't even need the eyes this time. Instead of bringing it straight on down she raised it a half inch first so it was an easy thing to pull his hand away. Gave it a lot of force, though. She was game, he gave her that much. He freed the spindle from the bar.

"Okay. My turn."

"No. Please. Just take the money. Just leave me alone, please? Enough, all right? All right?"

The husky voice had turned into a whine. The eyes were red with tears.

He smiled.

"Not enough, Claire. Not all right. But what are you worried about? You saw how tough it is. I'll probably lose anyway, right? Of course maybe I won't."

"I can't, please . . ."

"You can, Claire. You have to. See the gun? See this tubing at the end? It's called a silencer. I made it myself. That means I can shoot you three or four times if I want to without even killing you, you dumb piece of shit and nobody's going to hear it, the neighbors upstairs will never be the wiser. And *that*, Claire, is a world of pain, I promise you. You want it to go down that way? Fine by me. Different game is all. Nastier."

"Oh, Jesus! Why . . . ?"

"You know the little pffttt sound silencers always make in the movies? Doesn't happen. More like car door closing. So what'll it be?"

She thought of her widowed mother in Queens and how in another month it would be Christmas and then of her sister married three months almost to the day and pregnant out in Oregon and that she'd never visited, thought of the paintings just finished and half-finished and of David still not free of her nor her of him and she thought about the kitten who curled between her feet each night and who would feed her and take care of her and apprehended something of what the world would be like without her in it, an almost impossible concept just an hour ago but glimpsed now for a moment and thought *I'm so afraid, I'm so afraid of what I won't get to see and she put her hand down on the bar.*

. . . and now his control is complete. He can see it in her eyes. He can see she knows a truth he's known all along, that there is no help in this world, that what will happen will happen and no amount of pleading to god or Jesus or to the milk of human kindness will get you any goddamn where at all, that in the face of loathing as deep and strong as his is she is just another worker ant in an anthill he can bring down in a second, crush beneath his feet at any time he wishes—her hand on the bar says all of this to him, and the temptation is there to do it to her on the very first plunge of the spike, to bring it instantly into even more stark perspective for her, the perspective of flesh, of spilled blood, of pain.

Yet he resists that. He lets her pull away and listens to her gasp and the dull thud of the spindle against the bar and raises it again and watches her hand slide across the bar to submit a second time and wonders, is she hopeful? Does she see an end to this? Because he seems to have missed? That this might be true is delightful to him too because he can wipe it all away so quickly, he has lied again and he is very good at this, he has had practice and if hope is not yet there he can place it in her heart on this second try, bait his trap for the hungry animal which is all she is after all—hungry for the truth of what he knows to be.

And this time he can practically hear her heart beating, racing as she pulls away because yes! He can feel the hope there coiled in her like a snake—he has missed by a mile it seems to her and he can smell the stink of hope, its sudden sweet reek as he positions the spike above her hand a third and final time and then, prescient and sly and born of months and years watching his back, trusting his senses, he glances out the plate-glass window to the street . . .

"Who the hell is that?" he says.

And at first she can only think it's part of this game he's playing, this insane evil fucked-up game and she doesn't look up at all but only at her hand on the bar waiting for the courage to pull it away if she can a third

260 • Jack Ketchum

time but then the words and the tone of the words seem to spill through
to her and what she hears is unexpected, wrong in these circumstances, a
flat even tone as if he'd said well that's interesting, it's raining out and she
looks first at him and then at where he's looking and sees David on the
corner by the closed dark flower shop across the street. Their eyes meet
and he's scowling, puzzled and she thinks, oh no, oh god no, I was so
close, I might have finished this here and now. She remembers seeing him
down on the street across from her apartment building many nights ago
and drawing away from the curtain before he glimpsed her at the window
and remembers thinking how terribly sad it was for both of them and
how wasteful that she could never, ever have come out to meet him and
thinks *David, why in hell are you here again? What in hell have you done now?*

She holds his gaze and slowly shakes her head. Don't even think
it. The scowl disappears. Instead the eyes plead with her, confused and
uncertain. Eyes so well known and loved. She needs to deny these eyes.
For both of them.

"Who is he, Claire?"

"My . . . boyfriend. Ex-boyfriend."

"Ex?"

"We've broken up."

"So what's he doing here?"

"I don't know."

The man seems to think a moment.

She watches David take a step closer to the curb. She shakes her
head again. *No, goddammit*! Don't *do* this! *Please*, you fucking lovely
idiot, stay the hell *away*!

"I think you'd better invite him in, Claire."

"No."

"Oh yes. You have to."

"I won't."

"Yes you will. Or it's you first and then him. Twenty seconds is all I
need. He'll never know what hit him."

He closes the briefcase beside him and snaps it shut and slides the
spindle down the bar well beyond her reach.

He's ready to go now. The game is over. All of it over now unless she
brings David into this and if she does, won't it just begin again? To what
end? Why does he want this? What can he hope to gain? He can walk out
the door right now. Free and clear. Just walk away.

Her eyes go back to David. To hold him there. *Don't move.*

"Do it."

"I can't."

"You will."

She thinks—hard and fast as best she can. *She will not do this to him.* And there seems only one way to do that. To convince him that she's furious at him for being there. He ought to be able to believe that. He ought to have anticipated that reaction from her. She has every right to be furious—though she's not. Though seeing him again even under these terrible circumstances feels so tender that what she'd like to do is embrace him, hug him, sob into his shoulder not just for what this man has put her through tonight but for all they've lost and all they had. To do that one more time again. What she'd sworn she'd never do.

She moves out past the service station and turns and heads past the man to the door.

Outside on the corner David sees her long, purposeful, familiar stride but the look on her face is unfamiliar. It's a look he can't quite read. When he'd thought he knew them all. He's only just arrived here but already something feels wrong about her and he thinks, who's this guy in there? New boyfriend? Boss? But boyfriend doesn't feel right. Of course it's possible he just doesn't want to admit that she might already have one. Might already have replaced him.

But boyfriend doesn't feel right. Nor does boss. Something about her face, the look in her eyes.

A car passes and then another. Claire is at the lock now.

He steps out into the street.

Claire looks up from the lock and he's crossing, coming toward her and she feels the blood rush to her face, pulse pounding and she flings open the door because she will not expose him to this goddammit, she will not permit that and summons the most dismissive angry tone of which she is capable and shouts out into the still night air.

"DAVID! GO! GET . . ."

. . . OUT OF HERE! is what she means to say . . .

. . . but the sheer sudden size of her voice startles the man inside and he thinks . . . HELP! THE POLICE! *she's calling for help the stupid bitch* so he turns and fires and the flower blooms wet in her back and he hears the silencer like a door closing exactly as he's told her it would be and she falls spilled to one side, the glass door wedged open by her hips and he pulls the briefcase off the bar thinking *the fucking cop was right, he's finally had to shoot somebody* and the boyfriend is almost across the street closing the gap between them and as he steps over her body he sees her eyes flutter stunned and wide and the man is yelling *Claire! Claire!* loud enough to wake the dead, the man not exactly understanding yet he thinks but there's no way to know what he'll do once he does so as he turns a sharp right headed toward the subway at 72nd he fires again and watches, for a just a moment, a second flower bloom across the man's chest, watches him sink to his knees and fall and reach for her, the man's hand settling in her flung, tangled hair along the sidewalk, his hand opening and closing in strands of hair, unable to reach further.

He doesn't know if he feels fear. He might. Maybe he should.

But he knows he feels good.

David lies sprawled along the sidewalk. The sidewalk feels oddly warm to him. It ought to feel cold this time of year. He tries to move but can't. He tries to breathe and barely can. Is this shock? Death? What? He sees her lying near him in the doorway. If he focuses on her, on Claire, he might live, someone might come by.

That he might even want to live disgusts him.

She stares up, blinks into empty sky.

Tears again.

So many tears in this city. So much heartbreak.

Then none.

FOUR: CIVILIZATION?

In 1973, the psychologist Ernest Becker published a book that would win him a post-
humous Pulitzer Prize. It was entitled *The
Denial of Death*, and in it Becker argued
that civilization, that all culture, was an
elaborate defense mechanism protecting its members from the realization
of the reality of death. Civilizations
of all kinds were what Becker called
"hero systems," set up to provide con-
vincing illusions that enabled their citizens
to soldier on in the face of the unthinkable.

After 9/11, those who followed Becker wrote
that the terrorist attacks on the United States
were a product of the hero systems people needed to live, hero systems
that despite being necessary had a tendency to create evil in the world,
and that the attacks had reminded those of us in the West of our collective mortality. 9/11 attacked not only people but our culture, our sense
of security.

Writing for *Psychiatric Times*, Dr. James L. Knoll said, "The message [of the attacks of 9/11] was: 'Here is Death in all its arbitrary,

uncontrollable, horrific reality— All attempts at denial shall fail.'" He went on to argue that our task, after receiving this message, was to somehow work through these death fears, and even more to turn to our "innate capacity for inwardness and creativity—recalling, for example, the symbolism embodied in the myth of Orpheus, whose task it was 'to sing us back from death into a new way of being.'"

The stories in this next section do not achieve all that Orpheus did, but they are all aimed at examining the need for new songs, for new Civilizations. From King Kong to ancient Sumeria, from New York to the Moon, the following are all searching for new illusions, new symbols, that might make the arbitrary and inevitable destruction sure to come bearable at least for a few moments longer.

Douglas Lain is a novelist and short story writer whose work has appeared in various magazines including Strange Horizons, Interzone, *and* Lady Churchill's Rosebud Wristlet. *His first novel* Billy Moon *was published by Tor and was selected as the debut fantasy novel of the month by* Library Journal *in 2013. His second novel,* After the Saucers Landed, *was published in August 2015 from Night Shade Books.*

Thierstein.net reviewed "The Last Apollo Mission" this way: "What does it deal with, you ask? . . . I guess, in many ways, the story deals with the permeability of reality, to rather startling effect."

THE LAST APOLLO MISSION
Douglas Lain

On the Moon

Sitting at a folding card table inside the Apollo 11 space capsule, I take sips of cold coffee from a Starbucks coffee cup and shuffle through my screenplay. I'm trying to find the right scene and find my lines, but I can't focus. I'm shivering in a phony capsule made of plywood and fiberglass. The khaki shorts and sleeveless green silk blouse I'm wearing are inappropriate for the climate and temperatures on the moon, but Vaughn is using the Lost in Space replica spacesuit to explore the surface, and so I have to make do, huddling on a metal folding chair with my knees under my chin, while my boyfriend pretends to be an astronaut.

Watching him play golf out there, noting the way the Saran Wrap window pane distorts his image, I can't maintain my resentment. Yes, he's snug and warm in the spacesuit, but watching him through the porthole, seeing how the light is bent as it passes through the plastic wrap, I realize how unstable this moment is. The capsule itself is flimsy. There is almost nothing separating me from the vacuum of space.

How long were the original astronauts on the moon? How many lunar rocks did they collect, how many color photographs? How long will I be stuck here before we launch again? I should know this. I did my research when I wrote the script, but now that I'm here, the details aren't there for me. I just never expected to be involved in acting any of this out.

Pacing helps keep me warm, but I'm leaving footprints inside the ship. The grey and white sand that Stanley had shipped from England is underfoot inside the capsule. Another symptom of how hurried the mission has been. Everything is unfinished. There is no floor. This Apollo capsule was built for exterior shots. I'm not in a real space at all, but in a space that doesn't exist. I am in the part of the rocket that will never appear onscreen.

I kick the sand. I collect grains in the toe of my open sandal, launch the clump into the air, and then immediately regret this action when the cloud of sand expands inside the capsule. With less gravity the finer grains drift, and I start to cough. I stumble back and knock against the plywood exterior wall of the capsule, and for a moment it seems the craft will break apart, but then I find my bearings and everything holds.

I press my face up against the plastic film on the porthole and discover that, in this way, I can breathe without taking in dust. There is clean air at the edge, along the outer wall of the craft.

Looking out, I see Vaughn carrying the American flag. He is jumping several feet into the air with each step, and the light from the Earth is reflecting off his glass helmet.

We are on the moon.

Kubrick

I met Stanley Kubrick in the summer of 2001, right around the time I realized my writing career was over. It had taken me seven years to realize it, but the truth was that my career had ended before it had ever begun.

I should have never left the New School with just a Master's degree. If I'd stuck with the program, I could've been tenure track in some third-tier school somewhere in the Midwest. My friends did just that. Nicole Baker teaches creative writing and composition to depressive undergraduate girls and alcoholic, obese boys at the University of Texas, and Larry Moore is teaching at the University of Alberta, of all places, but

I'd been overconfident. I'd convinced myself that I could make good as a commercial writer. After all, my first published story was selected for Houghton Mifflin Harcourt's *Best American Short Stories of 1995*, and after that I figured an ordinary life as a college professor was beneath me. I stayed in New York, took a job at a used bookstore to make ends meet, and stayed up nights to write my first novel. Seven years later, I was still looking for a publisher and could no longer convince myself that the job behind the cash register at Church Street Books was temporary.

The moment before Kubrick strolled in to look at coffee table books and then offer me a job, I'd been in the back alley on a break. I'd finally caught up to my agent and was practicing my outdoor voice with her, holding the earpiece side of my cell phone in my fist and shouting into the microphone end.

"I'm still young," I'd shouted. "My ovaries still work, you Pepsodent zombie. You think it's over for me? It's not over."

The alley ran between the bookstore and the kitchen of an Indian restaurant with tiny windows painted purple and gold, and I could still smell fermenting curry when I stepped back behind the register.

Stanly Kubrick looked like any other celebrity, in so much as he drew the eye. His outfit, a tailored blue suit covered by a clean blue overcoat, was subtly color-coordinated without being cute, and while he wasn't handsome, there was something about the way he looked at me over the tops of his glasses, the way he stroked his scraggly grey beard and ran his palm over his balding head, that was charismatic. Attention flowed in his direction.

He stood in the second aisle, took a heavy hardback copy of "The Aviators of World War Two" off the shelf, and then put the tome back.

I approached him as casually as I could, said his name while his back was to me. He thumbed through chess books.

"Mr. Kubrick?"

He turned around and smiled at me. "Paula Austin?" he asked.

I froze at the sound of my name, at the way my name sounded when spoken by the director.

"Yes?" I said.

"I'm a big fan of your work," he said.

We were each of us speaking the others' lines. I took a breath and tried again, but the wrong words kept coming out of Stanley's mouth.

"What was that?" I asked.

"A very big fan of your writing."

"Ah . . . Thank you."

He'd read the story in the *Best of 1995*, the story entitled "A Broken Assemblage," and was much impressed.

"You were?"

"Very much impressed, yes. May I buy you lunch?"

"I'm not off work until seven."

"I want to hire you to write for me."

The Twin Towers

I looked up at the phallic monsters on the superblock, and at the expansive empty space between the towers. Kubrick paused for a moment by the glass and concrete arches and pointed at the bronze sphere in the fountain.

"Why is it that every public sculpture is supposed to represent world peace?" Kubrick asked.

"Does it?"

"Smooth and featureless, right?" Kubrick asked.

I crossed my arms and bit my lip. It was windy between the buildings and water from the fountain was caught by periodic gusts. Water droplets soaked through my thin blouse, and I wished I'd worn a sweater.

"It's a ball," I said.

"Yes?"

"Not a symbol for capitalism."

"You're saying that capitalism isn't a ball?"

Kubrick had keys for everything. He opened the huge double doors to the South Tower, pressed a button for the elevator, and then used another key inside the box. He turned the key and pressed the button for the basement, and took me down to the lunar surface.

The moon was underneath the World Trade Center. A man in a white oxford-cloth shirt, khaki pants, and a navy blue tie had a large compass in his right hand and a photograph of the moon in his left. He measured the surface of the giant globe, the model of the moon that filled the high-ceilinged room, and then compared the measurement with what was in the photo. I watched this from inside the elevator, stupefied by the dim spectacle of empty space and the giant globe, and then stepped forward onto the set.

Kubrick was gone. He'd been right beside me in the elevator, but when doors closed behind me, I looked around to find that the director had disappeared and, instead of Kubrick waiting for me by the moon, there were movie stars.

Nicolas Cage was wearing a white coat, holding a pocket calculator, and talking to the man who was measuring the moon. The actor had his sly smile going, the smile that always made me wonder how anyone so creepy looking could have ever made a career in Hollywood, while the girl with him was doing her best to come across as something more substantial than a seventeen-year-old with a media coach and a personal stylist. The three of them didn't really fit together, but it wasn't up to me to understand. I was just the writer.

"Nicolas Cage?" I asked.

"That's right. And who do I have the pleasure of meeting?"

"Paula Austin."

"Oh. Yes," Cage said. "The writer. "

The man with the compass and photographs explained that a dust storm would be nearly impossible to replicate at the scale Kubrick was asking for.

"We could do it in camera," the scientist said. "Or, if Stanley will let me, I could produce the effect digitally."

"I don't think Mr. Kubrick is going to allow CGI effects to pollute the project," Nicolas said. "Do you?" he asked the girl.

"No. He wouldn't want to pollute the project with CGI."

"You're going to star in the movie?" I asked.

"Me?" Cage asked. "No. I'm too well known."

"We're not acting in the movie. We're acting on the set," the girl said.

"Oh."

"You don't recognize her?" Cage asked. I shrugged. "Scarlett here was in *The Horse Whisperer*."

"Evans's book?"

"Redford's movie," Johansson said.

"Right."

"And now you're acting on Kubrick's set, but not in his movie?"

Scarlett smiled nervously at me and, for a instant, I thought I recognized her, but then realized that I was thinking of Molly Ringwald.

"Stanley is very detail oriented," Cage said. He pointed at the tracks that encircled the moon model, and then leaned in close to me and put his arm around my shoulder in a way that was a bit menacing.

"Look in the gaps," Cage said. He was too close, but his breath was very fresh. He smelled like organic mint and warm tea, maybe a bit like antiseptic soap. "Look," he repeated.

There were boxes, wooden boxes with glass fronts, in the spaces between the ties. These were Joseph Cornell's "Assemblages," and while at first I wasn't sure if they were authentic or not, eventually I came to believe in them.

The first box was entitled Solar Set and contained five tiny shot glasses, and each shot glass was held in place by tiny nails around the foot. Each glass contained a marble. There were two red marbles, two blue marbles, and one green. The next box contained an illustration of the moon taken from a nineteenth-century astronomy book. A yellow cork ball that ran along a wire track at the top was meant to represent the sun, and thereby the movement of time. I'd seen the box before at the Met, and I could still remember bits about the work that I'd picked up from the audio guide.

The next box contained a photograph of Lauren Bacall, the next one a clay pipe for making soap bubbles, and the next contained a paper cut-out of a green and red feathered parrot.

Looking at each assemblage as I moved in orbit around the moon I came to feel very strange. If these weren't the original works, if they were not the actual dream boxes made by the American Dadaist Joseph Cornell, then they were forgeries that made the distinction between copy and original irrelevant. What mattered was encountering life as something that could be preserved behind glass. Stuffed birds, blue and red glass marbles, feathers and clothespins, all were made into something more than what they were on their own, into something somehow more than real.

I moved to the dark side of the moon, where there was only a green light from the emergency exit sign. I struggled to discern what the assemblages on the dark side contained. I stared and stared, opening my eyes wide in the dark, until finally I picked up the box with shot glasses and marbles again. I stood up straight and looked around and realized that Scarlett Johansson and Nicolas Cage were gone. The movie stars had left and the entirety of the moon was dark.

Kubrick still wasn't anywhere to be seen, and the scientists in khaki pants and white dress shirts were gone. And I called out into the darkness a few times. I called out for help until I came to accept that I was alone.

I decided to find the elevator again. I crawled in the dark, heading in as straight a line as I could manage as I fumbled over wooden tracks and thick electrical cords.

I held onto what I thought was carpet until I saw the soft glow of the button for the elevator. There was only one button with an arrow that pointed up, and when I was inside it the only light came from the buttons for the floors. I reached out for a light switch and accidentally pressed the button for floor 76.

The elevator ascended and the overhead light slowly turned on. Dim at first, but then brighter and brighter as I made my way up.

Digital Transitions

My boyfriend Donnie told me that I ought to include a dog in the story. If Americans were going to go back into space, if there was going to be a return to the idealism of the '50s and '60s, a return to the stars, then I had to bring Fido along for the ride. Any idealistic public project that was going to take hold of the public's imagination in this new millennium would have to be cute.

"People want to believe in innocence, and that means animals. Puppy dogs, guinea pigs, maybe a talking insect? You need their unreserved sympathy," Donnie said. There was no reason to worry about the implications. It was a job, and that was all. He took a gulp of beer from a green bottle and then set the bottle down on the remote control accidentally.

On the television set, Jim Carrey made a face at the audience. His body seemed to be made out of rubber and he took his left leg and raised it over his head so that he appeared to be carrying himself on his own shoulder.

Donnie worked in animation as a freelance digital editor. He'd worked for Fox Animation, Warner Bros, Dream Works, and with Lucasfilm on a project called "Monkey Island" although he didn't like to talk about that one. Actually he rarely talked about any of his films. Once we watched Shrek together and he couldn't point out anything he'd done. He'd try to tell me, but his work went by too quickly or subtly. I could never see it.

"I edit so they don't notice cuts and jumps," he said. "If you really want to miss out on my best work, then look at Anastasia. That film has perfect transitions," Donnie told me. "Whatever problems there are in that film have nothing to do with what I did. What I did was invisible. The movie is seamless."

We were drunk in our studio apartment. Actually, Donnie was drunk, and I was working on catching up. I poured vodka and lemonade into an oversized red plastic cup and thought about all the smooth cuts, the little invisible spaces, in Anastasia.

Maybe Donnie was right. I needed a dog in the story, and not just any dog, but that dog the Russians had sent into space to die. I needed the Sputnik dog, and by Googling I found her name was Laika.

We would have never landed on the moon if it hadn't been for Laika. Without the Russians beating us, without the threat of communism, we would have never have gone. After all, there were no material reasons to go up. It wasn't as though we were expecting to find oil up on the moon, or diamonds or anything. There was nothing up there worth having, but still we had to get there first.

So yes, I needed a dog like Laika. After all, people would want to see an American version of Laika on the moon. I needed something tangible to motivate the audience and the characters.

"Richard Nixon," Donnie said.

"What?"

"Richard Nixon was president when they went to the moon," he said.

I went to get ice from our stainless steel refrigerator. Donnie didn't make consistent money; I was the one who paid the rent for our tiny little apartment, but when Donnie did make money, he'd usually make a substantial pile of it. We had a European refrigerator with a transparent Plexiglass front panel and a cold, clean, stainless steel freezer door. We had to keep the inside of the refrigerator clean because everything inside was always on display, but I enjoyed the discipline of that. I'd arrange the apples in a glass bowl and place them on a lower shelf. When I shopped I purchased items based on the color of the packaging, and ended up with a lot of greens and oranges. Perrier bottles and liters of orange soda are very pretty, I think.

The appliance seemed to match with the concrete walls in our unit. It was very clean, and it produced ribbons instead of cubes. Ice ribbons that came out of our Bosch freezer. They were curved like peppermint holiday candies. These ribbons wouldn't fit in a glass unless you snapped them into pieces, but the uniqueness of our ice made me feel like I'd arrived at something. I'd open the stainless steel door of the freezer, take an ice ribbon out of the metal bin, and feel as though I'd proven that art and everyday life could combine.

I returned to our bedroom and watched Jim Carrey dance with Lauren Hutton. She kept trying to bite Carrey, but he was too rubbery and agile for her. I put the ribbon of ice in my mouth so that it held my mouth open and then turned to Donnie to show him how ridiculous I looked, but Donnie's eyes were closed.

Maybe this Moon Mission could include the daughter of Christa McAuliffe? The story could be about how little Carly McAuliffe, now all grown up, was going to go to the moon in order to honor her mother's memory. Instead of the big ideological space race, this Last Apollo Mission would be a kind of coming-of-age story. It would be the story of reconciliation between a beautiful young astronaut and her dead schoolteacher mom. The side plot would be the story of a young jet fighter pilot struggling with alcoholism. He'd dry out when offered the chance to go back up there and make something out of his life.

The ice in my mouth slowly melted as I watched Jim Carrey close the lid to his own coffin. He had a stupid smile on his face and then he was trapped inside the box.

In 1969, the men who came back from the moon had used solar wind to power their craft, and they'd used a thin strip of aluminum as a solar sail. From the moon, they'd used lasers to measure the distance from the moon to Earth to within a fraction-of-an-inch accuracy, and they'd drilled an eight-foot soil sample. What kinds of practical projects could the new astronauts accomplish? Maybe they'd put a webcam on the American flag, or maybe they could build a sauna?

The ice in my mouth slipped from between my lips and to the orange carpet. I swallowed the rest of my vodka lemonade in one go and then climbed onto the couch next to Donnie. His eyes were closed, but when I cuddled up with him, he put his hands on my breasts and pressed against me. He put his tongue in my ear.

Richard Nixon had seemed happy for the astronauts when they got back. All the photographs show Nixon laughing, but maybe George Bush would be visibly disappointed when the astronauts made it back alive? He'd resent them for their success, and then finally admit that he'd wanted to go with them. They'd tell him that, while he might be president, he was no astronaut. And they'd tell him that nobody wanted to be stuck with him in the capsule. Not even the Republican astronauts wanted George Bush to come along for a ride in a cramped space capsule. Nobody wanted George Bush on the moon.

I took off my sweater and fetched the rust-colored knitted blanket off the back of the couch, while Donnie put his hands between my legs. He made it seem very natural so that I hardly noticed him doing it. He really was masterful with transitions.

Stripping like Barbarella

Donnie wants me to strip in the same way that Jane Fonda stripped during the opening credits for the film *Barbarella*. In the film sequence, Fonda floats weightless in her space capsule and removes her spacesuit. First she undoes the silver glove and then she removes the sleeve. She removes one leg of the suit and then the other. Her toes are pointed and her knees are bent. Her thighs appears to be perfect, her skin soft and smooth.

Perhaps the most erotic moment occurs when the tint in the glass of her bubble helmet dissipates. It looks as though the helmet is draining; all the bad black fluid disappears, and Fonda's oval face, her wide eyes and phony smile, are visible behind the glass.

We've been trapped on the moon for weeks, and I've made my desire clear to him, but he needs this stripping if he's going to perform the act. Donnie wants me to strip like Jane Fonda.

"We're stuck here, yeah? So we might as well live out the fantasy of it," he says.

"Your fantasy."

"Of course, yeah."

"What about my fantasy?"

This strikes Donnie as a welcome diversion. If I have a moon fantasy that he can fulfill, then we'll do mine first, he says, but afterwards I'll still have to strip like Jane Fonda.

"Well?"

"Well, what?"

I try to think of what it is that I want from him. I sit by the porthole, look out at the model of the moon outside, out beyond the Saran Wrap pane. I glance at the matte painting of an earthrise, and then close my eyes and try to fantasize, but the fantasies that occur to me like that, out there in space, don't appear to me as my own. I picture Donnie dressed in his spacesuit or as a hardhat worker and realize that the image is, if anything, homoerotic, but that works for me. I imagine climbing on top of him in a crater, or covering our bodies with moon dust and kneading his flesh like dough, but it doesn't take long before this image twists into something grotesque. My head fills with cartoon images. I picture Tom and Jerry doing 69 while floating in empty space. I picture Minnie Mouse tying up Mickey with her bow.

"I can't think of anything," I tell him.

Soon enough, I'm naked except for the space suit. I start by removing the thick rubber gloves for him. I unhitch the sleeve from the shoulder and slip my arm free.

"Are you even trying?" Donnie asks.

It isn't working for him. The problem isn't my body as compared to Jane Fonda's perfection, but rather the problem is the physical space inside the capsule. Fonda's striptease took place on a flat surface, and I'm trying to duplicate her actions, only in 3-D. Besides, looking around, I realize that there would be nowhere comfortable for us to fuck, even if he could get excited.

"Maybe you should hum the music from the movie as you take off your suit."

"How does the music go?" I ask.

But even Donnie can't remember the tune.

Rover

I sat with Stanley Kubrick in a battery-powered moon car and quietly ate my pastrami on rye. I was taking lunch on a facsimile of the rover, and was struck by how the gold foil wrapped around the legs of the lunar module matched the color of the inner layer of foil that wrapped our pastrami sandwiches. I wanted to discuss the first scene in the manuscript I'd emailed him that morning, but Kubrick was focused on eating. He was holding his sandwich with both hands and smacking his lips as he chewed, and I had to wait quietly under the umbrella-shaped antenna.

Then, when Kubrick finished his sandwich, he picked up the manuscript and started reading silently. He took small sips of coffee from a Starbucks coffee cup and mumbled the lines of dialogue under his breath.

"This isn't what I'm after," he said.

"What's that?"

"If I'd wanted to make a reality television show I wouldn't have needed a writer at all, correct?"

I took another bite of my pastrami sandwich and shook my head. "I'm not sure what you want," I said. "You're saying the characters are flat?"

Kubrick reached over to me then and did something I didn't expect at all. He took my sandwich away from me. He took my pastrami sandwich and held it up over his head as though he thought I'd try to snatch it back. When I made no such move he lowered the half-wrapped sandwich back down and took a bite of it.

It was a really good sandwich. The gourmet mustard had an aftertaste that complemented rather than contradicted the sandwich's rich, salty first impression, but Stanley Kubrick was eating it instead of me because he wanted to punish me for not taking the job seriously enough.

Stanley tapped the manuscript with his middle finger and then used his middle finger to point to the blank spaces between the lines of dialogue.

"Fuck the characterization. You're in the wrong form here. You've got no idea what a manuscript should look like on the page. You're wasting white space. There aren't enough words here."

Kubrick started the moon rover, and we drove off the grey sand and to the wooden tracks that encircled this first set. Kubrick drove the rover onto the tracks so that the wheels on the left side of the vehicle bounced along the wooden ties while the outer set of wheels gripped the smooth concrete floor of the WTC basement. We drove tracks away from the first lunar surface, around the giant globe of the moon, until we reached Kubrick's second lunar-surface set. On this version there was a blue and brown weather balloon tied to a seventeen-foot-long string. This was the distant Earth, and it bobbed gently on its tether. The sun was a projector behind a plexiglass window to the south of the set.

We jumped the track and drove across the lunar surface, finally stopping at an Apollo capsule that was just as realistic as the first, only smaller. This was the set for long shots, and Kubrick and I stood just as tall as the lunar module. He reached out to it, opened the hatch, and then stuck his head inside the craft.

"I hired you because you know Joseph Cornell's work," Kubrick said. He took his head out and then reached into the craft with his right arm and produced another assemblage box from inside the rocket. It was Cornell's dream box entitled *L'Egypte de Mlle Cleo de Merode*.

It was one of the few boxes that Cornell created that did not include a glass front but was instead a chest. Cornell had modeled this assemblage after a Votive cosmetic box and he'd tried to represent all of Egypt within it. The chest contained small glass jars or phials and each of these contained something of Egypt. One phial, for example, contained a photograph of the silent film star Theda Bara and was labeled "Cleopatra." Another bottle contained curls of brown paper and was labeled "Serpents of the Nile."

"Do you understand what I want?"

I shrugged.

"Each approach to art is also an approach to space," Kubrick said. "And for this space mission, I need a story that is real but abstract, that is personal but objective," he said.

"Tell me exactly what to do," I said.

"I can't do that. What I need from you is a new form," Kubrick said. "You have to help me create a new kind of space."

A New Art Form

I'd never been a fan of Stanley Kubrick. I considered him to be overrated. He was a middlebrow director who made pretentious melodramas, and I'd only ever seen maybe three of them. I'd seen *The Shining*, the one about Vietnam, and *2001: A Space Odyssey*. In fact, that last one didn't even count because I'd never managed to stay awake all the way to the end of it. I always fell asleep around the time the waitress walked on the ceiling, or else I'd pass out when the scientist stopped outside the lavatory to read instructions on how to use a zero-gravity toilet.

I had no idea what it was that Kubrick wanted from me. Asking me to write a new space or new form into being was not merely absurd, but sadistic. It was graduate-school talk; not what I expected from an American legend like Kubrick. So I ignored it.

I'd rewrite the script instead of rethinking it. I'd change the plot around, rearrange the characters.

In my new version it was McAuliffe's son who had the drinking problem, and then it was McAuliffe's son's male lover who drank, but each draft was worse than the last, and after two weeks of rewrites I decided to do it his way

If Stanley Kubrick wanted me to create a new kind of cinema, a new sort of movie, then my first step was to figure out what kind of movies he was already making. Skimming the biographies I found that he was most famous for his perfectionism. Kubrick spent years searching for a camera lens that would allow him to shoot *Barry Lyndon* using nothing but natural and candle light. I read that the street sets Kubrick built for *Eyes Wide Shut* were tremendously detailed and expensive, almost hyperreal. Kubrick's New York City streets were more detailed than real streets.

I watched all of his films. *Clockwork Orange* disturbed me, but only in the way that it was meant to disturb everyone. On the other hand, while I recognized that *Doctor Strangelove* was a comedy, it disturbed me in ways that were perhaps unintentional. It struck me that Kubrick had done something terrible to George C. Scott, and that something inside of Peter Sellers was broken, and I had almost worked out a way to break something in myself, but before I could figure it out, Kubrick's sound-stages were destroyed.

Nineteen hijackers managed to get past security at Boston's Logan International, Dulles International, and Newark, on September 11th. And that morning I was woken early, around 6:20 a.m. Eastern, by my cell phone. The device gyrated on my glass bedside table and made a clattering noise.

"Church Street Books," I said.

"They fucked us."

"Mr. Kubrick?"

"It's over. You can keep the retainer, of course," Kubrick said.

"Okay," I said. I glanced at the LCD screen on my cell phone to check the time, but somehow I'd turned on Tetris. An L-shaped block was falling.

While I listened to Stanley Kubrick swear at me from what I imagined was a phone booth in Times Square (Could I hear the buzz of neon lights over the traffic?), Mohammed Atta was taking a little yellow pill and staring out of the passenger side window of a BMW. Atta had had too much to drink at the Pink Pony, a strip club in Daytona, the night before. He reportedly was severely hung over, but I didn't know any of that at the time.

"Did you say that you don't want me to finish the rewrite? Am I fired?"

"The project is cancelled," Kubrick said. "They went the other way. Apparently the moon was just a contingency plan," Kubrick said.

Donnie rolled away from me on the futon, leaving a damp spot on my pillow. I looked at him. Donnie hadn't landed an editing gig for almost a year, and yet he always slept like a baby.

"Would you at least look at what I came up with? Maybe you could use it for another project?" I asked.

"Use what?" Kubrick asked.

The genre. I'd written the script from multiple points of view, but the effect was a single voice that could be acted out in space by multiple players.

"Shit," Kubrick said.

"You want me to email it to you?"

"No. Don't email me anything. I don't want to see it. Burn it. Burn everything."

"What time is it?" I asked

"Don't go into work today, Paula. Take a sick day," Kubrick said.

"Am I fired?"

But Kubrick didn't answer. Instead he hung up the phone, and I listened to the dial tone. I waited for the buzz in my ear to offer some kind of answer about what was going on.

I closed my eyes and lay back down, still half asleep, even, with my cheek on a pillow wet with Donnie's saliva.

Hypnagogic, I imagined sending an email to the sun. I imagined pressing Send and watching the code flying through space. I watched the ones and zeros burn as they touched the edge where the sun was hot. I imagined the sun as a golf ball, and thought about Buzz Aldrin getting drunk on the lunar surface. I imagined that Buzz was sweating.

After September 11th

For the first two weeks, the streets around Church and Murray were impassable, but even after Church Street was cleared of the debris—the broken filing cabinets, personal computers, and pulverized concrete—almost no customers visited the Church Street bookstore. Only the cork message board in the back of the store, next to the wire racks of the *Village Voice*, was getting us any foot traffic. The bulletin board was covered over with snapshots of the dead: photocopies of Polaroids, yearbook pictures, school photos, images scanned from drivers' licenses, and so on. Accompanying the photographs here were handwritten questions like "Have you seen our Johnny?" and demands like "Call this number if you see this girl!" accompanying the photographs.

Everyone wanted to believe that some of the people in the photographs might just be lost. They were dazed and confused and wandering the streets, but otherwise unscathed. I looked at the faces, the smiling dead men, women, and children. Most of them, their bodies, would never be recovered. I wondered how long it would take their families to give up looking.

For the first few days after the bookstore reopened, the space by the bulletin board was taken over by a stream of people who otherwise did not fit the usual demographic mix. There were older people and fat people in the store. There were black, yellow, brown, and red people.

But by the third day the demographics sorted themselves out, and the photographs that went up on the bulletin board were more glamorous. Our usual customers were students from the New School, or from NYU. Artists stopped in with illuminated color photographs. A dead woman looked at herself in a hotel bathroom mirror, and a handsome young man in his clean white suit stood in contrast to the spectrum of red and brown in the wood wall behind him.

Very little was required of me. The bookstore owner, a Slovenian immigrant named Slavi, spent hours standing by the cracked display window, next to his first edition copy of *The House at Pooh Corner*, staring out at the empty street. After awhile he wiped his nose with his hand, looked at his fingers for evidence, and then turned to me and asked, "Do you think customers will only want to buy from Americans now?"

I shrugged at him and retreated into reading. I didn't know the answer to his question, and he didn't really want an answer in any case. He just wanted to enjoy repeating the question.

While we waited, I read a book about the Marx Brothers. I flipped through a coffee-table book entitled *The Marx Brothers Scrapbook*, and watched another mourning family open the front door and wander to the bulletin board.

I read my book:

"Why a duck?" Chico asked. "Why not a chicken?"

Groucho answered, "No, viaduct. You know, like a bridge over water?"

"Ah, I see."

"Good."

"One thing though."

"Yes."

"Why a duck?"

I almost didn't recognize him at first, even though he was wearing the same exact blue suit he'd been in the first time. He smiled at me with the same mischievous grin, but when I spoke to him, he pretended not to hear me. Instead he strolled between the bookshelves and looked at cookbooks. Then he moved to literature. He took his time pulling trade paperbacks from the shelves and putting them back. He turned the corner and moved down another row, further away from the register. Finally he seemed to find what he was looking for and he approached me.

"Is this a first edition?" he asked.

I looked down at the book he'd selected—it was a beaten up paperback version of JD Salinger's *The Catcher in the Rye*. I turned the book over and found that, far from being a first edition, it had been printed in 1997. A new copy of *Catcher in the Rye* would have cost 5.95, but this was used and priced at two dollars.

"No, that's a first edition and I'd like to buy it."

"I don't understand."

"What does a first edition of *Catcher in the Rye* list for? You have a blue book?"

Slavi kept a current edition of the *Rare Book Price Guide* in a drawer by the register, and it listed a first edition of *Catcher in the Rye* at ten thousand dollars. I read the price out to Kubrick.

Kubrick wrote the check, but handed me a five-dollar bill. He turned to look out the plate glass windows at the front of the shop, but had to lean to the left in order to see past the owner. I put his book into a plastic bag for him.

"They made a mistake," he said. "But I won't make the same mistake they did. You're a talented writer, Paula. You should continue in that direction. Don't get sidetracked by this. Just take this money, and then you and we will be good and you'll be free of this whole nasty business."

"What nasty business is that?"

284 · Douglas Lain

Stanley Kubrick smiled at me. I'd asked the wrong question and made him angry, and his smile was the best, maybe the only, way he knew to express that fact to me. It was a smile that indicated that a certain kind of violence was being suppressed.

"Take the money, Paula. And then maybe take the time to write another novel."

"What was the mistake that they made, and why does their mistake mean that you should pay me $10,000?" I asked.

"Did you delete the manuscript you wrote for me?" Kubrick asked.

I smiled at him this time, leaned across the counter, and then reached out and took the check out of his hand. I waved the check in his face. It was a dramatic gesture, like something out of a movie.

"What does this bribe mean, Stan?"

"Write your novel, and send it to an agent. I'll write her name down for you."

Stanley Kubrick wrote the name "Nicole Aragi" on page one of the *Catcher in the Rye*, put the book back in its plastic bag, and then handed the bag over to me.

"How did you know ahead of time?"

"Careful what you ask me, Paula," Kubrick said.

"Did the attacks have anything to do with what we were doing? Were the attacks a way of making a new space?"

Kubrick stopped smiling. He grabbed his check out of my hands, tore it up into pieces, and then stuffed the pieces into his trouser pocket. He took the plastic bag from me, removed the *Catcher in the Rye*, and then walked back to the bookshelf where he'd found the book.

Stanley stood in the aisle for a moment, shrugged at me, and wiped his nose with his hand. He adjusted his beard with the palm of this same hand, pulling down on his chin, and then moved to the exit. He stepped around the owner, turned around one last time as if he had a parting thought, and then left. Kubrick stepped out the door and onto Church street, and by the time I got out from behind the register and across the store to the door to go after him, he'd disappeared down Vesey Street.

A Lime Green Convertible

When I spotted it rolling slowly down Broadway, my stomach clenched and I started shaking. It was probably a Ford Mustang convertible, definitely lime green, and I stopped outside of a Walgreens on the corner of Broadway and Warren, turned my back to the street, and stared at the display of Liquid Soaps and disinfectants behind glass. The antibacterial soap was the color of piss, and the bottles glowed in the October sun.

"Paula?" Nicolas Cage called my name from behind the passenger side window while Scarlett Johansson looked out the windshield and held the steering wheel with both hands. She blew a pink bubble with her sugar-free gum.

Johansson was wearing a green sweater and a poodle skirt, and she had her hair up. Now, rather than looking like Molly Ringwald, she looked like Olivia Newton-John. Nicolas Cage, on the other hand, looked only like himself, even though he was obviously dressed up like John Travolta. He was wearing a leather jacket and tight jeans, and he too wore his hair up, but in a pompadour.

"You remaking *Grease*?"

"Mister Kubrick asked us to talk to you."

"What about?"

"Get in," Cage suggested.

"I don't think so."

Nicolas Cage fumbled with the glove compartment, spilled the contents onto the rubber mat under his feet, and then pushed aside a Styrofoam cup, a car manual, what appeared to be ball bearings, and some Kleenex, until he found the pistol.

He rolled down the window with the crank, but unevenly at first. He had to roll the window back up and then roll it down again more slowly. When this was accomplished he pointed the gun out the window at me.

"Fuck, Paula. I mean, fuck!"

"What are you doing?" I asked.

"What does it look like I'm doing?" he asked. His voice was high pitched, and I realized that he was playing the scene for laughs. If the audience was laughing along with him, then his character would remain sympathetic even as he held me at gunpoint. "Get in the fucking car, Paula."

I opened the back door and slid in to the middle of the bench seat. Cage turned around and looked exasperated.

"Where are we going?" I asked.

"Shut up," he said.

"What do you want from me?"

"Just shut the fuck up, Paula!"

Cage produced a pillowcase with yellow sunflowers printed on it, from underneath the ball bearings on the floor. He pointed his gun at me—it was a grey and black pistol, not very large—and told me to freeze.

"Don't struggle with me, or I'll blow your fucking brains out," he said.

Scarlett blew another bubble and then purposely popped it with her tongue. She chewed her gum aggressively. She was overdoing it, overacting.

Nicolas Cage put the pillowcase over my head, but I could still make out their outline of the front seats, still see their two heads in silhouette. They were kissing, necking, but awkwardly, and when Cage pulled away from Johansson, a line of gum stretched between their mouths.

Starbucks

When they took the floral pillowcase off of my head, I found Nicolas Cage and Scarlett Johansson sitting across from me in overstuffed red chairs. They had changed out of their fifties-style Greaser costumes and into corporate uniforms. Scarlett was wearing the green apron with the usual Starbucks mermaid logo, while Cage wore Old Navy khakis, a button-down pink cotton shirt, and a Rolex watch.

The Starbucks didn't have any windows that I could see, but the space was filled with enough artificial light that I had the impression that it was still daytime. The tables around us were empty, but I heard a murmuring of customers from around the corner and down stairs.

"Here's your mocha," Johansson said.

"I didn't order any—" I started, but Nicolas Cage held up his finger to shush me. He wagged it back and forth at me.

"Don't contradict Scarlett, Paula. She works very hard and puts up with shit all day, the last thing she needs is you changing your order," he said.

"Look, you're very good, but could you break character for a moment and tell me what's going on?"

"Should I?" Cage asked. Scarlett sat down in one of the overstuffed chairs and took a sip out of the paper cup she'd just placed in front of me.

"Why not?"

"Okay, Paula. Okay, enough kidding around. You want information. You want to know what's going on?"

Were they going to shoot me? If so why had they taken me to a Starbucks, to a public space?

"Oh, is Starbucks public?" Scarlett asked. "I thought it was private."

"It's a private corporation."

The track lighting over my head intensified as the rest of the lights dimmed. The espresso machine stopped whirring, and I could hear the silence. Scarlett Johansson took the lid off of the coffee cup she'd been sipping from, and poured out glass marbles on the wooden table top between us.

"Those are from inside the boxes. *Those* are from the other side of the glass," she told me.

"Cornell's boxes?" I asked.

"Stanley wants you to tell us about him. About Cornell and his boxes," Nicolas Cage said. "That's what is going on, Paula. That's all. He wants you to tell us about Joseph Cornell, and why you chose him."

"Have you read my story?" I asked.

"Pretend that we haven't," Cage said.

"And then you'll let me go?"

"You'll be free to go anywhere you want."

The Broken Assemblage

"The Broken Assemblage" was my story about how the artist Joseph Cornell went about the process of dying in his little room, and how his sister Betty Ann coped with his demise. Her brother had been a Christian Scientist, he hadn't really believed in the outside world, and he'd left no real instructions for how to handle the affair of his death. Most of all he'd never indicated just what it was that he wanted her to do with his artworks, or more specifically his films.

She imagined calling Peggy Guggenheim, the millionaire heiress, but Betty didn't really want to talk to anyone who wore sunglasses shaped like television sets while posing for photographs with her toy spaniels, and while there were other collectors who might be interested, Betty couldn't remember any of their names.

"The Broken Assemblage" was about Mary Baker Eddy, the founder of the Church of Christian Science, who believed that the universe was really God's mind, and that since God was perfect and good, it only followed that sin was unreal. Betty's brother had tried to live out his relationship to God, to fill up on the righteous thoughts of Jesus, through his art, but even he had never fully succeeded. All Betty had to do, in order to realize how far from pure Joseph had been, was to read all the women's names in his art, to look at their photographs.

Rose Hobart, for instance, was an actress from the thirties, and her name was also the title of Joseph's first short film. All he'd done was rearrange the sequences of an old B movie and replace the soundtrack with music from one of his favorite samba records. Her brother had edited the images of Rose Hobart to make it appear that the starlet was staring at stars reflected in a pool of water. Rose Hobart looked at her own mirror image: she glanced over her shoulder at herself.

"The Broken Assemblage" was the story of Joseph Cornell eating store-bought jelly rolls and drinking cherry flavor Kool-Aid while working on his final film with Stan Brakhage. Cornell wrote down equations made of words on scraps of paper. He wrote, "Collage=Reality," and "metaphysics and purity."

Stan Brakhage was the filmmaker whose movies were all out of focus because he purposively broke his glasses in order to get a more authentic view of the universe. Stan Brakhage and Betty's brother were both children. They'd held onto something in childhood on purpose, and now that Joseph was dead, it was up to Betty to pick up all the broken pieces he'd left behind.

On the tiny screen in Joseph's room, the fold-up slide projector screen where the projected images of Rose Hobart were flickering, the actress was talking to a swami, and Betty found that she couldn't help but admire her brother's taste. The woman was quite lovely, and he had done something quite strange with her image. Lifted out of the usual flow of the movies, these scenes had a reality to them. He'd captured something about movies, something about what it meant to look at a movie that you forgot when you got caught up in the plot, and it really was beautiful and strange to see it. To sit in his studio, to find a half-eaten Hershey's chocolate bar on his nightstand, to watch his fantasies, it was as if he was still alive, or more like he was beyond life. There was something permanent about what was on the screen. Real life could never duplicate the quality.

My story "The Broken Assemblage" was a fantasy story, a strange tale about how Betty's own desires came into the world when she broke the glass on one of her brother's boxes. In the story, I intimated that she broke the "Soap Bubble" assemblage precisely because she came to understand that reality and desire are all mixed together. After watching her brother's film, she knew that his art was a way to keep reality, desire, and all the seductive images of the world at a safe distance. Betty wanted her desire to be in the world, so she broke the pane of glass on the box and let the ideas out into the air.

What I told Nicolas Cage and Scarlett Johansson was that, in the story, Betty's desires seemed less real to her after they'd been let out of the box. That she had broken open an assemblage entitled "Bebe Marie" and let the little girl doll inside the box free. She'd broken the frame, and then she found that the structures of her own life, all the little distances that had held her identity together, fell apart.

Betty's husband died shortly after Joseph's death, and her next-door neighbor's house burned down, which led to a series of misfortunes that shortly required Betty to move.

Betty ended up living in a state-assisted nursing home. Only a decade after her brother's death, she no longer knew her own name or how old she was, but was more and more convinced, every day, that she was a little girl. She was more and more convinced that she was lost in the woods, just like the girl in her brother's assemblage box had appeared to be.

I told Nicolas Cage and Scarlett Johansson that breaking the old frames wasn't a real option, but they didn't believe me. And when I insisted that finding a new space, a new form, had not involved seeking unmediated reality, when I insisted that I had given up on getting beyond the frame—well, they didn't seem to believe that either.

No Exit

I'm walking on the moon with Donnie, he's dressed in blue jeans and a black, turtleneck, long-sleeved shirt, while I'm fogging up the glass visor in my space helmet with each breath. I'm following him as he follows the wooden tracks around the lunar surface, then behind matte paintings, and then to the giant globe. Donnie is trying to work out exactly where we are and I keep telling him that we're in the basement of the World Trade Center.

"That's impossible," he says.

If we're not in the basement of the World Trade Center, then we're near the Fra Mauro crater. I try to explain it to him, but Donnie can't hear me through the safety glass on my space helmet. He stands on the tracks, and then steps into the space between the tracks, into one of Joseph Cornell's dream boxes.

When Nicolas Cage and Scarlett Johansson left us down here, they made sure to show me how all the dream boxes were already broken. The glass windows on each surreal display were cracked, shattered, or missing. And so there was nothing separating the necessary reality of Joseph Cornell's Christian mind from the contingent unreality of the stage set for us by Stanley Kubrick. Nicolas Cage and Scarlett Johansson told me that my new kind of writing was what gave me this chance to live directly. They themselves were just actors, always pretending, but since I'd be living on the moon, I'd get the chance to be real. I would be really real.

Donnie reaches out toward the moon and points to a crater several hundred miles north of our position. I bounce slowly down the track and try to tell him that he's pointing in the wrong direction, but as I said before, he can't hear me.

The space suit I'm wearing is heavy, but not as heavy as the real suits the astronauts wore. The original spacesuits weighed about 200 pounds on the moon and were made out of the twenty-five layers of plastic, fiberglass, and metal. My suit is skin tight, except for the fishbowl-style helmet and the white backpack I'm carrying. And Donnie is only protected from the vacuum of space by his black turtleneck shirt and blue jeans.

Back on the lunar surface I detach a high-tech scoop from the side of the lunar model and dig into the lunar sand absently. I keep digging until I hit the concrete floor.

"Where are we?" Donnie asks.

But he's asking the wrong question. The question isn't where are we, but who are we? Who are we that we could have ended up trapped so far down underground, all the way down here on the moon.

"You said there was an elevator?" Donnie said.

Donnie reaches out for me. He puts his hand on my space helmet and leaves a palm print there. He is so sure of himself with his hipster glasses and five o'clock shadow. He's accustomed to selecting between images, and I see him looking at me, at the reflection of the moon's surface on the glass bowl I'm wearing, and he's beginning to realize that he doesn't have a choice anymore. This image is real.

"Shit, Paula," he says. "Where the fuck are we?"

The Last Apollo Mission is underway, there is no such thing as up, but I don't have the heart to tell him. Instead I tell him there might be light out there, a green light for an emergency exit. I mouth the words to him so that he can read my lips. I look at Donnie from inside my glass helmet, and for a moment it almost seems as though he's understood.

"Where are we?" He asks it again, and again. And we circle around again, down the wood tracks, over the dream boxes, and then back. All the way back to the moon.

Gregory Feeley is known as both a critic and a fiction writer. His book reviews and critical essays have appeared in a variety of journals and newspapers, including The Washington Post *and* Foundation. *His first novel* The Oxygen Barons *was published in 1990, and since then he's published short stories and novels of alternative history.*

"Giliad" is a nonlinear tale that weaves past and present, game and reality, into a fiction about 9/11 and what it means for Western Civilization. SFSite.com described the story as follows: "The different viewpoints might appear to be disparate, but watch the skill of the transitions as the narrative shifts smoothly from one voice to the next, glides from present to past tense and then back again. The story is a brilliantly told Götterdämerung, its layers constructed so tightly that when the reader does finally perceive the whole there's a sense of the floor dropping away, revealing new possibilities of meaning."

GILIAD
Gregory Feeley

Trent's pleasure in being asked to ßeta-test *Ziggurat* deeply annoyed Leslie, who watched without comment as he slid in the CD but left when summer-movie music began to vibrate from the speakers as cuneiform characters appeared on the screen and slowly turned into the company's name. She was in the kitchen when he called her to come see something, and had nearly finished preparing lunch when he appeared at the door. "No, I'm not interested," she answered, ignoring his crestfallen expression. "Go role-play as Sargon, but don't tell me it's history. And that anachronistic Greek letter is pretty dumb."

"They're just showing off their HTML," he protested, hurt. "You say you hate not being able to underline in email." He took a sandwich, an act he made seem like a peace offering. "Was there really a king named Sargon?"

Leslie sighed. "Yes and he's certain to appear in the game, since his name sounds like someone out of *Star Trek*." Trent laughed. "You know what else they'll put in?"

"Gilgamesh?" he guessed after a second. Trent hated being made to feel he was being tested.

"Beer," she answered, handing him a bottle. "The Sumerians invented it."

"Really?" His pleasure at some bauble of fact was unmediated, like a child's. "And there were seven cities vying for supremacy?"

"In Sargon's time? I don't know." Leslie thought. "Uruk, then Kish . . ."

"Nippur, Eridu, Ur, Lagash, and Umma." Leslie looked skeptical, and he added, "I know, it depends on when."

"These are independent city-states? Then this would be before Sargon, or sometime after." She sighed. "I'll look it up, okay? But I don't want to deal with your game."

When she entered the office, however, a color map of the Tigris-Euphrates valley was glowing on the monitor. Trent was nowhere to be seen. Leslie pulled down her *Cambridge Ancient History*, and as she turned back toward the desk a half dozen cities appeared within the lopsided gourd formed by the two rivers. She stepped closer and saw that the symbols marking the sites were ragged-sloped triangles, ziggurats. Kish was nearest the stem, with the rest farther south; but after a second a constellation of features began to appear: the word AKKAD materialized just beneath the bottleneck, while stylized inverted V's, ominous as the peaks of Mordor in Tolkien's map of Middle Earth, rose to the east and became *The Zagros Mountains*. ELAMITES, AMORITES and GUTIANS threatened from the periphery. Leslie glanced at the speakers and noticed that the volume had been turned down.

Not wanting to sit with her back to the monitor as it cycled through these changes, she took her book into the bedroom. She could hear tapping from the living room, where the laptop was plugged in by the couch. She sat in the armchair—the squeak of sprawling across the bed would doubtless bring Trent—and browsed through the pages on Mesopotamia.

Reading history will send you repeatedly to the bookcase to consult other sources on the subject, unless the author has managed to catch you in the spell of his narrative (which means you are not reading history). This volume was so introductory that Leslie would have found herself standing up with every page, save that she did not own the books to consult. Finally she went to the back hallway and searched the double-shelved rows to locate an old paperback, *History Begins at Sumer*. Anecdotal and lacking an index, it led readers by the hand through successive "firsts"—first library catalogue; first farmer's almanac—with little discussion or analysis. She wondered whether the game designers had quarried it for local color.

Returning the books to the office, Leslie saw that the screen now showed a stylized face with dark holes for eyes and the corrugated beard of an Assyrian sculpture. She recognized it as a bronze head thought to be of Sargon, with its damaged eye-hole digitally restored. The image stared out at the viewer, its probable accompaniment muted.

"That's somebody," said Trent, who had appeared at the doorway.

"True enough," Leslie replied. "Ancient statues don't bear plaques, but they always turn out to be of specific gods or individuals—never some generic woman or warrior."

"How about epic heroes?"

"You mean like Gilgamesh and Enmerkar? They were probably historical figures."

"Enmerkar?" Trent said, startled.

"Sounds like Earwicker?" asked Leslie, smiling. He was already going to his shelf, pulling down the *Third Census* and the *Concordance*. After a minute he reported, "No . . . no references to Enmerkar or Gilgamesh. Rather surprising, when you think of it. Isn't the poem about the search for immortality, and bringing back the dead?"

"No, not really. Is that what fantasy writers think?"

Trent flushed at this, then sat down to consult one of his reference works. Leslie picked up the book on Sumer and tracked down the chapter on Gilgamesh ("First Case of Literary Borrowing"). Kramer's precis did make the poem sound more about seeking immortality than Leslie remembered. As Trent was doubtless about to find corroboration of this, she decided to withdraw the remark.

"Hey," she said suddenly, "pause that." She was pointing to the monitor, where the image of a desert landscape dominated by an enormous crumbling mound was undergoing digital transformation. By the time Trent had turned and clicked to freeze the image, the mound had risen into angular prominence, like an ice sculpture melting in reverse, and the surrounding wastes had sprouted small buildings. With a keystroke Trent restored the original photograph, and they gazed at the massive ruin, so decayed that the eye first saw it as a natural formation.

"I've seen that picture," said Leslie. "There's a modern structure on top, built by archeologists. It looks like a Crusader's castle."

"Really?" Trent drawled. "They must have edited it out."

Leslie explained that while the later Babylonians incorporated the various Gilgamesh poems into a single sequence that did include a quest for immortality, the Sumerian originals—composed during the period in which Trent's game seemed to be set, around 2500 B.C.—told a different story, in which Enkidu is physically detained in the nether world and Gilgamesh merely seeks to get him back.

"But it's the Babylonian version that everyone knows, right?"

"Well, yes." Leslie thought irritably that Trent was crowing, but he looked back to his reference book—an encyclopedia of fantasy, she saw—and she got it.

"That's right, the great man wrote about immortality, didn't he?"

It came out sharper had intended, but Trent didn't take offense. "He always said it wasn't immortality, simply an extremely prolonged life span," he said mildly. "He was far too obsessed with the end of things to preclude its eventuality."

And you had to be similarly obsessed to write his life, thought Leslie. Most of Trent's enthusiasms—*Finnegans Wake*, the works of James Branch Cabell, Wagner's *Ring*—were those of the great man, whom he was seeking, through a kind of literary archeology, to understand. That this required the intentness of the scholar rather than the enthusiasm of the dilettante was for Leslie its primary value.

"He would have hated computer games," Leslie pointed out.

"Certainly *these* games," Trent agreed. "He would have hated postmodernism's embrace of pop culture and mass media; he still believed in great modernist masterpieces rising above a sea of trash. Yet look at his best work: commercial SF novels, his 'serious' efforts unpublished. And his narratives are fragmented and decentered, mixing prose with verse and embedding texts within texts like—" He looked at the monitor, where overlapping windows had opened atop one another, and laughed at the too-to-hand analogy.

He had been gesturing unconsciously towards the top shelf, too close to the ceiling to hold any but small format paperbacks, and Leslie glanced up at their titles. "If you want to write about pomo sci-fi, why not the guy who wrote *The Simulacra*?"

"He's not as interesting," Trent said in a conspiratorial whisper, as though broaching heresy. "*My* guy isn't trendy; he's still out in the margins."

Images were appearing one after the other on the screen: an ancient map of Nippur, an artist's rendition of the walls of Uruk, a detailed relief of charioteers riding into battle. Scenes of war, which the city-states waged incessantly upon each other until they were conquered from without. Was this how players would busy themselves? An image of naked prisoners in a neck-stock was followed by a stele fragment of soldiers dumping earth over a mound of enemy dead.

"How do you win?" she asked. "Conquer everyone else, or just stay on top of your own small heap until you die of old age?"

"I'll let you know," he said. The screen was once more displaying the entire region, and Trent leaned forward to study it. "Why do they call it a river valley? The land between the rivers is wide and flat, with mountains on one side only."

"It's an alluvial plain." Except for the levées that gradually build up along the banks of the river and any canals, the land appears perfectly flat. But the basins defined by these ridges, too wide and shallow for the eye to discern, would determine the flow of water as it floods, an issue of gravest consequence.

"Annalivia, Annaluvia," Trent mused.

"Yes, dear." Outside, Megan's shout echoed off the tier of condo balconies across the grass, and she looked out the window. "Beta testers *play* with the product, right? They don't work at it."

"Not exactly, but I take your point." Leslie was already heading for the door, where Ursuline was blocking the threshold, evidently to alert her to anyone coming or going. She stepped over the sleeping labrador and padded quietly down the hall, leaving her book on the table outside their bedroom. Through the back screen she could hear the children's shouts, none pitched to the pain or alarm she was always listening for.

Four kids were visible or audible through the dining room window, circling each other on the trimmed lawn. Their game seemed improvised yet intuitively understood, and even the fluid shifting of rules that Leslie observed provoked neither confusion nor protest. What games did children play in the ancient world, without structures dedicated to their edification? Would the diversions of ancient Greece be more familiar to us than those of early Sumer, a culture twice as old and incomparably stranger?

Leslie took chilled coffee from the refrigerator, added ice, and stood watching out the kitchen window, a few degrees' different perspective. Without a ball or demarcated spaces, their game seemed the frolic of will in a field of limitless play, the impulse to sportiveness before it has touched a limit.

At one point the four children were all facing one direction, paused before a prospect invisible to Leslie. Something in their hesitancy immediately reminded her of the scene, shown earlier in this Kubrick's year on living room DVD, of the killer apes crouched warily before the slim featureless monolith. "It looks like the World Trade Center!" cried Megan, still weeks shy of her eighth birthday. "Where's the other one?" Trent had laughed, anticipating the coming scenes depicting life in 2001. "You'll see," he said.

The sun retained the brightness of midafternoon, though it was after five and Leslie, had she not taken a half-day from work, would be on the train home by now. The resumption of school still left what seemed an entire play day for Megan, who would go back outside for more than an hour after dinner. This plenitude, possible only in the first weeks of the school year, possessed the transient glamour of enchantment: one layer of time folded onto another. Partake while the feast is before you, she wanted to tell her daughter, who consumed her good fortune with youth's grassfire prodigality.

She brought a glass in for Trent, who had called up another map of Mesopotamia, this one showing the network of canals running between rivers and cities. "It's all connect-the-dots on a flat surface," he said in mild surprise. "I bet news travelled by boat and canal path, along these lines. Like a computer chip," he added after a moment.

"Watch it with the cute conceits," Leslie warned. She wondered whether the map's density of crisscrossings (which seemed to include all the thirty or so Sumerian city-states, not the just Big Seven chosen for gaming purposes) was largely imaginative reconstruction. How many of those first distributaries could still be discerned beneath millennia of subsequent history, flooding, and war? Perhaps through satellite photography, of which the last decade must have seen a lot.

Trent, angling his head to regard the map northside up, seemed to be thinking along the same lines. "The entire region is now part of . . ."

"Iraq, yes." Where children now perished for the imperial ambitions of their leaders, as had doubtless happened five thousand years ago.

Trent grimaced. "At least Great Games never pandered to the help-kill-Saddam market." He was reminding her that he had refused to get involved with a project called *The Mother of All Battles* nearly ten years ago, when turning down assignments was hard to do.

Leslie recognized that she was looking for a reason to dislike the game. "Ancient Sumer was such a strange culture, you're not going to gain a understanding of it by playing geopolitics."

"I don't think this is all wargaming," Trent replied as he clicked through a series of menus. "Here's a module on the economy of mud bricks. Look, you have to bake the ones that go into the bottom rows, or they will draw moisture out of the ground. And you need wooden frames to make them, which are expensive."

"That's not a mud brick," Leslie pointed out. "It's a clay tablet."

"Whoa, you're right." Trent backed up to restore a rectangular image that had appeared as a sidebar. "That might be a bad link." He scribbled for a moment on a clipboard next to the monitor.

Leslie leaned forward as Trent, exploring the program's architecture, followed a series of links that brought up more cuneiform images: tablets, cylinders, a pieced-together stele. "Wait, stop," she cried. The clay square on the screen was evidently small, as it contained only five rows of text. "I remember that one from college. See the first characters of the top three registers? They are 'Day 1, Day 2, Day 3.'"

"Really?" Trent studied the pictograms—a pair of curved lines, suggesting sunrise over the saddle between two hills, with one, two, and three vertical slashes beneath—while Leslie explained that the tablets dated from 3000 B.C., the dawn of writing, and that these three characters were for a long time the only ones on the tablet whose meaning was known. She had seen a slide of it in a history lecture, and when the teacher asked the class to guess she felt a thrill at the unmediated transmission of meaning, like current, across five thousand years. "How many hash marks till the base number?"

"The Sumerians had a sexagesimal system, based on factors of sixty, but their place notation progressed in alternating tens and sixes. It was very complicated."

"Hey!" Trent looked delighted. "So their system partook of both hex *and* decimal."

"Watch it," she repeated. "I didn't say hexadecimal." But Trent had already returned to the computer and was searching the game's list of tables.

Any history game that gave an explanation of the Sumerian notation system had a good chance of positioning itself out of the market, Leslie reflected as she returned to the living room. This one would have a tough time in any event, with *Civilization III*, the industry's 900-lb. gorilla, about (she remembered Trent saying) to burst onto the scene. She wondered whether games that big paid their beta-testers.

The living room window looked onto the front yard, away from the angled patterns of the condo complex behind them. Their lease allowed the owner to terminate on two months' notice if he sold the house to the developers, who evidently had plans to expand the complex next spring. This agreement reduced the rent but also, they learned, discouraged the owner from maintaining his property.

"History begins at Sumer." And ended, presumably, a few years ago, at least according to that silly book her Dad sent her one Christmas. Leslie worried less about inhabiting a post-historical world than a post-boom one, which seemed now to be fully upon them.

Trent was clicking rather than tapping, evidence he was venturing deeper into the game. Fair enough, late Friday afternoon in early September; it was anyway Leslie's turn for supper. The DSL being free, she plugged in the laptop's phone jack and went online, and spent the next twenty minutes (the ingredients for salad were already prepared) browsing through the pages that a search on *Sumer, Akkad, Mesopotamia* brought up.

Gamespace isn't textspace, which tilts the plane to create page, tablet, screen: upright to the eye like the drawings that words once were. Gamespace models the earth, a field of play for agents, not the gaze, to move through. Battlefield means battleground, its participants grounded as text never is. Sumer was a plain, even as its texts, lying forgotten beneath the successive accumulations of history, eventually become. You may claim equivalence, each plane perpendicular to its opposite, but the fallen tablets make clear which one subsumes the other.

Perhaps the computer game holds out the promise of genuine space, the three dimensions produced by intersecting planes. A surface isn't space at all, though references to "the white space" between words or "floor space" underfoot may seduce us into thinking otherwise. Leslie is undressing for bed, whose flat cotton expanse (it's too hot for blankets) extends unbroken almost to fill the room. Pulling a fitted corner back over the mattress, she causes a spray of rills—converging on an adjacent corner like improbably straight ridges—to widen and disappear. Every bedsheet is a landscape.

Sumerian scribes held their tablets at an angle while writing, as an old stele shows. So the act of writing takes place in space, even if it is read flat? Leslie plans to be asleep before Trent joins her; she is halfway there already. She can hear him in Megan's room reading about Greeks besieging Troy, with occasional glosses. There are probably also excisions of repeated lines, although Leslie can't hear them.

Scribes excised lines with a wet finger, smoothing the clay to blankness. Dried clay couldn't be altered, but fresh material was plentiful; Mesopotamia left no palimpsests like the scraped parchments of the West, too precious to discard. Leslie blanked texts at a stroke, words with no physical fixity dispersed even from the dance of forces that had briefly held them. Drawing the mouse across its pad, its faint drag pacing the ribbon she extended across the page, Leslie unworded the clumsy locution, restored the soothing emptiness, ready for words better chosen, as a child might fill in the surface she had scored. Scribes prepare their own tablets, but merchants are too busy, and Nanshe could push the set clay into the frame's corners with stronger fingers than her brothers, who preferred to scoop mud and hurl. She was not allowed to cut reeds but could bring them to her father, who let her lift the damp fabric and make marks on the pristine square so long as she smoothed them before he needed it.

A female scribe would be laughable, but women in merchant families were often taught to read. Nanshe plied needle, dowel, and chopping knife—awkwardly, but she could still hold a reed better than either brother. Carefully she positioned it between her fingers so that the nib was angled correctly, then sank it cleanly into the surface. The tactile pleasure of its yielding was intensified when she lifted the stylus to see the sharp wedge she had made. Twisting her fingers slowly, she added diagonal and perpendicular strokes: syllables, a word. She yearned to match her father's fluency, but the pride she took in producing a recognizable "wheat" swelled her heart, and she drew the cover back over the tablet without effacing it, a secret message for her father to find.

Dampness fled swiftly in the midday heat, and Nanshe stood up with the two frames in her arms and began to pick her way to the upper bank. Enannatum could bear them faster, but he and his friends were busy diverting a stream past their walled mud city, which would soon suffer attack from rival fortifications. Atop the rise, where a footpath paralleled the straight-ruled canal, Nanshe could see across leagues of fields, orchards, and low shaded houses. It seemed readily plausible that if she set down her frames and climbed the nearest tree she would see, wavering on the horizon, the walls of the enemy.

Writing, trade, and a premonition of the consequence: endless warfare and eventual destruction. Ineluctable modality of the geographical, the scribe thought as he rolled a fresh sheet into the platen; at least that if no more.

He was a half dozen pages into a science-fiction story, about a nuclear war fought with long-range bombers. Given time, the Soviet Union would doubtless be able to fire rockets half-way round the world, children of the V-2 with H-bombs as warheads. At the moment it didn't seem the world would wait that long.

"There's panic buying in the streets," called Cyril from the front hall. The scribe heard the clink of bottles in the paper bag, and the sound of the door being kicked shut. He realized that he had been unconsciously listening to the elevator ascending, and had set down the book and returned to his story in anticipation of Cyril's entrance.

"Just closing time for the liquor stores," he said calmly. "They're not open Sunday."

"I know panic when I see it." Cyril came in with a pair of bottles and an opener. "There will be fistfights in the grocer's, old ladies trampled in the crush."

"Well, we'll be sure not to hoard." He flipped off the bottle cap and took a deep drink.

"Whoever imagined Armageddon would arrive through the Suez? Hungary was galling enough. What's this?" Cyril lifted the book off the chair and read the cover. "*From the Tablets of Sumer*. A subsidiary of Pfizer?"

"You know very well what Sumer is," the scribe retorted. "And the tablets are dried clay."

"My people used stone. Actually, we took whatever God handed out."

"And look where that got—" said both men together. Cyril grinned blackly and tossed the book onto the desk. "Not a great title," he remarked.

"They'll probably change it for the paperback." The scribe typed the rest of his sentence, a brief rattle, and pushed his chair back.

The elevator began to descend back to the lobby, a rickety hum that did not register when he was typing or listening to music, but would start up during a lull to remind him that he lived in a hive. He had moved his family to Milford expressly to get outside the blast radius, and here they were back again, just across the river from Manhattan as Western Civilization seemed to be entering its death throes.

The basement shelter in Milford, with its blankets, chemical toilet, and emergency provisions, seemed in his imagination to lie still underwater. The image, literary and unreal, could not be contemplated in the intolerable present: it belonged to some other category of time. He imagined the occupants of a New York apartment building crowding down into the basement in the minutes before attack.

Cyril was leafing through the book. "Firsts?" he asked curiously. "Sumer was the beginning of civilization?"

"As we are its end. Great cities whose literate class is kept busy producing official documents, and so don't distract their masters. They found the Gilgamesh epic among thousands of temple inventories and official genealogies."

"First tame writers, eh?" Cyril commented. "Guess that's why they also had to invent beer." His own bottle, the scribe noticed, appeared to be bourbon.

"In their beginning is our end," he murmured.

"It's a cute idea," Cyril said, meaning that's all it was. "Is there a story in it?"

"I don't really feel like mining it for story potential," the scribe replied, a bit waspishly. Which wasn't really true, he realized: without thinking about it, he had been doing exactly that.

"I suppose you've been digging for references to Sumer in that damned thick square book," Cyril continued.

"It's not square; it's circular," he protested mildly.

"Found some already, I'll bet. Care to read me one? Go on; you know you want to."

With only a token show of reluctance, he pulled out the big book, supple-spined as a dictionary from frequent opening, and found the marked passage.

"Behailed His Gross the Ondt, prostrandvorous upon his dhrone, in his Papylonian babooshkees, smolking a spatial brunt of Hosana cigals, with unshrinkables farfalling from his unthinkables, swarming of himself in his sunnyroom, sated before his comfortumble phullupsuppy of a plate o'monkynous and a confucion of minthe . . ."

"A bigshot," Cyril commented. The scribe blinked at this, and jotted *lugal = bigshot* on a pad beside his typewriter. "Lots of bug imagery: drone, cigals, papillon—this is the ant and the grasshopper story, right?"

The scribe nodded. Cyril would love the *Wake* if he allowed himself.

"Dhrone also meaning throne, meaning the crapper. The great man's preoccupations never recede far, do they? I can bet what the 'unthinkables' are, but what about the 'unshrinkables'?"

"Pajamas, I think," the scribe replied. His mind flinched away from *unthinkable*. "There's a later passage, which contrasts 'Summerian sunshine' with 'Cimmerian shudders.'" Cyril looked about to smirk, and he added sharply, "Not Robert E. Howard's, but the land of shadows."

Cyril nodded wisely. "Sumer is igoin out," he said. "Lhude sing Goddamn."

There was nothing the scribe could add to that. The faint whine of an overhead jet, some 707 bound for Idlewild, reached them faintly through the window. The scribe looked at the pane, thinking about shutters. Flying glass; blast sites in the financial district, the naval shipyards. Apartments with a view of the Manhattan skyline might prove less of a premium.

"You're thinking story ideas." Cyril became very acute, not to say accusing, when he got drunk.

The scribe flushed. "The greatest temptation is the final treason," he began, then stopped: he seemed to have no more control over his words than his thoughts. "I was thinking about shudders."

Cyril laughed, then finished the bottle and set it on the floor. "Well, tell me what you decide."

The scribe's bottle was also empty, and it occured to him that when Virginia took the kids to a movie so he could entertain in the tiny apartment, he should be quicker in realizing that he had to go to the kitchen himself. Indurate though he was to alcoholic remorse, the scribe felt a stab of grief, that he had brought his family back to the targeted city, now near the endpoint of history.

And Cyril, who sometimes seemed to read minds (but likelier knew to follow one's stream of consciousness to where it pooled), said, "There's your title: *Last and First Gravamen*."

The scribe found he could not bear to contemplate the word gravamen. He was standing in front of the refrigerator, looking at containers of the juice, whole milk, condiments that he usually saw only at table. The quart bottle was cool in his hand, its heft comforting, but the hum of electricity and wisps of Freon-cooled vapor seemed fragile to evanescence, and the emanating chill breathed a message that he hoped not to hear.

Leslie was halfway through an aggravating Monday afternoon when Trent called with his proposal. "That game?" she said distractedly, waving away a colleague who had poked his head into her cubicle. Trent had fooled around with it all weekend, reasonable behavior for someone who spends his workdays editing documentation, but was expected to set it aside for Monday.

"I have been exchanging email with the developers, and they're planning a series of novel tie-ins."

"Novels? You mean, like Dungeon & Dragon books?" Leslie had seen such paperbacks in Barnes and Noble.

"Not gaming novels, but novels set in the game's era. They would be packaged to tie in with *Ziggurat*, but wouldn't follow its story line or anything—it doesn't have one, of course. Three novels, each one long enough for a slim book, and historically authentic, which is a selling point. But dealing with wars, trade conflicts, dynastic succession: just like the game."

Leslie didn't like the sound of this. She had met friends of Trent who had worked on such projects, which seemed a good way to earn six thousand dollars in four months rather than four weeks.

"What are they offering you?" she asked.

"They want to see a proposal, maybe two or three outlines. I told them about your history, and said you would be involved."

"In writing a novel?" Leslie was sure she was misunderstanding something.

"I'll do the work, I just need input for the outlines."

"Trent, this makes no sense." Her phone began blinking, a call routed to voicemail. "Isn't this game coming out in November? There isn't time for all this."

"It's been pushed back till spring; they're afraid of the competition from You-know-what. This repackaging is kind of desperate, and they need the books fast. I can do that, I just need to get the contract."

Leslie sighed. "We'll talk tonight, okay?" Another co-worker appeared, and Leslie waved her in. Another light went on and she jabbed at the button, too late. "Sit down, I just need to check my messages."

On the way home Leslie returned the weekend video rental to the library, where she checked the 930s shelf for books on Mesopotamia. She brought back several, which Megan studied curiously while Trent made supper.

"These must be very old people," she remarked. Then she added confidingly: "Daddy is reading me the oldest story in the world."

"The Sumerians were around long before the Trojan War. They probably invented the wheel."

Can something so obvious be startling? Megan looked surprised—of course wheels must have appeared at some discrete point—but said nothing until dinner, when her parents' conversation brought it back to mind.

"*Their civilization was stranger than those game designers realize. You can't write a popular novel about it without distorting everything.*"

"*Oh, come on—how strange can their motivations be? The cities fight over resources and influence, their churches slowly turn into bureaucracies, and individuals pray for solutions to their personal problems and worry about dying. Sounds familiar to me.*"

"*That's a gamer's-eye view. A novel would have to go inside the heads of one of these characters, and their value system—it's as far from the Greeks' as they are from us.*"

"They invented the wheel, so they wanted to be like us. The Pequots didn't have wheels, and Ms. Ciarelli read us a book about *them*."

Both parents stared at their daughter.

"That's an excellent point, dear. The Sumerians even had chariots, which they used in their battles just like the Greeks. Did I show you the images of them on the computer?"

"Not yet. Do they look like the ones the Greeks rode around the city walls?"

"We don't actually know what early Greek chariots looked like," said Leslie. "But Daddy is right, there are actual pictures of Sumerian ones."

"Even though they're older?" Megan thought for a moment. "I guess if you *invented the wheel*, you'd want to make sure everyone knew it."

Trent showed Megan images of Sumerian carts and chariots while Leslie washed up, then took her to the library to get a video. Leslie spent the hour reading about early Mesopotamia, the laptop beside her for taking notes. The glow of domestic contentment—the parents' eyes meeting after Megan said something wonderful could spark the most luminous serenity—still suffused the otherwise empty house, and this, plus perhaps the fact that she generally curled up in this armchair with a novel (the glass of wine also helped), shifted something within her, and the customs and practices of *kalam*, "The Land," began to suggest the most familiar and comfortable of stories: a Mystery (turning upon a former scribe's ability to enter a darkened chamber and read the clay tablets with his fingertips), a Melodrama (legal records told of wicked uncles challenging the legitimacy of their dead brothers' sons), a Gothic (involving the Sumerian custom of burying the family dead within one's house), and even a Romance (a marriage contract could bring the future bride, sometimes still a girl, into her husband's household without specifying who the husband will be, so that she grows up wondering which brother she shall marry). How easily the third millennium B.C. accommodated itself to the varieties of the twentieth century (or nineteenth century, if Leslie is honest) novel, the template of bourgeois sensibility.

Trent came down the stairs, hardcover in hand, with the careful tread of one leaving a child just asleep. Leslie smiled and waved. "Still on Book III?"

"For every category of ships I omit, I have to add an explanation for something else. She has already suggested that the story may last as long as the war."

Leslie laughed. "Switch to the *Odyssey*, fast! I'm surprised you have kept her interested so long in a story where no one travels."

"I suspect she's waiting for the captive princess to be rescued and flee toward home." Trent dropped into the couch opposite Leslie. "Raymond Queneau once said that all novels are either iliads or odysseys. He wrote one, *Odile*, that was intended to encompass both modes."

"As its title suggests?"

A look of astonishment spread across Trent's face. "I never thought of that."

Leslie shook her head fondly. "But does this rule apply to pre-Homeric literature?"

"Good question. The Gilgamesh poem would be an odyssey, wouldn't it?"

"Maybe the later versions, not the Sumerian one. No descriptive journeys, but lots of dialogue and social clashes."

"Huh." Trent pondered this. "So what do you call a Gilgamesh-Iliad? A Giliad?"

"Go to bed, Trenchant. I'll have something for you later." It was only after he had left, a grin on his face, that she realized what he was thinking.

He was asleep when she finally came to bed, the reading lamp on and a splayed book beside him on her pillow. *Hamlet's Mill: An Essay on Myth and the Frame of Time.* It was one of Trent's endearing qualities, that he fell in love with the assignments that were tossed to him: gave them his heart, which got bruised when they were kicked into some chute and later mashed flat in a change of plans. Entering the realm of novel tie-ins, land of the flat fees, he was already resolved to do more than asked. She shifted the book to the bedside table and slid in beside him, feeling an affection that flared brightest at the sight of her daughter's features visible in her sleeping husband.

As she pulled the sheet over her and darkness expanded beyond the bedroom walls, Leslie found herself thinking of the *Iliad*, seemingly more modern than the *Odyssey*, beginning with the war it treats already in progress and ending before its conclusion. Megan must already know the story of the Trojan Horse; will she be upset the hear of the burning towers, the slaughtered populace, and what awaits the victors who set out on triumphant returns? Gilgamesh was an iliad in that respect, too.

It is the last night of the end of history, and Leslie—who had been reading of the three tiers of cultivation in Mesopotamian farming—dreams of Nanshe climbing a tamarisk: emerging above the lower canopy of citrus and pomegranate to look across the grove, the date palms standing like aloof grownups surrounded by crowding children. Nanshe's playmates, feet planted among the cucumbers and lettuce, stood looking up as she scrambled higher, the breeze unimpeded in her hair. The sound of men raising the sluice gate carried clearly from the canal, and Nanshe imagined the water, trickling through the channels and branchings into the orchard, reaching at last to wet their toes. Their startled shrieks would rise like birds, and Nanshe would laugh and hurl down twigs.

"Your faces are tablets," she once cried, exulting at her friends' alarm, "I see what you really feel!" Father had been explaining to Enan-natum how a man's expression and posture can disclose his true feelings, vital skill for any merchant. Invisible in a corner, Nanshe listened. Now every visage contained characters effaced and rewritten, yet legible to her questing eye. The canopy is a face, where stirring leaves bespeak Ekur's stealthy efforts to climb. The horizon is a register, the line where dust storms, the winter rains, attacking armies will first inscribe themselves. The world is a tablet, a stele, the frameless burst of meaning that Nanshe, alone between the fruit trees and the unforthcoming sky, resolves to see hear feel for her own.

The rentals were returned unwatched, Trent's redaction of Helen and Paris's rapprochement left dangling. Cubicle workers stared transfixed before streaming video; officials disappeared into shelters; the skies fell silent. In the shocked still evening, the intolerable images replayed.

Connecticut, untouched by war in nearly two hundred years, got an upwind look. Leslie and Trent lived closer to Stamford than to Bridge-port, but it was toward the older city that Leslie traveled each day, to a thirty-floor gleaming wafer whose daily occupants flowed in and out on the nearby commuter trains. That afternoon, in response to a whispered comment by a ashen co-worker, she rode up to the roof and looked out west. It was there: a low smudge on the horizon, widening as it spread on its own terrible winds into Brooklyn and New Jersey.

No work was done next day, and the weeks that followed were tra-versed in a cloud of dazed grief. Megan, who had gotten (they later realized) a good dose of live coverage while her parents stood white-faced before the TV, had scary dreams about jets. Trent took a long time completing his assignments, then found new ones hard to get. It was somehow still that Tuesday, so violently nailed to history one could not pull free and move on.

"They now say less than ten thousand." No real numbers known at all, just vast uttered estimates, to be slowly refined by counting absences. From the hole in Pennsylvania, perhaps a salvageable black box. Amid horror,

Leslie found herself yearning for story: a cockpit transcript, defiant last let-ter, jubilant claim of victory. Which of you have done this? The loathsome Taliban of Afghanistan denounced the attack, Saddam Hussein hailed it.

Work resumed, though badly. Leslie had to tell her tech staff not to go to CNN.com so often. She came home to a consistently clean house, sign enough of how Trent wasn't spending his days. Megan's school held its postponed Open House, and they stood before her cubby and exam-ined her activities book, album of drawings, and her daily journal. Leslie turned to the journal entry for September 11, and they read:

Today somthing is going on but I don't know what. Marry came in and said somthing is getting wors. Somthing aubt a plane. But what that's the onley quchin I have. I'm probley going to ask her to tell me the ansor becas quechins are ejacashnal.

Trent shook his head. "You couldn't make up something like that," he said. Leslie looked at him with annoyed bemusement. Who said any-thing about making things up?

Their first trip to the City was a rainy Sunday excursion to the Brooklyn Museum of Art, where an exhibit on Japanese anime was about to close. They were quiet as they crossed the bridge to Queens, which afforded them a good look at the south Manhattan skyline. Trent perked up as they entered the lobby, however, and led Megan off to the fifth floor while Leslie checked the map for the Assyrian collection.

Most of the Mesopotamian exhibits were Babylonian, but Leslie found one extremely strange artifact from the era of *Ziggurat*: a teapot-sized terracotta jug bearing a chicken's head and four clay wheels. She stared at the thing, which looked more Dada than Sumerian, then read how such vessel carts could be dated to the mid-third millennium, but that scholars were divided as to whether they had been built as toys or for temple rituals. Leslie thought that the saucer-sized wheels were too crude for religious purposes, and noticed something that the descrip-tion hadn't mentioned, a half-ring emerging from the front of the vessel, from which a rope could be tied to pull the device. Of course it was a toy, though she could not imagine why wheels had been put on a pour-ing jug (it had two openings, one for filling from the top and a spout in front) rather than a chariot.

More compelling was a copper statuette on the opposite wall, of a man wearing a helmet with long curving horns and strange boots that

curled up extravagantly at the toes. His pointed beard and wide staring eyes reminded Leslie of a medieval devil, a conceit that would give
pleasure to a fantasy writer or a fundamentalist. The text noted that the
horns resembled those of a species of ram found in the mountain regions,
whose present-day inhabitants wore pointed slippers. So perhaps the figure had been made there: no one knew.

". . . It wasn't the actual film at all, just the video projected onto a
big screen, so we saw the clamshell version with its sides trimmed off."
Trent was talking about a kid's movie that had been shown as part of an
exhibit. It was raining on the ride back, and Leslie was concentrating on
the road.

"So what were these creatures like?" she asked dutifully. She was trying to get onto the Whitestone Bridge, but the lane for the turnoff was
stalled as a stream of cars, most bearing American flags, passed on the
left to cut in just before the exit.

"They were mammals, I guess: furry, with serene expressions. You
couldn't tell from the dubbing whether *totoro* was a made-up word or the
Japanese term for a forest spirit."

"Like Huwawa?" Trent was always gratified when she remembered
an earlier subject of interest to him.

"Hey, maybe. Huwawa fought back, but then the *totoro* were never
attacked. They *did* have enormous teeth."

Leslie wanted to ponder the nature of wheeled vessels, but consented
to discuss Gilgamesh and Enkidu's journey to the Cedar Forest to slay its
guardian. The strange passage held more interest than *Ziggurat*'s political
macaronics, and spoke (in some way) of the distances Sumerians had to
travel to get wood for their roof beams and chariots.

"Huwawa was supposed to be evil," Trent mused. "An odd quality
for a forest guardian."

"It was Gilgamesh who called him that," Leslie pointed out. "It
seemed pretty plain that he wanted to kill him for the glory. You will
recall that Enkidu, closer to nature, hated the whole idea."

"A *totoro* wouldn't kill anyone for the glory," Megan observed from
the back seat. "They don't need glory."

Her parents exchanged glances. "Good girl," said Trent. "More people should think that way."

After dinner Trent showed Megan a game board on his computer.
"Archeologists called it 'the Royal Game of Ur,' because the first boards

were found in the Ur royal cemetery. But other versions were found else-where, even drawn on paving-stones, so it wasn't just for kings."

Megan studied the irregularly-shaped board, which comprised a rectangle made of twelve squares and another made of six, joined by a bridge two squares long. Each square was brilliantly colored with one of several complex designs. "How do you play?" she asked.

"Nobody really knows. Some rules were discovered for a much later version, and it seems that each player threw dice to move tokens around the board. The two players each move in opposite directions, and can land on each other's tokens and bump them off, especially along the nar-row stretch here."

Megan reached out and traced her finger down on board's side. "Can we play it online?"

Trent shook his head. "Sorry, this is just an image of the original board. It wouldn't surprise me if there was a website somewhere to play it, though.

"Maybe the designers should add that feature to *Ziggurat*," he said later to Leslie.

"They know their audience better than you do," she replied. "You know what they would say? 'There's no place here for a *game*.'"

Trent laughed. "True enough. I like the narrow defile, though. It compels the player to move his tokens along the equivalent of a moun-tain trail."

"No mountain trails in Sumer. Were you hoping to give players a pleasant suggestion of the Khyber Pass?"

That night Leslie opened a file on her laptop and began to organize her notes on Sumer into something that could provide the outline of a novel. War had to be the theme of at least one book, Trent had said, and present in the background for the other two. Leslie decided to think about agriculture and water rights, a likelier cause for conflict than the poems suggest. Even a prosperous landowner would have no reason to read, but Leslie suspected that a middle-class audience would have prob-lems with an illiterate protagonist, so she invented a younger son who was intended to become a scribe. Worldly doings would dominate the action, but it was the kid sister who would prove the novel's secret pro-tagonist, and not merely for Leslie. *Women always constitute more of these books' audience than the men realize*, Trent had told her. You craft the book to please them, like the baby food that is flavored for the mother's palate.

She sketched out some paragraphs about a girl who helped her younger brother prepare practice tablets for school, while the older brother learned the family business with their father. Nobody knew how the clay tablets were made, though she could make some obvious guesses. Nobody knew the location of Agade, Sargon's magnificent capital. Leslie was tempted to set the novel there, though of course she realized she should use sites that readers would find in *Ziggurat*.

In fact . . . Leslie padded into the office, where the flexing trapezoids of Trent's screensaver moved silently across their bit of darkness. Trent used her own machine's better speakers to play music, so had left the *Ziggurat* CD in his drive, its icon present (she saw after tapping the side of the mouse) on the task bar at the bottom of his screen. She twirled the volume knob, then brought the cursor gliding down to click on the tiny pyramid. As the game instantly resumed, she brought the volume up to the lowest audible level, and the clashing sounds of battle faintly reached her.

Leslie clicked rapidly backward, undoing whatever war Trent had gotten himself involved in, then paused in the silence to examine the lists of artifact images. Might as well use implements actually pictured in the game, if you're going to write a tie-in. But the sub-directories showed few agricultural or domestic tools (the designers favoring scenes of splendor or warfare), and she found herself studying the gorgeous works of art, museum photographs—had the producer cleared the rights for these?—of enormous-eyed statuettes; gold jewelry of exquisite workmanship; goddesses carved of alabaster and serpentine, the later ones of Attic accomplishment, the earlier ones deeply strange.

What kind of culture could carve these stone figures, hands clasped reverently and eyes like saucers, and place them in their temples, presumably as stand-ins for individual worshippers? Their gaze was neither submissively lowered nor raised towards heaven; they were *looking at* their gods, with an alertness Leslie knew she could not understand. Did the temple's divine statues—made certainly of gold, meaning leaf covering perishable wood, which was why none had ever been found—gaze back, or were they intent upon other matters? The gods were sometimes taken from their temples and transported to other cities; vase paintings and cylinder seals showed them being poled along the river.

These were "idols," Leslie supposed, but it was foolish to conclude that they were literally worshiped, any more than those statues of the

Blessed Virgin that Connecticut Italians still carried to festivals. Carved images of supplicants stood before gilt representations of divinities in an enactment doubly signified, creating a field of force no instruments can measure.

Trent couldn't use this, though he might be interested in the "sacred marriage" hymns, which made clear that the new year's ritual ended in sexual consummation between the city's ruler (who assumed the role of the god Dumuzi) and a priestess who represented divine Inanna. More metonymy, although perhaps the gods were recognized as physically present in their surrogates.

Same with the food, she wrote in a file she was compiling for Trent's use. *Everyone knew that the food set out for the gods was actually consumed by the temple staff. Nothing is stone literal, it all hovers between levels of mediation, and we can't tell where to draw the line.*

This was evasion, and Leslie knew that Trent would brush it impatiently aside. The "Stele of the Vultures" was so named because one panel showed vultures flying off with the heads of slain soldiers, and there was no reason to believe that Sumerian armies showed mercy to their captives in any of their endless campaigns. Prisoners who could not be ransomed were killed or mutilated, and what else could you expect? the ancient world did not have POW camps. Trent's novelizations could not gratify the gamers' zeal for battles without acknowledging this truth.

The textbooks gave few women's names, but Leslie remembered a goddess known for mercy named Nanshe, and decided in the absence of evidence to the contrary that Sumerians sometimes named their children after minor gods. She added some more lines about the girl and her family, spent a few minutes reading news updates (a habit now faintly obsessive, but she couldn't help it), then took herself to bed. Drifting past shoals toward sleep, she thought of Nanshe, who spoke sometimes with the water-carrier, a great-shouldered man baked like a brick by the sun, who had been captured and blinded during a war years ago. He stood all day drawing water from the levée and carrying it along the road to the village square, the thick pole with buckets swaying at either end bowing across his back like an ox yoke. Mudu, the kids called him, as he had apparently said it once when asked his name.

"Were you a farmer?" Nanshe asked him as he walked back toward the well, buckets and pole slung easily over one shoulder. She felt pleased to have inferred this after watching his practiced motions with the shaduf—when temple servants were sent for water, they slopped and wasted effort.

"*La-ul,*" the man replied curtly. The intensifier suggested disdain for the question.

Nanshe was taken aback. "You weren't an artisan," she guessed after a moment; a blind potter or weaver could still ply his trade, or at least serve as assistant.

"*Sataru,*" he said simply. The verb meant to have incised, but Nanshe was slow to understand.

"You mean you were a scribe?"

Mudu didn't turn his face toward her, which was a relief, since his gaze was frightening. "Palace, not temple. Records."

His calloused hands did not look as though they had once held a reed. Nanshe looked at his powerful arms and back, which she had supposed been his since youth. Various thoughts contested within her, but her merchant's thrift won out and she protested, "Scribing is a valuable trade."

The man grunted. The sounds of men working the shaduf on the levée had evidently reached him, for he turned without pausing onto the path that led to the well, where he set down the pole and began to tie up the first bucket's handle. The polished crossbar over which the rope was slung squealed as he let the bucket drop, and he stretched his arms while they listened to the splash and then the glug of its sinking.

"Water is heavier than clay," he said suddenly.

Nanshe looked up at him, puzzled. "That's not true," she said. She started to say something more, then realized that speaking betrayed her location. She took a step back, and added, "Clay tablets will sink."

Mudu turned and began drawing up the rope. It occurred to Nanshe that he was probably saying that scribes do not carry loads all day. She was still trying to work out why the Palace hadn't ransomed him to his city, or set him to work keeping its own records, or otherwise turned his tangible value to account.

"How many years ago?" she asked. It occurred to her that he might have had children.

A shout carried faintly across the open air. Nanshe turned and saw an adult waving from the path bordering the adjacent field's far side, her mother's cook. She set off at a run, then whirled round to call "Goodbye!" to the slave. If Mudu had once been a palace scribe, he was something other than she had thought.

"If you like dallying at the well, you could bring home some water," Cook observed. She could not discern detail at a distance, or she would have cuffed Nanshe for speaking to the slave.

"You didn't send me out with a bucket," Nanshe observed. Then, "How long ago was the war with Umma?"

Cook laughed. "You sound like a tablet-house instructor." Nanshe scowled, and Cook pretended to flick water at her. "Which war do you mean?"

Nanshe began to say *When they brought back all the slaves*, but thought better of it. Sitting in the courtyard with a basket of legumes, she watched Cook cleaning a turtle with a small bronze knife, and wondered whether scribes impressed into battle for their city fought with better weapons than laborers. The household's other knives were flint, while vendors in the market sliced their wares with blades of clay. Was Mudu's weapon also carried back in triumph to Lagash; did it serve Ningirsu in his temple today?

Later Nanshe retrieved her doll from Sud, whose tiny clay soldiers had overrun it. Sitting in the shade of the poplar that arched over the house, she took a reed she had cut and positioned it beside Dolly's arm, as though it were a spear. The figure now looked like Inanna—Nanshe could not imagine an armed woman otherwise—and she reflected that if she took Dolly out to the house they had made for her in the tamarisk brush (Sud had helped, under the impression that he was building fortifications), then the knee-high mud brick structure, its thatched roof removable to disclose partitioned rooms within, would become perforce Her temple. Nanshe, who knew nothing of any temple's inner chambers, was thrilled at the thought of now gazing upon them.

As she lay that night with Dolly in her arms, the reed spear forgotten under the tree, Nanshe wondered whether she could recruit her mother's assistance in making Dolly a new dress for Festival. Attired like a prosperous merchantwife, Dolly would certainly

This isn't what my readers want. The plot must conform to a gaming scenario; any novelistic texture must grow in the cracks between.

Your readers? They are the game's readers; you're just brought in to entertain them.

Okay, I'm sorry. But if they're reading something I wrote, can I think of them as mine, even if the copyright isn't? At least for as long as they hold open the pages?

This is only a brief scene. Even a novelization can't be incessant action.

I'll give it a paragraph. One can introduce new themes in that little space, establish a counterpoint, okay? If I write more the editors will cut it.

Clay soldiers stood atop the house's perimeter, like invaders breaching the city walls. With an annoyed cry Nanshe swept them clear, but the point returned to her as she lay remembering: Sud thought in terms of armies because the lugals did; the cities did—it was the way things were. Perhaps the gods did.

War with Umma precluded trade with Umma, but Umma (Nanshe's father often said this) produced little that Lagash did not, and competed with Lagash for trade elsewhere. If the arrogance of Umma's people regarding water boundaries roused Ningirsu's ire, there was no reason why Lagash's merchants should question the will of the city.

Shock troops thunder across the plain, impossibly loud, each chariot drawn by two onagers. Lugal Eannatum's chariot commands *four*, and the songs will declare that it moved twice as fast. They far outpace the infantry, which disappears behind boiling clouds of dust, emerging seconds later, a forest of speartips glinting above their helmets, like figures marching out of a mountainside. The enemy ranks break and scatter, and though the chariots do not run them down as in song, no soldier stands fast to attack as they sweep through the line, causing spearmen to drop shields, spring away like panicked grasshoppers, trample each other. Umma's own chariots, fewer and slower, have not yet reached the advancing Lagashites, who see the rout, roar terrifyingly, and present speartips to the spooked Umman onagers. The plain dissolves into a swirling chaos of smoke, noise, and trembling earth, but the contest is already over.

The sickle-sword in Eannatum's hand would be portrayed in stelae and (now lost) wall paintings, the implicit metaphor—of his enemy falling like wheat before him—apparent to the most unsophisticated viewer. Sumer's plains, where nothing stands waving in ranked thousands but the wind-tossed stalks, themselves compel the image. Shall Ninlil, goddess of grain, bow down like grain before warlike Inanna?

As her city did before Inanna's. That is the story—Gilgamesh of Uruk's—he wants most to write, the wordstring that will reach from inscribed clay to etched polycarbonate. Beginning with young Gilgamesh's defeat of Agga's army and ending with the elder king building a shrine in subjugated Nippur, it will bracket the period (a few years, presumably, of his early maturity) when Gilgamesh gained and lost Enkidu, and so *must* deal with it, though in terms a gamer will not balk at. If Gilgamesh's triumphs over Kish and Ur are dramatized with suitable élan—Trent accepts that there must be several battle scenes—then the reader will sit still for the journeys to the Cedar Forest and the netherworld: perhaps even in the less familiar Sumerian versions. The harmonics of mythopoesis, echoing even from this profoundly alien culture, can inform any story, however strong its appeal to gamers.

He is trying to decide whether either *The Epic of Gilgamesh* or the earlier poems can be considered either iliads or odysseys. Declaring the *Epic* an odyssey is banal but probably unavoidable, just as "Gilgamesh and Agga," the only Sumerian Gilgamesh poem not to have been incorporated into the *Epic*, is an iliad in every respect. Role-playing games are all iliads, since they deal with battles, depict societies primarily in terms of their ability to sustain a war effort, and see individual psychology only through the lens of fitness for combat.

Longingly he thinks again of Enmerkar, the figure not in the carpet, whose presence in the *Wake* he yearns to discover. He suspects that Enmerkar and his friend Lugalbanda were the models for Gilgamesh and Enkidu, but the fragmentary nature of the few surviving tablets leaves this unclear. For these oldest of texts Queneau's schematic dissolves, and we are confronted with the stuff of myth, which Trent wants to rub between his fingers, raise to his nose. O show me the substrate of meaning, psyche's bedrock.

What did Lugalbanda cry when he awoke and found that his companions had left him for dead? The steppes of Mount Hurum, dry and desolate, must have seemed the Sumerian underworld, did he realize at first that he still lived? The tablet here crumbles into powder, the rest of the story is lost.

Enmerkar and the army commanded by his seven heroes succeed in subjugating Aratta (the poem could hardly have gone otherwise) and they return to Erech along their original route, intending to reclaim Lugalbanda's body and bear it home. Upon reaching Mount Hurum,

1. They find Lugalbanda, who has been roaming the steppes in despair. He
   1a. is overjoyed to see them, or perhaps reproachful, but
       accepts in the end his retrieval by his peers and his return
       to the land of the living.

1b. rages and does not forgive; the story becomes one of irreparable breach.

2. They do not find Lugalbanda, who
2a. has wandered deeper into the wilderness.
2b. has been taken away by the gods.

Trent imagines more pathways, a thorough exploration of the branching possibilities that, like books opened in dreams, can appear but not actually be read. Some he knows can't work: it's the Greek gods who take up petitioners *in extremis* and turn them into constellations. Nor can Lugalbanda break with Enmerkar; Sumerian myths don't deal with character conflict in that way. So Enmerkar and Lugalbanda are reunited; the ordeal of Lugalbanda abandoned is a wound that heals up by poem's end.

Such wounds make us feel what we can't understand: that's what myth is. Niobe, still weeping for her children though turned to stone, or the centaurs' anguished thrall to wine and lust, retain their power to claw at the reader. The *Wake* doesn't claw, though the great man, a lesser writer in every other way, knew enough to.

Untitled, obscure in meaning, often fragmentary, the two or three dozen narrative poems that exist in Sumerian versions seem too blunt and odd to move us as the Greek myths can. Except for the line about mankind being created from "the clay that is over the abyss," the only tale that Trent found deeply affecting was Lugalbanda's abandonment on Hurum and his undescribed reaction.

Mount Hurum is not on *Ziggurat's* map—no one knows where it is—and Trent recognizes that his novels must reside within the game's geography. He hovers above the plain, watching the words IRAQ and *Baghdad* fade away and the coastline press inward until it is resting against the city that now labels itself *Ur*. Trent begins to fall, slowly at first, then faster as the land below growing larger and more detailed until it tilts abruptly away, like the view from a plane pulling out of a dive, and he is skimming above a landscape that has lost its lettering and cartographic flourishes and assumed almost the realistic detail of a desert seen in the opening shot of a nature documentary.

A ripple breaks the horizon's flatline, and at once the ground flashing below is not sand but cultivated fields, divided by roads and levées. The structures ahead swell and gain definition, a great wall bristling with towers, its ramparts topped only by the central ragged pyramid.

The viewpoint circles the city center, temple and palace readily identifiable (Trent remembers close-ups of them) and the ziggurat's corrugated slopes rendered in vivid detail, then swoops down to alight in the central square.

The city is full but empty, for Trent knows (with the logic of dreams) that moving crowds would strain the resources of role-playing games: yet this is the Uruk of *his book*, anchored to the CD yet ranging freely, ungameably peopled by people. Trent moves through the throng in this confidence, secure in his characters' imaginative reality even as their bodies pass through him, or perhaps his through them. Cinched tight by the city walls, the crowded buildings radiated heat—unrelieved by winds—and a terrible stench, electronically imperceptible but evoked, made real in the mind's nostrils, by the twining long molecules of words, complex chains that twist to do anything, like wisps of smoke weaving themselves into firewood.

Stinks and gritty skin, heaped refuse and open water glimpsed from ramparts: immaterial perceptions electrons are too crude to trace. Why are words finer than particles, which are older than anything? The meaning of Sumerian myths elude us, but not because their tablets are fragmentary or our grip on their language infirm. Every word sprouts wings, turns metaphor, and flits off at an angle we hadn't seen. These angles are not ours, they disregard our geometry. This unbegetting language, spoken by no one, is hardware that only ran thoughts now incomprehensible, their myths a food our minds cannot digest.

No single stuff of myth, then, no wellspring feeding every people. To work in the digital realm is to accept this: the sentences you construct do not pretend to be transcriptions of spoken words, nor do your images seek validity as representations of nature, judged by their fealty to something. Music—always disconcertingly itself, especially when not giving tune to words—still plays while you play, but no longer serves only as dramatic accompaniment. Word, image, and tone alike emerge from the difference between 0 and 1, the contrast between fields of force that needs, can have, no touchstone.

Game-players don't know this; they blithely enter these regions (paying for admission), thinking them flat, directional. Assume our forest is merely your path, cheer yourselves after walking its length. Contention is stranger than you know, gamers, who strain at the lines we draw round you, roar at the points we dole out, and imagine yourselves at play in the fields of the board.

Trent frequently checked the online news outlets, a practice he justified on the grounds that it kept him at his desk instead of sending him into the living room to turn on the radio. Some days he merely glanced for new headlines; others he read to the bottom of what stories were available, searching for hints of the attack that was surely coming. He knew that Leslie was doing the same from work, and sometimes imagined them sharing a second in the pages of msnbc.com/news or www.bush-watch.net, invisibly present to each other.

When it came, the websites gave it headlines, although there was nothing more than reports of rocket bombardments. "It has begun," he said aloud. What someone had told him a dozen years ago, coming out of a late movie to students gathered on the sidewalks and word that Baghdad was under attack.

They ate dinner before the TV news: few facts, much commentary. "Word from halfway round the world," Leslie murmured, her thoughts on a different track than Trent's. "How long have most people waited for news of distant battles?"

"We're not getting much," he replied. Anchormen, bleating helplessly, were being replaced one by one with roundtable discussions. Trent cycled through the channels once more, then left it on public television.

"True; I was thinking of information reaching the strategic command, not the sorry populace. Do you think reporters will make it in before they flatten everything?"

"Afghanistan isn't Kuwait," Trent replied. "It's a big country, mountainous; far from the sea. You can't pulverize it from aircraft carriers."

"I don't know," said Leslie. She was sick with hatred for the Taliban, whose recent demolition of two immense Buddhas seemed their only assault upon something not living. But George W. Bush had declined to distinguish between them and al Qaeda, as though playing to a constituency that would regard such nicety as treason. His demands had been provocative and insulting, impossible to meet although the Taliban seemed to have tried. Yet had the Western nations invaded Afghanistan in the spring, she would have cheered.

"Is the President our foe?" Megan asked while Leslie was loading the dishwasher.

"In what sense?" she said, startled.

"I just heard Daddy on the telephone, and he was talking about our 'foe President.'"

On his desk Leslie noticed a photocopied page, with several sentences highlighted and scribbled dates and numbers in the margin. She squinted at the text, calling upon her grad school French. *Il y eut une attaque. Les villages insoumis . . .* There was an attack. The unsubdued villages illuminated themselves in turn, marking the progress of conquest, like the little flags in commercial cafes.

A shadow from the other side darkened the sheet, which she turned over to find a sentence in Trent's handwriting. *The resisting villages burst alight one after another, illuminating the path of victory, like the snapping banners of a streetside cafe.* The photocopy had been made with their scanner, his usual practice when he wanted to mark a passage from a library book.

"I hear you likened our President to Dario Fo," she said as they were getting ready for bed.

"I did?" He thought about it, then laughed. "He could be played by Dario Fo."

Reaching to turn off the light, she saw a book on the floor and turned it over to see the title. Her lips quirked: there was nothing to smile about, but confirmation of her husband's nature prompted an odd comfort. The photocopy had pleased her more than the scrap noting his daily progress, as though the assignment he had sought were a ditch to be measured in linear feet dug. He should have been writing books all along—books that encompassed history and literature, like the biography he had begun, rather than novelizations, mixing non-history with non-literature as though he was afraid to pull free of this world well lost. Could that last tug hurt as much as Trent seemed to fear?

She spoke of Trent when reluctant to speak of herself, her therapist had once noted, but wasn't she supposed to voice her cares? Trent had moved on, getting tech work and even a small grant, but privately raged, rejected (at least in his own mind) by a profession he should have rejected. It was only after tearing free, Leslie explained, that the wound could begin to heal.

"Do you think he is still suffering from that 'wound'?" her therapist asked.

"I'm sure he does." Leslie shifted slightly in the armchair, away from the view of Long Island Sound, and let her gaze rest on the pottery lining the book case. "It gnaws at him, that some people believe it, and that others won't declare they don't."

"Do you believe it?"

"No." This time she spoke firmly. "I've met her, remember? The whole industry is full of misshapen people who design games because they don't have the social skills to work in other environments. I mean—" she laughed—"I've got computer nerds reporting to me; I know about badly socialized people. But my guys don't claim creative temperaments. He shouldn't have been working for someone who lived with her boss, however stable she seemed."

"Does the fact that you believe him offer some solace?"

"You'd think it would." Leslie thought. "I guess it does, but not enough. He wanted to write a book called *Complicity*, a study of why people side with their peers' oppressors. I told him to stop it."

"And this was when Tobias was ill?"

"Right before he was born. It was still going on, afterward. Maybe that's . . ." She shrugged, her eyes suddenly stinging.

"That was four years ago," her therapist observed delicately. "This dispute may have exacerbated matters for Trent, since it struck directly at his role as a family man." She was reminding Leslie that she is not Trent's therapist. "That might explain his continued anger over professional problems that, by now, are ancient history."

Four years ago Leslie had been in bad shape, and the return of what she now recognized as clinical depression threatened to wash away the ground gained since. She began doing things only when she had to, and didn't pick up *Ancient Mesopotamia* at the library until they threatened to send it back. Trent made oblique comments on her listlessness, and even word that a Florida newspaper office had been contaminated by a rare form of anthrax—another grotesque intrusion from the world of techno-thrillers—failed to jar her out of numbed and ringing stillness.

Was everybody hurting? Leslie supposed so: the avidity with which her co-workers followed the war news smacked of self-medication. Updates rarely came during the workday, but she knew they checked regularly. Trent glared at the TV news, bitter and conflicted, while Megan, unselfconsciously mimicking the familiar Texas accent, asked about "the War Against Terra." Afghanis, caught in the irruption of renewed warfare as winter began to close the passes to their under-provisioned villages, experienced a brief rain of brightly colored food packets.

She sat on the couch, the household still after Trent had gone sullenly to bed, and considered her new book, whose full title proved to be *Ancient Mesopotamia: The Eden that Never Was*. It compared favorably with *Sumer: Cities of Eden*, the pretty Time-Life volume that the library already had on its shelves. *History Begins at Sumer* was unaccountably absent, but Kramer had contributed the text for another Time-Life title, *Cradle of Civilization*. Leslie was annoyed with Kramer for his tendency to make judgmental distinctions between "conquerors in search of booty" and "peaceful immigrants eager to better their lot," as though migrating populations' worthiness to move into a land depended on their adherence to some United Nations-like ideal of peaceful coexistence. Did that notion represent the spirit of the mid-sixties, or the spirit of Time-Life Books?

In the absence of Kramer's own tome, the earliest volume in Leslie's modest collection was A. Leo Oppenheim's *Ancient Mesopotamia: Portrait of a Dead Civilization*. Its forthright subtitle intimated Oppenheim's contention that Sumerian-Akkadian-Assyrian civilization was extinct and should be studied for its own sake rather than for its supposed value as the seedbed of human progress. Leslie found she preferred this austere honesty to the pious melioration that saw Gilgamesh, cuneiform, and the Code of Hammurabi as the first toddling steps of mankind's march.

The weeks that followed pulled Leslie in opposite directions: toward the fixity of the past and the lunacy of a fantasy future. She read with disbelief the mornings' news of anthrax spores mailed to TV studios and the nation's capital, with senators' offices contaminated and postal employees dead. The conclusion was inescapable: the United States was under attack by biological agents. The twenty-first century was turning out just as her teenaged sci-fi reading had predicted.

"They say it's Saddam." Trent was following the links from news reports on the spores' surprising sophistication to declarations by "fellows" at right-wing institutions that Iraqi responsibility was certain.

"Well, it certainly isn't the Taliban." The medieval theocrats who were regrouping in disarray under assaults from their warlord adversaries and miles-high bombers seemed poor candidates for the invisible attack that sent the world's superpower into panic, though perhaps (pundits mused) al Qaeda's penchant for low-tech operations staged within the target country had led them to obtain a cache of Soviet-era war germs. Such a theory did not require the hand of Saddam, but Leslie found it hard to push the reasoning further. The idea of pestilence blooming in the nation's nerve centers like sparks falling on straw left her disoriented. She did not fear for her own safety, but felt the axis of her being tilt vertiginously, a slow tipping into boundless freefall.

There were no further attacks, although a Manhattan woman with no traceable connection with the contaminated mails died of inhaled anthrax in Manhattan, and then another—a 94-year-old widow named Ottilie—in central Connecticut. Midway geographically, Leslie wondered if she should feel her family was in the crosshairs. She didn't, taking comfort in statistics. Word that spores might cling to letters that came through New Jersey moved Leslie to discard all junk mail at the curb.

A week later a letter was delivered sealed in a plastic wrapper containing a notice that the U.S. government had discovered traces of anthrax on the envelope and had subjected it to irradiation: it should be discarded unopened if it was believed to contain food or camera film. Leslie and Trent stared, unwilling to tear through the wrapper (the letter within was indeed junk mail) or to throw it away. It was an undoubted historical document, but to save the thing would make it a relic. Trent carefully photographed both sides with their digital camera and sold it on eBay for $85.

Cries for retaliation rose, angrier for being balked. Since Afghanistan could not be attacked twice, other targets were deemed plausible, usually Iraq. "Look at this," said Trent angrily, gesturing at his screen. "They're all so sure of themselves."

"I don't know why you're reading that at all," Leslie replied. "The chat boards of wargame fans isn't a place for political insight."

"These are my potential readers; I should know what they're thinking."

"I don't even believe that's true." Trent was clawing for a toehold, anxious for demographics that the Web couldn't give him. He showed more self-confidence with work that he respected.

Later she glanced at her screen and found a window open to the posts that had enraged him. Vaunting and aggressive, they bore the signature of angry, powerless guys desperate to be knowledgeable. *Let's do it right this time* and *Next time we nuke the K'abah* and *It's time we revisited The Land Between the Rivers*.

By this point Trent was convinced that the anthrax attacks had not been the work of Islamic militants at all. He suspected rogue forces within the American "bioweapons community," which had secretly developed the strain of anthrax. "Even the administration has admitted that the spores belong to the 'Ames strain,'" he argued, link-clicking deeper toward the documentation he sought. Leslie found his explanations painful to listen to, and she shrank without looking at those windows he left on her screen: laparoscopic images of warblog, like lab reports of current pathology.

Had Sumer suffered from pestilence? Though Leslie recalled no references to the plague, or even to disease as something contagious, it seemed incredible that cities of thirty thousand people, which created standing bodies of water and relied upon wells for drinking, were not periodically ravaged by pandemics, especially during wars. Perhaps Nanshe loses much of her family to cholera during a siege; it was a more plausible involvement than engaging her somehow in the business of battle.

No Sumerian myths mention plague; none of the images of piled dead picture it, nor is it mentioned in legal records. Mortality is ubiquitous, but the index entries for DEATH in Kramer's *Cradle* show an exclusive interest in the Sumerian afterlife, while those for *The Eden that Never Was* focus on the archaeology of grave sites. Gilgamesh showed no fear of catching Enkidu's fever, nor Enmerkar of Lugalbanda's. Death did not leap from victim to victim like a flea; each mortal possessed his own, patient and implacable. Whatever the hero's achievements in life, in the Land of No Return he wandered naked, like all the other dead, hot and eternally thirsty.

It was stifling on the second floor, the day's unseasonable warmth undispersed by the mild evening, and Leslie kicked away the damp sheets to rise and open windows. She continued through Megan's room and the baby room, now choked with books, opened the bathroom window (the tiles were barely cool beneath her soles and the toilet seat actually warm, as though someone had preceded her on it) and thence to the end of the hall, where the far window would allow a cross breeze. From there it seemed natural to descend the stairs, for the screened patio doors admitted the night air and she could walk around freely in the unlit rooms.

Opening the refrigerator would illuminate the uncurtained kitchen, and an attempt to fill a cup in the dark clattered the stacked dishes so loudly that she jumped back. Leslie wandered instead toward the front of the house, slowly—she sank her bare foot into the warm furry side of Ursuline, too torpid even to stir—but guided by the faint light coming from the office. Her own computer adjoined an open window so she sat at Trent's, where the monitor's low setting cast just enough light to see by. Trent never kept loose papers on his desk, but she could make out a page of his handwriting lying between *Odile* and *History Begins at Sumer*. She turned the light up slightly, and saw the journal Megan had given him for his birthday, blank sheets bound in dyed silk, held open between the two volumes. He had written in it with his fountain pen—another gift—and weighted the pages flat to dry.

If it had been a paragraph, manifest Dear Diary prose, Leslie would not have bent forward to read, but the two lines were centered like aphorisms, and there was something odd in the lettering. The monitor brightened slightly as the screen saver turned some corner in its workings, and the words leaped up at her.

ßeta-testing for ßeta males? And underneath: Real men write their own books.

The Montblanc rested in the gutter, a third object to disturb if she wished to turn back the page. Leslie sat back, feeling her face redden in the cool air. Seeking refuge for her gaze, she smacked lightly at the mouse, and the saver vanished, presented her a vista, dim in the darkness, on a burning city. Only the flames actually moved, the fleeing populace and spear-waving invaders caught as in a frieze, but the central building, one side lit by the conflagration, was a recognizable stepped tower, which its builders called "unir" and the successors to Sumer knew as "ziggurat."

Leslie moved her hands to the keyboard, hesitant lest she disrupt the game in progress. Within a minute, however, she had slipped past the undisturbed scenario and was reviewing Trent's interaction with the program, which proved to be the only one open. She checked the system documentation and saw, with a start, that the game had been running for days.

It was the work of a moment to settle in front of her own screen and search its flotilla of icons for Trent's preferred word-processing program. She ran it and found a list of textfiles: research on Sumer, downloaded online data, and *Ramparts.txt*, which proved to contain *The Ramparts of Uruk*, 56,917 words, last revised that afternoon. Trent had moved his work files onto her computer, presumably (it seemed obvious after a second) to allow *Ziggurat* to run unimpeded on his older machine. She had forgotten what gluttons for RAM these new games were.

The image was poignant: Trent keeping his writing files in a crevice between her hard drive's enormous programs—nothing takes up less room than text—while abandoning his own machine to the demands of *Ziggurat*. Doing his work at Leslie's desk, getting his email through the laptop, returning at intervals to his own computer where *Ziggurat* flourished, like a cowbird's chick, to consult with the creature that his own work not exceed it in grace or wit: this was austere to the point of penitential. Was Trent setting burnt offerings before the thing?

She clicked on another file, *BookTwo.txt*. It appeared to be mostly outline, but there was a title, *Wheels for Warring*. Leslie shook her head. It was just like Trent, to start with a safe title and have a better one ready for the next book.

The outline was followed by notes, which Leslie scrolled through idly. Some comprised bits of research that she had passed to him; others surprised her. *Only two types of personages are portrayed naked in Sumerian art: humiliated prisoners, and priests engaged in sacred ceremony. Why no sexual connotations?* Leslie shifted her bottom on the wicker chair and smiled. For Trent all nudity held sexual connotations. The dogwalker outside, glimpsing screen light falling on her breasts, doubtless felt the same. *Fragments of those statuettes of worshippers were found incorporated into the floors of the Inanna Temple. I.e., these objects remained sacred, even when no longer used?*

That lone blue eye in the display at the Met: they often used lapis lazuli for eyes (look at the blue-eyed ibex in the next case!), though they could never have seen such features. A legend of men with blue eyes?

"No, Jurgen, you must see my palaces. In Babylon I have a palace where many abide with cords about them and burn bran for perfume, while they await that thing which is to befall them." Epigraph? (No.)

Afghanistan is the opposite of Mesopotamia: a land crumpled into inaccessibility. Geographical barriers everywhere, the bane of invaders; while Sumer was open to all armies, the "Kalam" as flat as a board game.

Title for Book 3: A Game Without A Name. Problematic because the Sumerians of course knew its name; we don't. The game as metaphor for war; if it was also used for divination, then a guide to the Sumerian cosmos & psyche. Historians call it the game "of Ur" since that is where the first boards were found;

if I call it the Ur-game can I make allusions to the original FORTRAN "Adventure"? How many of Ziggurat's *players were even alive in 1975?*

Leslie created a new file, named it *Book3.txt*, and began to type. *Trent, you don't want to construct one of your novels around that board game. You are appealing to an audience that won't spend its money on books.*

You want to write about a female protagonist, preferably young and, though not herself powerful, able to glimpse its workings. If you must include that game, you can show her watching it played: it was laid out in the streets, remember? A little girl can watch almost anything unnoticed.

Women bring food, nurse the wounded, bury the dead. You want an aperture on war? Don't use the viewpoint of a young soldier; soldiers see almost nothing of the totality of war, they are brought in like a load of rocks and then hurled. Women see everything, and when it is over, they are often what is left.

The wind blew the smoke roaring through the streets, blinding the fleeing villagers and lofting scraps of glowing reed to settle like fireflies on the roofs not already burning. Scattered soldiers came at them, whom Nanshe first saw terrifyingly as the enemy, then realized with a greater shock were the defenders of Lagash. One flung away his shield as he sprinted past.

They had sought to watch the battle from the rooftops, but the wheeling armies had raised a cloud of yellow dust, immense as those seen in the sky, which obscured everything. The city wall was lined with spectators, who enjoyed a better view of the action, although the settlement across the canal was closer. Perhaps they saw the flank of battle shift then spill into the barley fields, concealed from the village by stands of date palm and poplars; perhaps the waving cityfolk had been trying to warn them. Nanshe could remember little of that disordered hour, of anxious inquiry between adults who blocked her view, the surmises and cries, people swarming down the ladders to shout questions, to call for their families, and finally to run.

Nanshe had become separated almost immediately, buffeted by legs and swinging arms. She tried to head home, but a cry to make for the city gates sent the crowd rushing against her, and by the time she emerged from the side streets she could smell smoke. Someone lunged for her, not the person she later saw stabbed with a spear, though events seemed alike unreal save what was happening now, grit biting her legs where she crouched. She could see Sud lying in the road, and started repeatedly when a large scrap caught in the rubble waved like a sleeve.

Smoke spattered the sky, and when night fell she thought it another gout from the burning market, to recede after some minutes. At some point she found herself stumbling over littered ground, eyes stinging in the darkness. Unnatural sounds reach her, a loud snap or the crash of walls. A groan from somewhere, and for an instant she imagined the slave moving confidently through the blackness, eyeless and unsmarting, calling out in an accent the marauders would recognize.

A shift in wind pushed aside smoke to disclose still-burning houses, flames from their collapsed roofs flickering through doors like glowing ovens. Occasionally Nanshe could hear a faint shout call down, and so knew the direction of the city walls. Lips cracked, she groped across open ground to the well, which she discovered surrounded by corpses. Desperation drove her to the exposure of the levée, where at last she fell forward to drink.

It is Gilgamesh come to subjugate Lagash, if you like, or else the Gutians sweeping out of the hills. Better perhaps a Sumerian enemy, for Nanshe had been assured that the armies would clash on the plains beyond the cultivated fields, or else before the city gates, and that soldiers would only kill soldiers. Hiding in the tamarisk brush, Nanshe understands only that what the boys had said about war was not true. She is not pondering the implications of this, any more than she is thinking about her parents or their smoldering home, for she is in a kind of shock. Alert to any movement in the brightening morning, she knows that nothing around her will proceed as she had been told.

Can you tell that story? The vaunting steles do not, nor any poems that officials preserved.

It cannot be reduced to a game, nor presented in terms of one. The metaphor itself is immoral.

A wail floated down the stairs, its eerie pitch catching the agelessness of the dreaming mind. Leslie left the room at once, negotiating the darkened floor's furniture and doorways with intimate familiarity. At the top of the stairs she heard it again, wavering between frightened and querulous, and went to her daughter's room. Megan was asleep but in distress, her head turning from side to side in the faint moonlight as her mouth shaped half-words. As Leslie approached, she saw the dim glint of open eyes.

"It's all right, honey." Experts advise that children having nightmares not be wakened, but her parents had learned how to offer Megan comfort without disturbing her. Leslie stroked her daughter's hair and murmured that everything was okay.

"I heard the plane and it scared me."

"Plane?" The Bridgeport Airport was a few miles away, and corporate jets sometimes landed late at night. Leslie tried to recall whether she had heard a plane a minute before.

"It sounded like a jet," Megan said lucidly.

Leslie doubted that her daughter had ever heard a non-jet engine overhead, but she took her true meaning. Storm-tossed but hearing the lighthouse, she realized with a pang that her misery did not matter, nor Trent's professional tribulations nor his baffled fury, but only her daughter's wellbeing, which she had heeded but not enough. "It's all right," she said, leaning forward to touch foreheads in the dark. "No more bad planes."

What is wrong cannot soon be put right—at least not what lies in the mind, which occupies not two or even three dimensions, but the infolds of a space no one has mapped. Leslie began attending her daughter more closely, reading to her at night (no Homer) and stopping with her for hot chocolate on their way back from the library or soccer practice. Megan worried about the school's winter pageant, holiday plans, a classmate's parents' divorce. She mentioned the World Trade Center only when discussing an assignment to summarize the week's news. What more concerned her was an image she had come upon while searching the Net with a friend's older sister: a condemned woman being forced to kneel while a Taliban executioner put a rifle to her skull.

"It's a horrible picture," Leslie agreed. She was furious that her daughter had been shown it.

"The people who did that . . . " Megan spoke with unaccustomed hesitancy. "They belong to al Qaeda, don't they?"

"Not exactly." If you want to get technical. "The Taliban let al Qaeda stay in their country, but they did not help carry out the attacks. The President insisted that they turn over Osama bin Laden, which they probably couldn't do, so he launched an invasion."

"I don't care," said Megan firmly. She was staring into the middle distance, where the woman kneeling facedown was visible to both of them. "I'm glad he's dead."

He wasn't the only one, though. As the death toll from the September attacks steadily dropped from the initial six thousand to just more

than half that, a reciprocal number, of those killed in Afghanistan, rose to match it. The first, dwindling value was widely followed and subtly resented—one couldn't actually accuse those refining it of unpatriotism—while the second, swelling one was neither: its extent (reported only on dissident websites) unacknowledged and enjoyed.

Leslie spoke twice with Megan's teacher, and even rejoined the listserv of women who had become pregnant the same month she had, which she had dropped four years ago. She read online reports of children experiencing anxiety and bad dreams, spoke to her therapist of Megan rather than herself, and watched her daughter: eating breakfast, doing homework, asleep. When troubled Megan was before her, she ignored everything else.

Rumblings from the shocked economy sounded dimly from work and home. Great Games, losing market share, cancelled its plans for a line of *Ziggurat* novels, and Trent (midway through the second book but not yet paid for the first) slid from stunned rage into depression. Leslie comforted him distractedly. Truckloads of rubble filed by the thousands, like a column of ants reducing a picnic's rubbish, from the still-smoldering wreckage of Ground Zero to Staten Island's Fresh Kills landfill, where it was sifted for personal effects and body parts. Troops of the "Northern Alliance" (a cognomen worthy of *Star Wars*) drove the remains of the Taliban into the mountains, which shuddered beneath the impact of enormous American bombs called "daisycutters."

Leslie wanted to spend the hour before dinner with her daughter, but Trent finally protested at cooking every night. Coming from the kitchen, she heard them sitting in the office together, discussing return trips to favorite movies.

"Dumbledore is kind of like Gandalf," Megan was saying matter-of-factly. "Except I don't think Gandalf would be very good with children."

"He treated those hobbits like children."

". . .But Sauron and Lord Voldemort are even more similar, aren't they?"

"Well, it's hard to put much spin on evil incarnate, isn't it?"

"Incarnate?" Leslie could hear her taste the word. "Is that what they call the 'evil-doers'?"

Trent groaned softly. "How I hate that term."

"Because *they* don't think what they're doing is evil," said Megan wisely. Leslie stood outside the doorway, leaning forward slightly to see them. "They think that God wants them to do this."

"That's right. And our culture—what the President calls 'Western Civilization'—believes that *we* are doing what God wants, though the government is careful not to say so in as many words. In the real world, your enemy doesn't oblige you by acting like Sauron or Voldemort."

"Or Darth Vader." Megan has a happy thought. "We'll be seeing Part Two of all three movies next year! Too oh oh too!"

"It must be the age of sequels."

"And the age of *Evil-doers*."

Trent laughed. "In movies, yes. In real life, it would be better if people were more careful about using that word."

"Or 'cowardly.'"

"Indeed." Trent looked at their daughter closely. "You still think about that?"

Megan shrugged. "Julie's Dad almost got killed." She paused, then asked, "Did Gilgamesh represent Western values?"

"Gilgamesh? He lived before there was a West, or a Middle East."

She is changing the subject, Leslie wanted to cry out, but Megan turned to face her father and said, "I'm sorry your book's not going to be published."

Trent blinked. "Heavens, dear, don't worry about that. Maybe someone else will publish it. Maybe I was writing the wrong book." He extended an arm, and Megan slipped under it. "That's an awfully tiny problem, if you think about it."

Lying awake, Leslie listened to her husband's steady breathing and wondered at the loss of his dream, the rout of the last ditch. He had told her in college that prose narrative was dead, that they stood at the end of its era just as the—had he actually said ancient Sumerians?—stood at its birth. Science fiction was the mode of the era, but its future masterpieces would not come in strings of sentences. The Web—he had charmed her by admitting that he too had reflexively read *www.* as "World War Won"— had blossomed in their college years from a jury-rigging of dial-ups to a vast nervous system, and Trent's vision of nonlinear, multimedia fictions—richly complex structures of word, image, and sound, detailed as Cibachrome and nuanced as Proust—seemed ready to take shape in the hypertrophied craniums of the ever-cheaper CPUs.

Trent seemed untroubled that the point of entry to this technology would be through electronic games, which were being developed solely for audiences uninterested in formal innovation and poststructural *différance*. He expected not to retain copyright to his early work, which would be remembered only as technical exercises and crude forerunners of the GlasTome. Its form would emerge by pushing against commercial boundaries from the inside. Even product, he told Leslie, could be produced with a greater or lesser degree of artistry.

When asked to reconcile this conviction with his love of novels, Trent replied that he also loved verse dramas. Reading the draft chapters of his biography of the great man, Leslie wondered at the wretched fellow's dogged attempts (remorselessly documented by Trent) to traverse the swamp of commercial fiction and pull his soles free of it later. Better to emulate the great man's own master: subordinate all to your work, let creditors and family wait upon your genius? Perhaps, as with the intervening James, fame will greet you anyway!

Lie down in bogs, wake up with fees. Trent had ended his unhappy sojourn in the land of the games without copyright or royalties, footloose into the barrens. *But we have our daughter, dear.* The occasional classes he taught, the magazine articles and the tiny fellowship, offered no visible path back to the realm where word and image alike danced in the flux of Aye and Nought. *But what you do is valued, and I love you.* An old colleague had offered the chance to beta-test and Trent had obliged, poor hopeful fool, been sucked in and spat out. *Write something about ancient Sumer.* Your banishing Eden beguiles then betrays you, leaving you stunned with grief, lost to truer pleasures, deaf to your lover's cry. It is the fracture of the unmalleable heart, the oldest story in the world.

It is Christmas Day, "a celebration of great antiquity," as the great man once put it. Dinner with Leslie's sister in Riverside Heights, their first trip to Manhattan since summer. Megan balks at going (she has heard some report of a possible "terrorist attack" over the holidays), and must be reassured that Caroline lives on the other end of the island from Ground Zero. Despite Christmas carols on the car radio and a half hour of *The Two Towers* on tape, she is moody and withdrawn.

"Are you still reading *Odile*?" Leslie asks, seeing the book resting in Trent's lap.

Trent picks up the book, studies a passage, then translates rapidly. "'For years I have deluded myself and lived my life in complete error. I thought I was a mathematician. I now realize that I am not even an amateur. I am nothing at all: I know nothing, understand nothing. It's terrible but that's how it is. And do you know what I was capable of, what

I used to do? Calculation upon calculation, out of sight, out of breath, without purpose or end, and most often completely absurd. I gorged myself on figures; they capered before me until my head spun. And I took that to be mathematics!'"

Leslie glances sidelong at him; she isn't sure if this is the point where Trent had stopped reading or a passage he had marked. "So is the novel both an iliad and an odyssey?" she asks carefully.

"Not that I can tell. I asked an old classmate, who wrote back last night: he says that the novel was written years before Queneau published that theory, and that the title was likelier a play on 'Idyll' and 'Odalisque.'"

"Oh." Leslie frowns. "Academics exchange email on Christmas Eve?"

"Why not? And now I can't remember where I read that claim—probably online."

"Did you search for the site?"

"Can't find it now."

Leslie gets her brooding family to the apartment of her sister, whose husband speaks with zest about the coming assault on Iraq. Caroline and Megan exchange whispers about presents in the kitchen, while Trent politely declines to be baited. Kubrick's film, sound muted, plays on the DVD; Leslie can see the second monolith tumbling in space. Sipping her whiskeyed eggnog, she thinks about 2002, the first year in a while that doesn't sound science-fictional.

On the third day Lugalkitun rode out to survey the damage, striding angrily through the village that had been destroyed when the battle overran its intended ground. Vultures took wing at his approach, though with insolent slowness, and a feral dog fled yelping after he shied a rock into its flank.

Beside the fields of an outlying farm he regarded the body of a girl, sufficiently well attired to be of the owner's family. Her clothing had been disturbed, either before or after death, and the king turned away, scowling. If the enemy had enjoyed the leisure for such diversions, they would also have paused to contaminate the wells.

Caroline asks Trent about a news item that appeared a few days ago announcing that a quantum computer, primitive but genuine, had successfully factored a number by using switches comprising individual atoms, which could represent 0 and 1 simultaneously. Is this still digital? she wonders. Trent, who was examining his gift—a new hardcover edition of the great man's *Cities in Flight*—offers a wintry smile and tells her that the spooky realm of quantum physics will make software designers feel like the last generation of engineers to devote their careers to zeppelin technology.

They go outside, mid-November weather of the warmest Christmas in memory. Down the street a circle of older women are singing, some of them wearing choir robes. A wind off the river blows the sound away, and Megan, looking anxiously upward, does not see them.

Near the burned house he came upon a toy cart, intact among so much rubble. Its chicken head stared as though astonished to find itself upended, and the king righted it with the tip of his boot. He had seen such contrivances before, and they vexed him. Miniature oxcarts and chariots he could understand, they were copies for children; but the wheeled chicken possessed no original—it stood for something that didn't exist. Set one beside a proper boy's clay chariot and you irresistibly saw both at full size, the huge head absurd in a way that somehow spilled onto the chariot.

The toy's wheels, amazingly, were unbroken: it rolled backward from his pettish kick. It never occured to Lugalkitun to crush it; a shadow cast by nothing is best left undisturbed. He looked at the ruins about him, pouring smoke into and summoning beasts out of the open sky. Neither emptiness above nor crowding below concerned him; his brown gaze ranged flat about his own realm, imagining retribution in full measure, cities aflame, their people in flight across the hard playing ground of The Land.

The wind shifts, and the last strains of melody—a gospel hymn—reach them. "Let's go listen," says Caroline, taking her niece by the hand. By the time they cross the intersection the choir is singing again, in a mournful, swelling contralto that courses through Leslie like vibrations from a church organ.

> *There is a balm in Gilead*
> *To make the wounded whole;*
> *There is a balm in Gilead*
> *To heal the sin-sick soul.*

Megan begins to cry. "I don't want a bomb," she sniffles, pressing her face against her mother's side.

Leslie and Trent exchange bewildered expressions. The notes soar into the air, fading with distance. Leslie pats Megan's shoulder, feeling wet warmth soak through her sweater. *My daughter is not well*, she thinks, deeply disordering words. Their wrongness reaches through her, and she tells herself furiously not to cry, that composure will calm her child. But the stone of resolve begins to crack, and two beads of moisture seep through, welling to spill free—their path will trace the surest route—and carve twin channels down her face.

—August 2001–July 2002

James Morrow is best known for the Godhead Trilogy, which includes Towing Jehovah, Blameless in Abaddon, *and* The Eternal Footman. *He is a literary science fiction writer whose work has garnered him World Fantasy and Nebula awards as well as a Golden Eagle for his short film "Children of the Morning." His most recent novel,* Galapagos Regained, *is out from St. Martin's Press.*

"Apologue" is a fable about both American power and Hollywood threats to the same. Here we see the old monsters defanged in the face of the attacks of 9/11 and we get a hint at how even these old celluoid nightmares might help us heal.

APOLOGUE
James Morrow

The instant they heard the news, the three of them knew they had to do something, and so, joints complaining, ligaments protesting, they limped out of the retirement home, went down to the river, swam across, and climbed onto the wounded island.

They'd always looked out for each other in times gone by, and this day was no different. The ape placed a gentle paw on the rhedosaur's neck, keeping the half-blind prehistoric beast from stepping on cars and bumping into skyscrapers. The mutant lizard helped the incontinent ape remove his disposable undergarments and replace them with a dry pair. The rhedosaur reminded the mutant lizard to take her Prozac.

Before them lay the maimed and smoking city. It was a nightmare, a war zone, a surrealistic obscenity. It was Hiroshima and Nagasaki.

"Maybe they won't understand," said the rhedosaur. "They'll look at me, and all they'll see is a berserk reptile munching on the Coney Island roller coaster." He fixed his clouded gaze on the ape. "And you'll always be the one who shimmied up the Empire State Building and swatted at the biplanes."

"And then, of course, there was the time I rampaged through the Fulton Fish Market and laid my eggs in Madison Square Garden," said the mutant lizard.

"People are smarter than that," said the ape. "They know the difference between fantasy and reality."

"Some people do, yes," said the rhedosaur. "Some do."

The Italian mayor approached them at full stride, exhausted but resolute, his body swathed in an epidermis of ash. At his side walked a dazed Latino firefighter and a bewildered police officer of African descent.

"We've been expecting you," said the mayor, giving the mutant lizard an affectionate pat on the shin.

"You have every right to feel ambivalent toward us," said the rhedosaur.

"The past is not important," said the mayor.

"You came in good faith," said the police officer, attempting without success to smile.

"Actions speak louder than special effects," said the firefighter, staring upward at the gargantuan visitors.

Tears of remorse rolled from the ape's immense brown eyes. The stench filling his nostrils was irreducible, but he knew that it included many varieties of plastic and also human flesh. "Still, we can't help feeling ashamed."

"Today there is neither furred nor smooth in New York," said the mayor. "There is neither scaled nor pored, black nor white, Asian nor Occidental, Jew nor Muslim. Today there are only victims and helpers."

"Amen," said the police officer.

"I think it's clear what needs doing," said the firefighter.

"Perfectly clear." The mutant lizard sucked a mass of rubble into her lantern-jawed mouth.

"Clear as glass." Despite his failing vision, the rhedosaur could see that the East River Savings Bank was in trouble. He set his back against the structure, shoring it up with his mighty spine.

The ape said nothing but instead rested his paw in the middle of Cortlandt Street, allowing a crowd of the bereaved to climb onto his palm. Their shoes and boots tickled his skin. He curled his fingers into a protective matrix then shuffled south, soon entering Battery Park. He sat on the grass, stared toward Liberty Island, raised his arm, and, drawing the humans to his chest, held them against the warmth of his massive heart.

COPYRIGHT ACKNOWLEDGEMENTS

ABOUT THE EDITOR

Douglas Lain is a novelist and short story writer whose work has appeared in various magazines including *Strange Horizons*, *Interzone*, and *Lady Churchill's Rosebud Wristlet*. His debut novel, *Billy Moon*, was published by Tor and was selected as the debut fantasy novel of the month by *Library Journal* in 2013. *After the Saucers Landed* is his second novel.

Lain is the publisher of Zero Books, which specializes in philosophy and political theory, and hosts the *Zero Squared* podcast, interviewing a wide range of fascinating, engaging people with insights for the new millennium: philosophers, mystics, economists, and a diverse group of fiction writers. He lives in Portland, Oregon, with his wife and children.